Eulalia!

BRIAN JACQUES

Illustrated by DAVID ELLIOT

PHILOMEL BOOKS

PHILOMEL BOOKS
A division of Penguin Young Readers Group
Published by The Penguin Group
Penguin Group (USA) Inc., 375 Hudson Street, New York, NY 10014, U.S.A.
Penguin Group (Canada), 90 Eglinton Avenue East, Suite 700, Toronto, Ontario, Canada
M4P 2Y3 (a division of Pearson Penguin Canada Inc.).
Penguin Books Ltd., 80 Strand, London WC2R 0RL, England.
Penguin Ireland, 25 St. Stephen's Green, Dublin 2, Ireland
(a division of Penguin Books Ltd).
Penguin Group (Australia), 250 Camberwell Road, Camberwell, Victoria 3124,
Australia (a division of Pearson Australia Group Pty Ltd).
Penguin Books India Pvt Ltd., 11 Community Centre, Panchsheel Park,
New Delhi 110 017, India.
Penguin Group (NZ), 67 Apollo Drive, Rosedale, North Shore 0745,
Auckland, New Zealand.
Penguin Books (South Africa) (Pty) Ltd., 24 Sturdee Avenue, Rosebank,
Johannesburg 2196, South Africa.
Penguin Books Ltd, Registered Offices: 80 Strand, London WC2R 0RL, England.

Published simultaneously in Canada.
Printed in the United States of America.
The text is set in 11/12.5-point Palatino.
Library of Congress Cataloging-in-Publication Data
Jacques, Brian.
Eulalia! / Brian Jacques ; illustrated by David Elliot.
p. cm.
Summary: On his way to invade Redwall Abbey, vicious and tyrannical
Captain Vizka Longtooth captures Gorath, the brave young badger whose
predicted destiny is to become the next Badger Lord.
[1. Badgers—Fiction. 2. Foxes—Fiction. 3. Animals—Fiction. 4. Fantasy.]
I. Elliot, David, 1952– ill. II. Title.
PZ7.J15317 Eul 2007
[Fic]—dc22
2007060022
ISBN 978-0-399-24209-0
1 3 5 7 9 10 8 6 4 2
First Impression

In honour of Peter McGovern,
a true friend and a great man

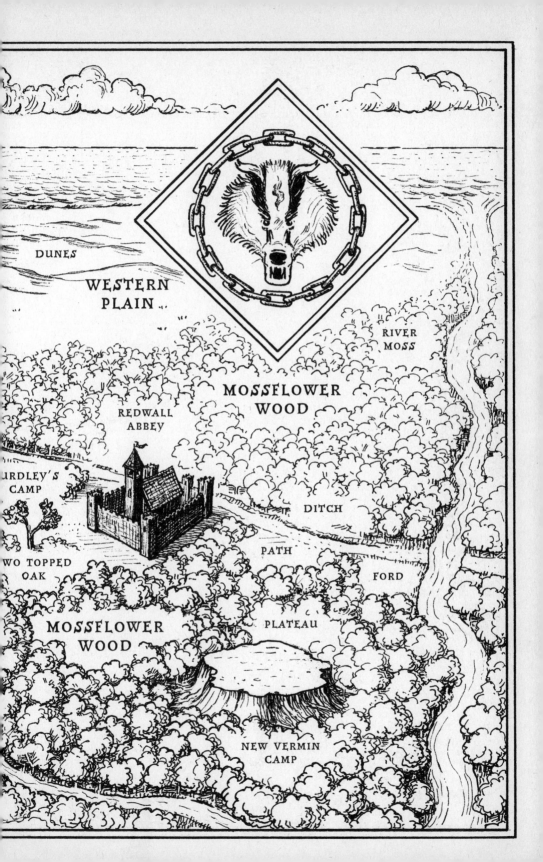

Prologue

Am I not fortunate, sitting in the forge chamber at Salamandastron? The fire is well banked up—I feel its warmth all around me, whilst I gaze out over our western shores at the sea. What an awesome sight, the vast deeps, on a moonlit winter night. Mountainous waves take on a silver sheen, powerful and mysterious as they thunder in from beyond the horizon.

Headlong, they crash in cascades of foaming spray upon the shore. Chuckling darkly over pebbles, and hissing secrets to the silent sands, as they are drawn back into the depths of boundless water. Nature, my friend, beautiful and fearsome, a hypnotic force few can resist. Goodness, how one's mind can wander, merely sitting here looking out from the forge room window. I must get back to writing my Chronicle.

It is a tale of several fates, each with its own destiny. Since I arrived at this mountain, I have set myself a pleasurable duty. From my own recollections, and information gathered from friends, both old and young, I recently put quill to parchment and began this Chronicle. Mayhaps when the story is finally told, my young daughter will enjoy reading it. I hope you will, too, my friend. Well, it starts like this . . .

BOOK ONE

Longtooth's Prisoner

1

It was a night for raiding. Beneath a dark, moonless sky, high seas ran grey and smooth to the shores of the Northern Isles. With her big single sail bellying smoothly, the vessel *Bludgullet* nosed shoreward, like some huge seabeast seeking its prey in coastal waters. Perched at the masthead, straddling the mainsail spar, the lookout, a small rat called Firty, was first to glimpse the glimmering, golden light on the far side of the saltmarshes. Noting the position of the illumination, he slid skillfully down a rope to the gently heaving deck.

Scurrying to the captain's cabin, Firty rapped on the door. He waited until a tall, golden fox emerged. The little rat tugged his ear in salute.

"Cap'n, dere's a light showin' ashore, dead ahead. I t'ink it might be sum sorta buildin', Cap'n."

Flinging a heavy cape across his shoulders, Captain Vizka Longtooth smiled, exposing a pair of oversized fangs. Firty swallowed hard. He, like every Sea Raider aboard the *Bludgullet*, had come to know the danger in Longtooth's smile.

"A buildin', ya say! Better sumthin' than nought on dis sun-fersaken shore, eh?"

The small crewrat nodded nervously, watching his cap-

3

tain reach for the mace and chain. It was a vicious weapon, a spiked iron ball on a thick chain, attached to an oaken handle. Firty crept backward, trying to stay out of his captain's way as he toyed with the mace and chain, swinging the spiked ball with a flick of his paw. The golden fox continued smiling, allowing the mace spikes to dent the woodwork of the cabin door. Firty tried to keep his eyes off the hypnotically swinging weapon.

"Will ya be goin' ashore, Cap'n?"

Vizka halted the swing of his mace; he fondled the spikes lovingly. "Aye, it wouldn't be gudd manners not t'call when dey left a light on fer us. Tell Codj ter rouse der crew. We're goin' visitin'!"

As *Bludgullet*'s keel ground into the shallows, the small, golden light stood out clear against the dark, velvet canopy of night sky. The vermin waded ashore, everybeast armed to the teeth, eager for booty and blood.

It was a night for raiding!

Lost in the deep sleep of total exhaustion, Gorath lay slumped by a glowing turf fire in the small farmhouse. There was a claw missing from one of the young badger's forepaws, his pads were thick with calluses and hardened scars. Wrestling half-buried boulders and uprooting scrubby tree stumps from the frozen earth was hard and punishing labour for a single beast. Gorath performed all his tasks unaided; his grandparents were too old for such heavy work. It was no easy life on the Northern Isles, both the weather and the land were hostile. Gorath, however, had youth on his side, plus unbridled strength, and an inborn tenacity. In short, he was like most male badgers, doggedly stubborn.

All Gorath knew of his early life had been imparted to him by his grandparents. His family came from the far Southern lands; both his parents were warriors who had fallen in battle during the Great Vermin Wars. The remainder of Gorath's family had been forced to flee the South.

4

The two old badgers took their little grandson in a small boat. They set off seeking a dream, a refuge of peace and happiness, where they could live without fear. They had heard tales of such places, the mountain of Salamandastron, and the Abbey of Redwall, legendary havens!

However, cruel fate and capricious weather shattered their dream. The aged badgers were landbeasts, with little knowledge of the sea. Their boat was blown far off course, and wrecked upon the rocks of the Northern Isles by a mighty storm. Gorath's grandparents stumbled ashore, carrying him between them, all three fortunate to be alive. That was how they came to a new life on the cold Northern Isles.

Their first few seasons ashore taught the three badgers some harsh lessons. A need for nourishment and shelter was paramount. Using timber from their wrecked boat, local stone, earth and moss, the grandfather built the house. Gorath and his grandmother foraged for food, whilst struggling to make the scrubland arable. It was hard, but they survived until their first meager crop came in, confirming that they were finally farmers.

Gorath grew to be a dutiful grandson, and a diligent worker. He never failed his grandparents, though as the seasons passed, one into another, things became more difficult for him. Wearied with age and illness, his grandparents grew unable to carry on working.

Thus it was that Gorath faced the hardships alone. He carried on clearing the windswept scrubland, planting, digging, coaxing and harvesting sparse crops from the thin soil. It was grindingly arduous work for a lone young one, but Gorath never complained. Sometimes in the long, dark evenings, when the wind dirged outside, Gorath would sit by the turf fire, listening as his grandfather told tales of Salamandastron or Redwall Abbey. How much truth there was in such stories, none of the badgers really knew, having never visited either place.

But the young Gorath was ever eager to hear more. He

5

was thrilled at the thought of Salamandastron, the fortress of warriors, ruled by Badger Lords, where none knew the meaning of fear. His grandfather taught Gorath a song about Salamandastron. Though the young badger never had cause or reason to be anything other than a peaceful farmer, something in the ballad wakened a feeling deep within him. It stirred warlike emotions, which made Gorath both excited and fearful, when he sang it as he worked throughout the daylight hours.

"Where wild waves break on West'ring shore,
that mighty rock mark well,
here live the free, the bold, the brave,
Aye, here the warriors dwell . . .
Salamandastron!
In dreams you speak to me.
Salamandastron!
Great fortress by the sea.

"Let evil ones come as they will,
our steel awaits them here,
wild fighting hares and Badger Lords,
will teach them how to fear . . .
Salamandastron!
Our battle cry rings far.
Salamandastron!
Come shout Eulaliaaaaa!"

Other times his grandmother told stories she had heard about Redwall Abbey. Gorath would gaze into the fire longingly. What a delightful place, the young badger thought. One immense home, built on happiness, peace and prosperity. Where many types of creatures lived in harmony, working, feasting and enjoying life together. Though Gorath was stirred by his grandfather's stories of Salamandastron, he also liked to hear about Redwall, with its gentle, more tranquil way of life. But what did it all mat-

6

ter now? Cruel fate and ill winds had denied everything to the young Gorath, leaving him far across the stormy seas, marooned on the harsh Northern Isles, with no means to follow his dreams.

These days, Gorath's main refuge came through sleep. Moreso as his grandparents had gone silent, they seldom told tales, or sang. They, too, withdrew into themselves, slumbering constantly.

The young badger lay by the fire, letting his eyes close, thinking how the weather had played a miserable trick on him. It had been a wild winter, followed by a false spring. In the space of a single night, all the crops, seedlings and fresh green growth, which Gorath had toiled upon, were blighted. Winter had returned with renewed fury, withering and freezing everything which had begun growing.

Gorath fell asleep with his grandmother's words echoing through his mind.

"If we have little else, at least we have peace on these Northern Isles."

And so they had.

Until that night, when the *Bludgullet* sailed in, and Vizka Longtooth decided that it was a night for raiding!

2

Gorath found himself thrust roughly into a waking nightmare. Hot scattered embers of the fire were kicked into his
face. Screams and roars echoed around the farmhouse
amid the flickering shadows and smoke. Instinctively the
young badger sat upright, grasping the closest thing to his
paw. It was the big, double-pronged pitchfork he called
Tung. But even as his paw fell upon it, a blinding pain exploded in his head. Dazed by the impact, he turned to see
what had struck him.

A big, golden-furred fox wielding a mace and chain was
standing over him. The intruder's long fangs glittered, as
he smiled in astonished amusement, calling to his crew,
"Dis wan haz der head like a rock I t'ink."

Before the stunned badger had a chance to dodge, the
golden fox brought the ball and chain crashing down
again.

Brilliant coloured lights and a cascade of shooting stars
thundered through Gorath's skull. He fell into a void of
agonised darkness.

How long he remained in that state, the young badger
had no way of knowing. Then strange visions began con-
fronting him, a mountain on the silent, sunlit shores of a
great sea. He was wading slowly toward it through the

waves. Standing on the tide line, over twoscore huge badgers stood watching him. They were armed with a selection of swords, axes, clubs and spears, each one a beautifully crafted weapon. Something told Gorath that these were not beasts from among the ranks of the living, but the shades of warriors who had passed beyond the pale.

One massive, silver-coated patriarch, far older than the rest, waded out to meet Gorath. He thrust a paw into the young badger's chest, his voice booming out over the sea. "Why come ye to Salamandastron?"

Gorath resisted the pushing paw, he did not like being shoved about. "Take your paw from me, old one!"

But the ancient continued pressing him backward. "Go ye to the Abbey of Redwall!" He pushed Gorath hard with both paws, sending him floundering into the sea. The young badger spluttered, spitting out the cold salt water.

"Lookit, Cap'n, der stripe'ound's alive!"

Gorath retched, as a weasel hurled a second pail of seawater into his face. He came awake to find himself onboard a large ship, surrounded by vermin, an evil-looking crew. Weasels, ferrets, stoats and rats, all fully armed and clad in tattered barbaric gear. Gorath was held captive, a thick, iron chain was padlocked tightly about his middle, the chain secured to the lofty mainmast.

Refilling his pail from over the ship's side, the weasel hauled it up on a rope and prepared to swing it at the prisoner.

"Can I give 'im annuver drink, Cap'n?"

The tall, golden fox, who had struck Gorath down, was leaning on the midship rail. Smiling, he revealed his long fangs to the captive. "Well, do ya still be t'irsty, stripe-'ound?"

Congealed blood from the dreadful wound on Gorath's forehead had stuck one of his eyes shut. The young badger stooped against the deck, his head was throbbing unmercifully. Saturated and shivering, he swayed as waves of nausea swept over him.

9

The golden fox kicked him, repeating the question.

"Be ya deaf as well as daft? Do ya wanna drink, stripe'ound? Speak!"

Gorath pulled himself upright against the mast, staring at his captor angrily. "I am not called stripehound, my name is Gorath!"

The fox ignored him, turning to the weasel with the pail. "Give der stripe'ound dat udder drink, Balid."

As the pail of freezing water sloshed over him, Gorath gasped with shock. The fox pointed at him with his mace haft.

"Yew got no name aboard my ship, except wot I calls ya. I'll call ya Rock'ead, 'cos yew got a skull t'ick as a rock. Aye, Rock'ead, dat's a good name, eh?"

The crew laughed dutifully at their captain's feeble joke. Balid, the water-throwing weasel, called out, "Sink me, Cap'n, 'e must 'ave a t'ick 'ead, if'n ye couldn't slay 'im wid two blows o' yer weppin." Balid had said the wrong thing, it was obvious by the pall of silence which fell over the crew.

The golden fox's heavy cape swirled as he rounded on Balid. "I'm Vizka Longtooth, cap'n o' der *Bludgullet,* an' I didn't kill dat 'un 'cos I wants 'im alive. So wot d'ye say to dat, Balid? Who did yew slay, tell me?" Vizka saw the weasel's paws trembling as he bowed in abject apology.

"Beggin' y'pardon, Cap'n, I was wid Codj. We never slayed anybeast. Alls wot we did was set fire to der farm 'ouse an' locked de two ole stripe'ounds inside, so they couldn't gerrout."

That was the second slip of Balid's tongue. It was also his last. With a maddened roar, Gorath launched himself at the weasel. The shortness of the chain prevented him from actually getting hold of Balid, but as the chain went taut, Gorath strained against it, lashing out with one paw. It connected with the weasel's neck, slaying him stone dead.

Suddenly, Vizka Longtooth was yelling. "Back! Get back,

all of ye! Stay outta dat beast's way!" The vermin crew needed no second urging, they scattered to the for'ard and aft deckrails, away from Gorath's reach.

Codj the fox, who was Vizka's younger brother and second in command, took up the big pitchfork, which he had taken from Gorath's unconscious body at the farmhouse. "Balid wuz my mate, I'll kill 'im fer dat!"

Vizka stayed his brother's paw. "No, ye won't. I wants Rock'ead kep' alive."

Codj scratched at his tail stump. "Alive, wot for?"

The golden fox chuckled, nodding toward Gorath. "Ye'd lose a sight more'n ya tailstump, if'n yew tried tacklin' dat 'un. Look close at 'im."

Both foxes watched Gorath carefully. He was making sweeping lunges at everything, from the limits of the taut chain which held him to the mast. His powerful, blunt-clawed paws were flexing, seeking to tear and destroy anything, or anybeast. Gorath was panting hoarsely, foam flecking over his bared teeth. Fearful roars emerged from his heaving chest. But it was the badger's eyes which struck terror into the beholders. They were suffused totally with dark red blood. The Sea Raiders' young captive had become transformed into a ravening beast, in the grip of some awesome madness.

Vizka took the pitchfork from his brother, showing his impressive teeth as he whispered, "Aye, Stumple, 'avin' no tail'd be der least o' yer worries if'n yer went near Rock'ead!"

Codj shot a resentful glance at his brother—he hated the nickname Stumple. It had come about after losing his tail in a fight when he was young. He spat sullenly in Gorath's direction. "Dat beast's crazy mad, 'e should be slain, I tell ya. If'n ye won't let me do d'job, then kill 'im yerself!"

Vizka called out orders to his crew. "Steer clear o' dat beast, don't feed 'im or give 'im water. Set course due south 'til I tells yer diff'rent. I'll be in me cabin wid Codj."

11

Keeping a safe distance from Gorath, the golden fox steered his brother round to the captain's cabin.

Pouring out two beakers of seaweed grog, Vizka gave one to Codj, explaining his reasons for keeping Gorath alive. "Lissen, I 'eard once about stripe'ounds like dat one. Some calls 'em Berserks, but ole Windflin said it was summat called der Bloodwrath."

Codj held out his beaker for a refill. "Ya mean Windflin Wildbrush, der great Sea Raider?"

Vizka nodded. "Aye, dat was 'im. Well, let me tell ya, Windflin was slayed by a stripe'ound wot 'ad der Bloodwrath. It was at dat place wid a funny name, Sammerstrong I t'ink, a big mountain castle, far down der sou'west shores. They says der beast wot killed Windflin was an ole stripe'ound called Asheye, a real mad Bloodwrath beast who couldn't be defeated."

Codj took a swallow of the foul-smelling grog. "Huh, 'e musta been a champeen fighter ter slay der great Windflin Wildbrush! But if'n Bloodwrath beasts are so dangerous, why do ya want to keep one alive? Best cure for any madbeast is to kill 'im quick!"

Vizka winked slyly at his younger brother. "Nah, ya don't turn a beast like our Rock'ead inta fishbait, 'e's vallible. I got plans fer 'im."

Codj was intrigued by his brother's words. "Plans?"

Vizka expanded upon his scheme. "Aye, plans. If'n I could break Rock'ead, an' tame 'im, jus' imagine dat! We'd 'ave a one-beast army, we'd be der terror of d'land an' sea!"

Codj was not wholly convinced. "Did ya see der way Rock'ead slayed pore Balid? Huh, one smack of 'is paw was all it took. I never seen nobeast wid dat sorta strength. So 'ow are ya goin' ter tame der beast if'n ye can't get near 'im?"

Vizka shook his handsome golden head pityingly. "'Tis a gud job I'm der brudder wid der brains. Ain't you 'eard dat 'unger an' thirst are de best tamers of all? We jus' keeps Rock'ead chained t'der mast, an' starve 'im inter my way

12

o' thinkin'. Hah, 'e'll do like I says, or perish, 'ow's dat fer a gud idea, eh?"

Codj was in awe of his older brother's wisdom. "No wonder yore cap'n o' der *Bludgullet*! Er, an' why are we sailin' south?"

Vizka commandeered the grog flask, as Codj was about to pour himself more grog. "We're goin' south 'cos dat's my orders. Aye, an' I ain't goin' down as far as dat Sammerstrung mountain. Let fools like Windflin get theirselves slayed by madbeasts. I tell ya, dere's lotsa places where der livin' is soft. Good vittles, loot an' plunder, dat's wot I'm after, Codj, an' I don't want ta fight for dem either!"

Codj stared ruefully into his empty beaker. "So 'ow d'yer plan on doin' all dat?"

The golden fox spread his paws disarmingly. "Rock'ead can take care of all der fightin' an' killin' fer us, once I got 'im trained proper."

All of this sounded quite good to Codj, but he still had unanswered questions. "But if'n we ain't sailin' for der stripe'ound mountain, where else are ya plannin' on goin'?"

Vizka poured him more grog. "Don't bother yore 'ead over dat, brudder, I'll find someplace. Yew go about yer bizness an' leave it t'me. I'll look out for ya, Codj."

But the stumptailed fox was still not satisfied. "Wot'll dis place be like?"

Vizka pondered a moment before answering. "T'will be a place where I kin rule, jus' like a king!"

Codj persisted. "Like a king, eh, an' worrabout me?"

The golden fox patted his brother's back. "Yew kin be cap'n o' der *Bludgullet*, dat's wot!"

The younger fox's tailstump quivered with joy. "Me, a real cap'n? Bludd'n'tripes, ya won't regret it, brudder. I'll be der best cap'n in all der seas, jus' yew wait'n see. Heeheehee, me, a cap'n!"

Vizka ushered him to the cabin door. "Aye, yew a cap'n. Now go an' keep *Bludgullet* onna straight south course, an'

13

don't strain yer brains wid too much thinkin'. Oh, an' remind der crew t'stay clear o' Rock'ead, an' not t'give 'im any vittles, norra crumb nor a drop, unnerstand?"

Grinning foolishly, Codj threw a clumsy salute. "Aye aye, Cap'n, unnerstood, Cap'n!" He held the salute, standing there grinning, until Vizka was forced to enquire.

"Well, wot d'ya want?"

Codj giggled inanely, winking several times. "Ain't ya gonna say 'aye aye, Cap'n' back ter me?"

The golden fox frowned. "No, I ain't, yore norrin charge aboard dis ship yet, I'm still cap'n, gerron wid ya werk!" He slammed the door in his younger brother's face.

Codj looked crestfallen, but only for a brief moment. He brightened up, swaggering off along the deck, practising his role of captain-to-be. Selecting a small, puny-looking rat, Codj jabbed his rump with Gorath's pitchfork, and issued him gruff orders. "Tell der steersbeast t'keep 'er on a south course! Make dem lines fast, an' swab dat deck! But firstly fetch me some vikkles from der galley! Go on, 'op to it!"

Pleasantly surprised that his commands had been carried out so promptly, Codj perched on the rail, out of the prisoner's reach. Making a great show of lip smacking, he applied himself to a bowl of hot soup and a tankard of beer, taunting Gorath. "Haharr, would ya like some vikkles, Rock'ead?"

The young badger crouched silently beside the mast, his forehead wound congealed into a huge, ugly scab. This had been induced by the late Balid, drenching him with pails of cold seawater. Gorath's dark eyes smouldered with hatred at his captor, but he did not rise to the mocking fox's bait. However, Codj continued as he ate.

"Mmmm, nice drop o' soup dis, made wid veggibles from yore farm it was. Beer's tasty, too, did yew brew it, or was it de old 'uns? Heehee, dey ain't got much use fer eatin' an' drinkin' now, 'ave they?"

With a sudden roar, Gorath charged his tormentor, giv-

14

ing out a strangled grunt as he was jolted to a halt by the chain. Shocked by the speed of the badger's rush, Codj jerked backward, spilling soup and beer over himself. Recovering himself, he sneered.

"Shame ya can't git yore paws on me, ain't it? Ya look t'irsty, I'll give ye annuder drink, eh!" Lowering a pail into the sea, Codj flung it over Gorath. The young badger stood unmoving, he did not even blink his eyes as the cold salt water lashed over him. Some of the vermin crew, who were watching, laughed at Codj's feeble attempt to rouse the prisoner further. This drove the stumptailed fox into a rage. He began shouting at Gorath. "Did ya like dat likkle drink, Rock'ead, d'ya want some more, eh? Ahoy, thick'ead Rock'ead, I said d'ya want some more, ye can talk, can't ya?"

Gorath stared unblinkingly at him, then spoke. "I can talk, but I don't waste my breath speaking to deadbeasts."

With an expression of comical surprise on his face, Codj looked around at his shipmates. "Did ya 'ear dat? De stripe'ound called me a deadbeast! Idjit, I t'ink Vizka musta knocked yore brains loose when 'e belted ya wid 'is mace. Can't ya see I'm still alive an' kickin'? See, I'll give ya anudder drink, jus' to prove it!"

Even as the contents of the pail sloshed over him, Gorath was still staring at his torturer. This time his voice was dismissive, heavy with contempt.

"You murdered my kinbeasts, so I'm going to kill you. I've said all I have to say to you . . . deadbeast!"

Dark blood began rising in Gorath's eyes, clouding them with the fury of Bloodwrath. At that point, Codj's nerve deserted him. Dropping the pail, he fled aft. Still dripping water, the young badger stood, staring after his mortal enemy.

3

With Salamandastron, his beloved fortress, at his back, Lord Asheye sat on his favourite rock, not far from the front entrance of the mighty mountain stronghold. Turning seaward, the ancient badger sniffed salt-laden air, mingling with the softer aroma of landward breezes. Producing a big, spotted kerchief from his dressing gown sleeve, he blew his snout loudly, and inhaled again. Ah yes, spring was finally done, it was the first day of summer. Tapping the butt of his yew staff against the rock, he hummed one of the Long Patrol hares' marching songs, singing along mentally with the tune.

> "Can ye see the golden gorse on the heath,
> an' dainty pale blue flax upon the plain,
> do ye feel the dewy grass underneath,
> then step lively, 'tis summertime again!
>
> "Oh we'll tramp, tramp, tramp!
> if the sergeant says we must.
> Aye, we'll left, right, left!
> 'til our paws raise up the dust!
> With me blade ever ready at my side,
> an' a knapsack full o' vittles on me back,

I'll go rangin' over hills far an' wide,
an' good comrades like you I'll never lack!

"Oh, we'll march, march, march!
'til our paws are droppin' off,
until it's one, two, halt!
Tell the cook to serve the scoff!"

Lord Asheye allowed himself a rueful smile. Those were
the days! Long gone seasons, when he would go roving
forth at the head of his Long Patrol. Some of those hares
had been sprightly paced, but he could outmarch them all.
Aye, those were the days of his strength and prime, full of
exuberant power and speed. In those times, there was none
to equal Lord Asheye. Nobeast possessed his reckless daring in battle.

He gripped his staff tight, sighed deeply, then released
his hold on the stout yew pole. Ah, but then . . . no creature
had the Bloodwrath like him. What had been a boon in
youth and war had become a curse in old age and peace-
time. Now the countless seasons weighed upon his sil-
vered fur like a millstone. Now he was paying the price for
that wild life he had led. The great badger's mighty frame
was bent with age, old wounds he had taken were a toll on
his stiff limbs.

But the worst penalty by far was his blindness. All those
blows and injuries he had sustained, whilst fighting heed-
lessly in the grip of Bloodwrath. Asheye had paid for them
with the loss of his sight. He heaved himself from his seat
on the rock, stepped awkwardly upon a small boulder and
tripped. Blowing sand from both nostrils, the once-great
beast reached out, scrabbling vainly for the staff, which
seemed to elude his paws. Lord Asheye smiled bitterly,
muttering aloud to himself, "As blind as a badger, hah,
where've I heard that before?"

A stout paw passed him the staff, and helped him upright. " 'T'wasn't me that said it, sah, you'd have prob'ly

taken my bonce off with a single biff, if I had, wot!" The
Badger Lord immediately identified the speaker by his
firm grip and drawn-out speech mode.

"Ah, Mull, take me inside, will you please."

Major Mullein Braggwuth Barshaw was a tall, distin-
guished hare. He wore the dark blue, silver-buttoned tunic
of Salamandastron's Commanding Scout Major. Other
hares, those of his rank and above, referred to him as Mull.
A strict disciplinarian, expert scout and formidable fighter,
Mull had been constantly at his Lord's side in the last few
seasons. The pair shared a friendship that went back a long
way. Mull steered Asheye toward the main fortress door,
chatting leisurely.

"Inside it is, sah, teatime doncha know, hot scones, dab
o' meadowcream, strawb'rry preserve, an' mint tea, wot! A
charmin' an' delicious daily ritual, sah!"

The old Badger Lord shuffled past the main door into a
vast, rough-hewn corridor, whose walls were adorned with
family crests, suits of armour, fearsome weapons and regimental flags. Lowering his voice, Asheye confided to his
companion, "Let's not go into the large Mess Hall. Have
them send tea up to my forge room, Mull. I need to speak
with you in private. Too much din in that Mess Hall."

Major Mullein nodded. "Right y'are, sah." He signalled
to a pair of young hares who were on their way to the
mess. "Tringle, Furps, nip along and see the Quartermaster Sarn't, will ye. Tell him to set out two trays of afternoon
tea for us, bring 'em up to the forge room, if y'd be so
kind."

The youngsters both threw the Major a smart salute.
Furp's sister, Tringle, smiled impudently at Mullein. "Both
with cream'n'jam, Major?"

Lord Asheye glared her way in mock severity. "With
extra cream and jam, young miss. Oh, and Furps, remember which is your left paw and which is your right. Don't
go tripping and spilling any, eh."

Furps bowed awkwardly and stumbled against Tringle.

"Oh er, ah, hmm, no trippin' an' spillin', do m'best, y'lord-ship, I certainly will, wot!"

Both young hares shouted simultaneously, "On y'marks! Get set! Go!" They bounded off at top speed. Major Mullein chuckled.

"Stap me, sah, those two haven't stopped racing against each other since the day they were born."

The old badger made a shrewd observation. "That's because they both want to be runners in your Scout Patrol, Mull."

The Major was surprised that Asheye concerned himself with such small details. However, he hid his feelings with a languid drawl. "Do they really, I hadn't noticed, sah."

Lord Asheye's forge room was the traditional retreat of every mountain ruler, going back in time to the first Badger Lord. It had a raised fire at its centre, which was never allowed to go out. Charcoal, seacoal and driftwood were piled along one wall of the room, which had all the trappings of an armourer: two anvils, a quenching vat, a ready supply of metal and well-seasoned timber. The metal for blades, the timber for handles and hafts. There was also a bellows, a barrel of oil and bunches of secret herbs, used in the making of weapons. On the wall opposite the door was a long, open windowspace, facing the shore and the western sea.

Lord Asheye sat on the low, wide sill, beckoning the Major to sit beside him. Mullein had been in the forge room many times, yet he still could not help staring in wonder at the weapons which hung from its walls.

Most of them were made for Warrior Badgers, huge spears, hefty shields, stout longbows with arrows almost as tall as himself, and swords. Such swords they were, legendary weapons of massive proportions, broad-bladed, double-pawed hilts, far too heavy for any but a Badger Lord to wield.

19

Asheye spread his big, greasy forge apron on the sill between them as a knock sounded on the door. "Ah, the tea. Come in, please!"

It was the first time Furps and Tringle had been permitted to enter this inner sanctum. Their heads swivelled from side to side, trying to take in everything.

Major Mullein hid a smile, cautioning them, "Eyes front, chaps, look where you're jolly well goin'. Lose that tea an' I'll have your tails for dinner, an' your guts for garters."

Wobbling slightly, the two young hares made their way to the sill and placed the trays down gingerly. Lord Asheye gave their ears a gentle tug.

"Well done, you two. Now, let's see who'll be first back to the mess. On y'marks . . . get set . . . go!"

They flew off like twin arrows, with the Major shouting, "I say, shut that door on y'way out! Oh never mind, I'll jolly well do it myself, wot!" He rose and went to shut the door. "Now, sah, what were y'wantin' to chinwag about, eh, wot?" Mullein spread a substantial-looking scone with strawberry preserve and thick meadowcream.

Lord Asheye ignored the food, lowering his voice as he confided to the Major. "This is for your ears alone, Mull, not to go beyond this room. Understood?"

"Indeed, sah, mum's the word, wot!"

Asheye nodded his great silver head. "Good beast, Mull, I know I can depend on you, so listen carefully. Since the turn of the last moon I've been having dreams. . . ."

The Major interrupted with a chuckle. "Know what y'mean, sah, I get 'em m'self. Some pretty odd ones, when I've been scoffin' cheese'n'pickles for supper in the mess."

Asheye gave a deep snort of irritation. Mullein knew he had said the wrong thing and apologised.

"Ahem, most dreadfully sorry, m'lud, bloomin' silly of me t'mention it. Pray continue, sah!"

The old Badger Lord carried on with what he was saying. "Being blind has sharpened my perception, made me face things more rationally. Though what rhyme or reason there is in the voices of long-gone Badger Lords I cannot say. But I trust in them, and I feel instinctively I must heed their words.

"They have told me of my fate, and mark this, the ones who speak to me in dreams cannot be ignored. This is what I have learned. It is decreed that once the autumn leaves start to fall, I will not be seen again at Salamandastron. So it must be."

Mullein protested. "Not you, sah, why, you've got absolute scads o' seasons to go yet!"

The ancient badger's immense paw covered his gently. "Now, now, don't go upsetting yourself, my friend. It comes to us all sooner or later. The thought of passing on does not worry me unduly. I've had a fine, long life, much longer than I deserve really, considering the wild path my Bloodwrath led me down. In my dreams I have spoken with the great heroes of Salamandastron, Lord Brocktree, Sunflash the Mace, Boar the Fighter, Urthclaw, and others too numerous to mention. They all tell me one thing: Redwall Abbey will soon be in grave danger!"

Major Mullein sprang from the windowsill, his paw clamped on the sabre hilt at his waist. "Then with your permission, m'lud, I'll arm up the Long Patrol an' get 'em marchin' for the Abbey today!"

Lord Asheye beckoned Mullein to sit down. "If it were that simple, you'd have been on your way with the Patrol three days back."

The Major's long ears rose stiffly. "Then what the deuce is holdin' the confounded job up?"

Asheye turned his sightless gaze toward his friend. "The new Badger Lord."

Major Mullein was back up and pacing the chamber. "New Badger Lord, what new Badger Lord? Nobeast told me about any new Badger Lord!"

Asheye waited until the Major slowed his pace. "Listen, Mull, I told you I would not see another summer here, so who'll rule Salamandastron when I'm gone?"

21

Mullein came to a halt, stamping his footpaw. "But what's all that got to blinkin' well do with Redwall bein' in danger? Really, sah, I'm all at sixes an' flippin' sevens with your dreams'n'riddles!"

Asheye reached out and clasped his friend's paw. "Then sit down and be patient. Here, pour me some tea and I'll explain as best as I can." The Badger Lord sipped his drink slowly, only continuing when he felt the hare had calmed down. "This Badger Lord who will succeed me, I have learned that he is still a youngbeast. However, he is possessed of an even more ferocious Bloodwrath than was ever inflicted upon me. Our Long Patrol will not be needed at Redwall Abbey because he is fated to be there when the danger arrives. But before he can ever rule this mountain, he must be tested in the fires of battle. Now do you see?"

Mullein stroked his bristling moustache. "Indeed I do, sah. The Lord of Salamandastron must be as wise as he's strong an' warlike. But how will we know this chap, what does he look like, sah?"

Lord Asheye turned his face to the sea. He sat silent, feeling the gentle wind upon his face. Major Mullein watched the old Badger Lord closely, waiting for a reply. There was a long pause, then Asheye suddenly began speaking as though he was in the grip of a trance.

"Who will defend Redwall Abbey,
in its days of peril and strife?
The beast who shuns both armour and sword,
torn from the simple life.
He with destiny marked on his brow,
who walks with the banished one.
Send forth a maid to seek out the Flame,
to rule when the old Lord is gone!"

Asheye rose, shaking himself like one waking from sleep. "Great seasons, where did that come from?"

Major Mullein tried not to sound surprised. "Must've

been your dream chaps who put it into your head, m'lud. Beggin' y'pardon, but you've never been one for the jolly old poetic verse an' all that, wot! Well, stap me, sah, looks like Redwall's in for a bit of a ding dong. Hmm, an' there's a Champion on the horizon, one who'll flatten the flippin' foebeast, if I'm not mistaken. Sounds like an odd chap from your description, wot? Never heard of a Badger Lord who shuns armour an' bloomin' swords. What I really don't understand is the bit about destiny bein' marked on his brow, an' as for walkin' with a banished one, an' sendin' out a maid to seek for a flame . . . if y'don't mind me sayin', sah, the whole thing's got me flippin' well flummoxed."

Asheye took a sip of his tea, which had now grown cold. "Well, old friend, I had no idea that I was going to speak such a rhyme, so you'll excuse me if I confess to being as baffled as you are. However, it does explain a few things from my dreams. The coming trouble at Redwall, and the arrival of a Warrior. Also, the fact that this other badger will rule here in my stead, always supposing that he lives long enough, or isn't defeated in battle. As for the rest, I'm truly puzzled. Where's the maid that we must send forth?"

Mullein twirled his moustache briskly, and stood both ears to attention, always an obvious sign of his displeasure. "Hmph! So that's why I'm not allowed to sally forth with the Long Patrol, sah, a confounded maid is the one for the blinkin' task, accordin' to your sources. Hah, I question the wisdom of a load of long-gone badger spirits. I mean, what possible use would one maid be in the midst of an invasion upon Redwall, eh, wot?"

The ancient badger patted his friend's paw. "Now, don't get your whiskers in an uproar, Mull, I'm bound to obey the voices of past mountain Lords. So, how do we choose this maid whom we must send to solve our problems? Any suggestions, Major?"

The discussion was interrupted by a series of urgent knocks upon the door. Mullein rattled his sabre hilt. "Yes, stop knockin' the bloomin' door down. Come in!"

It was Corporal Thwurl, a tall, droopy hare, with a mournful countenance. His nose was swollen, one ear was askew, and his left eye was a puffy slit. He saluted Mullein. "Major, sah, wish to report, sah, ruckus in the mess, sah, Assistant Cook's gone bonkers, sah!"

Lord Asheye rested his forehead against the windowsill, sighing wearily. "Not Mad Maudie again. Deal with it, would you, Major Mullein? No, wait, bring her up here. We'll see what she has to say for herself this time!"

When Corporal Thwurl left, Asheye and Mullein waited in stony silence for several moments. Then sounds of a tussle echoed up the stairway outside. Apparently it was the offender being brought to the forge room by four guards. She was very vocal.

"Yah, gerroff, you swoggle-toothed bounders! If I could jolly well get free I'd biff your snouts off! Just you wait, I'll poison your porridge, I'll sabotage your salad, I'll destroy your duff, I'll . . . I'll . . . wahoo!"

Stuffed into a floursack, which was fastened at her neck, the miscreant was hauled into the room and dumped upon the floor. There she struggled, coming out with more colourful oaths at all and sundry. Mullein drew his sabre, roaring.

"Silence, marm! Be still, ye fiend, cease that din!" He slashed downward, neatly severing the drawstring of the sack, and releasing the young haremaid. Lying flat on the floor, she wiggled her ears and threw the Major a salute. "Most kind, sah, thank ye!"

Mullein silenced her with a glare, turning to Thwurl. "What're the facts, Corporal, make your report."

The droopy-faced Thwurl pawed tenderly at his nose. "There was complaints h'in the mess, Major, h'about the soup. It was too 'ot, sah, this h'assistant cook 'ad loaded it with red pepper, wild ransom, an' that 'otroot stuff, wot otters likes to h'eat."

The assistant cook interrupted from her prone position.

"Too hot, my auntie's pinny! Barley soup's as dull as blinkin' dishwater, it needed livenin' up!"

Lord Asheye growled out from his windowseat. "Silence, miss, stand up straight, to attention! Corporal Thwurl, carry on with your report, please!"

"Well, sah, h'I told 'er wot h'I thought of 'er soup, an' she struck me on the nose with 'er ladle, sah, then she went h'on to further h'assault me, an' several h'others, sah. We 'ad to subdue 'er by stuffin' 'er h'in a sack, sah. Whereupon she continued to shout h'insults at h'us, an' . . ."

Major Mullein waved Thwurl to silence. "Yes, yes, I get the general drift, Corporal. Assistant Cook, what have you to say for yourself, do you wish to refute the charges, wot?"

Assistant Cook Mad Maudie (the Hon.) Mugsberry Thropple fluttered her eyelashes endearingly at him. "Only to say, Major, that I'd do it all again if that puddenheaded oaf said nasty things about my soup, only next time I'd punch him in his other eye, too, so there!"

Lord Asheye shook his great head sternly. "That's quite enough of that, miss. Corporal, you and the guard may leave now. Major Mullein and I will deal with this, thank you."

When the escort had departed, the badger resumed his seat on the windowledge. He spread his big paws despairingly. "Maudie Thropple, what are we going to do with you, eh?"

Mad Maudie, as she was known to the mountain hares, shifted guiltily from one paw to the other, murmuring, "Really, I don't know, m'lord, what's anybeast goin' t'do with me, that's what my old pa used t'say."

Major Mullein waggled his ears knowingly. "My old friend, rest his memory, Colonel Thropple. What a gallant and considerate creature he was. Don't you remember any of the lessons he taught you, Maudie?"

The young hare smiled brightly. "Oh indeed I do, sah, Pa

taught me to box, an' I've been Regimental Champion of the Long Patrol for six seasons now!"

Mullein squinched his eye into a jaundiced stare at her. "We know that right enough, m'gel. You've also been on more charges than any other hare I can recall. You've served five terms in the guardhouse, and had three final warnings about your conduct, wot!"

Maudie stared at the floor. "Sorry, sah."

The Major's tone hardened. "Sorry, is it? Well, let me tell you, missy, sorry's not good enough this time. You've tried the patience of everybeast on this mountain far too long, ain't that right, Lord Asheye, sah?"

The badger nodded. "Yes, it is, Major. Maudie, you leave us no alternative. It gives me no pleasure to drum you out of the Long Patrol. At dawn tomorrow you will leave Sala-mandastron!"

In the stunned silence which followed, Lord Asheye listened to the haremaid's tears splashing on the forge room floor. There was a loud sniff from Mullein, then he approached the Badger Lord and whispered in his ear.

"I say, sah, we've never drummed a hare from the jolly old regiment. Couldn't ye find some alternative for young Maudie? I've known her since she was a mite, the daughter of my old comrade Colonel Thropple. I used to bounce her on my lap when she was nought but a babe."

The Badger Lord could not explain his next statement. The words tumbled unbidden from him. "I think there's a lot of good in you, Maudie Thropple, so in memory of your father's fine name, I'm going to give you one last chance. The Major and I have decided that you shall go on a most important mission. It will be both dangerous and demanding. Are you willing to go?"

Mad Maudie scrubbed the tears from her eyes with a floury paw. "Oh, rather, sah, say the bally word an' I'm off like a flippin' lark after a ladybird!"

Major Mullein was still registering surprise at Asheye as he spoke to the haremaid. "Right, off y'go, pack a light

26

kit an' weapon, apologise to the Corporal and those others you biffed, then report back here for instructions."

As the forge room door slammed shut, Mullein wheeled upon the Badger Lord. "What'n the name o' blue blazes made y'say that, sah?"

Asheye shrugged. "I don't know, Mull, but I think Mad Maudie's the one who'll get the job done. Don't you see yet? She's the maid who will fulfill my dream!"

4

Abbot Daucus was a brisk, energetic mouse in his mid-seasons. On this particular afternoon his energy was being sorely taxed, as he searched Redwall Abbey high and low, accompanied by Granspike Niblo, the plump, old hedge-hog who was Abbey Beekeeper. Daucus paused at the foot of the attic stairs, waiting for Granspike to catch up with him. Both creatures, panting heavily, sat down together on the stairs. Daucus scratched at his scrubby, ginger-tinged beard.

"Well, marm, apart from these attics, that's the whole of the Abbey building we've been through, from the wine cellars to the dormitories. I don't think we've missed anything, have we?"

Granspike stared enquiringly at the Abbot. "The kitchen larders, he could've hid himself there?"

Daucus discounted the suggestion. "No, I searched them myself, whilst you were going through Cavern Hole. Confound that young Prink, where does he get to? More important, where do our goods and chattels go, where does he hide them?"

Granspike rose wearily, dusting her apron off. "Dearie me, Father Abbot, I was wrong an' you were right. We should never have taken Orkwil Prink into Redwall. Both his parents were a bad lot, ramblin' an' thievin' like wildbeasts. 'Tis true enough, what was said about 'em, a Prink'd steal the eyes out o' yore head if'n you didn't watch 'em. Four seasons of that rascal is more'n enough for any Abbey. Aye, an' Master Prink has sorely tried everybeast within Redwall. I think he's run out o' sympathy from all, includin' meself!"

Daucus patted the good hedgehog's spines carefully. "It's not our fault, Gran. We couldn't refuse a young 'un a roof over his head and food. It's his mother and father I blame, deserting him and running off like they did. Ah well, no use going over all that again, come on, let's go and take a look through the attics."

He picked up the lantern they had brought along and began climbing the spiral staircase. They had ascended only a few steps, when a deep, rumbling voice echoed up to them from the lower dormitory floor.

"Bee's you'm up thurr, zurr h'Abbot, wull ee bestest cumm daown. Oi've founded ee likkle scallywagger!"

Daucus immediately recognised the caller, Foremole Burff, the leader of Redwall's quaintly spoken moles.

Granspike Niblo's voice went squeaky with relief. "Thankee, Mister Burff, we'll be right down!"

Foremole Burff was waiting on the dormitory landing. He tugged his snout respectfully. "Zurr, marm, you'm axcuse oi furr not coomin' up thurr, oi'm gurtly afeared o' tall places!"

Knowing the moles were soildiggers, and afraid of heights, Daucus smiled understandingly. "I'm not too fussy on them myself, Burff. Did I hear you say that you'd caught Orkwil? Where is he now?"

Foremole Burff pointed a hefty digging claw in a downward motion. "H'in ee gate'ouse, zurr, an' he'm gurtly well guarded, burr aye!"

As the trio trooped downstairs, Granspike shook her

head. "In the gatehouse, I might've knowed it. Father Abbot, we should've searched from the outside and worked inward, 'stead o' doin' it the other way about."

Daucus heaved a long sigh. "Not to worry, the main thing is that young Prink has been caught."

By the time they had reached ground level, and were crossing Great Hall, others were hastening to join them, everybeast speculating.

"Has he been apprehended, the villain?"

"Aye, Skipper's holding Orkwil in the gatehouse!"

"So that's where he was hiding?"

"No, they just took him there so he couldn't escape."

"Well, where was his secret hiding place, d'you know?"

"No, but we'll soon find out, come on!"

Out the Abbey door they paraded, down the front steps onto the gravelled path between flower beds and lawns. A high sandstone outer wall ran foursquare around the Abbey grounds; it had a walkway on top, and battlements. Each section of the wall had a small wicker gate built into it, with the exception of the main threshold gate. This was the western ramparts, containing the big oaken main gate; it had a gatekeeper's lodge built against the wall. Either side of the gate, two flights of stone steps ran up to the threshold walkway. More Redwallers had congregated around the gatehouse area.

Abbot Daucus paused at the gatehouse door, surveying the crowd who were gathered there. He frowned. "Have you nothing else to do but hang about here? Friar Chondrus, no meals to prepare, Sister Atrata, no patients to attend in sickbay? Please disperse and go about your chores. The Elders and I can deal with this matter. You will all get your goods back, I assure you."

A group of Dibbuns, Redwall's Abbeybabes, was seated on the bottom of the wallstairs. Daucus cautioned them, "I hope you little ones aren't thinking of climbing those steps to the walkway?"

A tiny squirrel named Dimp shook his head severely at the Father Abbot, answering for his companions. "We all be h'Elders, us goin' inna gate'ouse, an' 'ave a word wiv naughty Orkwilt!"

Granspike shooed them off with her apron waving. "Ho no yore not, liddle sir, time for you lot t'get washed up for dinner. Folura, Glingal, tend to these Dibbuns will ye."

The two identical otter sisters began herding the Dibbuns to the Abbey pond. The babes squealed and ran off, in an attempt to escape. They stood little chance against the swift ottermaids. The Redwallers around the gatehouse had duly dispersed.

Daucus smiled approvingly at his companions. "Good. Shall we go in now?"

Orkwil Prink's usually sunny disposition had deserted him. He sat on the floor of the gatehouse with Rorc, Skipper of Otters, and Benjo Tipps, the big hedgehog who was Redwall's Cellar Keeper, standing either side of him. There was a rope tied about Orkwil's waist, each of his custodians held an end. Also in attendance were Fenn Bluepaw, the Abbey's squirrel Recorder, and an old watervole lady, Marja Dubbidge, Redwall's official Bellringer. The hubbub from outside had ceased, creating a silence inside the little gatehouse, which was heavy with foreboding. The young hedgehog's head drooped miserably, he stared at the floor, not daring to raise his eyes as the new arrivals entered.

Abbot Daucus pulled up a stool, and sat facing the miscreant, studying his demeanour, before turning to Benjo Tipps. "I understand from Granspike that he was discovered hiding in your cellars, is that correct?"

The stout Benjo tugged his headspikes respectfully. "Aye, Father Abbot, 'tis where he was. Though I don't know why I never knew it afore today. My ole eyes ain't all they was, an' my hearin' could be a lot better. Young rip! Must've been comin' an' goin' as he pleased, an' all without my knowin'."

31

Daucus consulted Foremole Burff and Skipper Rorc. "So, Granspike says you found him hiding inside an old barrel, was any of his hoard there?"

Orkwil raised his eyes and spoke for the first time. "I never kept any of it in the barrel, sir, all's I had there was a few vittles, a lantern an' my notebook."

Daucus made a gesture at the rope around Orkwil's waist. "Remove that thing, Skipper, I don't like it. He isn't going to run anywhere now. What's all this about a notebook, Orkwil, why did you need to keep a notebook?"

Fenn Bluepaw glared over her small spectacles at the young hedgehog. "So that's where my season songbook disappeared to! I bound it myself, specially, and I hadn't written a single song in it yet. You rogue, I wager you helped yourself to my best charcoal writing sticks, too. Rest assured I'll count them, when I get back to my study. I know exactly how many I had!"

The Abbot interrupted his Recorder. "Miz Bluepaw, this isn't getting us anywhere, kindly hold your peace. What was the notebook for, Orkwil?"

Freed of the rope halter, Orkwil felt better, some of his former easy manner returned. "Oh, the notebook, Father, that was to keep track of everything I borrowed. . . ."

"Huh, borrowed?" Marja Dubbidge snorted. She was immediately silenced by a glare from the Abbot, who beckoned Orkwil to continue. The young hedgehog warmed to his subject.

"Aye, borrowed. I never meant to keep anything for good, after awhile I'd return it. Like your silver belt buckle, Foremole, sir."

Foremole Burff wrinkled his velvety snout. "Boi okey, oi never h'even knowed et wurr stole'd, oi found it t'uther day, unner moi pillow!"

Orkwil spread his paws magnanimously. "You see, I give it all back, sooner or later. What I do is, when I borrow something I list it in my notebook. Then when I return it, I cross it off the list. Though one or two things I hold on to for a long time, because I like them so much. Sorry, Father."

Daucus continued his interrogation. "And where, may I ask, are all these missing items, if they're not in your barrel?"

The young hedgehog twiddled his paws, grinning mischievously.

"Riddle me ree don't read my mind,
inside my book your goods you'll find!"

Skipper's rudderlike tail clipped Orkwil's ear. The big otter warned him with a growl, "Mind yore manners, Master Prink. Speak proper to the Abbot, an less o' yore gobbledygook!"

Granspike still had a soft spot for Orkwil. She tut-tutted at Skipper, and placed a paw about the young one's shoulders. "I think wot he means, Father Abbot, is that there's writin' in his book, tellin' us where t'find all the goods he took. Ain't that right, Orkwil?"

The grin reappeared on Orkwil's face, he nodded. "That's right, clever old Gran!"

The old hogwife suddenly snapped. She smacked him hard on the cheek, shouting, "Don't ye start gettin' smart with me, young hog! Clever ole Gran, indeed. Who was it found ye half-starved an' weepin' out in the woodlands, after yore no good ma'n'pa had run off on ye, eh? Who was it brought ye to Redwall an' begged to get ye taken in? An' this is all the thanks I gets for it!"

Orkwil broke down then, he sobbed and hugged Granspike. "Oh Gran, Gran, I'm sorry!"

She took his tearstained face in both paws. "Why, Orkwil, why? Wot made ye do it?"

Abbot Daucus passed him a kerchief. "Come on, young 'un, blubbering doesn't solve things. This isn't the first time you've been caught thieving. Now don't give me that injured look, you know as well as anybeast here, thieving is the only name for it. Sneaking away the property of good, honest Redwallers, and holding on to it for as long as you please. What other name is there for it? Why do you do it?"

Orkwil Prink shook his head in bewilderment. "I don't know, Father, whenever I see anything I like, well ... well ... I just have to have it, so I take it!"

Fenn Bluepaw was heard to mutter, "It's in his blood. From what I've heard his parents were both the same, shifty, feckless robbers!"

Skipper interrupted her. "Yore wrong, marm. Robbers are those who hurts others to take wot they wants. Orkwil never hurt nobeast."

Marja Dubbidge was on Fenn's side, she argued back, "Mebbe he didn't beat us up t'get our goods, but he still hurted us. I was very hurted when he took my best knitted mittens. You did, didn't you?"

Orkwil nodded. "But I was going to give 'em back."

The watervole pointed an accusing paw at him. "Then where are they, eh? Yore a nasty, young sneak thief!"

At this point, Abbot Daucus felt things had gone far enough. He stood up, kicking the stool aside and raising his voice. "Silence! This is not the way Redwallers are supposed to behave, stop all this bickering right now!" There were shamefaced murmurs of apology from some, then the peace was restored. Daucus waited until he had calmed down sufficiently to continue. "You will all receive your possessions again in good time. Orkwil, speak truly now. Is there anything you took which cannot be returned? Tell me."

The young hedgehog shook his head slowly. "Not that I can think of, Father, only food from the kitchens, and some cider from Mister Benjo's cellar."

Benjo Tipps recalled the two flagons of Special Pale Cider, which he had been storing for the Midsummer Feast. He bit his lip, and held the silence. Then Daucus put the question to them all.

"Orkwil Prink has admitted what he has done, it isn't the

first time he's been caught stealing. We've never had any Redwaller thieving from his friends before. Now, what do you say we do about it? Other times I've put him to scouring pots in the kitchens, or confined him to the dormitory, but it seemed to have no effect on him. So I ask you, what is his punishment to be?"

There was a momentary pause, then Marja Dubbidge was heard to whisper to Fenn Bluepaw, "I'd send that young villain packin', away from our Abbey, 'tis all he deserves!"

Granspike Niblo uttered a strangled sob. "Oh no, don't say that, give 'im a chance!"

Foremole Burff spoke, contributing his sensible mole logic. "Oi'd send 'im aways from ee h'Abbey, but only furr wun season. May'aps 'twill teach ee young 'un a lessing."

Abbot Daucus shook his mole friend's paw heartily. "Thank you, Burff, that's the ideal solution. Are we all agreed on that?"

Everybeast held up their paws, with the exception of two, Fenn and Marja. The Abbot stared levelly at them, Skipper and Benjo glared at the pair, Granspike gazed pleadingly at them. For a moment, nothing happened. Then bit by bit, the Recorder and the Bellringer raised their paws. The Abbot gave a beaming smile.

"Good, then that's a full show of paws, thank you!" His face turned stern as he addressed the parolee. "Orkwil Prink, you are not permitted to enter Redwall Abbey for the space of one season, until the first autumn leaves appear. We hope that on your return to us, you will appreciate this place, and become a useful and honest creature among your friends. The life you must lead outside these walls will perhaps teach you a lesson. You must fend for yourself, find your own food and shelter, and avoid harm. Granspike Niblo will give you some stout clothing, and Friar Chondrus will provide you with sufficient plain food to last three days. Make good use of your time out there, think of us, as we will be thinking of you. Above all, do not

35

steal anything which does not belong to you. I hope you return to us as an honest and more resolute young creature. You may go, and may good fortune be with you, Orkwil!"

Evening sunlight shaded the western flatlands, turning the outer walls to a dusty, warm rose. Descending larks sang their Evensong as Orkwil rambled away north, up the dusty path outside Redwall Abbey. He heaved a gusty sigh, wiping the last of Granspike's tears from his brow. Turning, he took a backward glance at the Abbey. The huge sandstone edifice stood serene and unchanging, from bell-tower to arched windows, with stained glass reflecting the sinking sun in rainbow hues. Shouldering the staff which carried a food pack tied to one end, he turned away, sniffed and wiped his eyes.

Ah well, he'd gotten off fairly lightly, considering the offenses he'd perpetrated. The good old Abbey would still be there on his return at autumn. He'd be a reformed character by then. But meanwhile . . .

He wasn't being hunted, lectured at, tied up in the gatehouse, interrogated or told off. Here was the open road before him, the woodlands, plains, hills and streams to roam unhindered. Free as the breeze, and with nobeast to tell him how he should behave. Orkwil Prink leapt in the air and shouted aloud. "Yeeehaaaahoooooh!"

5

The ship *Bludgullet* nosed its course through heavy seas, heaving up and down with a constant seesawing motion. A squall had hit during the night, sweeping out of the north, bringing with it gusting winds and pelting rain. For the young badger chained to the mast, there was no shelter, he was out there alone on the heaving deck. However, the wild weather did bring one blessing with it, fresh rainwater. Gorath lay flat out, beneath the centre of the huge, square sail, with his mouth wide open. Raindrops, puddling in a crease of the canvas, came trickling down, providing him with a much-needed drink of clear, cold water. When he had taken his fill, Gorath crawled back to the mast. He sat with his back against it, awaiting the passing of the storm, and the dawn of a new day.

Gradually the rain ceased, though the seas still ran high, with the ship dipping up and down as it ploughed southward. Daybreak revealed a dark, sullen sky, with ponderous cloudbanks in the wake of the vessel. Rising, falling, with the horizon glimpsed between foam-crested greeny-blue waves of mountainous proportions, up and down, up and down.

That was when Gorath got his first taste of seasickness. The wound he had received on his forehead, formed into a thick scab of dried blood, still throbbed painfully. This, with the bucking of the ship, brought on a spasm of retching. The young badger slumped over, wishing that death would release him from his cruel predicament.

From the cabin doorway, Vizka Longtooth and his first mate, Codj, watched Gorath. Vizka passed Codj a length of tarred and knotted rope. The golden fox's long fangs showed as he whispered instructions.

The other, smaller fox nodded, then enquired, "Yarr, Cap'n, but why do ya want t'stop me?"

Vizka shoved him toward the badger. "'Coz dat's my orders, t'ickead, jus' do like I says!"

Codj shrugged, and swaggered off swinging the rope. "I do like ya say, yore da cap'n."

Gorath had closed his eyes, trying to gain respite from his suffering in sleep, when the knotted rope struck his back. He wheeled about to see his enemy swinging the rope. This time it struck him on the side of his jaw. Codj snarled at him; standing out of range of Gorath, he continued wielding the rope.

"Up on yore paws, Rock'ead, who sez ya could sleep, eh?"

Gorath was too sick to do anything about it, he crouched by the mast, covering his head with both paws.

His tormentor continued to flog at him with the knotted rope. "Gerrup, lazybeast, stan' up straight when I speaks to ya!"

Vizka came hurrying up and snatched the rope from Codj. "Leave dat pore beast alone, go 'way!"

The mate did as he was bidden, leaving them alone. Vizka crouched a safe distance from his captive, and began to speak in a wheedling tone. "Pore Rock'ead, wot ails ya, are y'tired?" Gorath stayed as he was, making no answer. Vizka cocked his head, trying to see the badger's face. "Are ya sick, is dat it? I gotta good cabin an' a bunk, all nice'n cosy, 'ow would ya like t'sleep der, eh?" There was still no

38

reaction, though Vizka could see that his prisoner was saturated and shivering. "D'ya wants vittles, we got good food, plenny t'drink, too." He watched the young badger keenly, for any response. Still getting no answer, the golden fox stood up. "I'm der cap'n 'ere, jus' tell me wot ya wants an' I'll give it to ya. Dat's a fair offer, eh?"

Gorath did not even open his eyes to look at the fox.

Vizka pulled his thick cloak tight about himself. "Cold out 'ere, I'm goin' to me cabin. But yew ain't goin' nowhere, Rock'ead. Sooner or later y'll speak ter me. Or y'll die, chained ter dat mast!"

Vizka did not go to his cabin; instead, he went to the main cabin, on the deck below. Codj was there with some of the vermin crew. He caught the knotted rope that Vizka tossed to him.

"Ya wants me ter go an' flog 'im agin, Cap'n?"

The crewbeasts made room as their captain sat down at the mess table. "Nah, dat'n's 'ad enough fer now, leave 'im 'til later."

One of the crew, a hulking ferret called Grivel, commented, "Dat stripe'ound'll die iffen ya flogs 'im too much. Cap'n near killed 'im wid 'is ball'n'chain. Can't be too far off dead now, if'n ya asks me."

Vizka smiled at Grivel. "But I didn't ask ya, did I?"

Vizka Longtooth was always at his most dangerous when smiling. Grivel did not fancy a confrontation with his captain, so he fell silent.

The golden fox rose, staring at him pointedly, almost challenging him to speak. "I'll decide wot 'appens t'the stripe'ound. Rock'ead's a young beast, an' a strong 'un. A bit o' starvin' an' beatin' won't do 'im no 'arm. You jus' watch, I'll bring 'im round ter my way o' thinkin'. Same as I'd do wid anybeast, eh, Grivel?"

The hefty ferret stared down at the tabletop, avoiding his captain's smiling eyes. "Aye, Cap'n, wotever ya say."

Without warning, Vizka dealt Grivel a swinging back-pawed blow, which knocked him out of his seat, flat on his face. Vizka laughed, looking around at the other vermin in the cabin. "Pore Grivel, can't 'old 'is grog, if'n y'ask me!"

The crew knew what to do, they laughed aloud with their unpredictable captain, every one of them. Vizka issued orders. "When vittles is ready they'll be served up on deck. I want y'all to sit where dat stripe'ound can see ya. Watchin' yew lot eatin' might stir up 'is appetite. Look as if yore enjoyin' dinner, make Rock'ead feel 'ungry. Codj, you keep an eye peeled on 'im, I'll be in me cabin if'n ya wants me."

Grivel waited until Vizka had gone from the cabin before he picked himself up, wiping a smear of blood from his lip. A large, fat, one-eared rat named Feerog, who was Grivel's messmate, shot him a warning glance.

Codj headed for the door, calling over his shoulder, "I'm gonna keep watch on der stripe'ound." Vizka and Codj were very close, so the crew did not say anything until he had gone out on deck. Once the captain and first mate were not present, Grivel spat blood upon the floor.

"Did ya see dat, why'd 'e pick on me, wot did I say?"

Feerog supported his friend. "Yarr, sometimes der cap'n will belt ya jus' fer lookin' at 'im d'wrong way. It ain't right, mates!"

Grivel poured forth his grievances against the captain of the *Bludgullet*. "Aye, an' why'd we waste a whole season sailin' round der Northland coasts, wot's ter be gained there, eh?"

There were nods, and mutters of agreement as Feerog took up the cause. "Couple o' sacks o' veggibles an' some grain. Huh, an' a crazy stripe'ound. We coulda been in the southern isles, at least 'tis allus warm there."

A runty old weasel, Snikey, spoke his piece. "Cap'n must 'ave 'ad 'is reasons, any'ow we're sailin' clear o' the Northlands now, ain't we?"

Grivel's voice was thick with bitterness. "But we ain't bound fer no southern isles, are we? I'll wager der cap'n's got dis ship 'eaded for the Western shores, an' ye know wot dat means, don't ya?"

Feerog slammed his knifepoint into the mess table. "Aye, Vizka Longtooth wants ter do wot Windflin Wildbrush couldn't. Kill dat ole stripe'ound an' 'is rabbets, an' make 'imself king o' der mountain!"

Snikey shrugged. "I'd sooner live on a mountain than be stuck aboard dis tub all me life."

This was the chance Grivel had been waiting for. Grabbing Snikey, he head-butted the runty old weasel hard. Still holding Snikey, he kicked open the cabin door, and flung him, half-stunned, out onto the deck, growling at him. "We ain't gittin' slayed in battle, jus' ter make Longtooth famous. An' remember this, ya liddle sneak, one werd to Vizka or Codj, an' yore a deadbeast!" Slamming the door, Grivel winked at the others. "I caught 'im a good 'un, split 'is nose, stinkin' tale-carrier. I've never trusted dat weasel!"

A black rat, called Durgy, shook his head. "Ya did der wrong thing there, mate, everybeast knows Snikey's the cap'n's spy, 'is mouth'll 'ave t'be shut fer good, or 'e'll go blabbin' ter Longtooth."

Feerog pulled his knife from the tabletop. "Yore right, I'll see to it dat Snikey slips off nice'n'quiet-like."

Late afternoon found the weather still overcast, but calm. Gorath stayed huddled against the mast, where he had been since early morning. The pangs of seasickness had left him, and the pain in his wounded forehead had calmed somewhat. Nobeast had bothered him all day, though he was aware of Codj watching him from a distance.

Then the cook, a greasy, bloated ratwife, dragged a cauldron along the deck, halting where she knew the chained prisoner could not reach. Taking the lid from the cauldron, she began stirring it, yelling in a shrill voice, "Come an' get yore vittles, afore I tosses 'em overboard!"

The aroma of cooked food assailed Gorath's nostrils, and he realised how desperately hungry he was. The crew lined up with their bowls and dishes as she began slopping out steaming ladles of the mixture. Even Vizka attended, holding out a basin, and questioning the cook as she filled it to the brim with the mixture.

"Mmmm, this smells good, wot is it, Glurma?"

She gave Vizka a snaggletoothed grin. "Me own special skilley, Cap'n, carrots'n'turnips, oats an' herbs, wid lots o' shrimp an' mackerel in it!"

Vizka winked broadly at the vermin crew, who were sitting out of Gorath's reach, eating their meal. "Yarr, dat'll put der twinkle back in yore eyes, buckoes!" They made a great show of blowing on the hot skilley and scooping it up, some with their grimy bare paws.

Vizka knew just how far the chain would allow his captive to roam. Carefully, he placed the filled bowl out of the young badger's reach, and began coaxing him. "Come an' taste it, friend, ya must be starvin', eh?" Gorath uncovered his head and stared at the bowl, but he made no move for it. Vizka continued taunting. "Good vittles, shrimp an' fishes from der Northland coast, an' veggibles from yore farm, try some."

Gorath rose; he staggered forward to the end of the chain, reaching out. The crew laughed uproariously at his vain attempts to reach the bowl. The badger gave up, and went to sit with his back to the mast.

The golden fox dipped a paw in the bowl and sucked it. "Real good dis is, Rock'ead. Tell ya wot, I'll move it closer if'n ya speak ter me."

Gorath locked eyes with the smiling fox, but kept silent. Something in those eyes made Vizka feel nervous, the smile fell from his face and he snarled.

"Widout food yore a deadbeast. Speak!"

Then the badger spoke. "You will die before I do. You, and that other one." Here he nodded toward Codj. "And as many of these scum as I can take with me. So don't waste your time talking, I don't speak with beasts who are already dead to me."

Vizka leapt up, quivering. "You'll beg me ta die afore I'm done wid ya!" He kicked the bowl, sending it into the sea. The golden fox strode back to his cabin, with Codj trotting in his wake.

"I told ya we shoulda killed 'im, Cap'n!"

Vizka shoved Codj into the cabin ahead of him. "Shut yore mouth, idjit, der crew can 'ear ya!"

Nobeast noticed Durgy sidle up to the rail and sit beside Snikey. The runty weasel was licking inside his empty bowl, when the black rat murmured into his ear softly.

"Did ya see dat? Waste o' good vittles, der way our cap'n kicked dat bowl o' skilley overboard. I coulda ate dat extra bowl, couldn't you, mate?"

Snikey stared into his empty bowl. "Aye."

"Den why doncha go an' gerrit, spy!"

Snikey fell backward into the sea from the rail, a look of shock on his face, and Durgy's blade between his ribs. Grivel and Feerog quickly filled the vacant space at the rail. Durgy nodded at the sea.

"Snikey's just gone ter get more skilley."

6

There was not a single cloud on Maudie (the Hon.) Mugs-berry Thropple's horizon. The young haremaid did not even feel the weight of the haversack on her back as she skipped blithely along the dunetops. She, among all other hares at Salamandastron, had been chosen to go on this most important quest. Once more, she went over the instructions, which had been drummed into her by Lord Asheye and Major Mullein.

"Find a bloomin' badger. One who knows not his own strength. A beast from the simple life, who shuns armour, an' knows not the sword. Er, what else? Oh yes, he's got destiny marked on his blinkin' brow, an' er, what next?"

She paused on one paw, wrinkling her nose. "Er ... er ... gottit! He walks with a banished one, an' a flame, that's it. Find him an' haul the blighter back to the jolly old mountain. Oh, well remembered, that, maid!" Still balancing on one paw, she took stock of her position.

To the west, the great sea was an expanse of turquoise and blue, twinkling under a clear summer sky. Below her was the coastline shore, sweeping up into the dunes. Ahead, and off to the right, lay heath, low hills and scrubland, with a fringe of treeline in the distance. Not having the faintest idea where she was going, Maudie picked up a pawful of sand. She tossed it into the air, calling aloud, "I say, Mother Nature old thing, which way do I go now?" Incoming sea breezes blew the sand grains off toward the distant trees. Maudie threw a casual salute to the sky. "Thankee, marm, the woodlands it is!"

Setting herself a brisk pace, she marched off, still trying to repeat the instructions. "Find a blinkin' badger with destiny marked on his armour, or somethin' like that. Er, one who shuns the simple sword for life, an' walks with a confounded fear of a flamin' banished one. Oh, my giddy aunt! Not to worry, Maudie old gel, you'll know the blighter when you trip over him, wot!"

Having spent her first night out camped in the dunes, Maudie had broken her fast in the early morn, with a dried crust of oatbread and a swig of water. She complained to herself as she marched through the scrubland.

"Huh, a skinny old crust an' a single gobful of water. What sort of food's that to give an expert cook? I'll bet the chaps back at the mess are crammin' their fat faces with all kinds of fascinatin' fodder. Right, that's it! As soon as I get the chance I'm goin' to whip up a good cooked lunch for m'self!" The thought of hot food cheered Maudie up no end. Never downhearted for long, the incorrigible haremaid broke out into song, making up the words as she went along.

"Oh, I love nothin' better than a meal that's served
    up hot,
so stir your stumps there, Cooky,
an' let's see what you've got.
A pie, a pastie or pudden,
a flan, a stew or cake,
to save a poor maid starvin',
let's see what ye can make.
Me tummy's a-rumble, apple crumble
just might halt its din;
a fair old scoop of mushroom soup,

would stop me growin' thin.
You'd win my heart with a damson tart,
I'd wolf it at one bite,
an' follow it up with a fruitcake
at dinnertime tonight!
Oh, serve more salad, I fear my ballad
is coming to an end,
take pity on me with a fresh pot o' tea,
'cos I'm fading fast, dear friend.
Pretty soon, I fear, you well may hear
this maiden's final moans,
tell Mama not to weep, or to lose any sleep,
when they find her daughter's bones!"

As she trilled the last notes of her song, Maudie became aware of a mole. He was trundling along a few paces behind her, pulling a small wheelbarrow. He was an old creature, dusty and ragged. Moreover, he was weeping copiously. The haremaid halted, and the mole bumped into her, probably because he could not see through his tears. Maudie gave him her kerchief, enquiring gently, "I say, old lad, are you alright?"

The mole blew his snout resoundingly, then snuffled. "Hurr, missy, that'n bee's the saddest likkle song oi ever hurrd en all moi loife."

Maudie felt quite upset, so she started comforting him. "It's not true, y'know, just something I made up. There now, dry your eyes an' stop cryin'."

The mole did as he was bid, though he looked rather rueful. "But oi do luvs a gudd, sad song, marm, thurr b'ain't nuthin' loike a gurt ole weep, makes a body feel better roight h'away."

Maudie gave him a small curtsy. "Oh well, I'm sorry I stopped you bawlin', if y'like that sort o' thing. You just jolly well carry on if you like weepin', wot!"

The mole tugged his snout politely (as good-mannered moles do) and extended his paw. "No, no, oi'm over et

46

naow, miz, oi bee's called Bungwen ee Hurmit. You'm must've bee'd gurtly 'ungered to be singen' ee song loike that 'un."

The haremaid shook Bungwen's paw. "Actually I am a mite peckish for some hot vittles. My name's Maudie, pleased t'meet you, Bungwen."

The mole sat on his barrow, which was loaded with roots, tubers and berries. He smiled affably. "Mouldy, that bee's a noice name. Oi tell ee wot, Miz Mouldy, iffen you'd push me'n ee barrer to moi dwellin', oi'll treat ee to an 'ot lunch, wudd that suit ee?"

At the mention of a hot lunch, Maudie seized the barrow shafts. "I say, splendid! You just roar out the directions, old fellow, an' you've got a lunch guest!"

Bungwen's dwelling was a cave dug into the side of a hill. Heaving himself from the barrow, he beckoned Maudie inside. "Cumm ee in, Miz Mouldy, this yurr's moi 'umble 'ome!"

It was indeed humble, but comfortable, a small cave, with ledge seats padded thick with dried grasses. It contained a stove, built from rock slabs and chinked with solidified mud.

The hermit mole poured Maudie a beaker of dark liquid from a jug. "Naow, you'm set thurr an' sup that, miz, 'tis moi own tansy'n'coltsfoot corjul. Oi'll make moiself bizzy with ee stew, t'woant be long en cummen!"

It was rather dark inside the cave, but there was enough light coming in from the entrance to distinguish things. The cordial was chilled, and tasted delicious. Maudie sipped it as she watched Bungwen tending to the cauldron on the stove. Some of the herbs he was adding to his stew were very aromatic.

"Hurr, wot brings ee owt yurr, miz, bee's you'm losted?"

The haremaid shook her head. "I'm not lost, I'm on an important mission. By the way, have you seen a large badger type roaming your neighbourhood—huge, hefty,

47

fearless-lookin' type? I think he carries a flame, an' has a banished one with him. Don't suppose you've spotted the chap, wot?"

Bungwen stirred the cauldron, tasting a small drop. "Only ones oi sees round yurr bee's they rarscally sandy blizzards, miz, they'm woan't leave oi alone." As he spoke they heard the wheelbarrow being upturned outside. Bungwen put the lid on his cauldron, and brandished the ladle. "They'm smelled moi cooken an' cummed to steal et!"

Mocking, hissing voices came from outside.

"Gizzzzzz vittlessssss, ssssoilmoussssse!"

"Give vittlessss to ussss, or elsssse!"

Maudie restrained her friend from dashing outside. "I say, steady on, old lad, who are those blighters?"

Bungwen growled. "Oi tole ee, miz, they'm blizzards, narsty bunch o' villyuns!"

The haremaid flexed her limbs in a businesslike manner. "Right ho, 'nuff said, matey. Now you stay out o' this, an' I'll toddle out an' educate those bullies!"

She strode resolutely out of the cave, assessing the situation at a glance.

About a dozen male sand lizards were scattering the contents of Bungwen's barrow about. Their emerald green flanks glistened in the sun, dark, reptilian eyes flickering hither and thither, seeking more mischief. When they saw Maudie, the group froze, staring balefully at her.

She glanced coolly back at them, issuing orders like a nursemaid dealing with unruly youngsters. "Clean the sand out your ears an' listen to me, you blitherin' bunch. Kindly put that barrow back the way you found it, an' clear off, smartish, wot!"

One, bigger than the rest, reared up on his tail. "Ssstay out of our biznessssss, longearsssss!"

Maudie began bouncing on her footpaws, milling her forepaws in small, tight circles. "No point talkin' t'you foul felons, wot! You need two swift lessons, one in manners, the other in the noble art of hare boxin'. Right, defend y'self, sir!" She shot out a quick, thudding hook to the lizard's jaw, sending him flat on his back. Not for nothing was Maudie (the Hon.) Mugberry Thropple, Regimental Boxing Champion of the Long Patrol. She threw herself upon the startled bullies, yelling the war cry of perilous hares. "Eulaliiiaaaa!"

With all four paws going like pistons, the haremaid sent her foes scattering. Thunderous punches, and punishing kicks, rained savagely on the reptiles. She was everywhere at once, jabbing, swinging, feinting, uppercutting and lashing out fiercely with her footpaws. "Blood'n'vinegar! Forward the buffs! Eulaliiiaaaa!"

With lightning precision, Maudie managed to overcome the lizards, even stopping the few who tried to sneak off. The beaten reptiles cowered on the ground, squeaking and whimpering abjectly. The avenging haremaid stood over them, scowling sternly.

"Up on y'paws now, you slimy crew. Set that barrow upright an' place everythin' back in it neatly. Stir y'stumps!"

The sand lizards tottered about, nursing bruised heads and fractured tails as they did Maudie's bidding.

Bungwen the Hermit was awestruck. "Boi okey, Miz Mouldy, oi never see'd ought loike that afore. You'm surrpintly a gurt, moighty wurrier, burr aye!"

Maudie winked broadly at the old mole. "Think nothin' of it, old top, glad to be of service, wot! Here, you lizard types, form up in a line now. Quick's the word an' sharp's the action, jump to it, laddies! Now, let's hear you apologisin' to Mister Bungwen."

The reptiles were forced to bow politely as they hissed, "Ssssorry, sssssir!"

Bungwen nodded, grinning from ear to ear, as Maudie stamped up and down behind her vanquished foes, treading heavily on their tails as she cautioned them.

"Sorry? I should jolly well think so, you pan-faced, twiddle-pawed, string-tailed, misbegotten lot! Now begone from here this instant, and just let either of us catch you in these parts again. By the left, we'll make you weep for a full season. Now get out of our sight!"

Bungwen thoroughly enjoyed sending the bullies on their way with good solid kicks to their nether parts. Paw in paw, the mole and the haremaid swaggered back into the cave, with Maudie chuckling, "Well, that certainly worked up my appetite, wot!"

Bungwen watched in amazement as Maudie downed several bowls of the hot stew. "Beggen' you'm pardun, miz, but oi'd be afeared to meet ee if'n you'm bee'd proper 'ungry!"

The haremaid nodded, holding forth her beaker for more cordial. Eating was a serious business with Mad Maudie, leaving her no time for idle chitchat. After taking a brief nap, she gave her host some rudimentary boxing tips, and made him a gift of her sling and pouch of slingstones, which she seldom found use for.

"Well, time for me t'be movin' on, old thing, I should make the woodlands by early evenin'. Goodbye, an' remember, don't take any old lip from those bullies, give 'em the old one-two if they ever show their warty snouts around here again, wot!"

Bungwen Hermit shook Maudie's paw warmly. "Oi'll do jus' that, miz, an' thankee furr yore cump'ny. You'm take gudd care of eeself naow. Hurr, oi'd watch owt furr surrpints on ee scrublands, thurr bee's one or two slitherin' abowt this season. If'n ee sees a gurt owlyburd, doan't be afeared of 'im, ee's a gudd friend o' moine, name o' Asio Bardwing. May'aps ee's see'd this badgerer you'm lukkin' furr. Goo'bye Miz Mouldy, gudd fortune go with ee!"

Bungwen stood atop his hill, waving and weeping, as the haremaid set off in the late noon sunshine. He blew his snout loudly, and called out to her, "Pay ee no 'eed to moi tears, miz, oi dearly do luvs a gudd ole blubber!"

Maudie felt sad to leave him, but she straightened her shoulders and strode out resolutely for the woodlands. The countryside was quiet, save for the usual heathland noises, droning bees, the chirruping of grasshoppers and the high trill of descending skylarks. Keeping a wary eye out for snakes, she sang an old barrack room ballad to herself.

"O Corporal I'm weary, can't ye hear me,
when do we stop for tea,
I feel I'm goin' out o' my mind,
would you like to come with me!

"Right, left, left, you clod,
here comes the awkward squad!

"Pass me a flagon from out o' the wagon,
the fat old Sergeant said.
the cook says he can't read the cookery book,
so he's makin' a broth of his head!

"Right, left, left, you clod,
here comes the awkward squad!

"The Quartermaster's goin' faster,
he ain't goin' to halt,
the Colonel's a nut as we all know,
an' I think it's a Major fault!

"Right, left, left, you clod,
here comes the awkward squad!"

Maudie chuckled to herself, recalling the season she was put in training. All the recruits were so dim and clumsy that they were named the awkward squad. The treeline was in plain view now, stately beeches, spreading oaks, and shrubby elders were easily discernible. Maybe that was where Bungwen's friend, the owl Asio Bardwing, lived.

There was no discernible sound from behind her, but a sudden instinct caused the haremaid to turn around. She thought she caught a swift flash of shiny green flanks top-

51

ping a mound, but then they vanished from sight. She thought that it could be the sand lizards following her, bent on some sort of revenge for the beating she had meted out to them, but she could not be sure. Maudie reasoned that it would not do any harm to let them know she was ready and able for them. Unshouldering her knapsack, she made an elaborate show of rolling up her tunic sleeves, and spitting on her paws, in a truculent manner. Then she yelled out a challenge.

"Come for another dose, wot? You snotty-snouted sneakers! Well, here's the gel who's jolly well ready for ye, show yourselves if ye bloomin' well dare! You blighters are dealin' with a Long Patrol Boxin' Champion. Did ye know Big Stinky Wothers, eh? Well, he didn't last one round with me. Aye, an' Nutpaw Jarkins, Sideswiper Smythe, an' Fearless Frink Maclurch. I laid them all out, despite the fact that they were proper pugilists! Hah, I could whip the flippin' lot of ye, with one paw tied behind m'back. So come on, who'll be first for a good helpin' o' paw pudden, ye lily-livered layabouts?"

There was no reply from the scrublands.

Maudie shouldered her pack and pressed on, muttering to herself darkly. "Just let 'em try, they don't call me Mad Maudie for nothin, wot! Sand lizards, hah, they'll be slit gizzards by the time I'm finished with 'em!"

She reached the trees whilst it was still daylight. Gathering some firewood, the young haremaid set about lighting a small fire, in the shade of an oak. Rummaging through her pack, she came up with some chestnut flour, dried berries and hazelnuts. Adding water to the flour she kneaded it into a firm, stiff dough. Sprinkling it liberally with nuts and berries, Maudie rolled it out into a long sausage shape. After coiling it around a green stick, she proceeded to cook it over the flames. The result was an appetising, if somewhat curiously shaped, cake which she called a Throppletwist, in honour of her family name.

Bungwen had tucked a flask of his cordial into her knapsack; it complemented her supper quite nicely.

The haremaid sat with her back against the oak, eating her Throppletwist, which was cooked to the greenstick, and sipping cordial. Maudie was a garrulous creature, and often held conversations with herself.

"Wonder if Corporal Thwurl's nose is still swollen? Big, droopy-faced rule stickler, I should've jolly well given him a cauliflower ear, wot! I'll bet some of the chaps back at barracks would go green if they could see me now. Assistant Cook, sent out on a blinkin' secret important mission, eh. 'Strewth, if I make a bloomin' good go at this, Lord Asheye'll prob'ly promote me to Colonel Cook in Charge. Hoho, C.C.I.C. I'd liven 'em up a bit, wot?"

Maudie put on what she imagined was a doddery commanding voice, issuing orders to all and sundry. "Hawhawhaw, you there, young feller me laddo, fetch me a bumpkin o' Fine Fettle Olde Cider, there's a good chap. I say, Corporal, wot'syourface, Thwurl, yes, you sah. Kindly slice me a scone, an' bung some raspb'rry jam on it. Don't stand there catchin' flies with y'mouth, jump to it, laddy buck. Ah, this is the jolly old life, wot wot!"

She chuntered on to herself as the evening sun dipped into the western horizon. It was comfortable, sitting by the little fire, taking supper in the warm afterglow. Maudie had been walking all day, apart from the few hours she had spent with Bungwen Hermit. The young haremaid let her eyes slowly droop shut. She was hardly aware of the two sand lizards, each holding the end of a rope. They scampered on either side of her, racing around the oak trunk, which Maudie had her back to. She blinked and sat up straight. "What the bloom . . ."

The reptiles raced by her again, meeting up at the rear of the tree, where they swiftly knotted the rope. Maudie strained at her bonds, but her body and forepaws were bound tight to the oak. She was trapped. The haremaid's first reaction tumbled forth indignantly. "I say, let me loose, you sneaky rotters, or it'll be the worse for you. Flippin' cads!"

The rest of the lizards slithered out of cover to confront her. The largest of the bunch, the first one she had attacked earlier, came right up to Maudie. There was a blotchy swelling on the side of his jaw. He hissed viciously at her, pointing to the injury. "Sssee thissss? Now you will sssssuffer for it!"

7

Orkwil Prink spent his first night away from Redwall beneath an overhang of bushes on a ditchside. It was the first time since his infancy that he had not slept in the Abbey. The young hedgehog's former joyous mood deserted him as soon as night descended.

He found himself flinching whenever anything moved in the breeze; imaginary shapes in the darkness frightened him. Even the nocturnal woodland sounds sent a shudder through Orkwil. Miserably, he crept along the northern path. Then he tripped and fell into the ditch.

Luckily, there was very little water in it, but there was quite a bit of mud. Panicked, he floundered about, sloshing through the malodorous mire. Bush fronds, dangling down, tangled into his headspikes. Orkwil gurgled in terror. Had some hideous beast of prey caught him? He struggled to free himself, and then realised it was merely an overhanging bush.

Sobbing with relief, Orkwil hauled himself up the ditchside and found shelter amid the dense vegetation. Perching between two thick branches, and plastered with smelly mud, he wished fervently to be back safe inside Redwall. But alas, that would not be possible for a full season. He wiped away a muddy tear, thinking, *That's if I live that long!*

Oh, for the dear old Abbey. Laughing and joking with friends, by the fireside in Cavern Hole, a delicious supper, maybe hot soup and toasted muffins. Then up to the dormitory, and his little truckle bed, for a peaceful night's sleep, between lavender-scented quilts, with a soft pillow for his head.

Orkwil licked at his salt tears, then spat away the mud. Here he was, through no fault of his own, none of that lot back there understood him. Mouldy old Elders! Trouble with them was that none of them could take a little joke. Huh, they all got their stuff back, didn't they? Well, nearly all. Still, that was no reason to turn a harmless little hog out into the wilds. It was their fault he was stuck in a ditch, covered with slutch. Orkwil managed to extract a plain oat scone from his bundle. He gnawed at it, thinking up recriminations to heap upon his tormentors' heads.

Suppose he got trapped here and couldn't get out, what then, eh? A huge storm might come, with torrents of rain, and the ditch would fill up, into a raging river, to wash him away and drown him in the process. Probably Granspike Niblo would find his young battered body, when she was out gathering watercress. Orkwil pictured the scene. His limp carcass being carried back to Redwall, on a stretcher strewn with woodland blossoms. The Dibbuns howling with grief, and the Elders having to accept the blame for their harsh sentence. Hah, they'd be sorry then, especially that Marja Dubbidge, and Fenn Bluepaw, seeing as it was they who started all his misfortunes. Father Abbot Daucus would shake his head sadly and say that no youngbeast would ever be banished for a full season again. Redwallers had learned a stark lesson from young Orkwil Prink, a good little creature, cut off in his tender seasons.

Orkwil finished his plain oat scone, feeling very self-righteous. At least he had done something good for all the other young Redwallers. Saved them from such harsh punishments in the seasons to come. Well, of course he had. He wagered they would probably raise a memorial over his grave in the Abbey grounds. Aye, and hold an Orkwil Prink rememberance day, once every summer. At this point, Orkwil could not hold himself back from shouting aloud.

"And that'll teach you all a lesson, won't it?" His cry disturbed two blackbirds that were nesting in the bush, which shook as they fluttered off. What was that? Orkwil wondered. He crouched there, shivering, until he fell into weary sleep, clinging to the branches.

Is not the light of day a wondrous thing? It banishes all fears and worries of the previous night. Warm sunlight shafting into the leafy bush canopy wakened Orkwil. He stretched his paws, yawned and promptly fell from the shelter of the bush, down into the ditchbed ooze. Uttering some very fruity oaths, which would have earned him a good dressing-down at the Abbey, he scrambled back up onto the pathside.

Wolfing down another plain oat scone and an apple, Orkwil breakfasted as he resumed his journey, regardless of the foul-smelling mud, which was caked thick on his spikes. As he trudged along, an idea began forming in the young hedgehog's mind. Maybe he could find a friendly little family of woodlanders, dormice or bankvoles. They would probably live in a snug little cottage, somewhere along a riverbank. He could become useful to them, helping with the everyday chores. Then he could pass away a pleasant season, with a roof over his head, and vittles aplenty. Maybe he would stay with his new friends for more than a season, perhaps two.

Orkwil giggled aloud. They'd start getting worried at Redwall, when he didn't turn up at autumn. Probably wear their paws out, sending search parties to look for him. Now, where was the nearest river on the northern path? It had to be the River Moss. He'd heard Skipper Rorc talking about it. There was a ford that crossed the path, someplace further up, Skipper had said so.

With a lighter heart, and a renewed spring to his paws, Orkwil forged onward. He halted at noon, peering up the path, not sure whether the shimmer in the distance was from the heat haze, or the ford waters. Plumping himself down on the mossy bankside, he undid his bundle. There were only more plain scones and a flask of pennycloud cordial. The young hedgehog pulled a face. "Measly little rations, they're prob'ly having a great lunch back at the Abbey, out in the orchard, like they always do in summer. All kinds of trifle, an' pudden, strawberry fizz, an' all that. Hmm, what's this?"

Opening a small package, which he had not noticed before, Orkwil was delighted to find about a dozen candied chestnuts. He chuckled happily. "Good ole Granspike, bet she slipped them in for me!" He was stuffing them down when he felt a sharp pain in his back. "Yowch!" Orkwil turned and saw a magpie, about to peck him again. Angrily, he lashed out at it, shouting, "What d'ye think yore doin', be off with ye, bird!"

The magpie, a handsome black and white fellow, merely hopped back a pace, and stood with its head on one side, staring impudently at the young hedgehog.

Orkwil raised a clenched paw threateningly. "Ye cheeky wretch, I said be off!"

The magpie leapt forward, pecked at Orkwil's paw, and skipped nimbly backward. The young hedgehog was furious.

"I'll give ye such a clout . . . I'll . . ."

The bird gave a mocking cackle. "Raaaahakarr!"

Orkwil retaliated then. He grabbed the staff, which his bundle had been tied to, and swiped at the magpie. It hopped out of range, and Orkwil ran at it, swinging the staff. "Ye hard-faced featherbag!"

The magpie flew up, then hovered, cackling raucously, but staying just out of the staff's reach. Orkwil sought about and found a pebble, which he flung at the bird. This time it dodged to one side, then flew across the path, into one of the trees bordering Mossflower Wood. Orkwil brandished the staff at it.

"You start pesterin' me again an' I'll break yore beak!" He turned back to his lunch, only to find it all gone. The plain oat scones, and the remains of his candied chestnuts, were missing. Only the kerchief his bundle had been wrapped in lay on the ground. The uncorked flask had been tipped over, and all the pennycloud liquid had spilled into the ground.

Orkwil was furious, more so when he was greeted by a chorus of harsh cackles from the nearby trees. A group of about nine magpies was perched in the branches, gobbling down his supplies. He waved his staff and ran at them, thwacking away lustily. The scavengers merely flew up to higher branches, where they continued eating their plunder and mocking him. Chattering with rage, the young hedgehog hopped and leapt, trying to reach them with his staff.

"Ye scum-beaked thieves, ye patch-faced robbers, just let me get my paws on ye!"

Safe in their high position, the magpies performed little strutting dances, adding to Orkwil's anger. This did not improve matters. He redoubled his efforts, hurtling himself at the tree trunks, throwing pawfuls of earth, and any stones he could find.

It was a futile exercise, though it took Orkwil some time to realise this. He ended up flat out on the path, huffing and blowing for breath, completely worn out. The magpies continued their derision, even dropping leaves and pieces of twig down on him.

After awhile, Orkwil wearily stood up and walked away from the scene, with the birds' scornful cackles echoing in his ears. The ditchmud had set hard between his spikes, it was heavy, uncomfortable, and itched him unmercifully. He became sullen and morose again. How far was it to this river ford, he needed a long soak, and a good bath. The nerve of those birds, too, stealing all his supplies like that.

Thieves and robbers, that's all they were! Then he recalled that the same thing had been said of himself, only a day ago at the Abbey.

Noontide shadows were lengthening when Orkwil saw the ford, running across the path up ahead. Stumbling and staggering with exhaustion, he tottered forward, grunting with the effort of placing one footpaw in front of the other. On reaching the ford, he lay on his stomach in the shallow edge, letting forth a sigh, which sounded like a deflating balloon. Water, fresh running water! Orkwil sucked up huge draughts of the clean, cold liquid. Then he rolled into the ford and went deeper, allowing the current to carry him downriver for a distance. Grabbing the hanging branches of a willow tree, he halted his progress. His footpaws just barely touched bottom, the river came up to his chin. After ducking his head several times, Orkwil clung there, feeling the soothing current washing him clean and refreshing his body. *What a wonderful thing riverwater is,* he thought. Then he noticed the watervole watching him from the far bank. Redwall Abbey had taught Orkwil manners, he nodded amiably to the creature. "Good day to ye, sir."

The watervole was a big, bushy old beast, his dark brown fur heavily streaked with grey. He squinted at the young hedgehog, snapping out a reply. "Never mind what sort o' day 'tis, what're ye trespassin' round here for, eh?"

Orkwil put on a friendly smile. "I'm sorry, I didn't know I was trespassin', I was only taking a bath."

The watervole nodded, first up-, then downriver.

"Plenty o' river both sides, without dirtyin' up my stretch. Are ye stealin' my watercress, is that it, eh?"

Orkwil shook his head, still acting friendly. "No, sir, honestly. Matter o' fact, I've had all my supplies stolen from me. Back there, down the path. It was a bunch o' magpies that did it."

The watervole smiled maliciously. "Serves ye right then, don't it. No thievin' magpie'd get near my watercress. Not my fault yore vittles got pinched, 'tis yore own! Nobeast takes a bath round here 'cept me, so get movin', 'edgepig!"

Orkwil had been building up a dislike for the watervole. He was about to deliver a few cutting insults, when the watervole suddenly spoke cordially to him.

"Do y'see these big clumps o' watercress growin' by the bank, matey? Would ye pick some of 'em for me?"

Orkwil saw his opportunity to do what he had been planning. Help somebeast out, who lived by the river. Maybe this watervole wasn't such a bad old codger. There might be a chance that he could live with him for the season, helping out. Holding his chin high, he waded across, to where the watercress grew in profusion. "Certainly, sir. My name's Orkwil Prink, now you just let me know when I've thrown enough watercress over. Here comes the first lot!"

He began heaving bunches of the plant to the watervole, who caught them eagerly, stacking them high. The young hedgehog went to his task with a right good will, conversing as he did. "This looks like good, fresh cress, sir, what'll ye be makin' with it, a salad?"

The watervole nodded. "Aye, salad, though that'll do for lunch tomorrow. I'm goin' to make a big pot o' my favourite, watercress, mushroom an' watershrimp soup."

The young hedgehog chuckled. "Sounds wonderful, I've never tasted a soup like that before, sir."

The watervole clambered out onto the bank. He picked up a bow and arrows. Notching a shaft to his bowstring, he sneered, in a cold, hard voice, "An' yore not likely to taste it, Orful Stink, or wotever yore name is. Now leave that watercress alone, an' get out o' here, afore I puts an arrow in yer. Go an' find yore own food someplace else, you ain't gittin' none o' mine. Move!"

Orkwil was shocked by the watervole's meanness, and told him so in no uncertain terms. "Why, ye nasty old skinflint, y'selfish, crafty, graspin', cressgrabber! If I'd have known . . ."

61

The watervole aimed the arrow, drawing back his bow-string threateningly. "Shut yore mouth, 'edgepig, an' make yoreself scarce. I'll give ye a count o' three, then I shoot!"

By the look in his mean little eyes, Orkwil knew that he was not joking. He immediately began swimming back to the ford.

Evening was setting in as Orkwil waded from the water. He sat dejectedly on the ford bank, smarting with indignity from his treatment by the watervole, and listening to the rumbling growls from his stomach. He was hungry. Orkwil cast about, in an effort to find some food, but he was pretty useless at foraging for himself.

That was the trouble with being brought up in an Abbey, he reasoned bitterly. If you wanted food, you went to the kitchens, and they fed you. Aye, and it was all deliciously cooked, too. There was no grubbing around in the soil, or searching the wilderness. Orkwil knew that young ones learned about such things as self-survival at Abbey school. But he was always missing, hiding away somewhere in a barrel, the result being, he never attended. Life wasn't fair, he concluded. But he picked himself up and began foraging about for vittles.

It was dark by the time he returned to the ford. All he had managed to gather was some dandelion roots, a few berries that the birds had missed, an apple that was hard and green and a plant that he surmised was edible, but he was unsure whether to eat the top or the bottom of it. He drank a bit more water, and sat down to think hard about a solution to his predicament.

It came to him suddenly. He had been branded a thief, so why not be one, properly, at least it was one thing he was good at. He flung the bits he had gathered away, waded to the other side of the ford, then set off downriver along the bank. Orkwil knew when he was in the area of the water-vole's home, he could smell the soup on the fire.

Now, how to separate one miserable, fat beast from one

steaming pot of soup? That was the problem. It was solved for him when a rustling in the underbrush caused Orkwil to dodge behind a sycamore. It was a pair of vermin, a big, brutish river rat, and his equally sly-looking mate. They, too, had smelled the soup, and were figuring out how to lay paws on it. The vermins' solution was simple. The big male rat produced a hardwood club.

"It'll be that ole watervole, I've spotted 'im round 'ere afore. We'll just charge in, knock the livin' daylights outta the ole fool, an' rob 'is vittles!"

His mate took a saw-toothed knife from her ragged smock. "Aye, drag 'im out onto the bank, then when we've ate the food, we kin 'ave a bit o' fun with 'im!"

Orkwil had never encountered hostile vermin before. He was horrified at their savagery. Peeping around the sycamore trunk, he watched as they searched the bankside. The female found the entrance to their victim's home. Smothering her sniggers, she pranced about, waving the knife in anticipation.

Her mate brandished his club, muttering a warning. "Don't yew go stickin' 'im with that thing right away, couple o' taps on the noggin with this'll send 'im t'sleep. We can play games with 'im later. Alright, foller me!"

They vanished into the entrance. Orkwil had a sickly feeling in the pit of his stomach about what was going to happen next. He stayed behind the tree trunk, trying to reason things out. Really speaking, it was none of his business. The old watervole had been very nasty to him, why would he want to help a creature like that? Then there was the question of two fierce river rats, carrying weapons. They were obviously killers. Suppose they'd caught *him*, would the watervole come running to offer his help? Huh, hardly!

The spikes on the young hedgehog's back stood rigid, as agonised squeals and cruel laughter issued forth from the victim's dwelling. There was a moment's silence, then the river rat emerged, dragging the watervole by his footpaws, and calling to his mate.

"Fetch that soup out 'ere, I'm starvin'. Heeheehee, did ye 'ear the way this 'un squealed? Bumblin' idjit, wouldn't 'old still so I could knock 'im out proper. Huh, 'e near fell in the soup twice!" He set about binding the unconscious creature with a rope he had found in the dwelling.

His mate staggered out, bent double with the weight of a cauldron full of hot soup. She set it down, licking her paws. "Mmmm, s'good soup, this, fulla watershrimps!"

Both rats leaned over the soup, dabbing their paws in, alternately blowing and licking on them, as they planned their captive's fate.

"We could shove 'im in the empty soup pot with a few rocks, an' see if it'll float in the river. Heeheehee!"

"Nah, best if'n we jus' puts 'im inna pot, lights a fire under it an' cooks 'im. Watervole soup, heehee!"

It was at that moment Orkwil decided he could not cower in hiding from the vermin, something had to be done immediately. Grabbing his staff tightly, he leapt out of hiding and charged the rats. Fortunately, they had their backs to him, and did not see the young hedgehog until too late.

One mighty whack of the yew staff between the club carrier's ears knocked him out cold. As the rat crumpled to the ground, his mate whirled around. She drew her knife swiftly, but Orkwil, aided by the speed of panic, was even quicker than she.

Crack! He hit both her paws, sending the knife flying. *Thud!* He thumped the butt end of his weapon hard into her stomach. As the river rat doubled over, with the breath whooshing from her, Orkwil struck again. Thwock! Right on the crown of her head. The vermin stood staring at him for a split second, then her eyes crossed as she tumbled facedown on the riverbank.

Orkwil was shaken from snout to spikes with the audacity of his rapid attack. It took him a few moments to regain his composure. Never having been involved in serious combat before, he had to think about what to do next. Of course, tie both the rats up before they came to.

He loosed the rope from the unconscious watervole, and dragged the rats, one by one, to a nearby beech tree. Placing their backs to the trunk, Orkwil tied their forepaws together, so they had the tree in a backward embrace. Then he attended to the vole. Grabbing some bankmoss and mud, he piled it on the old creature's head wound, and spoke to him. "There, you'll live to grumble again, old misery. Though you don't deserve any help, after the way you treated me. So I'm going to charge you a bowl of soup for my help. I think that's fair enough."

Orkwil got a bowl from inside the dwelling. He filled it, and drained it, three times before he was satisfied. The watervole was beginning to stir, groaning feebly. Orkwil placed the empty bowl alongside him, and took his leave. "I've left ye those two rats to deal with, old 'un. I don't suppose they'll get much mercy from ye, though. Oh, an' thanks for the soup, 'twas very tasty!"

This time, instead of going back to the ford, he headed downriver a short way. Not far from the bank, he found a large patch of ferns. A sudden weariness overcame Orkwil Prink. This was due to the excitement brought on by his first fight, plus the three bowls of soup, which he had guzzled with unseemly haste. The young hedgehog made his way to the centre of the fern bed and curled up there. Within moments he was fast asleep.

He was also sinking slowly into the ground, because Orkwil had unwittingly chosen to sleep in a swamp.

8

Once the *Bludgullet*'s lookout sighted land off the portside, Vizka Longtooth gave orders to heave to, and follow the coastline. The weather had become milder and was considerably warmer. It had been four days, and Gorath was still chained to the mast. The young badger had received nothing to eat, or drink, apart from a few mouthfuls of rainwater. He looked gaunt and ill, with his head wound now solidified to a hardened scab, which stuck out on his brow like some grotesque decoration. But he would not give in, either to blandishments, starvation or beatings, which were regularly inflicted upon him. The golden fox, however, still lived in hopes of converting Gorath to the life of a Sea Raider.

It was a calm summer morn, and Vizka was taking breakfast, as usual, just out of reach, but well in sight of his prisoner. He spooned warm oatmeal and honey from a bowl, making much show of enjoying it, as he taunted Gorath. "I'll wager ye worked 'ard ter grow dese oats, an' yore honey is jus' der way I likes it. Sweet'n'thick!"

The badger kept his head down, not bothering to look up at his tormentor. Vizka held the partially filled bowl out to him.

"Ye knows yer like it, Rock'ead, cummon, talk ter me, d'yer want some, eh?" When he received no reaction, the golden fox merely emptied the remainder of the bowl over the side. "I had enough o' dat, let d'fishes eat it!" Vizka picked up the length of tarred and knotted rope. "Ha, lookit wot I found, d'yer wanna taste o' dis, eh?" He was about to swing it, when his brother, Codj, approached, pointing landward.

"See, Cap'n, a river, crossin' der shore, off dat way!"

Shading his eyes, Vizka peered at the wide estuary. It ran across the sands, into the sea. "Anybeast knows dis river? Ask der crew, brother."

Codj saluted, going off to the main cabin, where some of the crew were breakfasting. He returned with Glurma, the fat, greasy ratwife, who was ship's cook. She had served on other ships before coming aboard the *Bludgullet.* Vizka nodded toward the river.

"You know dis place, eh?"

Glurma wiped grimy paws on her stained apron. "Aye, Cap'n, dat's der River Moss, runs out o' Mossflower Country."

Vizka signalled his steersbeast to take *Bludgullet* in closer. "Big river, did ye ever sail up it?"

The ratwife gnawed at a dirty paw claw. "Long time back, afore yew was borned."

The golden fox cuffed Glurma's paw away from her mouth. "Tell me 'bout it!"

Glurma sniffed and spat into the sea. "Sailed up dere wid Cap'n Boljan, in der *Sharkfin,* lookin' fer Red Abbey- walls. Never got dat far, though, only to der fordplace. Shrewbeasts, an' h'otters, 'undreds of 'em, druv us away. Mad fighters dose shrewbeasts an' h'otters, we wuz lucky ter gerrout alive. Huh, never went back dere!"

Vizka Longtooth mulled over the information, murmur- ing, "Yew was lucky t'git anyplace in a vessel liddle as der *Sharkfin.* An' wid Boljan, too, hah, dat 'un was scared've 'is own shadder. Red Abbeywalls, eh?" Vizka suddenly realised what the cook was trying to say. "Ye mean Redwall Abbey, was dat der name o' d'place?" The golden fox suddenly seized the ratwife, shaking her. "Redwall Abbey! Wot did Cap'n Boljan say about it?"

Glurma struggled to free herself of the golden fox's grip. "I'll tell ye if'n y'stop rattlin' me bones!" Vizka released the cook, who spoke willingly. "Aye, Redwall Abbey, dat's wot Boljan called it. An' 'e knew der way, 'cos 'e 'ad a chart. It wuz straight up der River Moss, carry on through der trees, 'til ye comes to a ford. Den yew abandons ship, an' marches south down der road fer mebbe a day or more, an' ye kin sight it, plain as a pikestaff. Biggest place ye ever clapped yore eyes on, an' der richest, too. Dat's wot Boljan said!"

Gorath still sat beside the mast, his head hanging low, and both eyes closed, the picture of a hopelessly beaten prisoner. However, inside his heart was thumping wildly, he had heard everything the cook had said. Redwall Abbey! This was the land of Mossflower that his grandfather had told him of. Suppressing the quivers of excitement that threatened to betray his feelings, the young badger slouched even lower, allowing his wounded forehead and muzzle to touch the deck. He listened carefully to what was said.

Vizka Longtooth issued orders. "Drop anchor an' furl dat sail. Codj, git all paws up 'ere on deck. I got summat ter say!"

With its prow facing inland, the *Bludgullet* rode at anchor in the river mouth. Gorath raised his head a fraction. He stared across the shore, to the coarse-grassed dunes, and the woodland fringe in the distance. Somewhere out there the Abbey of Redwall lay basking in the still summer haze. The golden fox flicked him across his back with a long, knotted rope.

"Looks nice, don't it, Rock'ead? But yew won't be seein' none of it, 'til ya learns some sense, or starves t'death. Makes no diff'rence t'me, 'tis yore choice."

Vizka Longtooth leaned on the tiller, waiting until all his crew had arrived. The deck was jam-packed with vermin of all types, eager to hear their captain's pronouncement. The golden fox took Gorath's pitchfork, Tung, pointing landward with it. "Ye've all 'eard o' Redwall Abbey, I wager?" A murmur of anticipation ran through the ranks. He gave it time to die away, then continued. "Dere's some says 'tis only a pretty story, an' others says 'tis real. The biggest, richest place anywheres. Well, wot d'ye say buck-oes, would ye like to find out?"

The vermin crew roared their approval. Now Vizka was really talking, this was better than scrounging around the barren Northern Isles, robbing impoverished farms. If there was such a place as the Abbey of Redwall, what secrets, and treasures, lay waiting there to be taken?

The fox captain's long teeth gleamed as he smiled. "Aye, mates, Redwall Abbey, dat's where we're bound! But mark ye, I only wants loyal crewbeasts at me back when I takes dat place on. Are ye wid me, eh?"

Brandishing a bristling array of weapons, the crew roared aloud. "Aye, Cap'n!"

Suddenly the tines of the pitchfork were pointing at the ferret, Grivel, and the two rats, Feerog and Durgy. Vizka's tone was almost cajoling them. "Haharr, an' worrabout yew three, which one of ye'd like ter lead der shore party to Redwall?"

The trio jostled one another as they strode forward, each pointing to himself.

"I'll do it, Cap'n!"

"Pick me, Cap'n!"

"Y'can trust me t'do der job, Cap'n!"

Codj gave his brother an injured look, figuring that he had been passed over as leader of the shore party. Vizka

69

winked at Codj, widening his toothy smile. Codj kept wisely silent, knowing the coming danger to somebeast, which his brother's smile always heralded.

Vizka waved the pitchfork at his crew. "Avast, who o' these three do I choose?"

Now everybeast was shouting out, calling the name of the one they fancied. The golden fox let them carry on awhile, then waved the pitchfork for silence.

"I think we should let 'em choose atwixt 'emselves, by test o' combat. Last beast standin' alive gits der job!"

Shrieks of delight echoed from the barbaric crew. "Aye, Cap'n! Test o' combat! Aye!"

A ring was quickly formed, with the three contestants at its centre. They stared uneasily at each other, then began circling. Each knew that nobeast refused an order from Vizka Longtooth, whose smile had become a wide grin of enjoyment. He signalled with the pitchfork. "Haharr, go to it, me lucky buckoes, no mercy an' no quarter. We'll see who's fit ter be der leader!"

Grivel had his cutlass out halfheartedly, he shrugged at Feerog. "We ain't got no choice, mate!"

Feerog did not hesitate; whipping out his sword, he ran Grivel through. As he did, the big, black rat, Durgy, jumped him from behind. Durgy did not have a sword, but he was expert with his dagger. Feerog gave a gasp of surprise as the blade plunged between his ribs, he collapsed silently. It was all over in the twinkling of an eye. A hush fell over the crew as they gazed at the two who had just met death.

Durgy turned to face his captain, pointing to himself with the dagger. "I think it'll be meself who'll be leadin' yore shore party, Cap'n!"

Vizka shook his head. "Not after ye've slayed three o' my crew, Durgy."

Codj looked puzzled. "Three? But dere's only two of 'em."

Vizka was enjoying himself, he nodded affably to the crew. "Three if'n ye counts pore Snikey. Durgy an' 'is two

70

mates was plottin' agin me, but Snikey 'eard 'em, so Durgy did 'im in, an' tossed 'im o'er der side. Ain't dat right, mate?"

Durgy was at a loss for words. Vizka winked at him.

"Thought ye'd fooled me, didn't ya, but der cap'n o' de *Bludgullet* knows everyt'ink. Don't 'e, Cooky?"

The fat, greasy cook, Glurma, nodded.

The crew knew then who had informed on the plotters.

Glurma ducked off silently to her galley. One or two of her vermin shipmates cast glances of disgust at her. But Vizka distracted their attention, carrying on with his summation of the good times ahead for his loyal crew.

"Belay, buckoes, I nominates Codj t'be der shore party leader. We'll take dis Redwall Abbey, an' loot it down to der stones. Loads o' booty fer all paws, eh!"

At the mention of looting and booty, the crew cheered lustily. Everybeast was firmly on the golden fox's side.

He leaned on the pitchfork, smiling indulgently at them. "Aye, booty, grog an' vittles fer my trusty cullies!" He paused, shaking his head sadly. "All 'cept fer one, an' I'll leave 'im to yew, ain't no room aboard *Bludgullet* fer mutineers. Harr, 'tis a sad day for yore ole cap'n. I'll go an' mourn in me cabin."

The circle of drawn weapons closed in on Durgy.

Vizka Longtooth paused before entering his cabin. He listened to Durgy's last scream, and heard the splash as his carcass hit the water. Then he wiped away a mock tear. "Harr, a sad day indeed!"

That evening the Sea Raiders poled their vessel up the navigable channel across the sands. Codj commanded two squads, both tugging on hawsers attached to the ship's bows. By dusk they were into the dunes. Gorath stared at the sandy walls, either side of the deck. Freedom had never looked so near, yet been so far from him. The young badger waited until the crew took to their bunks and hammocks. When the decks were deserted, he inspected the chain that held him to the mast. It was neither old nor thin, but a thick, solid iron chain, which could not be broken by any score of strong beasts. The lock went between two links, holding the chain tightly about his waist, a big lock, stout and secure. He did not know who was the key holder, though he suspected it was either Vizka or his brother. Gorath knew nothing of locks, this was the first one he had ever encountered. His big, blunt claws made no impression on it, though he tugged, heaved and even bit at the thing. Somehow, someway, he had to free himself, and escape from these vermin. He had to reach Redwall if he had any chance of staying alive.

Hunger, weariness and anxiety cast him into a sleep that was more of a faint than a slumber. He dreamed of a mouse, a fearless-looking creature, who wore armour, and carried a shining sword. The mouse spoke words into his exhausted mind.

"To perish midst vermin will not be thy fate, watch for the young thief, be still and wait!"

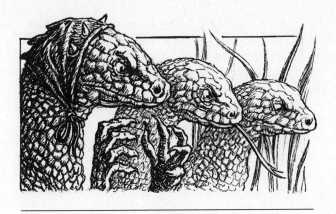

9

Mad Maudie (the Hon.) Mugberry Thropple was neither a whiner nor a pleader. Being surrounded by lizards, and bound to a tree, did nothing to dampen her fighting spirit. When the big lizard leaned over her, hissing and threatening, the haremaid managed to give him a hard kick in his green, mottled stomach. The big lizard gave a curious gurgle, and collapsed clasping his injured midriff. Maudie booted out again, dealing him another kick in the back, at about the spot where she imagined a lizard's bottom would be. Then she gave him a piece of her mind.

"Now then, you slinky blighter, pay attention! You don't frighten me in the slightest, not you, or those other caddish types skulkin' over yonder, wot!"

The big sand lizard crawled out of Maudie's reach. His face had taken on a sickly pallor, but he staggered upright, hissing viciously. "You will die forrrr thisssssss!"

Maudie twiddled her ears at him. "Yah, boo an' sucks t'you! Just wait'll I get loose, I'll boot your blinkin' tail into the middle of next season, you great, slithery wretch!" She wriggled and tugged at the rope, but to little avail, it still held her fast to the trunk of the oak. Whilst she struggled, Maudie kept an eye on the reptiles.

The big lizard had gone over to consult with the others.

73

They huddled together, making lots of lizardlike noises, and constantly pointing in the haremaid's direction. Maudie kept her spirits up by shouting insults at them.

"'Strewth, a fine lot you bounders are, d'you have to hold a full-blown conference to decide a simple maiden's fate? Hah! What's all the hissin' for? You sound like a load of old kettles, boilin' away at teatime. Now, if I were you, which I'm jolly well glad I'm not, I'd go an' find some types who'd be scared of you. Off ye go, an' frighten some frogs, or torment some toads, wot!"

As if taking her advice, the lizards dispersed, hither and thither. Maudie wrinkled her nose.

"Funny, maybe they've decided to heed my flippin' wisdom. Hmm, they're an odd lot, really, payin' attention to me. P'raps I've got a hidden talent as a lizard lecturer?"

However, after a brief interval the lizards returned, each one carrying several pebbles or pieces of rock. Still keeping out of Maudie's reach, they placed the lot in a heap. Now the big lizard came forward, he picked up a good-sized pebble. "You will die the death of a thoussssand sssstonessss!"

Maudie saw him throw, she ducked her head to one side. The pebble bounced off the oak, followed by another smaller one, which grazed her ear. Maudie winced.

"Ouch! I say, pack it in, you rotters, where's your sense of fair play? Yowch, that hurt!" A sharp piece of rock had struck her footpaw. Suddenly, an unearthly screech rent the air!

The lizards stopped what they were doing and fled in silent terror. An owl landed at Maudie's side, it was a magnificent bird, with feather tufts on its head like short ears. Huge, yellow eyes blinked at the haremaid from a rounded, white face. Maudie could not help flinching as the savage, hooked beak flashed toward her. The rope was sliced through with a single slash of the owl's beak. His head swivelled around, almost in a full circle as he addressed the haremaid.

"Whoohooooh! Ah've no doubt that thee'll forgive me, tarry there, lass, ah'm fair clemmed for t'want of a lizard!" He swooped off like a mammoth moth, great, rounded wings creating a loud, clapping sound as they smacked together on the downswing.

Maudie instantly remembered the name of the owl, which Bungwen Hermit had told her to watch out for. "Asio Bardwing, and just in the nick of flippin' time, too! Wonder where he's tootled off to, wot?"

Blowing on the ashes of her fire, Maudie added more wood, and got it burning again. It was now fully night. Maudie sat patiently by the small blaze, waiting to see if the owl would return. She was starting to nod off again, when he winged in. Perching next to her he nodded, then gave a tremendous belch. "Buuurp! Manners, owld lad! Ah'm right sorry t'be so long, lass, but ah'm right partial to a taste o' lizard now an' again. Yon big scoundrel won't bother thee n'more, nay!"

The haremaid gazed in horrified fascination at the tail of the big lizard, which was still hanging from the side of the owl's beak.

He noticed, and sucked it in with a quick slurp. "Beg pardon ah'm sure. Wot's tha name, lass?"

Maudie rose, treating him to a small curtsy. "My name's Maudie, sir, you must be Asio Bardwing."

The owl's yellow eyes went even wider. "Whooooh, how'd thee know that, are ye magic?"

Maudie chuckled. "Actually, I was told your name by an old friend of yours, Bungwen Hermit."

Asio shook his big, feathered head. "Never heard o' the beast, ah reckon you're magic. Maudie, eh? Bah gum, that's a reet grand owld name, mah Auntie Cordoolia had a second cousin, on Uncle Wilfrum's side, her name were Maudie, gradely owld duck she were. So then, Maudie lass, wot's thee doin' round here?"

The haremaid explained. "Actually, I'm lookin' for a badger, large, hefty warrior type, carries a flame an' walks with a banished one. I don't suppose you've seen him?"

Asio's head swivelled almost right around. "Thou supposes reet, lass, 'appen ah've not seen anybeast apart from thee this season. Couldn't thee see this badger with thy magic?"

Maudie added twigs to her fire. "Really, I'm not at all magic, honestly."

Asio waved a talon, which was almost the size of a small dagger, in Maudie's face. "Fie on thee, ah knows magic when ah sees it, lass. Ah'll wager thee can read claws, am ah reet?"

Maudie did not like being ungracious to her rescuer, so she humoured Asio. "Read claws? Well, just a little bit."

Asio hooted happily. "Whoohoohooh! Ah knew thee could, the moment ah set eyes on thee, lass. Here, read mine. Wot does the future hold for me, will ah wed an' have little 'uns, ah dearly would like to have a mate."

Maudie had seen fortune telling performed, at the barrack room in Salamandastron, to pass time on long winter evenings. It was all in fun, of course, a bit of harmless trickery. She had never seen it done on a bird, however, but Mad Maudie was always game for anything.

"Righto, old chap, let's see your claws."

Asio held up one foot, tipped with four murderously long, curving claws. Maudie gulped at the sight of them.

"Er, righto, now hold 'em still an' let me see what I'll jolly well see. Your name is Asio Bardwing, right?"

Asio nodded solemnly. As Maudie strove to think of her next question, he marvelled, "Aye that's reet, lass, Asio Bardwing of the Big Bardwing nest. How did thee guess that?"

Maudie suddenly realised that she was dealing with an owl who had complete memory blankness. Accordingly, she played her role to the hilt, murmuring darkly, "I know

76

this because I am Mad Mystic Maudie. Do you know a mole they call Bungwen the Hermit?"

Asio gasped. "Aye, old Bungwen the mole, I remember him now, bah gum, he were a good little bloke!"

Maudie made several passes over his claws with her paw. "Silence now, O feathery one, for I see destiny in your blinkin' claws, wot. I am getting a message from the Big Bardwing Nest, from somebird called Auntie Cordoolia, do you know such a creature?"

Asio looked flabbergasted. "Well, blow me down, she knows Auntie Cordoolia! Wot's her message, lass, er, mad Misty wotsyername, tell me?"

Maudie peered closely at the big owl's talons, and saw scraps of the big lizard still sticking to them. She felt slightly nauseous, but continued. "She says you have a long and happy life ahead of you, if you eat less lizards, and more vegetables."

Asio clacked his hooked beak disgustedly. "Ah were never fond o' vegetables, but ah'm quite partial to green things, frogs, toads, newts, lizards. Go on, wot else does she say?"

The haremaid intoned in a dirgelike voice, "She says you will meet a very pretty young owl. When you do, you must mind your manners and treat her kindly."

Asio clenched his talons with joy, almost taking off Maudie's nose as she reared back. "Tell me more, more!"

Maudie continued, "If you treat her like a toff, she'll jolly well marry you, and lay scads of bloomin' eggs. There, that's all I can see, everything's gone fuzzy!"

Asio thrust his beak to within a hairsbreadth of her nose. "Wot's a toff?"

Maudie shrugged. "Oh, er, a nice sort of chap."

The owl's eyes circled dreamily. "An' y'say she'll lay eggs, eh! Eggs, that's where little owls come from, tha knows. Bah gum, lass, thankee kindly!"

Maudie shook her head, as if coming out of a trance.

"Oh, think nothin' of it, old bean, us magic hares do this sort o' thing all the flippin' time, wot!"

Asio hopped up into the branches of the oak. "Ah'm beholden t'thee, lass, bide there 'til ah get mah owlyharp, an' ah'll sing thee a song." He rummaged about in the foliage until he came up with a beautiful little harp. Hopping back down to the fireside, Asio began tuning it and getting his voice into pitch, whilst he posed dramatically.

Plinkplinkplink . . . "Toowhoohoohoo!" Plinkplink . . .

The haremaid felt like covering her ears, it was the most dreadful, tuneless din she had ever heard. But she sat smiling, and looking appreciative, out of courtesy.

The owl's chest puffed out like a balloon, as he launched into his discordant song. It was actually an owl courtship ballad, containing many drawn-out hoots.

"I've spoken to your pa and to your mother,
    too, whoohoo,
they've given me permission for to woo, whoohoo,
so now I can come calling upon you, whoohoohoohoo,
If I say I love you will you love me, too, whooooooooh!

"Cows go moo and doves can coo,
some fish blow lots of bubbles, too,
but only owls can woo hoo hoo!

"We'll fly into the sky so high and blue, whoohoo,
I'll catch butterflies and moths for you, whoohoo,
you'll be the happiest owl that ever
    flew, whoohoohoohoo,
I'll stay forever true, my dear, to you, whooooooooh!

"For limpets limp round in a crew,
they stick together just like glue,
but only owls can woo hoo hoo ooooooooooh!"

Maudie's ears were still buzzing from Asio Bardwing's hoots, long after he had ended his song. Despite her suffering she clapped enthusiastically, with both ears and paws, in the approved hare manner. "Oh I say, super hunky dory, wot, well done, Asio!"

The owl preened his feathers and took a bow. "Aye, it were rather gradely, even though ah say so m'self. Hearken, lass, shall ah sing thee another?"

The haremaid protested vigorously. "Good grief, no, you must save that spiffin' voice o' yours, in case an attractive young owl flaps by. Please don't wear your blinkin' beak out on my behalf."

The owl put aside his owlharp reluctantly. "May'aps yore right, lass, 'ey up, are y'not feelin' well?"

Maudie lay back, with a paw draped across her brow, doing her best to look pale and interesting. "Oh, I'll be alright, just achin' a trifle, from the rocks those lizardy blighters chucked at me. I feel a bit tired that's all."

Immediately Asio became the model of sympathy and help. "Right, you lay down there an' get a good owld sleep, lass. Ah'll see to the fire an' keep it goin'. Don't worry about owt now, ah'll be up in yon tree, keepin' an eye out for thee until dawn."

That night Maudie slept safe and sound, knowing she had no need to worry about sneak attacks, with Asio Bardwing in the tree overhead, protecting her.

Maudie rose refreshed, dawn had already broken, promising a warm summer day. Woodland birdsong could be heard far and near as Maudie blew on the fire embers, coaxing them into life with twigs and dried moss. She liked the woodlands, they were a pleasant change from heathland, mountains and shoreline. The shadow and light of trees afforded sunlit swards, placid dimness and dappled aisles amid the big ancient trunks.

Stretching and yawning, Maudie looked up into the oak foliage. She was not best pleased by what she saw. There was the owl, fast asleep.

Muttering to herself, the haremaid laid out some scones,

for toasting. "You have a good night's sleep, an' ah'll watch out for thee, lass. Hah, the bloomin' old fraud, I could've been jolly well murdered in my own bed, with him snorin' his confounded beak off right over my head! Hmph, I'll let the blighter snooze on for that, see if he gets any brekkers off me? Fat chance! Anyhow, a cad like that prob'ly doesn't eat respectable tuck, wot! More likely he stalks the blinkin' neighbourhood scoffin' any wretched reptile that blinks an eye at him! Sleepin' on duty, too? By the left, he'd be on a fizzer if old Major Mull caught him nappin'. . . ."

"Whoohoo, is that toastin' scones ah smell?" Asio came flapping down from his perch, almost knocking Maudie flat with a heavy buffet from his wings. "Well, ain't this grand, toasty scones, an' ah see thee've got honey t'spread o'er 'em, too. Ecky thump, lass, th'art a little treasure an' no mistake!"

The haremaid thought of enforcing her ban on the owl's breakfast, but one look at the wicked talons stuffing a scone between the razor curves of the lethal beak changed Maudie's mind. However, she was not her normal cheerful self, and treated Asio coolly as they shared the scones. After they had eaten, the owl began pacing back and forth, swivelling his head. "Ah've been thinkin', lass!"

The haremaid replied snootily, "Oh really, is that where the noise was coming from!"

Asio chuckled. "Nay, pudden'ead, owls don't make noises when they think!"

Maudie immediately felt sorry for her waspish remark. "Sorry, what was it you were thinkin', old lad?"

The owl explained. "This badger thou art lookin' for, ah can tell thee, hide nor hair of him ain't been sighted hereabouts all season. But if there was such a beast in the land, ah'll wager somebody at Redwall Abbey would've spotted 'im. Aye, Redwall, that's the place, lots o' travellers visits there, lass!"

Maudie's ears stood up straight. "Oh, corks, I've just remembered, that's where I was ordered to go. Redwall. Oh, I'd dearly love to visit that jolly old heap, I've heard so flippin' much about it, from the chaps at Salamandastron who've been there. I say, Asio, you don't actually know how t'get there, do you?"

The owl winked a huge yellow eye at her. "Ah did once upon a day, but ah've forgotten now. Still, never fret, lass, ah know who does, an' ah can take ye to 'em as well!"

Maudie began packing her scant belongings. "Splendid, right, lead on, O feathered matey. Er, by the way, who exactly is it that you know, wot?"

Asio pecked at a few scone crumbs that had stuck to his talons. "Hasn't thee heard of the Guosim?"

The haremaid stood, ready to leave. "Oh, y'mean the shrew chaps, Guosim. 'Guerilla Union of Shrews in Moss-flower,' first letter of each word, that's how they got their name, y'know, Guosim! I came across 'em one time, when I was out with the jolly old Long Patrol. Pretty odd bunch, the Guosim, singin' and feastin' one moment, then arguin' an' scrappin' the next, wot!"

The owl's yellow eyes widened in awe. "Well, blow mah feathers away, lass, ah never knew that was wot the name Guosim meant! Mossflower's Shrews in Union of Guerillas. How dids't thou remember all that? Ah were right when ah fust met thee. Magic, that's wot thee are, lass, magic!"

Maudie did not provoke further discussion with Asio by arguing. She followed him as he set out into the deep woodlands. The owl flew gracefully slow, keeping near to the ground, and gossiping constantly.

"Ah were plannin' on poppin' o'er to visit the shrews, but ah went an' forgot. Woe to birds that gets owld, that's wot ah says, lass. This head o' mine has gotten like a leaky pot, nothin' stays long in it these days."

Maudie nodded. "Just as long as you know which way we're goin', old chap, don't want t'get jolly well lost."

Asio hooted scornfully. "Get lost goin' to Bulrush Bower?

Ah could find mah way theer blindfold, an' with both wings tied behind mah back, lass."

They ploughed deeper into the vast woodland tracts, to areas where the tree canopy was so dense that only a soft, green light prevailed. It was mossy underpaw, and silent, the monolith trunks of giant trees reared upward, like columns of black stone.

Asio winged toward a soft pool of golden radiance, which could be seen some distance off, remarking, "Ah'd have t'be daft to miss Bulrush Bower, sithee, there 'tis, lass. May'ap we'll be in time for lunch."

Maudie perked up at the mention of food. "Indeed, they sound like a jolly lot, can you hear 'em singin', listen."

Sure enough, the sound of rough bass voices, both old and young, became plain as they drew closer.

"Ho, truss up me troubles an' toss em away,
go sink 'em deep down in the waters,
even fathers an' mothers have grandparents, too,
one time we were all sons an' daughters. . . .
Guosim! Guosim! Bind 'em sling 'em douse 'em!
With a gee and a you and an oh oh oh,
an ess and an eye and an em em em!
Oh Guosim I'm one o' them!"

Maudie found herself skipping along to the catchy air.

Asio merely muttered grumpily. "Huh, wot's all that supposed t'mean?"

The haremaid chided her friend. "Why should it have to mean anythin', it's just a jolly happy song, an' I for one blinkin' well like it!"

Bulrush Bower was a small pond in a clearing. It was, of course, fringed entirely by bulrushes. The place was packed with Guosim shrews, small, spiky-furred beasts with long snouts. Each one wore a coloured headband and a broad, buckled belt, into which was tucked a little rapier;

their only other clothing was a short kilt. They showed no fear of their two visitors, though one fellow, an aggressive-looking type, drew his sword, barring their way. "Where d'ye think yore off to, eh?"

Maudie bowed formally, she knew how to deal with creatures like this. Her tone was cool and distant. "I'm a messenger from the Lord o' Salamandastron, take me to your chief. Don't stand there lookin' useless, put up that blade, an' bloomin' well shift yourself, laddie buck. Sharpish, wot!"

The shrew immediately did as he was bidden, they followed him, with Asio murmuring, "Marvellous! Ecky thump, ah knew the lass were magic!"

A large area of the sunny sward had been covered with picnic tablecloths, it was spread with scores of pies, each one with a cream topping. A fat-bellied shrew, with over-large ears, was striding around amid the pies. Dabbing his paw into odd ones, he would taste it, then pull a wry face. Turning to meet the visitors, he wiped his lips with a kerchief.

"Asio Bardwing, yore a day late, the festival started yesterday. I suppose you forgot as usual. Hello, who's this, a friend o' yourn?"

Asio blinked several times, revolving his head. "This is er, er . . . oh, tell him who thou art, lass!"

The haremaid held out her paw. "The name's Maudie Mugsberry Thropple, sah, from Salamandastron."

The shrew seemed impressed, he shook Maudie's paw in a grip like a steel nutcracker. "Salamandastron, eh? Welcome, miss. I'm chieftain o' these Guosim an' my name's Log a Log Luglug."

Log a Log was always the given title for a shrew chieftain. Luglug pointed to his oversized ears. "Don't even bother askin' how I came by the name o' Luglug, or ye could find yoreself in trouble." Picking up a pie, he offered it to them. "I'd like ye to try this, an' tell me wot ye think.

Our best cook an' her mate are off visitin' relatives. So some of the young 'uns volunteered to 'elp out with pie makin'. Wot ye see is the results of their efforts."

The pies looked appetising enough, but a taste from each of Luglug's guests confirmed his worst fears. After just one bite, Maudie and Asio pulled horrible faces, reaching for water to wash away the taste. Asio squinched his eyes hard.

"Burst me beak! Art thou tryin' t'poison us, Luglug?"

Maudie's ears shot up stiffly as she gasped out, "By the left! Pie, d'ye call that? Guuurrrgh! It's enough t'give you the clangs'n'collywobbles for ten seasons. What did they blinkin' well put in it?"

Log a Log Luglug shrugged. "Some fruit from three seasons back, swampvetch, stinkweed, pounded ransom, an' swine parsley. The usual stuff young scallywags put in when they wants to upset their elders. I wish we had a decent cook with us, I really do."

Maudie was not normally one to volunteer, but she saw an opportunity to curry favour with the shrew chieftain. "Say no more, sah, I'm the very chapess you're lookin' for, I was assistant cook at Salamandastron. Now, where's the bloomin' galley, an' some fresh ingredients, wot?"

Luglug called some of the older shrews over. "Show Miz Maudie the supplies, an' get a good fire goin' under them clay ovens. Do as she tells ye, an' mayhaps we'll get somethin' good to eat t'day." He shook his head irately at the array of dreadful pies. "Dig a hole an' bury these, as deep as ye can!"

Maudie had a sudden idea. She approached Luglug, whispering in his ear, "'Scuse me, sah, but how about this for a wheeze . . ."

Luglug listened to the haremaid's scheme, then he grinned broadly and smote her heartily on the back. "I don't know wot a wheeze is, but if'n that's wot ye call it then I'm all for it!"

He hailed a passing young shrew. "Ahoy, Dinger, was you one o' the pie-makin' crew?"

Dinger and several of his young friends smirked maliciously. Their culinary atrocities had not gone unnoticed. Dinger took a sweeping bow. "Aye, me an' me mates made 'em special for ye!"

Luglug selected two pies, passing one to Maudie. The shrew chieftain winked at Dinger. "That was good of ye, but we ain't greedybeasts, we'll share em with ye!" *Splaaattt!* The pie caught Dinger square in the mouth. Maudie's pie came a respectable second, landing flat on the forehead of a young shrew close to Dinger. A few of the young shrews got behind Maudie and Luglug, pelting them vigorously with the cream topped pies. That did it! Within moments, Bulrush Bower became the scene of a fully fledged pie fight. Amid howls of laughter, the dreadful missiles flew back and forth between young shrews and their elders. Pies squelched into faces as the shrews slithered and slipped to take aim, or to avoid flying pies.

When the first pie was launched, Asio fled into the cover of a spruce tree, being of the opinion that owls were pretty poor pie fighters. Not so with Maudie and Luglug; caked from tip to tail with squashed cream, crust and filling, they battled on heroically, giggling, gurgling and falling over backward whenever they were hit. It was enormous fun while it lasted, but finally the pies ran out, and everybeast sat down amid the slutchy residue.

Asio flew down to a lower perch, casting a jaundiced owl's eye over the haremaid and the shrew chieftain. He pointed a wing accusingly at them. "Thou wert the ones that started all this, look at the mess of ye, ah've never seen owt like it!"

Young Dinger rose from the debris, blowing pie filling from the tip of his snout. Exchanging reproving glances with Asio, he shook a paw at Luglug and his contingent, exclaiming, "Old 'uns these days, I don't know, wot's the world coming to, eh?"

The statement caused roars of unbridled laughter from

all the Guosim. Heaving themselves upright, and supporting one another, the entire shrew tribe tottered into the pond shallows to clean up.

There were willing paws aplenty to help Maudie with her cooking, by midnoon her offering was ready. The haremaid did not attempt anything fancy, she prepared food that was plain, but satisfying. Flatcakes with nuts and berries, fresh fruit salad, some shrew cheeses, chopped celery stalks and a cordial of dandelion and burdock. The Guosim chieftain complimented her as they sat eating together.

"This is a perfect feast for a happy summer's day, I can't remember the last time I had so much fun!"

Young Dinger called out, "Aye, me, too, Chief. Wot d'ye say we do this once every summer, pie fight an' all?" There were shouts of agreement from the Guosim.

Asio helped himself to another flatcake. "Mayhaps thou could call it Mad Maudie Day!"

Luglug clinked his beaker with the haremaid's cup. "Mad Maudie Day it'll be, thank ye, friend, if'n there's anythin' we can do for ye, just ask me anytime."

Maudie was in like a shot. "Er, actually there is, sah, I was wonderin' if you could possibly show me the way to Redwall Abbey. I need t'get there, doncha know?" She explained the mission Lord Asheye had sent her upon, asking if the shrews had seen the badger with the flame, who walked with the banished one.

Log a Log Luglug stroked his snout reflectively. "Ain't seen nobeast like that 'ereabouts, miz, a badger like that'd stick out like a lantern at night. As for takin' ye to Redwall, well, that's quite a journey. But nothin' a Guosim couldn't manage. I'll do ye a deal, though: you stay 'ere an' cook supper for us this evenin'. Then first thing tomorrer we'll break camp an' take ye to the Abbey. Is that a bargain?"

Maudie shook Luglug's outstretched paw. "Rather, I'll say it is, how'd you like a drop of woodland broth to sup round the fire tonight, wot?"

Mad Maudie (the Hon.) Mugberry Thropple had been trained by the best cooks at Salamandastron. Even the great Lord Asheye always asked for seconds when she served up broths, which were her speciality. That evening she produced a woodland broth which had the Guosim savouring every drop.

Asio assured the shrews solemnly, "Ah tell thee, yon lass is nowt but magic, an' thee can tek mah word on it!"

After supper, Maudie sat by the campfire with the Guosim as the young ones sang and danced. It was a soft summer night, with the darkened skies reflecting starlight upon the still surface of the pond at Bulrush Bower. Tomorrow she would start the journey to Redwall, and see the fabled Abbey for herself. Asio was dozing, though he opened one eye, to comment on the Guosim music.

"Hmm, tain't too bad, mayhaps ah'll give 'em a song later."

Maudie muttered under her breath, "I blinkin' well hope not!"

The owl craned his head forward. "Wot did thee say?"

Maudie smiled. "I said, save it for tomorrow, wot!" She watched the little shrewmaids dancing as Dinger and his friends sang the melody.

"Honour your partner, hop one two,
twirl round twice, now tap that paw,
curtsy low, my pretty shrew,
altogether turn once more.

"Guosim maids are small and fair,
nimble as the day is long,
they wear ribbons in their hair,
as they dance we sing this song.

"Two steps forward, one step back,
point that footpaw, shake it round,
grace and charm you'll never lack,
tripping lightly o'er the ground.

87

"Guosim maids are neat and bright,
such a lovely sight to see,
spinning round in pale moonlight,
pray, miss, save a dance for me!"

Two elders continued the air with flute and drum, whilst the singers joined the maids, each taking a partner and twirling gracefully off around the lakeshore. Luglug nudged Maudie, whispering quietly, "Ole Asio's fallen asleep, now ye won't 'ave the pleasure of 'earing him sing."

The haremaid whispered back, "I've already heard him sing, an' it wasn't any bally pleasure!"

Luglug chuckled. "Aye, so have I, an' I'd much sooner put up with his snores than his singin', thank ye!"

Gradually the usual Guosim hubbub died down, the dancing ended, and the musicians ceased playing. Round the fire, and the lakeshore, Luglug's tribe lay down for their much needed rest. There was no need of coverlets, it was a warm, windless night. Maudie stretched out on the moss, imagining what Redwall Abbey would look like, as she fell into a slumber. Soon the only sound in the woodland depths was the gentle snoring of Guosim shrews, and the odd crackle as the campfire died into embers.

It was in the gray gloom which precedes dawn, when everybeast was wakened by the piercing wail of a shrewmum.

"Waaaaah! Where's my liddle Dupper?"

Maudie knocked Asio sideways as she sprang up. She joined Luglug, and several others, who were running to the lakeside. The Guosim mother was scurrying about distractedly, waving her paws.

"Dupper, where's my baby? Waaaah 'e's gone!"

The haremaid took charge of the situation. Grabbing the shrewmum by her flowery apron, she halted her, calling sternly, "Please be still, marm, you'll mess up all the tracks. Now, when did y'last see Dupper, wot?"

Guosim scouts spread out into the surrounding trees, as the mother explained tearfully. "I 'ad Dupper in me paws last night, when I went t'sleep. Oh, where's the pore liddle tyke got to?"

The gruff voice of a Guosim scout came from the north corner of Bulrush Bower. "Over 'ere, mates!"

Maudie bounded to the spot, ahead of everybeast. She could tell, by the horrified look on the scout's face, and the ominous drag trail of tracks, what the shrew was going to say.

"The liddle 'un's been taken by a snake!"

The word struck terror into the Guosim, just the word snake sent them into a gibbering panic. It was Asio who got order, with a deafening hoot. "Whooooohooooo!"

Maudie could see by the state of the shrews that they would not be of any use to her. She nodded to the owl. "Right, quick's the word an' sharp's the action, laddie buck, we've got t'get that babe back, and jolly well soon!"

Luglug countered grimly. "Not much chance, miz, once a snake's got ye, that's that!"

The haremaid grabbed the rapier from Luglug's belt, and thrust it into his paw, whispering to him, "Bad form, sah, wot? You're supposed t'be a blinkin' chieftain among shrews. Look at the example you're settin' 'em. A little baby'll die if ye don't do anythin' about it. Now c'mon, stiff upper snout, wot!"

Luglug gritted his teeth. "Yore right, Miz Maudie, let's get after that evil worm right now!"

The owl, the haremaid and the shrew chieftain sped off into the still darkened woodland depths.

10

Bludgullet was now sailing through the Mossflower woodlands, away from its normal habitat of the open sea. It was
a novelty to the vermin crew, sunlight and shade, the absence of wind and tranquil, waveless waters. The only bar
to their pleasure was that the ship had to be poled upriver.
Without the aid of sail, and with the current, however
gentle, running against them, they were forced to propel
their vessel to its destination.

Vizka Longtooth kept to his cabin, leaving Codj and a
stoat named Bilger in charge of the crew. The pair patrolled
up and down the ranks of vermin crewbeasts, who were
sweating at their long paddles, punting the ship along.
Codj flicked a knotted rope's end about idly, he was se-
cretly scared to use it. Some of the crew were vicious, bad-
tempered beasts, who would not take kindly to being
whipped. It was slow progress, and the crew soon became
disenchanted with the rustic surroundings. They began
complaining aloud.

"Yowch, I'm bein' eaten alive by h'insecks!"

"They ain't h'insecks, they're midges."

"Huh, they might be midgets, but they got giant teeth!"

"Ain't there no cool water t'be 'ad aboard dis tub?"

"Aye, an' we ain't stopped once fer vittles, I'm 'ungry!"

"I'm gittin' splinters offen dese paddles."

"Yew ain't gittin' splinters offen der paddles, dat's wid scratchin' yore 'ead, mate!"

Codj sniggered openly at his clever remark. The recipient of it, a hulking, boulder-headed weasel, snarled at him.

"D'yer think yore funny, Codj Stumple? 'ow would yer like me t'bust dis paddle o'er yer stumpy be'ind?"

Codj was nettled by the remark about his lack of tail, but he did not fancy his chances against the big weasel. Pretending he had not heard the insult, Codj stalked off to his brother's cabin.

Vizka was rocking in a hammock, sipping grog. He eyed Codj irritably. "Worrizit now, annuder mutiny on our paws?"

The smaller fox fidgeted with the strands of his rope end. "It's dat lot out dere, nothin' but moan moan, alla time. Wot am I s'posed ter do? Yore der cap'n."

The golden fox heaved himself from the hammock, and peered out the open door at the sky. "It's gettin' on fer eventide, tell 'em t'down paddles an' rest fer the night. Anythin' else ter report?"

Codj shuffled his footpaws awkwardly. "Ain't much drinkin' water left."

Vizka lashed out, cuffing his younger brother's ear. "Well, don't tell me, thick'ead, lower der barrels inta der river. Dis is fresh water we're sailin' in, or didn't dat thought seep into yer brain?"

Codj tried to leave the cabin quickly, but Vizka caught him tight, by his tail stub.

"Next ye'll be tellin' me we're low on vittles. Organise a shore party, an' gerrinta dat forest out dere. Huh, d'place must be fulla fruits'n'roots, birds, an' eggs, an' all kinds'a vittles. Do I have ter tell ya everyt'ink, eh?"

Codj tried to justify himself. "But warrabout der stripe'ound, who's gonna watch 'im?"

The golden fox shoved his brother contemptuously out through the cabin door. "Don't talk stupid, dat ole Rock-

'ead ain't goin' nowheres, wid an iron chain holdin' 'im t'the mast. Der stripe'ound'll be dead inna few days. I wuz watchin' 'im dis mornen, 'e ain't gotten long ter go now."

Gorath lay slumped alongside the mast, largely forgotten amid the new surroundings. The huge scab on his forehead protruded even further, his matted fur clung to his bones, like an ill-fitting garment. The young badger looked for all the world like a beast close to death. However, behind his closed eyelids, a fierce glimmer remained in his eyes. Deep inside Gorath, the will to live, and the desire to avenge his kinbeasts' deaths, burned like an unwavering flame. He did not fear death, his only concern was that he might die leaving his enemies alive.

In the early evening, Codj, heading a party of six, which he had paw picked, managing to omit the big, tough, mean crewbeasts, were foraging in the woodlands. It soon became painfully obvious that Sea Raiders were totally ignorant of woodland produce. Codj was bombarded with enquiries from the vermin of his party, about matters which were a mystery to him.

"Ahoy, Codj, didyer reckin dis is a vittle, it's some sorta juicy, green, rooty thing?"

Codj shrugged. "I dunno, take a bite an' try it."

"Yuuurrkk! Tastes 'orrible, all sour'n'bitter!"

The questions began to rile Codj.

"Where's all der red, rosy apples round 'ere, Codj?"

"Aye, an' where's all der trees wot dose strawberries grows on, eh?"

"Dere should be loads of stuff 'angin' from dese trees, dis is supposed ter be a forest, ain't it?"

"I likes soup, where does der stuff grow wot ye makes soup out of, dat's wot I'd like ter know?"

Codj brushed away a wasp that was trying to land on his muzzle. "Aye an' I'd like ter know, too!"

A skinny rat called Firty cupped a paw to his ear. "Wot's dat?"

Codj looked around, walked into a beech trunk and roared at Firty, "Wot's wot? Take no notice if it ain't sumthin' yer can eat. Now shurrup!"

But Firty had definitely heard something. "It's somebeast yellin' out. . . . Listen!"

Orkwil Prink was the most weary and miserable of creatures, having spent half the night and a full day trapped in a marshy swamp. He had wakened from his sleep in the fern bed when foul-tasting, brackish water leaked into his mouth. The danger of his plight dawned upon the young hedgehog rapidly. During the night, he had wandered into the fern grove, thinking it a reasonably safe place to snatch a few hours' sleep, only to find he had walked straight into a swamp. It was the ferns that had buoyed him up long enough to fall asleep. Then they had collapsed under his weight, he was sinking!

Orkwil managed to grasp onto nearby fern stems, and haul his head free of the mess. He held on tightly, gasping for breath, and spitting out swamp water. Inevitably, he felt himself sinking again. Heaving upward, Orkwil managed to raise his body slightly. Furiously he began scrabbling about, hoping to find firm ground, but his efforts were all in vain. The weight of the miry sludge clogged around the young hedgehog's spines, dragging him down again. He had no idea of where solid ground lay, it was difficult to see anything in the darkness of night.

Salvation came in the form of a branch; it scratched his snout as he floundered about. Orkwil grabbed the limb, pulling it downward until he could hang on properly. It was an alder tree that had saved his life.

Now Orkwil Prink was suspended in a sort of limbo, half in and half out of the swamp, unable to go anywhere. He hung there, calling out at intervals. "Help! Somebeast save me! Help!" But no help came. Dawn broke slowly, to find him still hanging on to the alder, his voice down to a croak, and his paws numb with fatigue. Now he could see the rest of the tree. Orkwil figured that the alder trunk was rooted to the edge of the swamp, but he had no chance of reaching it. Long hours had taken their toll, now he had only the energy left to cling on for dear life. He wept bitterly as he pictured his inevitable end.

How deep was a swamp, did it reach the earth's core? No search party would ever find his poor young body. His voice was down to a hoarse whimper, he tried it. "Help, oh heeeeelp." It trailed off miserably.

As the morning wore on, Orkwil somehow contrived to wriggle his paws until they became entwined in the alder twigs. Now he did not have to hang on, he merely hung there bemoaning his fate, and composing his own eulogy, revelling in his own misery.

"A fine young 'un gone, and all for what?
Some mouldy ole soup, an' that ain't a lot!
Alas an' alack for pore Orkwil Prink,
stuck in a swamp without vittles or drink,
he hung there, brave beast, not darin' to budge,
his head in a tree, an' his bottom in sludge.
His last thoughts were of friends at the old homestead,
would they know that their young hog was dead,
and would they weep sadly o'er his empty cot?
Those bandy-pawed elders, the snotty-beaked lot!
Aye, Orkwil's departed, but who'll shed a tear,
who'll blub on their salad, or cry in their beer?
And who'll even notice one dark, stormy night,
a small, muddy hog ghost, a pitiful sight.
Will they say, friend Orkwil, come, welcome indoors!
Or, you filthy young wretch, have you wiped
    those paws?"

As the hot, noontide sun beat down on the swamp, Orkwil ceased his blubbering and fell asleep out of sheer weariness. In the early evening he was wakened by a cloud of winged insects trying to sample his head. Unable to stop them, Orkwil yowled piteously. "Yah, gerroff me, you horrible villains! Can't ye leave a pore young creature to perish in peace? How would you like it, stuck in a swamp with midges gnawin' at yore snout, an' buzzin' down yore ears!"

A short distance away in the woodlands, Codj and his party heard Orkwil's protests. The stump-tailed fox drew his sword, pointing with it. "I t'ink it's comin' from over dere."

The little rat, Firty, grinned smugly. "See, I tole ya sumbeast was shoutin'."

Codj liked bullying anybeast smaller than himself. He rapped Firty's paw with the flat of his blade. "Seein' as yew 'eard it first, yew kin go in front, go on smart mouth, lead on!"

Firty ventured forth gingerly, registering his protest. "If 'twas Cap'n Vizka, 'e'd go first, I betcha!"

Codj pricked his tail with the sword. "Well, I ain't Cap'n Vizka, so move yerself, or I'll chop yer tail off!"

"Then Firty'd be a stumple like yew, haha!"

Codj wheeled on the party, who were shuffling behind him. "Who said dat?" He eyed the five blank-faced vermin sternly. "Cummon, own up, who's insultin' me be'ind me back, eh?" All five stayed silent, Codj waved his sword at them. "If'n somebeast don't talk soon, I'll make yez sorry. Now speak up, buckoes, who said it, eh?"

The standoff was broken by Firty's squeal.

Codj turned to see him standing at the edge of the ferns. "Worra yew skrikin' like an ole ratwife for?"

The small rat showed his muddy footpaws. "I ain't goin' in dere, it's all squelchy!"

One of the party, an old stoat, called out, "Wotjer mean, squelchy?"

Firty jabbed his paw furiously at the fern bed. "I mean squelchy enuff to sink ye down over yore ears!"

Orkwil's impassioned plea was loud and clear now. "Oh take pity on me, kind sirs, help me, I beg ye!"

Jungo, a fat weasel, who possessed a single tooth, giggled. "Huhurrhurr! Sumone t'inks we're kind sirs, dat's nice!"

Codj silenced him with a glare, then issued orders. "Spread out, but don't go fallin' in de squelch. See who's makin' all dat noise!"

It was Jungo who found Orkwil. "It's an 'edgepig, 'e's stuck inna squelch, I kin see 'im. Over 'ere, mates. Huhuhurrr! A likkle 'edgepig!"

Codj was first to locate the spot where Jungo was calling from, he glared to and fro irately. "Where in de name o' blazes are ye?"

Orkwil's voice rang out hopefully. "I'm here, sir, in the swamp!"

Codj slashed angrily at the ferns with his sword.

"I'm not talkin to yew! Jungo, where are ye, oaf'ead?"

The slow-witted weasel's voice came from over Codj's head. "Hurrhurr, I'm up in dis big tree, I kin see de 'edgepig!"

The rest of the foraging party arrived at the alder. Codj beckoned upward with his blade.

"Gerrup dere, yew lot, an' don't come down wirrout dat 'edgepig, de cap'n'll wanna werd wid 'im!"

All of the Sea Raiders were skillful climbers. A solid tree was easier to scale than masts, spars and rigging on the open main. It did not take them long to lasso Orkwil with a length of rope. They heaved together, and he shot out of the ooze with a gurgle and a plop. The vermin swung him back and forth on the rope, releasing it when Orkwil was close to the alder trunk. He landed with a muddy squish, right next to Codj, who leapt aside, snarling, "Watch where yer splash dat squelch!"

The young hedgehog began unfastening the rope, which was noosed about his middle. "I'm sorry, sir, didn't mean to splash you. My name's Orkwil Prink, I've been stuck in that confounded swamp since last night. Thanks to you and your friends I'm safe now. Phew! I couldn't have lasted much longer in there, I can tell ye!"

The fox's footpaw stamped down on Orkwil's stomach, knocking the wind from him, and stopping him from untying the rope. Codj put his swordpoint to Orkwil's throat. "Gabby liddle 'edgepig, ain't yer? So then, Orful Stink, where do ya comes from, eh?"

The other vermin had descended from the tree, they laughed at Codj's little joke. It took Jungo a moment to catch on, then he guffawed appreciatively. "Huhurrhurr-hurr! Orful Stink, dat's a good 'un!"

The young hedgehog sighed. "That's twice in two days somebeast's not said my name right. It's Prink, not Stink. Orkwil, not Awful. Orkwil Prink, if y'please!"

Codj sneered, pricking his captive's throat with the swordpoint. "If y'please? Well, don't 'e talk pritty. I asked yew a question, Orful Stink, where do ya come from? Ye'd better speak afore I starts carvin' ya!"

Orkwil answered quickly. "I'm from Redwall Abbey, sir, but I was on a short trip, y'see, an' I wandered into that swa . . ."

Codj hauled him upright sharply. "Redwall Abbey, eh, yore jus' the bucko we're lookin' for. Vizka'll want to talk wid yew! Lash 'im up good an' fetch 'im along, mates!"

Orkwil knew it would do no good to protest, the vermin looked like a primitive and murderous crew. Moments later he was bound by all paws to a spearpole, and carried off, swinging upside down between two weasels.

11

It was dusk by the time they arrived back aboard the *Bludgullet.* Vizka Longtooth cast a glance at the mudcaked young hedgehog, who was trussed to the spearpole. He shook his head pityingly at his younger brother. "Dat's der queerest kind o' vittles I've seen in a while. Wot d'yer want luggin' dat filthy 'edgepig aboard of a nice ship like dis?"

Codj flourished his sword, pointing it at Orkwil. "Jus' guess where dis 'edgepig comes from."

The golden fox wrinkled his nose. "A swamp by the smell of 'im!"

Codj nodded. "Aye, dat's where we found 'im, but do yew know where 'e lives, eh?"

Vizka stared levelly at his brother and smiled. It was that dangerous smile, which Codj had come to know so well. Vizka reached for Gorath's pitchfork. "I'm gittin' tired o' yore liddle games. Tell me, afore I does sumthin' I'll be sorry for later. Where does 'e live?"

Codj answered promptly. "Redwall Abbey!"

Vizka flung the pitchfork, it stuck deep into the mast, quivering. Grabbing his brother in a hearty embrace, Vizka pounded his back soundly. "At last ye've done summat right, Codj! Haharr, strike me anchor an' gut me grandpa, a beast wot actually comes from Redwall Abbey? I knowed dat place was real, I jus' knowed it!"

Bending down, Vizka brought his face level with the captive. "Wot's yer name, liddle muddy matey?"

The young hedgehog replied wearily, "Orkwil Prink, sir."

The golden fox threw back his head, roaring with laughter. "Haharrharrharrr! It suits yer well, Orful Stink! D'ye hear that, mates, the 'edgepig's called Orful Stink!"

The crew laughed dutifully, nobeast dared not to, even Codj. Orkwil closed his eyes resignedly, not even bothering to correct his captor.

Vizka signalled to Bilger. "Sluice 'im down an' clean 'im up, get rid of Orful's Stink. Hahaharrr, that's a good 'un, eh!"

The pails of river water which splashed over Orkwil were both clean and refreshing, he even managed to catch a swift drink. Vizka smiled his famous deadly smile, the long fangs protruding.

"Now lissen, mate, me'n my crew wants ter pay yore Abbey a nice liddle visit. But we don't knows 'ow t'get there. Ye looks like a sensible young 'edgepig, so yew tell me 'ow, an' I'll take yore werd fer it, eh?"

Orkwil shut both eyes tight and clenched his teeth. The very idea of this barbarian fox and his evil crew going to Redwall did not bear thinking about. Though he was cringing with fear inside, Orkwil decided that no matter what happened to him, he would not divulge the location of the Abbey, which had suddenly become so dear to him it meant more than life itself.

Codj prodded the captive with his sword. "Ye'd better tell der cap'n wot 'e wants t'know, or yer name'll be Orful Sorry."

Nobeast laughed at Codj's pun.

Vizka smiled, stroking his two long fangs as he viewed Orkwil's show of resistance. "Lissen, 'edgepig, I knows yer can 'ear me. Tomorrer morn I'm gonna git the galley fire burnin', good an' 'ot, an' I'm gonna stick a spit over it. Now I ain't sayin' no more, I'll jus' leave ye for de night, to t'ink about wot I'll do to yer. Never fear, by der time Longtooth's done wid ya, yore name'll be Orful 'elpful. Haharr, 'ow about dat, mates, Orful 'elpful?"

The *Bludgullet*'s crew laughed obediently once more, even Jungo, who had not understood his captain's joke.

Vizka issued orders to his brother. "Cut 'im loose, an' chain 'im next to Rock'ead fer the night. Wake me early tomorrer, d'ye hear? Oh, an' keep an eye on our 'edgepig through the night."

When they came to cut Orkwil's bonds, he kicked and fought furiously. Bilger, Firty and Jungo had to hold him still as Codj severed the rope with his sword. Between them they dragged Orkwil to the mast, where Gorath lay chained. The badger appeared to be either unconscious or dead. Codj was not about to check on Gorath's condition, he stood with his sword ready, as Bilger and the others took a loop in the chain, and padlocked it around Orkwil's waist. Gorath suddenly stirred, so they got out of the way speedily.

Codj beckoned to his messmates. "Let's go an' git some vittles an' grog, the 'edgepig ain't goin' anyplace . . . unless the stripe'ound eats 'im!"

Jungo scratched his tail. "Do stripe'ounds eat 'edgepigs? I didn't know dat."

Firty gave him a playful shove. "Codj wuz only jokin'."

Jungo thought about that for awhile, then called out to Orkwil as they headed toward the galley. "Don't worry if'n der stripe'ound eats yer, mate, 'e's only jokin'. Hurr-hurrhurrr!"

When they had gone, Orkwil tapped the badger gingerly. "How did you come to be captured, friend?"

Gorath opened his eyes, his voice sounded hoarse and slow. "I'm from the Northern Isles, they burned my house, and slew my grandparents. The one they call Longtooth battered me down with a ball and chain. I woke up chained to this mast. I don't know how long I've been on this ship, lost count of the days. My name is Gorath." He held out a huge, workworn paw. Orkwil clasped it.

"My name's Orkwil Prink, I'm from Redwall Abbey."

The big, young badger suddenly became alert. "Redwall Abbey! I've heard about it, Orkwil, is it as marvellous as they say?"

The young hedgehog's eyes filled with tears. "Even more marvellous, Gorath, I've come to realise that now. That golden fox, Longtooth, he wants to go there with his vermin. I'm sure they plan on attacking it. Listen, friend, we've got to get to Redwall before they do. Could you make it?"

The badger's reply was tinged with bitter irony. "Why of course, Orkwil, but there's a little matter of a steel chain and an iron padlock holding me to the mast. Only for that I'd love to go to Redwall with you. I see you're locked up, too, how do you plan on leaving this ship?"

The young hedgehog inspected the padlock that held him to the chain, then he took a glance at Gorath's lock. "Huh, that shouldn't be too hard, mate, I've dealt with better locks than these rusty ole things."

The badger seized his friend's paw. "D'you mean you could open these locks?"

Orkwil winced. "Aye, providin' you don't break my paw, you've got a grip like a pike's jaw. Find me somethin' like a pin, or a nail, an' I'll have us free in a jiffy!"

They sat there, scanning the deck keenly, but there was no sign of anything useful. Then Orkwil pointed. "What's that thing sticking in the mast?"

Gorath's heart leapt as he caught sight of the object. "That's Tung, my pitchfork. The fox must've forgotten he threw it. He walked off and left it there!"

Orkwil cautioned Gorath. "Keep yore voice down, mate. . . . Whoops!"

Being locked close to Gorath on the chain, Orkwil was

suddenly swung into the air as the badger reached up and grabbed the pitchfork, which he pulled loose with a few good tugs. Orkwil hit the deck with a bump, gabbling out instructions to his big friend.

"Get down an' lay low, hide that thing before anybeast comes up on deck, hurry!"

Gorath lay flat, concealing most of the pitchfork with his body. Orkwil kept watch, assuring himself that all was quiet above deck. He ran his paws around the mast, searching until he found what he needed.

"Now go nice'n'easy, friend, there's a nail stickin' out a bit, right about where my paw is now. Could you lever it out quietly with one o' the prongs of your fork?"

Whilst Orkwil kept watch, Gorath probed at the nail-head. Getting the prong of his weapon beneath the lip of the nail, he levered carefully at it. The nail gave a slight creak, then it began to move, bit by bit. Gorath wiggled it from side to side, until it loosened. Putting the pitchfork aside, he braced himself. Gripping the nail in his big, blunt claws, he heaved away, yanking it free of the mast timber.

They both sat with their backs to the mast, as Orkwil took the nail and went to work. He twiddled it in the key-hole of Gorath's lock. The badger watched anxiously, whispering, "What's happening, is it opening?" He fell silent as the young hedgehog glared at him, wiggling the nail back and forth. Orkwil grinned.

"A good thief can open any lock. There!"

The padlock lay open. Gorath breathed a huge sigh as he loosed the chain from his middle.

Orkwil chided him, "Be still, bigbeast, give me a chance to get my lock off. Wait . . . wait . . . ah, there it goes, mate!" The chain clanked to the deck. Orkwil was about to rise, when he sat back down speedily. "Be still, somebeast's comin'!"

It was Codj, coming to check up on the two prisoners. Halting where he knew he was out of the badger's reach, the stump-tailed fox peered through the darkness at them both. He was surprised to see Gorath sitting upright, though he could not see that the captives were free. Codj turned away, heading back to his cabin, commenting aloud, "Still alive, eh, Rock'ead, huh, wot keeps ya goin'?" He half-turned as something sounded behind him, but Codj was too late. Gorath's huge paws were around the fox's neck, and he was whispering in his ear.

"I'll tell you what keeps me going, the need to slay my kinbeasts' murderer. Tell me again how you locked them in a farmhouse, and burned them alive. Tell me!"

Orkwil watched in horrified fascination as Gorath shook the already dead fox like a rag. He ran to the badger, tugging at his simple, homespun tunic. "Come on, mate, leave him, we've got to get away from here. We must get to Redwall an' sound the alarm!"

With the limp form of the fox still clenched in his paws, Gorath turned to face the young hedgehog. Orkwil gasped with fear. The badger's eyes were blood red, his teeth bared like a madbeast. Gorath was in the grip of Bloodwrath. Then something very odd happened. Gorath dropped the carcass of his foe, picked up both Orkwil and his pitchfork and slid over the side of the ship, into the River Moss. By the time they reached the bank, he appeared quite calm. Orkwil attributed his friend's sudden change to the cold riverwater.

"Which way to your Abbey, my friend?"

Orkwil pointed. "Go east, we'll cross to the other bank when we're safe out of this area."

They set off into the nightshaded woodland, with Orkwil leading the way. He had been walking rapidly for awhile, when he noticed that Gorath was dropping behind. The badger's pace was noticeably slower, and he was having to stop, leaning on the pitchfork, with his huge striped head drooping. The hedgehog waited until his friend caught him up, one look at Gorath was all he needed, Orkwil shook his head.

"Yore in bad shape, everythin' is catchin' up on ye. Rest, an' vittles, that's what y'need, matey. Sit down."

Gorath slumped wearily to the ground. His head wound, thirst, starvation and cruel treatment had finally taken its toll. That, with his brief attack of Bloodwrath, had left him as weak as a Dibbun.

Orkwil scratched his headspikes, trying to think what to do. The answer came to him in a flash, he took command, issuing Gorath with orders. "I've got it! I know this neck o' the woods, mate. Now you stay here, keep that Tung thing with ye, but don't move, sit right here. I think there's a big, ole bed of ferns hereabouts, stay clear of it, 'cos it's a swamp. Someplace along the bank there's a fat, greedy vole. That beast's got two things we need, vittles an' a place to rest. You stop here, I'll come back for ye as soon as I can. Understood?"

Gorath rose with a grunt. "I'm coming with you."

Orkwil folded his paws resolutely. "No, you ain't, I said yore stayin' here!"

"And I said I'm coming with you!"

The pitchfork prongs were a spike's breadth from Orkwil's snout. He hardened his voice as he glared at Gorath. "That's what I said, yore comin' with me. Now stop arguin' an' let's get movin', bigbeast!"

The bankvole was quite a good cook, by woodland standards. He was sitting on the edge of the river, just outside of his dwelling, savouring the aroma of a large, speckled trout. Only the previous day he had netted it in a reed snare. It was not often that such a feast was to be had, speckled trout were cunning and swift on the River Moss, but voles, particularly old and greedy ones, were equally sly and quick.

The watervole had been up most of the night, preparing himself an epic breakfast. He had dug a firepit, laying his ingredients on the white-hot charcoal embers. A layer of fresh watercress and dandelion leaves, with fragrant mint, pennywort and sorrel. Next came the trout, stuffed with mushrooms and some almonds he had been saving for such an occasion. Topping the lot with a layer of dock-leaves, he covered the pit, and its contents, with loam. Soon it would be baked to a turn.

Sipping a beaker of his own home-brewed cider, the watervole sniffed the delicious aroma permeating through the loam.

"Mmmmm, is that baked trout I can smell, marvellous!"

The vole's paw reached for the club, which lay beside him, as he snarled viciously at Orkwil Prink. "So, it's you agin', well, I'm ready for ye this time, 'edgepig. Try anythin' wid me an' ye'll join those two water rats, weighted down wid rocks in the swamp!" Waving the club, he scrabbled around with his free paw, and came up with a long dagger. "Aye, I'm good'n'ready, so make yore move, if ye dare!"

Orkwil shook his head, feigning sadness. "Well, there's gratitude for you, after me savin' his life. If I'd known he was goin' to be so nasty I wouldn't have invited you along, my friend."

The vole looked over his shoulder, to see whom the young hedgehog was addressing. His jaw dropped at the sight of the huge badger carrying a pitchfork. Dropping both club and dagger, the terrified beast took to his paws and fled into the woodlands.

Orkwil began raking the loam from off the cooked trout. "Dearie me, I never knew voles could run as fast as that. D'you think it was somethin' I said?"

Squatting down beside the cooking pit, Gorath helped to lift the delicious repast out onto the bank.

"Who knows, perhaps he didn't feel very hungry?" For the first time, Orkwil saw his friend smile. Indicating the fish, the young hedgehog smiled back. "I'll wager you feel hungry, mate. Look, why don't you stop here, eat your fill and rest. I can make it to the Abbey alone, yore too weary an' ill to travel far. I'll get help sent out to you, just take it easy, you've been through enough."

Gorath used the vole's dagger to share out the meal. "Eat up and don't talk so much, Orkwil. I'm coming with you, just as I've been ordered to."

The young hedgehog looked oddly at his companion. "Ordered to, wot d'ye mean?"

Gorath explained, "While I was chained to the mast of that ship, I saw things in my mind. A mouse who carried a sword spoke to me, he told me to watch for the young thief. You told me yourself that you were the thief, remember, when you were opening the locks. That mouse halted my Bloodwrath. Do you know what Bloodwrath is?"

Orkwil shook his head, so Gorath continued.

"My grandparents called it the affliction of Badger Warriors. It is a rage for battle that cannot be stopped. When the Bloodwrath strikes I lose all control of myself. Nothing can stand against me in my lust for slaughter, nothing but death itself."

Orkwil's voice sounded very small. "I saw it on the ship, when you seized the fox, it looked as if yore eyes were filled with blood."

Gorath nodded. "Aye, that was Bloodwrath, I would have attacked that full vermin crew. But in this weakened state, they would have overcome me with their numbers. It was the sword mouse who brought me out of it. He appeared in my mind, and told me to go to Redwall with you. So don't try to stop me, little friend, eat this food and we'll be on our way."

Orkwil began wolfing down the food, talking with his mouth full. "Right, I'll try not to stop you, mate. Anyhow, I lost my staff in the swamp, so I couldn't really, could I?"

Gorath passed the vole's club and dagger to him. "You'd best take these."

Orkwil could see Gorath was smiling. He brandished

the weapons, slitting his eyes fiercely. "There, how do I look now, eh?"

The young badger managed a straight face. "Oh, very savage, a real terror I'd say!"

Orkwil took a last mouthful of food and licked his paws. "Come on, then, let's go to Redwall, mate! Oh, before I forget, there's something there that I want you to see."

They set off along the bankside together, the badger's curiosity was aroused. "What's that?"

"Just a friend of yours, the sword mouse, is that what you called him?" Orkwil winked broadly, and would not say anything further.

Dawn glimmered through the trees onto the River Moss. Vizka Longtooth lay asleep in his cabin, gradually coming awake to the sound of voices outside his cabin door.

"Yew tell 'im, Glurma, 'twas ye wot found 'im!" Firty's remark was followed by the cook's denial.

"Ho no, mate, yew see'd 'im afore I did, I was on'y da one who tripped up over 'im on me way t'the galley."

Jungo interrupted Glurma. "Why don't youse both tell de cap'n t'gether?"

Firty rounded on him irately. "Why don't yew tell 'im, bigmouth, go on. March in dere an' say, 'Cap'n, I got news for ye, Codj is dead'!"

The cabin door flew open, knocking Firty flat, and smacking the rat cook in her bulging stomach. Vizka grabbed Jungo by the neck. "My brudder dead, where, 'ow?"

The hapless weasel's windpipe was constricted, he gurgled, "Gollawolla me, Clap'n, yer krokklin' me!"

Glurma rubbed her stomach with one paw, gesturing with the other. "Over dere by d'mast, 'e's over dere!"

The golden fox rushed to the spot. Hardly paying any attention to the crumpled figure of his brother, he stared wildly around, yelling, "Where's der stripe'ound an' dat 'edgepig?"

107

Bilger, who had just appeared on deck, took in the situation at a glance. "Gone, Cap'n!"

It was the wrong thing to say. Vizka felled him with a hard blow, and jumped up and down on him, roaring, "I kin see dey're gone, mud'ead! But who saw 'em, an' where've dey gone to?"

The rest of the crew had turned out to see what all the commotion was about. Vizka rounded on them. "Don't jus' stan' there, do sumthin', go an' track 'em!"

Keeping her distance, Glurma the cook called out, "None of dem kin track, Cap'n, we ain't got a trail follerer aboard!"

Vizka kicked the prone form of Bilger. "Den go an' find one an' bring 'im back 'ere!"

There was a mass scramble as the vermin followed Bilger to the rail, nobeast wanted to stay aboard with their captain in his present mood. About ten made it into the river, when Vizka halted the rest.

"Git back 'ere, it don't take all of youse to find a tracker. Line up there, where I kin see ye!"

The remainder of the crew formed a haphazard line. They stood staring at the deck, as Vizka paced up and down in front of them, glaring.

"Wot a crew, eh? Y'spends yer lives snorin' an' eatin', huh, dat's when yer not swiggin' grog. Lettin' prisoners escape, dat's all yore good for!" He went to the tiller and leaned on it, shaking his head. "An' dere's my pore brudder, deader'n a stone. Codj was worth more'n all of ya put t'gether, now 'e's gotta be laid t'rest. Dogleg, Patchy, find some sailcloth an' wrap Codj up in it. Bind it round wid dat chain, so 'e'll sink. Firty, make up some nice, fittin' werds to say for when my brudder goes overboard."

The two stoats, Dogleg and Patchy, parcelled the carcass of Codj up in a length of sailcloth. They bound it with the chain which Gorath had been locked to. Six crewbeasts bore the bundle to the rail, where they balanced it. Firty stepped forward at a nod from his captain, and dirged the eulogy he had hurriedly put together about Codj.

"Parcelled up in sail an' chain,
we won't see young Codj again,
'e's goin' down where der fishes play,
one shove'll send 'im on 'is way,
while all 'is good ole shipmates wail,
fer one pore fox widout a tail!"

Vizka gave the bundle its required shove, sending it overboard. The golden fox wiped water from his eye, which some of the crew mistook for a tear, but it was only caused by a splash as Codj hit the river. A shout came from the bank foliage.

"Ahoy, Cap'n, we found ye a tracker!"

Bilger and his mates scrambled aboard, dragging with them a creature who was not having the happiest of days. It was the watervole. Bilger sent him sprawling with a well-aimed kick. "Dis ole hairy mouse knows der way to dat Abbey place, Cap'n, an' 'e sez dat stripe'ound an' de 'edgepig robbed 'is brekkist jus' afore dawn."

The prisoner attempted to rise, but Vizka booted him flat again. "Wot's ya name, 'airy mouse?"

The watervole snapped abruptly, "I'm a vole!"

Vizka allowed him to stand upright. "Well, if'n ye wants ter stay alive, vole, ye'd best tell me where Redwall Abbey is."

The captive indicated with a sullen nod. "Upriver to the ford, an' south down the road, as far as I know."

Vizka tweaked his captive's snout until tears poured from the vole's eyes. "Yer a feisty ole crab, ain't ya? Well, let me tell ye, I'm der cap'n o' dis ship, so ye'd best show me some respeck, or yer'll be a dead 'airy mouse!"

Still tweaking his victim's snout, Vizka gave orders. "Weigh anchor an' get under way, we'll pole 'er upriver t'der ford. Dogleg, give dis 'un a paddle an' put 'im ta work. Fasten 'im on a lead, we don't want 'im slippin' away. Hah, we might need an 'airy mouse when we gits ter Redwall."

By midnoon of that hot, summer day, *Bludgullet* had progressed well. The vole stared at the entrance hole to his dwelling as they sailed past it. He silently cursed the bad fortune which had thrown him into the paws of Vizka Longtooth and his Sea Raiders. His reverie did not last long, though. A sharp tug on the tethering rope tied around his neck dragged him back to reality. Bilger was shouting at him.

"Keep movin', get dat paddle a-pushin', move yer wobbly ole bottom or I'll move it for ya!"

The watervole spat on his blistered paws, glaring at his taskmaster, as he punted deep with the long paddle.

Soft evening shades were draping over the land as Orkwil and Gorath waded across the River Moss, where it forded the path. Orkwil pointed south. "If we push on, I reckon we might get to the Abbey sometime after supper."

Gorath began plodding wearily down the path. "Do you think there'll be any supper left over?"

Orkwil matched his big friend's flagging pace. "There's always food to be had at Redwall, mate, anytime of the night or day, you'll see."

12

It was fully dawn when the trio slowed their headlong dash through the woodlands. Luglug beckoned to a strata of sandstone ledges, dotted with bushes and shrubbery. He drew his rapier.

"That place looks like snake land t'me, go careful now. Serpents like these shaded places, with lots o' nooks an' crannies, an' ledges where they can sun themselves."

Maudie whispered to Asio as they crept forward, "Looks jolly silent an' sinister t'me. I wouldn't be at all surprised if the neighbourhood was crawlin' with flippin' snakes, bet there're adders, too, wot!"

The owl scoffed. "Snakes are nowt but snakes, lass. Adders, subtractors, they're all a load o' sneaky worms t'me. Ah've never been fond o' the slippery things."

Maudie froze, fixing her eye on a movement, about halfway up the ledges, by a slender rowan tree. "Luglug, I think I've found our snake. See it, up there, coiled around that rowan root. There's the babe, too!" They ducked behind an old spruce, peering out to get a better assessment of the situation.

Asio blinked. "How's the liddle tyke, my eyes ain't too good from this distance. Is the babby hurt, d'ye think?"

The shrew chieftain shaded his eyes, staring hard. "I

think I saw him move. Aye, he moved again, see? So, baby Dupper ain't been bitten yet, or he'd be stiff as a board. That's an adder, though, I'm sure!"

Maudie kept her eyes on the ledge. "How d'you know, by the thing's markins?"

Log a Log Luglug wrinkled his snout. "Can't make out any markins, it's in the shade. I can smell it from here, though, that's an adder!"

The owl was skeptical of Luglug's judgement. "Nay, lad, all snakes smell the same, it could be a slow worm for all thou knows!"

However, Luglug was adamant. "That's an adder, I tell ye!"

Maudie treated them both to a severe wiggle of her ears. "Will you chaps stop squabblin' an' help me to figure out how we're goin' to rescue little wot'sisface. There's no way we can sneak up on that slimy rotter, he'd see us comin' from up there on the ledge. By the time we crossed the flat area and climbed those rocks, the blighter could've done away with the poor mite, an' scoffed him t'boot. So, let's stop bickerin' about snake smells, an' face up to the confounded problem!"

Luglug shook his head. "Pity we never brought a bow an' arrows along."

Maudie stamped her footpaw, but quietly. "Really! I'm lookin' for solutions, sah, not wishful blinkin' thinkin'! Asio, any ideas rollin' about in that feathered bonce of yours, wot?"

The owl blinked his huge, yellow eyes. "Aye, lass, ah'll back off a touch, then fly up high in t'sky, then zoom in an' give yon worm ecky thump, just like ah would wi' a lizard!" Before Maudie or Luglug could protest, or agree, Asio shuffled rapidly backward and was lost to view.

The shrew chieftain blew a sigh of frustration. "It's no good talkin' to that stubborn ole fool. Come on, miz, we'll start advancin' careful like, so we can give him some help, if'n he does wot he's goin' t'do!"

Nipping quietly from tree to bush, the pair stole forward, with Maudie keeping an eye on the snake and its prey, as Luglug watched the sky for signs of the owl. They reached the base of the ledges. Maudie stared upward.

"This is goin' t'be the tricky part, old chap, wot. No sooner do we start scalin' these ledges than that villain will spot us, we'll stick out like toads on a thimble!"

Without warning, a tremendous din rang out from above: Asio's hooting and screeching, mingled with little Dupper's wails, and the vicious hissing of the snake.

Maudie began bounding up the ledges. "Come on, mate, Asio's arrived. Blood'n'vinegar! Eulaliaaaa!"

The sandstone was weathered, soft and rounded, with no real pawholds, but Maudie and Luglug scrabbled up it as if their lives depended on it. They arrived on the scene in the midst of the hubbub. The owl was gripping the reptile's body in his talons as they attacked one another, beak for fang, in a furor of coils and feathers. The shrewbabe was howling lustily, trying to crawl away from the conflict.

Maudie leapt in. Snatching the infant up, she hurried him out of harm's way. Luglug circled the fight with his rapier at the ready, trying to get a good thrust at the snake. It came a moment later, when the snake lunged, openmouthed, for a strike at Asio. The shrew chieftain thrust the blade right down its throat, dodging to one side as its tail thrashed furiously. The owl held it tight in his talons until he was sure the snake was dead. Luglug retrieved his blade from the reptile's mouth, saluting the owl with it.

"Got the brute, just as it was goin' to strike ye!"

Asio flung the snake's limp carcass over the ledge with a scornful flick of his hooked beak. "Goin' to strike me? Thou must be jestin', lad, yon great string o' scales must've bitten me about four times in all. Aye, he put up a gradely scrap, though, ah'll say that for 'im!"

Maudie was wrapping the shrewbabe back in his little

shawl. Concern registered in her eyes as she stared at Asio. "Are you quite sure, old lad, that filthy rotter got his fangs into you four blinkin' times, wot?"

The owl blinked. "It were either four or five times, ah weren't countin'. Still, yon worm's slain now, an' the babbie's safe. That's all wot counts, lass!" Asio's legs seemed to buckle, he wobbled a pace or two, then squatted down, his head nodding forward as he watched Luglug cleaning off his blade. "Whoo, ah feel right tired out, 'appen ah'll need a liddle nap afore we carry on back 'ome." He winked lazily at Luglug, then chuckled. "Yeh great pudden'ead, yon worm weren't no adder, it were nowt but a grass snake. Ah were right, weren't ah?"

Putting his rapier aside, the shrew knelt alongside Asio, patting his wing gently. "Aye, mate, you were right, no doubt about it."

The owl's eyes were blinking rapidly as he turned to Maudie. "Ah may forget one or two things, but when ah recall 'em ah'm always right, eh, lass?"

Still holding the shrewbabe, Maudie hurried to Asio's side. However, the great yellow eyes had fallen shut, for the last time. The haremaid knelt, pressing her face against his downy cheek feathers. "My poor, old, brave, muddle-headed friend, you've earned a perilous warrior's rest. Sleep well, Asio Bardwing!"

Maudie and Luglug laid him where he had fallen, they built a neat cairn of sandstone slabs over Asio. It was mid-morning before the task was finished. The shrewbabe was hungry, he began whimpering for his breakfast. Maudie rocked him soothingly, as Luglug recited a few lines over the owl's resting place.

"Friend of the Guosim, courageous one,
it is time to bid thee farewell,
round campfires at night thy name shall live on,
for great stories of thee I will tell!"

Maudie passed the little one to the shrew chieftain. Taking Luglug's rapier, she saluted her fallen comrade, yelling aloud the Salamandastron war cry, in tribute to him. "Eulaliiiiiiaaaaaa!"

They returned to Bulrush Bower in time for lunch. Little Dupper's mother was overjoyed to get her baby back unharmed. Luglug and Maudie told her of the owl's heroic sacrifice, how Asio had saved Dupper by doing battle with the adder. The shrewmum was greatly moved, she proclaimed from that day forth, her little one's name would be changed, from Dupper to Asio. Both Maudie and the Guosim tribe were in complete agreement with the decision. They ate a simple lunch, shrewbread, apples and some cheese. When all their baggage was packed, Luglug gave orders.

Shrews are notoriously noisy, they gossip and shout constantly. To gain silence Luglug had to shout out his official title, Log a Log, in an ululating call. Maudie was startled; for such a small creature, he had a resounding voice.

"Logalogalogaloooooog!"

The Guosim ceased jabbering and listened to their chief. Luglug was very brief with his announcement. "Get the liddle 'uns on their lines'n'harnesses! Rigril an' Teagle, yore in the scoutin' coracle! Porters an' portagers, move out! We're bound for the Abbey o' Redwall, by the crookstream an' ripples!"

The Guosim cheered this news to the echo, Redwall was a great place to visit. Everybeast bustled to their chores. Maudie watched the process, sorting out in her mind what it all meant. She saw parents fastening small woven harnesses around the waists of their infants, and others packing equipment upon their backs. Rigril and Teagle had raced off, as soon as Luglug told them they would be in the scouting coracle. The rest, who were mainly sturdy looking males, followed the two scouts. Luglug explained what was happening.

"That gang who've gone ahead are the portagers, miz. Guosim goes everywhere by logboats, rivers'n'streams, that's the way we travels. Ye see yon fir grove, we've stowed our logboats there. They've got t'be carried, portaged y'see, across t'the crookstream. A shrew needs strong paws an' a broad back to be a portager!"

Maudie saw Guosim, or at least the bottom halves of them, emerging from the grove. The shrews were carrying six fine, long logboats. She chuckled at the sight. It looked like upside down vessels, each with many pairs of legs, tramping away into the woodlands. Luglug did not appear amused.

"There's nought funny about portagin', missy, 'tis a fair ole trek afore we reaches the crookstream an' ripples. We'd best take the lead, c'mon."

Maudie hurried to catch up with the bristly little Log a Log. "I know there's nothin' funny about havin' to carry the jolly old boats, wot. But it looks rather comical, don't it? I say, those portagin' chaps mustn't be able t'see a bally thing, how do they know which way to go, wot?"

The Guosim chieftain explained. "That's why we'll be walkin' in front o' the first logboat. The front shrew will follow our footpaws. The next beast follows his, an' so on. When yore portagin' all ye can see is the ground 'neath yoreself, an' the footpaws o' the one in front of ye."

Having reached the lead position with Luglug, the haremaid looked back. Behind her was a well-ordered procession, the line of logboats, followed by Guosim porters, carrying bundles of camping equipment. To the rear of the porters came the little ones. Each was tethered to their family members by a harness and a lead rope. Bringing up the tail end of the column came a score of young warriors, each with drawn rapier, eager and willing to prove themselves in the event of an attack. Maudie concluded that though Guosim shrews were noisy and argumentative, they could be very well ordered, when each had a specific task to perform. The logboat carriers struck up a sort of marching shanty, to keep their footpaws in time with each other.

"We ain't no sailors on the sea,
in ships decked out with sails,
there ain't no call for cap'n, mate or bosun,
but we knows more o' paddlin' boats,
on river, pond or stream,
than anybeast wot ever sailed the ocean!

"Gimme a good ole logboat,
that's the craft to keep me fit,
when a logboat ain't carryin' a Guosim,
well, the Guosim's carryin' it!

"I bet there's no saltwater beast,
a-headed back to home,
who's reached the land an' heard his cap'n order,
'All paws on shore now lift this ship,
an' carry it on yore 'eads,
it looks t'me like we've run out o' water!'

"Gimme a good ole logboat,
that's the craft to keep me fit,
when a logboat ain't carryin' a Guosim,
well, the Guosim's carryin' it!"

Twilight was already covering the woodlands when they reached their destination. The place Guosim called the crookstream and ripples looked peaceful enough to Maudie. She organised supper as the shrews tethered their logboats to the bank, loading them, so they would be ready to move on the morrow. A foraging party brought in some button mushrooms, scallions and early acorns, which Maudie used as a filling for the pasties she was making.

Luglug commented as they sat beneath the bankside willows, "I tell ye, Miss Maudie, I ain't never tasted pasties as nice as these in all me seasons. Er, how would ye like to become a Guosim cook? The job's yores if'n ye want it. In fact, I'll make ye Grand Guosim Chef, an' give ye a staff of helpers. Wot d'ye say?"

The haremaid shook her head. "Sorry, 'fraid not, sah, I'm a Salamandastron hare of the Long Patrol. Couldn't imagine m'self balancin' a whoppin' great logboat between my ears, an' singin' portagin' songs. Besides, I've got a jolly old mission to complete. Couldn't very well do that an' toddle off t'be a blinkin' Guosim chef to boot, wot!"

Luglug looked crestfallen, but he made no further mention of the subject.

Maudie was wakened at the crack of dawn next morning. Still yawning, she was thrust into the prow end of the lead logboat, alongside a young shrew named Osbil. The vessel lurched off from the bank, powered by fourteen Guosim, all paddling energetically. The haremaid nodded to her companion. "G'morning, I say, aren't we supposed t'be paddlin', or something like that, wot?"

Osbil replied, without taking his eyes off the stream ahead, "Have ye ever paddled a logboat afore, marm, do ye own yore own paddle?"

Maudie shook her head. "First time I've been in a bloomin' boat, old lad, jolly good, isn't it, 'fraid I don't have a perishin' paddle. S'pose I might borrow yours, wot?"

Osbil continued peering upstream. "Huh, s'pose ye might not borrow my paddle, marm, nobeast in this tribe touches another 'un's paddle, t'aint done. If'n it's the first time ye've been in a logboat, then ye'd be hopeless as a paddlebeast. Takes at least four seasons t'train a Guosim paddler. Them's our rules, marm!"

The haremaid sniffed. "Oh, golly gracious now, can't have me breakin' the flippin' rules, can we. But why aren't you paddlin'?"

Osbil answered without looking at her. "'Cos I'm first

prowspot, got t'keep me glims on the course ahead, especially as this is the lead logboat."

Maudie gestured upstream. "Well, don't let me stop you, old chap, you keep your eye . . . glims peeled, if that's a prowspotter's job. Er, pardon me askin', but what's my purpose aboard this jolly old logboat, wot?"

Osbil winked, and gave Maudie a swift grin. "Prowspotter's mate's supposed to sing, so the paddlers can keep in stroke. Just like when yore marchin'."

The sun broke through the foliage which formed a canopy over the crookstream, causing a lacy effect of light and shadow. Dragonflies hovered on the reed-fringed banks, watching the logboat flotilla as it passed by. Crookstream was aptly named, it was a real switchback, with more twists and turns than a corkscrew. Looking back, Maudie marvelled at the skill of the Guosim paddlers. She could see Luglug, standing in the stern of the last logboat, enveloped in a rainbow of spray. As they pushed upstream against the playful, gurgling waters, Maudie broke out into an old Long Patrol barrack-room song, hardly a march, she thought, but quite a good tune. The haremaid had a strong voice, which rang out loud and clear.

"Oh, soldier, I'm askin' ye, where would ye like to be, all on a winter's day?
As onward you push, through the snow-driven slush, on your cold an' weary way,
with dew on your nose an' your ears solid froze, an' ice from scut to eyes.
Tell me, tell me, give me a big surprise!

"March on! Left, right! One, two an' a-three!
At last I've found an officer,
who's like a mother to me!

"Oh, Sergeant Maclain, I don't wish to complain, it ain't like me to moan,
but on this winter day, I'd just love you to say,

119

that I should've stayed at home,
with a mug of hot soup, an' me ears all a-droop,
in an armchair by the fire,
O Sergeant, Sergeant, that's my heart's desire!

"Eyes front! Ears up! Whiskers stiff'n'straight!
one more word from you y'wretch,
an' yore through the guardhouse gate!"

The Guosim laughed aloud. Like anybeast who had to obey rules and orders, they appreciated the sentiment of Maudie's song. One bold, young shrew even shouted out, "Yore Sergeant sounds just like our Log a Log, miss!"

He was silenced by Luglug's stern voice from the rear. "Aye, an' one more word from you, mate, an' ye can get out an' push. Now dig those paddles deep!"

As they progressed further upstream, the shrewbabes began to get restless and disobedient. Two of them even leapt into the stream. They were hauled in immediately, and scolded by their family members.

"You liddle rogue, you might've been drowned!"

"Aye, either that or eaten by a big fish!"

Maudie remarked to Osbil, "It's just as well they were on harnesses and leads."

The prowspotter pointed to a long, silvery gleam under the surface. He yelled out a warning. "Ahoy, pike inna water!"

The haremaid saw the pike as it headed for the reeds, avoiding a salvo of slingstones from the Guosim. "Great seasons, look at the size of that villain, wot!"

The great fish's green-gold bulk slid silently off and was lost among the reeds. Osbil commented, "That thing'd take a full-growed Guosim afore ye could wink. As for the little 'uns, huh, they wouldn't make much more'n a snack for a monster like that!"

Throughout the morning Maudie came to realise that besides being a thing of beauty and wonder, the crookstream could conceal a host of dangers. Osbil pointed out more pike, a great eel and a number of hunting barbels, all lurking beneath the smooth surface, savage predators in their own domain.

At midday the logboats pulled into a shaded inlet. Maudie joined Luglug in a stroll along the bank, to stretch their limbs. A shout from around the bend heralded the return of the scouting coracle. Rigril and Teagle came ashore to make their report. "We made it up as far as the ripples, they look a bit lively today, Chief."

Luglug shrugged. "I never knew a time when those ripples wasn't lively. Teagle, wot are ye chewin' yore lip for?"

Teagle was a good scout, well-versed in woodland ways. She explained her concern to the Guosim chieftain. "Two bends up, by the big rock, where it's shallow an' pebbly, we saw a lot of woodpigeon fly overhead, doves, too, an' a few thrush an' blackbird."

Rigril nodded in agreement. "Aye, Chief, an' there ain't no great wind, or signs o' storm. Somethin' scared those birds. Drivin' 'em south, we figgered."

Luglug looked from one to the other. "Vermin, d'ye reckon?"

Teagle stopped gnawing at her lip. "Brownrats, I think. We spotted two of their scouts, but I think they saw us first. Anyhow, we got out o' there fast!"

Maudie took note of Luglug's anxious frown. "Tell me what's on your mind, sah, perhaps I can help. Member of the Long Patrol y'know, an' all that, wot?"

The Guosim chieftain patted her paw, smiling tightly. "Mayhaps ye can, if yore as good at tactics as ye are at cookin'. Let's talk about it over lunch."

The meal was not a cooked one, since they could not risk a fire. As an apology for some of their previous culinary atrocities, the younger shrews put together a very tasty woodland salad, with cheese, hazelnuts and oatbread. While they ate, Luglug explained the position to Maudie.

121

"There's a horde o' Brownrats been roamin' this neck o' the woods for a few seasons now, an' I tell ye, they're a bad lot! Their chief is a big 'un called Gruntan Kurdly, he's a born killer, an' he ain't no fool. Ole Gruntan's got a mind sharper'n a dagger."

Maudie helped herself to more salad. "Indeed, an' what d'you think the blinkin' rascal's up to, may I ask?"

Luglug spread his paws meaningly. "Nothin', if'n his scouts ain't seen our scouts. But, if'n they did spot Rigril'n'Teagle, then we're in the soup, an' here's the reason why, miss. That place by where the big rock sticks up, 'tis a perfect spot for an ambush. The stream runs shallow o'er the pebble bed, an' 'tis slow goin' paddlin' a logboat. So, if'n Gruntan knows we've got to pass by there, he'll be layin' in wait for us, take my word!"

Maudie let her ears flop to half-mast (a thing she often did when pondering a problem). "Hmm, I see. Tell me, d'you think he'll have both banks covered, or will he just have his scoundrels waiting on one bank, wot?"

The shrew chieftain scratched his tail. "Prob'ly both banks. Don't get me wrong, Miz Maudie, I ain't scared o' fightin' those rats, but we got liddle 'uns along with us, wot do I do about the babes? We could chance makin' a run for it, 'cos when we reach the ripples, the current runs the other way, downhill. Nobeast would catch us once we was on the ripples."

Maudie was staring at the coracle, moored to the bank. "D'you think we could get all the little chaps, plus two good paddlers, into that thing, wot?"

Teagle raised her eyebrows. "It'd be a bit of a squash, marm, but me'n'Rigril could prob'ly manage it."

Maudie addressed her next remark to Luglug. "What d'you have in the way of weaponry, old lad?"

The shrew counted items off on his pawpad. "Every Guosim has his rapier, most carry slings an' stones, an' there's around a score of us with bows an' arrers. Of course, if'n push comes to shove, a paddle's as good a weapon as anythin', miss."

The haremaid winked at her friends. "Well, huzzah for us, I say. We can work a flanker on the rotters, bit of a reverse pincer, as I've heard old Major Mull call it. Yes, that's what we'll jolly well do, wot!"

The shrew chieftain gazed blankly at Maudie, he could think of only one thing to say. "Wot?"

It had been said of Gruntan Kurdly that his mind was teetering on the brink of madness. Or to put it in Brownrat parlance, he had butterflies in his head, lots of them. However, no Brownrat, or any other vermin, dared to mention this to the warlord's face. The rare few who had were long dead, or, as Gruntan himself put it, had suffered a dose of the Kurdlys.

Gruntan Kurdly was the biggest of all his horde, both in height and girth. Brownrats smeared themselves with dyes and ochres, mainly yellow and blue, adorning themselves with the bones of their enemies, giving the horde a savage appearance. But none could outdo Gruntan in colour, or barbarity. He was a virtual rainbow of daubs, stripes and blotches of all hues. Around his huge waist, he sported a wide belt hung with skulls, ranging from birds to reptiles, with a few vermin craniums. These were a reminder to his horde, to show them who was warlord.

Gruntan sat on his litter, atop the high rock, watching preparations down below for the proposed ambush. His dozen litter bearers, several of whom were big females, hovered around, rendering him every attention. The Brownrat warlord was inordinately fond of hard-boiled eggs. The horde had recently ravaged the woodpigeon nests, so there was a plentiful supply for their leader. Three of Gruntan's daughters were kept busy shelling the eggs, whilst their father wolfed them down as he questioned his two scouts.

"Haharr, an' wot did ye see downstream, me beauties, eh?"

Notwithstanding the shower of boiled egg fragments which he was forced to face, Noggo, the chief scout, reported. "Sh'ews they was, Boss, Grousen sh'ews, loads of 'em."

Gruntan spat out a bit of shell, cuffed the ear of the daughter responsible, then continued. "Grousens, ye say, an' did they 'ave 'andsome likkle boats wid 'em? Hoho, I needs some of those boats."

Biklo, the other scout, nodded eagerly. "Aye, I counted them meself, six long 'uns, an' a likkle round 'un, wot their scouts used, Boss!"

Gruntan's eyes grew dreamy as he imagined himself being transported along peaceful streams by boat. He liked boats. For a rat of his size and weight, the warlord was surprisingly quick; suddenly, he grabbed Noggo by the throat. Gruntan whispered hoarsely to him. "Noggo, me ole matey, was you spotted by the Grousens?"

Gulping, the scout tried to shake his head. "The sh'ews never saw us, on me oath, Boss!"

Gruntan released Noggo. He let his sly, glittering eyes rove over both scouts, popping another egg into his mouth. "Hearken t'me, mateys, an ambush only works if'n it's unexpected. T'wont be no ambush at all if'n ye've been seen by the Grousen sh'ews. So, tell me agin, was you spotted by 'em, eh?"

Noggo and Biklo shook their heads vigorously, replying in unison, "No, Boss, we wasn't spotted!"

Spearing another egg on one claw, Gruntan waggled it at the two scouts as he issued his customary warning. " 'Cos if'n you was, guess wot'll 'appen to ye?"

Noggo spoke for them both. "A dose of the Kurdlys, Boss."

Gruntan devoured the hard-boiled egg swiftly. "Haharr, right first time, me beauty!" He beckoned to Stringle, a tall, thin rat, who was his first officer. "Git down there, an' see

124

that the crews are well stowed out o' sight on both banks. Keep yore eyes peeled up 'ere on me, I'll give ye the signal when they're comin'."

Stringle saluted with his spear and loped off. Gruntan Kurdly lay back on the litter, with a sigh of satisfaction, chewing happily on another egg. "Noggo, tell me when ye see those sh'ew boats hovin' into sight, will ye? Haharr, there ain't nothin' like some trim likkle vessels to ride the waters on!"

Sounds of the stream, gurgling softly over its pebbled bed, echoed up from below. Gruntan's eyes began to flutter, a half-eaten egg slipped from his paw. He was just about to start a nice nap, when Noggo shook him.

"Ahoy, Boss, 'ere they comes!"

From the top of the tall rock, the logboats looked small as they negotiated a bend in the stream. They were placed with two close to each bank, the coracle was in midstream, flanked by the remaining two boats. Gruntan murmured, "Come on, me beauties, come to ole Gruntan Kurdly!"

BOOK TWO

A Thief Absolved

13

Evening shades were turning the ancient walls of the
Abbey to a dusty rose pink, the soft air was still warm from
the long summer day. Little Dimp heaved himself laboriously up the north wall steps, toward the outer walltop.
Each stair was an effort for the tiny squirrel, but he was de-
termined to succeed. Down below on the lawn, two more
Dibbuns, a mousemaid named Flim and an infant molemaid, Jorty, stood wagging their paws at Dimp. Dibbuns
were forbidden to climb the steps, or to be alone up on the
ramparts. Both the tiny maids were shocked at the antics of
Dimp, and told him so.

"Cumma down now, naughty squiggle, you not ap-
posed t'be uppa there. Comma down, me say!"

"Hurr, you'm getten inna trubble, zurr Dimp, fall on ee
skull'ead, or sumpin'. Coom ee daown, yurr!"

Dimp made it up onto the high walkway. He did a brief
jig, calling scornfully to the pair below, "Ho, go an' boil
yore bottims!"

Squeaking with shock at Dimp's turn of phrase, the little
maids threw their pinafores over their faces and dashed off.

"Hi, hello there, is anyone on the wall?"

Dimp went to the battlements, he began scrambling up,
to see who was hailing the walltops from outside. "H'I'm

onna guard h'up 'ere, wot you want?" Levering his chin over the battlement, Dimp stared down. He had never seen anybeast the size of a badger in his life, and certainly not the huge, gaunt creature in a ragged smock, wielding a gigantic pitchfork. The Dibbun fell back onto the parapet, speechless with fright.

Orkwil was further along to the right of the main gate, when Gorath hailed him.

"There was somebeast up there a moment ago, a little squirrel, I think. I may have frightened him off."

The young hedgehog came scurrying back to his friend's side. He looked up to the walltop. "Listen, friend, you'd better make yourself scarce. Hide in the bushes, I'll speak to whoever it is." Whilst Gorath concealed himself at the north woodland edge, Orkwil began hailing the ramparts. "Hello up there, anybeast about? We need to get inside!"

Flim and Jorty were halfway across the lawn when they bumped into Fenn Bluepaw. The Abbey Recorder confronted the little ones sternly. "What's all this squealing and shouting about, why aren't you two inside, getting ready for bed?"

Jorty jumped up and down on the spot. "Marm, et bee's Dimp, he'm bein' gurtly naughty!"

Flim could not wait to inform on Dimp. "An', an', an' guess wot he sayed, marm, Dimp sayed the bot word to us. Ho good my gracious, it was h'awful!"

Fenn Bluepaw looked from one to the other. "'Bot word,' what's that supposed to mean?"

Flim could hold back no longer. "Dimp told us to boil h'our . . . bottims!"

Jorty nodded vigorous agreement. "Hurr aye, an' he'm cloimbed oop on ee walltops, marm!"

The bottom remark went unheeded. No sooner was the walltop mentioned than Fenn stamped her footpaw wrathfully. "Off to the Abbey, you two, this very instant! I'll deal with Master Dimp!"

Flim and Jorty watched the Recorder striding purposefully to the north wallsteps, where Dimp could be seen, cowering in the shade of the battlements. The little mousemaid scowled darkly. "Hah, I not like t'be Dimp, Sista Fenn prolibly chop his tail off for bein' naughty!"

Jorty giggled. "Hurhur, or she'm moight boil his bottim!"

Flim clapped a paw to her little friend's mouth. "Goodness me, you've sayed bottim now!"

They trundled off to the Abbey, giggling together.

Orkwil yelled up to the walltop, for the second time. "Anybeast about, we've got to get inside, it's urgent! Hello up there, who's that?"

Fenn Bluepaw appeared at the northwest gable, her face the picture of indignation. "So, 'tis you, Orkwil Prink? The thief who was banished for a season. I shouldn't even be talking to you! Go on, be off, you scoundrel!"

The young hedgehog spread his paws, pleading. "But marm, ye don't understand, I've got to speak with Abbot Daucus, or Skipper, it's really important!"

Fenn picked little Dimp up, turning her face away from Orkwil, and remarking scornfully, "Huh, first a thief, and now a liar, you haven't changed much. Well, you can stand there fibbing all night, but you're not entering this Abbey!"

Gorath had watched the exchange from the cover of some bushes. He left his hiding spot and came to stand beside Orkwil. The badger, not knowing his young friend's predicament, decided to reinforce Orkwil's plea. Cupping both paws around his mouth, he bellowed out to anybeast that might have been within hearing range, "Listen to me, or you'll be sorry when Redwall is attacked!"

Skipper Rorc emerged from the Abbey for his evening patrol of the grounds, which was more in the nature of a leisurely stroll to walk off a big supper. He heard Gorath's resounding voice, and hurried toward the north wall. On the way, he passed Fenn Bluepaw, who was hauling along a reluctant Dimp. Skipper nodded. "Evenin', marm, d'ye know who's doin' the shoutin' out there?"

The Recorder squirrel sniffed. "Pay no attention, 'tis only Orkwil Prink trying to get back into our Abbey. Come on, Dimp, don't drag your paws!"

The squirrelbabe pulled back. "Mista Skip, that not Ork'il, it's a monister wiv a hooj fork, I saw 'im!"

Skipper was already running for the wallsteps, he called back, "It didn't sound like Orkwil, I'd best take a look!"

A moment later the otter was on the walltop, staring down at the bedraggled, weary pair. "Wot's all this about an attack, young Prink, an' who's that giant ye've got in tow?"

Gorath spoke for himself. "I'm Gorath. I don't know who you are, sir, but there's a whole crew of sea-raiding vermin who'll be here before too long. Take it from me, that's a fact!"

Skipper vanished from sight, shouting to Orkwil, "Take yore friend to the main gate an' I'll let ye in!"

Abbot Daucus was cutting a slice of yellow cheese to have with his pear as an after-supper dessert, when the door of the Great Hall burst open. Skipper Rorc strode in, flanked by Orkwil Prink and the biggest badger the Abbot had ever seen. Daucus rose hastily from the table, addressing the badger. "If you enter our Abbey as a friend, there is no need to carry a weapon, sir!"

Gorath looked at his pitchfork, Tung, as if just noticing that it was in his paw. He bowed slightly, placing it on the table. "Forgive me, I didn't mean to frighten anybeast. I came here with Orkwil, to warn you that your Abbey may soon be attacked by vermin, a large crew of them, headed by the fox they call Vizka Longtooth—" Gorath broke off, he seemed to wilt, clutching the support of the table. He staggered slightly, slumping down on one of the benches by the table side.

Orkwil spoke. "Gorath's my friend, he was captured on

132

the Northern Isles by the vermin. They had him chained up to a ship's mast. He's been beaten and starved."

The Cellarhog, Benjo Tipps, immediately started shoving food from the table in front of the big, gaunt badger. "Pore beast, 'ere, matey, you take yore fill o' good Redwall vittles. Aye, an' there's plenty more where they came from. Orkwil, you can tell us the rest, eh?"

Abbot Daucus took charge then. "Everybeast out, please, I want this hall cleared. Friar Chondrus, bring more food, and some hot soup if you can manage it. Now you just sit still there, Gorath, we'll take care of you, my friend."

The badger tried to nod, but his head fell forward onto the table, and his eyes started to droop.

Daucus gave more orders. "Sister Atrata, kindly fetch your medicines from the sickbay, and any assistants you may need. Skipper, will you and your daughters clear the table off? See if you can lay our friend on it, with a pillow for his head. Orkwil, come to my room, you can enlighten me on the situation. Benjo, you'd better come, too, and Skipper, please join us when you're done here."

The vessel *Bludgullet* took longer than expected to reach the ford. Overhanging trees, narrow banks and outcrops of rock had to be negotiated to ply the ship upriver. Vizka was forced to admit that whilst a ship at sea could be fleet and nimble, forcing it upland, through a woodland river, was no easy task. The golden fox took command of the operation. He did not spare the rope's end with tardy paddle pushers, driving them to their limit with lashes, blows and curses.

The crew sweated and toiled throughout the night, scratched by foliage, lashed by their captain and plagued by midges and stinging insects. It was backbreaking work. Whenever a rest was called, the vessel would drift backward with the current, and the anchor would have to be dropped.

The sun had been up for some considerable time, and

there was still no sign of the path or the ford. Vizka kicked the watervole, who had slumped to the deck with fatigue. "Gerrup on ya hunkers, 'airymouse, are ye shore dis is de right way to der fordplace?"

The watervole was hungry, sick to his stomach and resentful. He curled a lip at the *Bludgullet*'s captain. "Huh, which way can this river go, except t'the ford, eh?"

Vizka hauled the unfortunate beast up by the rope, which was tethered about his neck. He bit the watervole's ear until his victim squealed with pain. "I never ast ya fer smart remarks, just a straight answer. So, are we bound der right way fer dat ford?"

The watervole whimpered as he nursed his torn ear. "Yes, yes, this is the right way, sir, I swear it!"

Even as he spoke, one of the vermin, who was in the water, hauling on a headrope, sang out. "Dere's some sort o' path crossin' der water up ahead, Cap'n, dis river's gettin' shallower!"

Vizka Longtooth released the rope, letting the watervole slump to the deck. He patted the wretched beast's head. "Well done, bucko, you was right, dat'll be der ford." The golden fox glanced about at his crew as he called out a halt. "Drop anchor, an' moor 'er t'der bank."

There was an audible groan of relief from the vermin crew, they flopped down, panting and gasping from their night-long efforts. Vizka knew they were totally exhausted, but he was artful at dealing with his creatures, to get his own way.

"Youse two, Baul an' Widge, stop 'ere ter guard der ship. All d'rest of ya, git ready ter march by mid-mornin'." Vizka put on his dangerous smile, watching the crew for signs of protest, or rebellion. They hung their heads in sullen silence, not even daring to sniff or mutter. Vizka strode up and down, nodding. "Good, good! I gives ya my word dat by tonight ye'll be feastin' like kings, an' sleepin' in Redwall Abbey. So, wot d'ya says ter dat, me buckoes?" He strode off to his cabin, not waiting for a reply, knowing that they would do as he ordered. Or die. Pausing at the cabin door, he turned, pointing at the watervole. "Jungo, yore in charge of dat 'un, make sure 'e don't try ter escape."

Jungo hauled the vole over by his neck tether. "Huhuh, I'll watch 'im like a mudder duck wid an egg, Cap'n. Ahoy, hairymouse, you knows 'ow mudder ducks watches their eggs, don't ya?"

The watervole shook his head. "No sir."

Jungo knocked him flat with a swift kick. "Huhuhu, dey sits on 'em, like dis!"

Abbot Daucus, Benjo Tipps and Skipper Rorc had been joined by Granspike Niblo. They listened intently as Orkwil related his story, telling of the coming danger from Longtooth and his vermin Sea Raiders. Granspike hugged Orkwil fondly.

"You see, Father Abbot, I allus knew there was good in this young feller. Even though he were banished for the season, Orkwil came back to warn us!"

Daucus smiled at the young hedgehog. "Indeed he did, you are a credit to your Abbey, young Prink!"

Orkwil immediately perked up. "Does this mean I'm not banished anymore, Father?"

Skipper gave Orkwil's snout a playful tweak. "I should 'ope not, matey, we'll be needin' beasts like you to defend the walls. How many vermin d'ye reckon Longtooth has with him?"

Orkwil scratched his headspikes. "I never had time to count 'em, but there must be more than eight score at least. What are we going to do if they attack Redwall? We don't have many trained warriors, and it may be some time before Gorath is well enough to fight."

The Abbot gathered both paws into his wide sleeves. "Redwall was never a military stronghold, we'll do what we've always done in times of attack. Our walls are strong enough to face any onslaught of vermin, we'll defend, right, Skipper?"

The burly otter nodded. "Right, Father. Meself an' ole Benjo here, we've both had a bit of past experience with rovin' vermin. Seems t'me this lot don't sound a lot different, we'll deal with 'em atween us, one way or another. How would ye like t'be an officer o' the guard, young Prink? I think he'd suit the job well, eh, Benjo?"

The Cellarhog winked at Skipper. "Aye, why not, all young 'uns got to grow up sooner or later. I wish that the badger was fit to fight, though. My spikes! Have ye seen the size of him? I'll wager he could do some damage wid that pitchfork o' his!"

Orkwil was bursting with pride at his unexpected promotion. Feeling very important, he ventured an opinion. "My friend Gorath is a real warrior, I've already seen him slay one creature, when we were on the vermin ship. He told me that he suffers from Bloodwrath."

The Abbot sat up straight in his chair. "Great seasons of slaughter! D'you mean to tell me the badger lying on Great Hall table is a beast of Bloodwrath?"

Orkwil hastened to assure his Abbot. "I wouldn't worry too much, Father. Gorath told me that he was saved from the Bloodwrath by a vision of a mouse who carried a great sword."

Pushing his chair to one side, the Abbot rose. "It must have been Martin the Warrior! Come with me, friends, let's take a closer look at this badger."

Down in Great Hall, Gorath was sitting up on the edge of the large banqueting table. Friar Chondrus was refilling a bowl from a cauldron of leek and mushroom soup, whilst Foremole Burff held forth a plate of carrot and turnip pasties. The huge young badger accepted the soup and a pastie, grunting. "My thanks, friends, this is wonderful food!" As he ate, Sister Atrata, who was standing up on the table behind her patient, worked on some of his other wounds. Orkwil approached him boldly.

"How are you doing, mate, feeling better?" As Gorath

raised his face from the soup bowl, Orkwil gasped and took a backward pace.

The thickly crusted scab, which had formed over the large wound that Vizka had inflicted with his mace and chain, was gone. Centred in the middle of his white forehead stripe was a deep scarlet shape, resembling a large flame. Gorath looked oddly at his friend. "I'm feeling a bit better, what are you staring at?"

Before Orkwil could reply, Sister Atrata explained. "I was bathing that dreadful injury on his head, with some special herbs and hot water, when the scab came loose. It was the size of a small plate. Well, I didn't know how severe the wound was, so just kept on bathing until the scab fell off. I'm afraid no more flesh or fur will ever grow in that spot again. However, the wound beneath was protected, and kept clean by the dried blood which had formed the scab. It isn't raw, or moist, and Gorath says it doesn't pain him anymore."

The badger touched his wide, flame-shaped wound. "It feels fine, thank you, Sister. Could I see it?"

Abbot Daucus extended his paw to Gorath. "If you feel well enough to walk, there's a polished shield on the wall, in an alcove over there. I've seen many a pretty young Redwall maid using it as a mirror. Come on, take a peek at yourself, friend, it's not so bad."

On reaching the alcove which contained the shield, Gorath staggered right past it. He pointed at the Redwall Abbey tapestry, his voice sending booming echoes around Great Hall. "It's him, it's the warrior with the sword. There!"

Orkwil grasped his big friend's paw. "Hah, see, told you there was somebeast you might want to meet—that's Martin the Warrior!"

Gorath sat down on the floor, gazing at the woven figure. "He saved my life!"

It was impossible not to be impressed by the likeness of

Martin. His eyes seemed to follow every creature, they were kindly eyes, but brave and resolute. Orkwil had always thought there was something very comforting in looking at Martin, he felt reassured by the sight of the warrior, as did every Redwaller. The Abbot placed something in Gorath's paws, it was the warrior's sword. Though it looked no bigger than a long dagger in the badger's massive grasp, he admired it greatly.

"This is a marvellous blade, whoever forged it must have been a master of the armorer's craft." The badger leaned toward the tapestry as if listening to something. He beckoned to Orkwil. "Would you please bring me my weapon?" Orkwil did as he was requested.

Gorath held the pitchfork until it was close to the tapestry. "This is not a real warrior's thing, but I call it Tung, it isn't as wonderful as your sword, but it has always served me well." Gorath laid Tung alongside Martin's sword by the tapestry. Without another word, he curled up on the floor and slept.

Sister Atrata whispered to Orkwil, "He seems to like it there, I'll bring him blankets, and a pillow. Your friend is still not recovered."

The party tip-pawed away from the sleeping badger, with the Abbot murmuring softly to Skipper, "Anybeast who can talk with Martin is a friend of Redwall."

Benjo Tipps agreed. "Aye, you could tell they was talkin' to each other, just by watchin' Gorath!"

Orkwil cast a backward glance at his friend, slumbering deeply, watched over by the greatest warrior of all. He whispered in Martin's direction, "If you can, sir, get Gorath well, so that he can help us to face those vermin!"

Did the eyes of the figure on the tapestry blink? Or was it just a trick of the flickering candlelight?

14

Brownrats secreted behind rocks on both sides of the crookstream watched eagerly as the little flotilla of log-boats drew closer. Gripping clubs and spears, they awaited Gruntan Kurdly's signal. Their plan was simple, a straight charge into the shallow, running water would catch the unsuspecting Guosim shrews by surprise. It would be the perfect ambush. At its deepest part, the crookstream ran less than waist high, owing to its heavily pebbled bed.

Gruntan had left his litter, he lay flat on the top of the high rocks, overlooking the scene. He kept up a constant, muttered conversation with himself as he kept track of the logboats. "Haharr, now lemme see, there's two logboats to the right bank, an' two t'the left. Then there's two more in midstream, wid the liddle round boat betwixt 'em. Once they gits level wid this 'ere rock, I'll send my mob out, an' we'll give 'em thud'n'blunder!"

"Er, shouldn't that be blood'n'thunder, Boss?"

Gruntan glared at his scout, Noggo, who with Biklo was lying alongside him. "That's wot I said, izzenit?"

Biklo pointed out the error. "No, Boss, you said thud'n'blunder, not blood'n'thunder."

Gruntan grabbed both scouts' ears and banged their

heads together. "Avast there, y'swabs, wot sounds better, blood'n'thunder, or thud'n'blunder, eh?"

Noggo blinked hard, trying to uncross his eyes. "Thud'n'blunder, Boss, I likes the sound o' that!"

Gruntan tugged their ears roughly before releasing them. "Aharr, matey, an' so do I. Blubber thrunder it is then!"

Both scouts edged out of his reach, saluting. "Aye aye, Boss, blutter thrumble, or wotever ye say!"

Maudie was in one of the midstream boats, she looked across to Luglug in the other. The shrew chieftain was scanning both banks keenly. "Those rascals ain't much good at hidin', miss, I kin see 'em crouchin' in the rocks both sides of us."

The haremaid allowed her paws to stray near the bow and arrows lying close to her. "Yes, I've spotted the blighters, too, they're all painted up like a dellful of bloomin' daisies. Not the best idea if you don't want to be jolly well seen, is it? So, what d'you say, old Lugathing, we know they're there, an' they know we're here. Shall we open up the ball?" She signalled Rigril and Teagle, who were holding the coracle, filled with shrewbabes, between both logboats. "Right, off y'go chaps, give them paddles a good whack, an' don't stop for anythin'. Good luck!"

Then things developed swiftly. The coracle shot off, with the babes squealing lustily as spray cascaded around them. Luglug roared to the four logboats skirting the banks. "Logalogalogaloooooog!"

They began launching showers of slingstones at the rats in the rocks.

Gruntan Kurdly sprang upright on his high perch, bawling furiously, "Don't just sit there, ye block'eads! Chaaaaarge!"

His first officer, Stringle, leapt upright. "Youse 'eard the boss, cummon, charge! Charge! Ch . . ."

A well-aimed slingstone cracked him on the jaw. He

140

slumped backward as the other Brownrats came out of hiding. Without somebeast to lead them, they came cautiously forward. Gruntan danced with rage, flinging grass, soil, shale, anything to paw, as he yelled. "Don't stan' around waitin' for winter! Charge, ye fools! Chaaaaarge!"

Now the boats closest to shore began to speed up, half the crews paddling, as the other half continued slinging. Maudie stood erect, a shaft notched upon her bowstring. "Right, give 'em blood'n'vinegar, chaps. Eulaliiiiaaaaaa!" She loosed her arrow, bringing down one of the vermin, who was splashing through the shallows toward them.

The Guosim archers were ruthlessly efficient, they fired off salvos of arrows into the charging rats as they entered the crookstream. Maudie saw Guosim still hurling slingstones into the forward flank of vermin, as she notched up another arrow, shouting. "One more time, then let's get out of here. Shoot!" Another rain of arrows cut the air, then the Guosim dropped their bows and started paddling energetically.

Now the logboats that had been close to shore came to midstream, ahead of the two carrying Maudie and Luglug. All six craft carried on upstream, their paddlers working hard. The coracle had rounded another bend, and could not be seen, but the logboats were hard in its wake.

Gruntan Kurdly was beside himself with rage, he hopped and danced on top of the big rock, ranting and raving. "Get after 'em, stop 'em, ye blitherin' blisters! I wants those boats, ye sluggardly laggards! Out! Git yore useless bottoms out o' the water an' run along the banks, ye brainless blunderers! 'Tis ten times easier runnin' on land than 'tis in a stream! Are ye deaf, daft or ditherin'? I said git out an' run along the bankside!"

Some of the rats could not hear him clearly amid the stream noise, they continued wading through the water. Gruntan hopped and jumped wildly on top of the high rock, bellowing dreadful oaths and curses. Then he jumped a fraction too far, and disappeared over the edge.

Noggo stared in bewilderment at where Gruntan had been. "Huh, where's the boss gone?"

Biklo shrugged. "I think 'e fell, 'cos 'e's not 'ere no more, mate!"

Noggo scratched his tail awhile, then he giggled. "Well, 'e can't slay us now, can 'e? The sh'ews musta spotted us, 'cos they was ready for the ambush. The boss said if'n we was spotted, then we was in fer a dose o'the Kurdlys."

Biklo suddenly realised they had been given a new lease on life, due to their leader's mishap. He began chuckling. "Mebbe ole Gruntan fancied 'e was a bird, hahahahaha!"

His companion sniggered uncharitably. "Heeheehee, that's wot comes of eatin' all those eggs, mate. I reckon 'e turned into a Kurdlyburd!" Both rats sat down. Overcome by merriment, they laughed until tears rolled down their cheeks. Then an agonised wail arose from below.

"Yeeeeeeeooooow . . . ooh, 'elp me mates, owow-aaarrrrgh!"

The laughter froze in their throats, Noggo and Biklo crawled to the edge of the rock and peered downward. About halfway down the rockface, a big, old, gorse bush sprouted out of a crevice. Gruntan Kurdly was hanging there, painfully suspended in the thorny branches, wailing.

"Yowch, ooch, yeeek! 'elp me afore this thing breaks!"

Noggo called down instinctively. "We'll 'elp ye, Boss, stay there!"

Gruntan's voice reached new peaks of indignation. "Stay here? Where d'ye think I'm goin', fer a paddle in the water! Get a rope down 'ere t'me, quick!" Looking down, Gruntan spotted his first officer. "Ahoy, Stringle, organise some 'elp an' git me outta this!"

Vermin were called away from chasing the logboats, to assist their leader out of his predicament. The task was eventually achieved, with lots of ropes and harnesses. Gruntan Kurdly was hauled up to the top of the rock, screaming and yowling every pawlength of the way. The big Brownrat was pierced by long, sharp gorse thorns, from tailtip to ears. Whilst a team of helpers worked gingerly to remove them, he glared murderously at his two scouts.

"I should peel the hides off'n ye both, aye, an' sling youse into that bush. But I'm givin' ye another chance, git after those logboats an' see where they're bound!"

Wordlessly, Noggo and Biklo dashed off to obey the order.

Maudie and the Guosim had problems of their own. The coracle containing Rigril, Teagle and the shrewbabes had run too far ahead of them. The waterway called the crook-stream'n'ripples was a curious phenomenon. Once they were past the pebbly shallows of the gorge, the water deepened drastically. Even though they were paddling against the current, the going became smoother as they came in sight of a fork. It was there that the water went two ways, following a diverted course to one side, which the Guosim had named the ripples. This tributary thundered off downhill.

Luglug stood in the prow of his logboat, shouting to Rigril and Teagle, as they were swept into the slipwater at the fork. "Pull 'er out, keep to yore midstream, don't let those ripples draw ye in afore we gets to ye, mates!"

Whether he could be heard over the rushing waters and the excited cries of the shrewbabes Maudie could not tell. However, she could see the trouble which the coracle was in. Rigril and Teagle were paddling furiously, trying to hold the little circular craft back, but it bumped against a rocky nub, just beneath the surface.

A groan of dismay arose from the crews of the six pursuing logboats. The coracle had begun to rotate, bouncing off the underwater rock, and slipping right into the ripples. As it hit the opposing downhill current, the paddlers' oars became useless. Spinning like a top, the coracle was lost to sight, skimming swiftly downstream on a perilous course.

Luglug was bellowing. "Put yore backs into it, Guosim, we've got t'catch 'em!"

Maudie watched breathlessly as the shrew paddlers put all their might into their efforts. Compared with the coracle, the logboats had to struggle against the slipwater at the fork. Immediately they had to back water, and avoid going into collision with one another, as the long, pointed logboats hit the ripples. Gousim rowers dug paddles deep, leaning back, trying to stop their boats going into a spinning motion. The six craft raced off downhill, leaping and juddering into white clouds of enveloping spray.

Maudie put her mouth close to Luglug's ear, she yelled aloud, "These ain't ripples, they're rapids!"

The shrew chieftain's voice was almost lost amid an increasing thunder of water as he bellowed, "Save yore voice an' hang on tight, miss, there's a big 'un comin' up!"

Maudie heard herself scream as the logboat shot off into thin air. It was then that she realised that the "big 'un" was a waterfall.

15

Abbot Daucus had issued orders that neither of the Abbey bells was to be tolled. If vermin invaders were heading for Redwall, it was not advisable to pinpoint the building's position too soon by ringing its twin bells. Orkwil stood watch on the walltops, with Skipper Rorc, Foremole Burff, and Benjo Tipps. They took the northwest corner of the ramparts, which was the most likely vantage point to catch sight of the Sea Raiders, who would obviously be headed down the path toward them.

Orkwil felt very grown-up and important in his new role. Armed with the dagger and club he had gained from the water vole, the young hedgehog peered out into the darkness.

Leaning over the battlement beside him, Skipper whispered, "No sign o' them yet, mate, how far behind ye do ye figger those villains were?"

Orkwil shrugged. "Can't say really, Skip, but that big, golden fox won't hang back when he finds me'n Gorath gone, an' his brother slain into the bargain."

Benjo rubbed his eyes, concentrating on the path. "Ain't much moon showin', 'tis real gloomy out there. This is the part I don't like, the waitin'."

Skipper let his chin rest on the battlement. "It must be

midnight now, mebbe they've made camp, restin' up until daylight. Don't forget, they're in strange country, so they might feel like goin' carefully."

Orkwil shook his head. "I don't think careful is a word Longtooth is accustomed to. If he knows the way, he'll be comin' nonstop for Redwall!"

Contrary to Orkwil's opinion, Vizka was an extremely careful creature, especially when it came to his own personal safety. Even now he marched at the centre of his crew, well protected on all sides by vermin bodies. It was past the midnight hour, the path ahead was in total darkness, Vizka cursed softly as a weasel blundered into him. "Ya clumsy oaf, gerrup in front an' send der scouts back ter me!"

The two stoats, Dogleg and Patchy, came marching back. They had the vole on a rope lead, stumbling behind them. Dogleg thrust the prisoner in front of Vizka. "Dis 'un sez 'e kin see der Redwall place, Cap'n!"

The golden fox seized the vole's neck roughly. "Ye'd better be tellin' der truth or I'll gut ya!"

The vole managed to gasp out, "'Tis up yonder, not far, ye'll see it yoreself soon."

Vizka gave orders to the weasel Magger. "Get der crew down dat ditch aside o' de path. Tell 'em t'wait dere an' be quiet. Jungo, Bilger, come wid me, bring dat hairy mouse wid ya!"

Glad of the unexpected rest, the vermin crew slid into the dry ditch. As Vizka and the two crewbeasts went cautiously forward, the watervole pointed ahead. "There 'tis, see, Redwall Abbey. Can I go back to me river now, sir? I've showed ye the way."

Vizka showed his fangs in what he thought was a friendly smile. "Ye did well, hairy mouse, I'll let ya go soon, but first dere's a liddle job I wants ya to do fer me. Jungo, give 'im yore sling an' stones. Bilger, take off'n yer shirt an' scarf."

The vole looked bemused as Vizka rigged him out in the

146

filthy oversized shirt, and draped the scarf about his head like a turban. The golden fox fitted a stone in the sling and placed it in the vole's paw, commenting, "Haharr, don't 'e look like a salty ole Sea Raider now!"

Jungo chuckled. "Huhuhuh, looks real pretty, don't 'e?"

The vole hitched up his floppy shirtsleeves. "Wot am I dressed up like this for, sir?"

Vizka nodded at the Abbey walls as they loomed up in the night. "Yore gonna announce us as visitors. Now, 'ere's wot ya say. Shout out nice'n loud, 'Ahoy in dere. I'm a pore, starvin' seabeast, let me an' me mates in so's we kin get some vittles, kind sirs.'"

The vole stared disbelievingly at Longtooth. "But nobeast'll hear me, they'll all be well abed by now."

Vizka patted his back reassuringly. "Yew let me worry about dat, fatmouse, jus' do as yer told. Go on, an' shout out loud'n'clear now, y'hear?"

The vole scratched his thick fur. "An' then I'm free t'go?"

The golden fox nodded amiably. "Aye, free as a burd. Now yew go an' deliver der message, we'll wait right 'ere." He drew his two crewbeasts into the woodland fringe, watching the vole walk off toward the wall.

Bilger sniggered, sensing his captain's intentions. "Jus' testin' der ground, eh, Cap'n?"

Jungo looked puzzled. "Testin' der ground, wot's dat?"

Vizka cuffed his ear lightly. "Pay attention an' watch dose walls."

Orkwil was first to spot the movement on the path below. He cautioned his friends, "There's somebeast down there, can't make out who 'tis in this dark, but I'll wager that 'un's a vermin!"

Skipper peered down at the strange figure. "Stay where ye are, don't come any further!"

The vole stood still as he carried out Vizka's order to the letter. "Ahoy in there, I'm a pore, starvin' seabeast, let me in so me an' my mates can get some vittles!"

147

Orkwil recognised the vole by the tone of his voice. However, before he could do anything, Benjo Tipps flung an oakwood burl, which he used as a barrel stopper. It hit the vole squarely between both ears, felling him. Orkwil gasped at the speed with which the Cellarhog had acted. "Mister Tipps, that wasn't a sea vermin. He's a vole who lives up near the ford!"

Benjo chuckled grimly. "Then why didn't he say so? Looked like a vermin, said he was a seabeast, an' if'n I ain't mistaken, he was carryin' a weapon. Wot d'ye say, Skip?"

Skipper Rorc nodded. "That's a loaded sling he was totin', ye did the right thing, mate. It could've been a trap, no use standin' round an' chattin' with vermin. Strike now an' talk later, that's wot I always do! Now then, young Prink, can ye see any more o' the villains out there?"

Orkwil stared hard, but there was no sign of movement. "No, Skip, there's nobeast about that I can see. D'you think Mister Tipps has slain the vole, he looks awful still just lyin' there."

Benjo patted Orkwil's headspikes. "Don't worry, young 'un, he ain't dead, but he'll have a headache that'll last a day or two when he wakes. If the coast is clear enough after dawn we'll fetch him inside."

"Er, fetch who inside, may I ask?" Friar Chondrus emerged onto the walltop, Granspike Niblo was with him. They brought food for the wall sentries.

Foremole Burff ladled himself a bowl of mushroom soup. "Et wurr summ voler, dressed oop loike ee vermint. Hurrhurr, ole Benjo bringed 'im daown with one shot!"

Orkwil and his friends tucked into fresh, crusty bread, cheese and hot soup, each feeling rather pleased at their night's work thus far.

Vizka Longtooth and his two crewbeasts retreated stealthily back to the ditch. Dropping down into the dried ditchbed, the golden fox left his crew sleeping, but wakened the weasel Magger, whom he had come to rely on as his second in command.

Magger noticed the absence of the vole. "Where's der 'airymouse, Cap'n?"

Vizka put aside his mace and chain. "Oh, dat one, we left 'im lyin' around someplace, but de 'airymouse taught me a lesson tonight. Dat Redwall place, it ain't no Abbey fulla soft woodlanders. Gettin' in dere ain't gonna be easy."

Magger replied hopefully, "We've fought battles afore, Cap'n, an' we ain't never lost. Yew kin do it if'n anybeast can, nobeast stands agin Vizka Longtooth an' wins!"

The golden fox leaned back against the ditchside. "So ye say, but I ain't never fought no stripe'ound."

Magger looked questioningly at his captain. "De stripe-'ound, 'ow d'yer know 'e's in dere?"

Vizka explained. "Dat 'edgepig was up on der wall, I 'eard 'is voice, dat's 'ow I knows our Rock'ead's in de Abbey, dey escaped t'gether didn't they?"

Bilger, who was half-asleep, opened one eye. "Does dat mean ya ain't gonna try an' take Redwall, Cap'n?"

Vizka picked up his mace and chain, his eyes and his long fangs gleaming in the darkness. "I nearly slayed dat stripe'ound last time I 'it 'im wid this. I'll finish der job next time, you see. Afore dis season's out I'll be cap'n o' Redwall, plannin' an' brains, dat's all it takes!"

On the walltops, Granspike Niblo was clearing away the supper bowls. She smiled fondly at Orkwil. "I'm glad to see ye back 'ome an' behavin' yoreself, Orkwil. You did a good job here t'night, defendin' our Abbey an' sendin' those vermin packin'."

The young hedgehog passed her his empty bowl, shaking his head. "We knocked one ole vole senseless, Gran, that's all. The vermin are still out there, I think Redwall has some hard days ahead. By the way, how's my friend Gorath comin' along, is he better yet?"

149

The old Beekeeper shook her head. "He's gettin' better, but that big feller isn't fit yet, not by a long straw. Pore beast's been through a dreadful time, if'n ye ask me."

Foremole Burff chuckled. "Aye, marm, but you'm wait'll ee badgerbeast bee's well agin. Hurrhurr, then ee'll see summ sparks a-flyin', boi okey ee will!"

16

Maudie felt she was in the middle of a nightmare in broad daylight. As the logboats soared out over the waterfall they were enveloped in a milky fog of spray, tinged through by a broad spectrum of rainbow colours. The haremaid had released her hold of the logboat, as had the Guosim crews. All about them the air was filled with the roar of cascading waters. It was the strangest of sensations, plunging downward amid all the noise and colour, seeing others falling alongside her, some still holding their paddles. Maudie even had time to think about what had happened to the coracle, and its cargo of shrewbabes. Would the logboats land on top of them? Those poor babies, it didn't bear contemplating. . . .

Splaaaash! Kabooooom!

The Guosim crews hit the water. Maudie was immersed in a world of swirling blue, green and white, with the dull boom of the waterfall echoing in her skull. She was whirling about, like a leaf in a hurricane, water filling her mouth, nostrils and vision. Her body was swept sideways, as she felt herself thrust upward, paws flailing in all directions, toward the surface.

"Whoa, matey, gotcha, up ye come now, bucko!" A huge, fat otter had her by both ears, in a viselike grip.

The pain of being hauled out by her ears was momentary, Maudie felt herself flung up onto a mossy bank, as though she were a bundle of washing. In swift succession, several Guosim were slung onto the bank beside her. Luglug was one of them, he sprawled alongside the haremaid, both coughing and spitting out water and weed fronds. The big otter banged his rudder down on their backs, helping them to expel the debris from their lungs. He pointed to Maudie, laughing as he bellowed out to an equally big female otter, "Hohoho! Lookit this 'un, Kachooch, did ye ever see a shrew with a set o' lugs like that?"

Maudie managed to gasp indignantly, "I say, d'you mind, I'm a blinkin' hare, not a shrew!"

The big female, Kachooch, helped Maudie upright, winking cheerfully at her. "Take no heed o' Barbowla, me deary, he's only joshin'."

Luglug gave the big male's rudder a hearty tug. "Barbowla Boulderdog, you ole gullywhumper, wot are you doin' in these waters? I thought you was livin' on the East River Moss."

Barbowla hauled another shrew from the water and casually tossed him ashore. "Log a Log Luglug, ye whiskery ole knot'ead, don't ye know any better'n tryin' to paddle logboats o'er the ripples? Good job me'n the family was here t'pull yore acorns out o' the soup."

Luglug retrieved his paddle and inspected it for damage. "Didn't have much choice, mate, we was on the run from Kurdly an' his Brownrats. Did ye manage to rescue our liddle 'uns, they was swept away ahead of us."

Kachooch beckoned along the bank with her rudder. "Bless their liddle spikey 'eads, they're in the holt, playin' with me'n Barbowla's grandbabes. Shame on ye, lettin' 'em get away from ye like that!"

Maudie intervened. "It wasn't our fault, marm, we were fightin' off the rats, y'see."

Kachooch pursed her lips angrily. "There's far too many

152

o' those brown, ratty murderers for most honest beasts to fight off. They does as they pleases around Mossflower these seasons!"

Barbowla towed an upturned logboat further down the bank, to where a number of his sturdy sons and daughters turned it upright with a joint heave. "That Gruntan Kurdly's like all bullies, he'll meet his match one fine day, an' I hopes I'm around t'see it. Come to the holt an' take a bite with us, yore Guosim's all safe'n'sound. There should be plenty o' plugs'n'dips to go round."

Luglug smacked his lips noisily. "Plugs'n'dips, eh, lead on, me barrel-bellied bucko!"

Maudie accompanied Kachooch, enquiring, "Beggin' y'pardon, marm, but what in the flippin' name o' seasons is plugs'n'dips?"

The big otterwife chuckled. "You'll soon find out, missy."

The otters' holt was on an island further downstream, they took the logboats and paddled to it. Barbowla and his extended family had built the holt like a small fortress, from log and stone chinked with moss and rivermud. Inside it was a scene of comfortable chaos, homely and welcoming. Barbowla and Kachooch had a large number of sons and daughters, all of whom had partners and broods of small otters. Together with the Guosim, and their babes, there was a considerable number of creatures to feed.

Maudie found herself ensconced in a corner, with Kachooch and her eldest daughter, Belford. The haremaid was given a wooden skewer and a clay bowl, whilst Belford went to the main cooking fire in the centre of the holt. Maudie went also, just to see what was going on. There was a massive cauldron into which the cooks were adding a mixture of cheese, cornmeal and finely chopped herbs. The haremaid's curiosity as a cook overcame her. She asked Belford, "I say, it all smells jolly appetisin', what exactly are they doin'?"

The ottermaid took up a pan. "That's the dips, they say the herbs are a secret recipe. I'll get our dips, you go over there an' get the plugs."

Maudie went to the other side of the fire, where more cooks had a couple of old iron shields, which they were using as roasting pans. She watched them pounding hazelnuts and chestnuts with chopped mushrooms. Pouring honey over the mixture, the cooks made it into lots of tiny cakes, roasting them on the shields. They sizzled as they rolled about, until they were hot and a deep brown colour.

One of the cooks filled a trench-shaped platter, passing it to Maudie. "Yore plugs, mate. Go easy, they're hot. You'll enjoy 'em, if'n you haven't tasted 'em afore!"

The haremaid curtsied politely. "Thank you, I'm sure I jolly well will, wot!"

Back with Kachooch and her daughter, Maudie skewered one of the plugs, dipping it into her bowl, which had been filled with the steaming mixture from the pan. She had to nibble at it delicately, because it was all very hot. However, Maudie voted plugs'n'dips as among the tastiest food she had ever eaten.

"Absobloominlootly scrumptious! Why've I never had this before? Top marks, you chaps, eleven out of ten I'd say!"

One of the cooks, a young fellow with a fine voice, began singing an old otter ballad, in praise of the delicacy.

"When I was a babe my ma would say,
Guess what I made for dinner today,
blow on your paws an' lick yore lips,
'cos I've cooked up some plugs'n'dips!

"Oh plugs'n'dips you can't go wrong,
you'll grow up so big'n'strong,
ain't no bones or stones or pips,
just good ole fashioned plugs'n'dips!"

154

Barbowla joined Maudie and the two otters, helping himself to plugs'n'dips. The haremaid marvelled at how he could swallow them down hot at a single go. The otter chieftain patted his stomach and winked at her. "I tell ye, Miz Maudie, you got to learn to git yore share an' scoff it quick, when you got a family the size o' mine. Moreso when the likes o' Luglug an' his famine-faced gang joins ye for dinner. Huh, lookin' at the size o' them shrews I allus asks meself, where do they put it all?"

Maudie smiled at the big, friendly otter. "Serves you jolly well right givin' the Guosim such wonderful vittles, old chap. I hope Log a Log Luglug thanked you properly for rescuing his shrews, wot?"

Kachooch refilled Maudie's bowl. "Ah, away with ye, missy, we don't need lots o' fancy compliments for doin' wot any decent beast would. Dearie me, though, I'm still chucklin' at that coracle full o' Guosim babbies!"

Selecting a fat plug, Maudie skewered it. "I expect it was quite a task, finding them all in that rough water, how did you do it, marm?"

Kachooch shook with stifled laughter. "We didn't have t'do a thing, they didn't even get their liddle paws wet. The coracle came down, whirlin' like a sycamore seed, with the babes gigglin' an' chortlin' like it was all a big game. Well, there must've been about six or seven of us in the water at the time, we never even saw it comin', did we, Bel?"

Her daughter, Belford, grinned ruefully. "Certainly didn't, Ma, it landed right on our backs, an' skidded across us, straight onto the bank!"

Barbowla showed Maudie the top of his head. "Aye, an' I've got a patch o' fur missin', 'cos I was the one it landed on first!" Barbowla's face was such a picture of injured dignity that Maudie had to struggle to look sympathetic.

"Must've been pretty painful for you, sah. Sorry about that, but we were on the run from the enemy an' all that, y'know. Pity you were injured, eh wot!"

155

Barbowla nodded. "Thankee, miz, but it ain't nought to weep over. I'm more worried about Kurdly an' his rat horde. If they're trailin' you an' the shrews, then 'tis for sure they'll bump into us. We wouldn't stand a chance agin the numbers Kurdly commands."

Maudie realised the position their arrival had put the otters in. She grasped Barbowla's paw firmly. "Indeed, sah, that's why I suggest you come to Redwall with us, that'll put your family out of harm's way, wot!"

Kachooch practically wriggled with delight. "Ooh, Redwall Abbey! I allus wanted to visit there, ain't that where yore cousin Rorc is, Skipper?"

Barbowla shook the haremaid's paw. "Good idea, miz, I'd like to visit the Abbey, ain't never been there afore." He glanced warningly at his wife and daughter. "Not a word o' this to the others, y'hear. The length o' time they takes gettin' ready for a journey, Kurdly'd be here attackin' afore they're half-packed."

Belford contained her excitement. "Yore right, Pa, we'll just say the family's joinin' the Guosim to guide 'em along the stream apiece. Maudie, d'you think Luglug would object to takin' our babes along in his logboats? The rest of us are all strong swimmers, we don't need to ride in boats."

Maudie reassured the otters. "Rather, I'm sure our Log a Log would welcome your plan. Come on, Barbowla, let's have a quiet word with him."

Luglug immediately agreed with the plan, taking them to one side, and lowering his voice. "I'll go along with anythin' you say, mates, but we'd best do it right now. Two o' my rearguard scouts have spotted the rats, they're startin' to climb down the rocks either side o' the falls. Just leave things as they are an' git yore liddle 'uns into the logboats, matey. The way I figgers, it'll be a close-run thing to shake off those Brownrats an' make it to Redwall Abbey!"

Barbowla's eyes narrowed craftily. "I knows the waterways twixt here an' Redwall better'n most, beggin' yore pardon, Luglug. There's lots o' streamlets an back cuts, dead ends an' marshes. Let me lead the way, mate?"

Luglug nodded briefly, explaining to Maudie, "He's right, there's quite a few places an otter can go, where a logboat crew might not see a passage."

The haremaid threw a smart salute to Luglug and Barbowla. "Right y'are, chaps, quick's the word an' sharp's the action, wot, forward the blinkin' buffs I say!"

A party of twelve litter bearers lowered Gruntan Kurdly's carrying stretcher gingerly onto the rocks at the head of the waterfall. The huge Brownrat chieftain moaned and winced as his body made contact with the damp stones. Stringle, the rat officer, approached Gruntan, he had to shout, to make himself heard above the roar of the waterfall.

"Noggo an' Biklo just reported that they've seen the sh'ews, an' some riverdog otters, they're sailin' off, below there, in the logboats!"

Irately, Gruntan cupped a paw about his ear, bellowing, "Wot's that, speak up!"

Stringle shouted louder. "Riverdogs an' Guosims, Boss, sailin' off in logboats. . . ."

Gruntan swung a heavy walking stick across Stringle's shins, causing him to break into a hopping dance of pain. "Wot'n the name o' bursted beetles are ye talkin' about? Silverlogs wailin' on a blow there wid frogstoats? Away, ye blitherin' buffoon, an' see wot those sh'ews are up to! Ahoy, somebeast move this stretcher, afore I'm soaked an' drownded!"

Amid more howls and groans from Kurdly, the bearers moved the litter onto drier ground. Bandaged and poulticed with evil-smelling unguents, Gruntan winced as his healer, Laggle, approached. The old, wrinkled, female rat was carrying what looked like a pair of rusty pincers. She mumbled as she turned her patient roughly, facedown, removing swathes of grimy dressing.

157

"Gorra get those gorse spikes out afore they fester, still plenty left in yore tailparts, 'old still now!"

Gruntan squealed like a stuck pig as Laggle went to work with furious energy. "Yow! Wow! Yeeeeek! Ye dodderin' ole murderer, I'll 'ave ye gutted an' roasted for this. Ayaaargh!"

Smiling with satisfaction, the healer showed him a hefty gorse spike. "I just dug this 'un out o' yer be'ind, nice, ain't it? There's a few more in there, but they're stuck deeper'n this, bigger ones, they are. Once they're out I'll clean the wounds up wid rock salt an' boilin' water. Oh, stop whingein' like a baby will ye!" Chuckling maliciously she went to work again. "Mebbe ye won't feel like eatin', I'll take care o' those waterfowl eggs they're boilin' for ye."

The six logboats, plus the coracle, shot off downstream. Barbowla and all the able-bodied members of his family swam in formation around the flotilla. The shrew and otterbabes were virtually uncontrollable, they packed the next to last logboat, which became a scene of chaos. Dancing, singing, quarreling and squealing, they never let up for a moment. Some even leapt overboard, but were soon rescued by the otters.

It was a shrewmum named Frenna who solved the problem. She poured a few flagons of dandelion and burdock cordial into a cauldron; into this she mixed the contents of a few small vials. Placing the cauldron in the midst of the infants, Frenna strictly forbade any of them to drink it, saying it was only for grown-up creatures. She sat at the stern of the logboat, with her back to the little ones. Immediately, like all babes who have been told not to do a thing, they fell upon the mixture and drank it. Fenna signalled to the shrew paddlers. Gently they began to hum and sing a leisurely song.

"Hear the stream flow softly, slowly,
see the waters calm and deep,
floating on and on forever,

158

slipping, dipping into sleep
Way hoooo my baby oooooh . . .
Take me to the lands of dreaming,
there small birds do sing so sweet,
calm noontide sails into evening,
where the sun and moon both meet.
Way hoooo my baby ooooooh . . .
Hush, you stream, be ever tranquil,
silent now each paddle blade,
trees o'erhead lean down to kiss you,
sunlight warm and cool dark shade.
Way ooooh my baby oooooh."

Sitting in the lead logboat with her Guosim friend Osbil, who was still acting as prowspot, Maudie was pleasantly surprised at the silence which had fallen over the vessels. Looking back, she saw the otter and shrewbabes in the second boat, they were all sound asleep. "Well, who'd have thought a few verses of gentle singin' could send those little bounders to dreamland, wot?"

Osbil continued prowspotting as he replied. "Aye, that an' a few drops o' missus Frenna's shuteye potion. 'Tis nought but simple herbs, but it does the job every time, believe me, mate."

Barbowla swam alongside the logboat, issuing directions to the Guosim paddlers. "Better step up the pace, buckoes, Kurdly's rats have all reached the bottom o' the falls, they'll be right on our tail afore long. Stay straight on this course, but keep yore eyes peeled for a big, white willow tree to yore right. I'll direct ye from there."

Osbil saluted with his rapier. "Straight ahead it is, I'll watch out for the willow."

Log a Log Luglug had stationed himself in the coracle, with Rigril and Teagle. They kept to the rear of the log-boats, constantly watching behind for the first sign of Kurdly and his Brownrats. It came sooner than they had anticipated.

Teagle spied about twoscore of the vermin front-runners in the distance. "Here they come, mates, all painted, well-armed an' ready for the slaughter. They're still a fair way off, but comin' along fast!"

Luglug groaned. "Aye, an' they're comin' along the left bank, too, we could've done without that!"

Rigril shrugged. "Makes no difference, look, there's another lot just appeared on the opposite bank!"

Luglug beckoned to an otter swimming alongside the coracle. "Git up front, matey, tell 'em to put on as much speed as they can. We need to get round that bend up ahead!"

Word went along the line of logboats, on Luglug's command they went into a formation of pairs. Grimly every Guosim bent to their paddles. Headropes were thrown out to the otters. With strong otters to each rope, they sped along in front of the vessels, increasing the overall speed as they towed skillfully. All this was done in complete silence. At this point nobeast wanted to wake the little ones, and cause extra confusion.

Stringle strode back along the right bank, to where the main body were coming from the foot of the waterfall. At the centre of the lines, Gruntan Kurdly was propped up on his carrying litter. Stringle made his way through to the Brownrat leader. "They been spotted, Boss, paddlin' along the stream up yonder, those streamdogs, too. Hah, won't be too long afore we catches 'em up now."

Gruntan did not even acknowledge Stringle's report. He was applying himself greedily to some cold plugs'n'dips, which had been looted from the otters' wrecked holt. Stuffing his mouth with plugs, he drank deeply from the cauldron. The cold mixture slopped down his chin, onto his bandages. Stringle stood waiting until his gluttonous leader could talk.

Gruntan belched aloud. Wiping a grubby paw across his mouth, he announced, "Hmm, that ain't bad grub, it'd taste better if'n it was 'ot, though. Lissen, don't slay all those streamdogs when ye catch 'em. Keep one o' them alive, I'd like to know 'ow they makes these vittles." Gruntan wiped his dip-slopped paw on the head of a nearby litter bearer, wincing as he sat up straight. "An ye say you've caught 'em, eh?"

Stringle shook his head, correcting Gruntan. "No, Boss, I only said we've spotted 'em, an' it won't be too long afore we catches 'em."

Gruntan glared at him peevishly, gesturing. "Then don't stand there a-flappin' yer jaw, go an' catch 'em! I gotta 'ave those sh'ewboats!"

Stringle knew there was no point in talking to his boss when he was in such a mood. He saluted and dashed off without further ado.

Gruntan shifted position, wincing again at another thorn, which Laggle had not yet discovered embedded in his rear end. There was a sound from the ranks behind him. What was it, a sneeze, or a snigger? Whirling his head around, he narrowed his eyes suspiciously. "Somebeast laughed just then, who was it, eh?" The horderats remained silent. Gruntan fixed one rat with a stare which commanded an immediate answer. "You there, ugly mug, who was it wot laughed?"

The rat's throat bobbed up and down nervously. "It wasn't me, Boss, I swear on me oath it wasn't!"

Gruntan crooked a grimy claw at him. "Come over 'ere!" He watched the unfortunate approach on shaking paws. "Move yoreself, I said come over 'ere, stan' there!"

The rat stood close to his leader, right on the spot he had indicated. He tried one last plea. "It wasn't me wot laughed, Boss, honest!"

Gruntan bent his head close to the rat. "Well, let's 'ear ye laugh now. Go on, laugh!"

The rat made a feeble attempt. "Er, haha."

Without warning Gruntan seized the cauldron of cold dip and upended it over his victim's head, leaving him

161

wearing it, like a monstrous helmet with mixture dripping from it. Gruntan dusted his paws off. "Now let's see ye laugh that off! Hahaharrr!"

The rest of the Brownrats laughed dutifully along with their boss, until he turned on them, bellowing, "Wot are you lot laughin' at? I never told ye t'laugh! Now get movin', double-quick, afore I really give ye somethin' to laugh about!"

Officers roared out orders as the ranks marched off at a rapid pace. Gruntan Kurdly was jounced up and down on his litter, pierced deeper by hidden thorns. However, he gritted his teeth and endured the pain, concentrating on a prize of six logboats.

17

Once the logboats rounded the bend, they were out of sight from the rats. Maudie marvelled at their speed, they were going so fast that they were sending up bow waves. The shrewmum Frenna had covered up the babes with quilts and blankets; they slept on, blissfully unaware of everything.

Maudie was first to see the tree, she nudged Osbil. "Aha, one white willow straight ahead on the right!"

The Guosim shrew patted Maudie's back. "We'll make a prowspotter out of ye yet, miss!"

Barbowla came streaking through the water like an arrow. "There's thick bush the other side o' that willow. If'n ye look careful there's a hidden stream there, too. I'll go an' mark the entrance, we needs t'be in that cutoff, behind those bushes, afore Kurdly's crew arrives!"

A dismaying thought struck Maudie. "Er, a moment old chap, are you sure you've thought this plan through, right?"

The big otter forestalled her objection. "I knows wot yore goin' t'say, miz. If'n the rats comes along the bank on that side, they'll be bound t'see us, 'cos they've got to cross the very cutoff water that we're hidin' in. Is that wot you was goin' to say?" As Maudie nodded, Barbowla held up a paw. "Don't fret yore pretty, long ears, Miz Maudie, 'tis already taken care of. Now trust me an' git movin'."

Gasping for breath, and exhausted by their efforts, the Guosim paddled their final logboat behind the bushy screen. Luglug, Rigril and Teagle slid in with the coracle. The shrew chieftain had the same misgivings as Maudie. However, before he could speak, Barbowla silenced him.

"Let's 'ave every able-bodied beast out 'ere on the bank with me. Come on, we've got to provide a bridge for the vermin to cross. Luglug, get yore strongest shrews, mate. Aye, an' tell 'em to bring their paddles along, we needs all the muscle we kin get!"

Barbowla led his contingent of Guosim and otters to where a large, fallen tree trunk lay covered by fern and shrubbery. Suddenly the plan became clear to Maudie, she winked at the big otter.

"I say, well done, sah! If we bridge the sidestream with that trunk, then scoot away double-quick in the jolly old logboats, we could fool 'em. Old Kurdlywotsit an' his foul mob should cross the bridge, thinkin' we've carried on along the mainstream. What a super wheeze, they'll go right past us, wot!"

Barbowla began clearing away shrubbery. "No time for gossipin' now, miz, those villains'll be here soon. There's a good growth o' rush an' bush up yon sidestream, we can lay low there until they pass. Ahoy, let's git this ole log a-rollin', you Guosim, use yore paddles to move it. We need t'be quick!"

Everybeast bent their backs to the task. Shrews dug their paddles under the trunk and levered away with them. Maudie joined Barbowla's brawny family, hauling on three stout ropes.

At first nothing happened, then Luglug took over. "On my command, crews . . . One, two, heave!" The trunk began to slide across the ferns and damp moss.

Maudie gave a whoop. "That's the stuff, chaps, keep the blighter movin'!"

Beetles, worms and all manner of crawling insects fled for fresh cover as they were exposed to the daylight by the shifting of their shelter. An old Guosim shrew, who was watching the bankside, whispered hoarsely, "Keep yore voices down now, an' git a move on. I think I can see 'em in the distance!" His urgent entreaty lent power and speed to their limbs, the trunk moved rapidly along, until they were at the sidestream.

Barbowla and his otters leapt into the water, helping to shift the huge log, as the shrews put their paddles to the broken tree's base. Once it was bridging the water firmly, everybeast swiftly trampled the area surrounding both sides. This was to make it look as though the trunk was often used as a crossing. Without taking breath, the shrews were back into their logboats, paddling furiously off down the sidestream, with the otters towing and pushing each craft.

Maudie crouched at the stern of the last boat, alongside Osbil the Spotter, whose keen eyes picked up movement back along the bankside.

"I can see the painted scum, they'll be at that trunk afore long. I wouldn't be surprised if'n they spotted us!"

Maudie glanced upstream, to where the coracle, and the leading logboat, were slipping into the shelter of over-hanging trees and rushes. "Not to worry, bucko, we should just about flippin' well make it. Duck your head, old lad, an' hope for the best!"

Barbowla and Kachooch thrust the stern of the last log-boat under cover, just as the leading score of Brownrats arrived at the decoy bridge. Kachooch slipped silently along the line of boats, whispering a caution. "Don't paddle, stay still! If'n they look up this way an' see any movement of boats or trees, they're bound to see us. Lay low now, an' not a sound out of anybeast!"

At the tree-trunk bridge, a dispute appeared to have

arisen. Kurdly's leading rat, Stringle, was calling across the mainstream to the scout Noggo, who was with a large contingent on the far bank. "Can ye see any sign of 'em upstream?"

Noggo shrugged as he shouted back, "I can't see 'em from 'ere, wot'll we do?"

Stringle sat down in the centre of the log. He looked this way and that, then scratched his head. "Best wait 'ere 'til the Boss arrives!"

Noggo could see the sidestream from the opposite bank. "D'ye think they've gone up there?"

Stringle spat contemptuously into the water. "Yew thick-'eaded dolt, 'ow could they sail through this log I'm sittin' on? Huh, if'n brains was vittles you woulda starved to death when ye was born!"

More rats began arriving on either side of the stream, until both banks were crowded. Everybeast waiting on the arrival of their leader's stretcher.

Peering from beneath the leafy foliage, Luglug grunted. "I can't see a thing, wot's goin' on back there?"

Maudie and Osbil had the best view. Through a screen of rushes the haremaid gave her assessment of the situation. "Looks like there's some sort of confounded conflab goin' on. Wish they'd jolly well move on an' pick someplace else t'do their jabberin'."

Osbil commented, "Somethin' should be happenin' shortly, here comes ole fat-bottom Kurdly on his litter."

One of the shrews clanked his paddle against the logboat's side. Luglug cautioned him in a severe undertone, "Belay there, mate, d'ye want the vermin to know we're here?"

The shrew apologised. "Sorry, Chief, I swiped at a wasp wot was buzzin' round me snout, huh, I missed it!"

The shrew chieftain glared savagely at him. "I won't miss you if'n you makes any more noise, I'll splinter that paddle atwixt yore ears. All of ye, keep yore heads down, an' not a murmur out of anybeast!"

Gruntan Kurdly was on the same bankside as Stringle, grunting with pain he sat up straight on the litter, staring at his officer. "Well, wot are ye waitin' for, next season?"

Stringle tried explaining. "I er, thought we'd better wait fer you, Boss . . . er, I think we've lost 'em. . . ."

Gruntan exploded. "Lost 'em, worra ye talkin' about, lost 'em, 'ow could any fool lose six logboats on a straight stream?"

Stringle pointed across at Noggo on the other bank. "Well, that scout couldn't see any sign of 'em up ahead, an' I couldn't see 'em either. So we waited for yore orders, Boss."

Noggo called across, trying to sound helpful. "I was sayin' to Stringle, they might've gone up that sidestream, Boss."

Gruntan Kurdly cast a glance at the tree trunk which bridged the sidestream, he looked across at Noggo. "An wot, pray, gave ye that bright idea?"

Noggo shrugged. "Well, they had t'go somewhere, an' they ain't on the mainstream, so I thought they might've cut off up there, Boss."

Noggo was sorry he had spoken. Gruntan pointed to the bank, where he was sitting upon his litter. "Get over 'ere, now!"

Noggo looked at the stream separating them both. "Wot, y'mean swim, Boss?"

Gruntan bellowed aloud, "No, I mean fly, ye dimwitted dolt. Get over 'ere right now!"

Noggo leapt in and swam across. A moment later he was standing, trembling, alongside his leader.

Gruntan indicated the tree-trunk bridge. "Tell me, 'ow did they git six logboats over that?"

Noggo had his answer ready. "Carried 'em, Boss, they

was carryin' their boats when me'n Biklo first spotted 'em. Sh'ews kin carry boats, y'know."

Gruntan winced as he pulled a gorse thorn from his tail area. "Right, we'll wait 'ere whilst you go an' take a look. Give us a shout if'n ye spot 'em."

Noggo knew he had no choice, he set off along the less well-defined and more muddy sidestream bank.

Osbil whispered to Maudie, "There's one of the vermin comin' toward us, what'll we do?"

The haremaid murmured as she watched the approaching Brownrat, "Keep lyin', doggo, he might not come up this far. But if he does, don't fret, I'll jolly well stop the blighter. In fact, I'll stop him cold!" Going into a crouch, ready to spring, Maudie clenched her paws tightly. Everybeast in the boats held their breath.

Noggo was talking softly to himself as he neared the rushes and overhanging trees. "Huh, that's wot I get fer tryin' t'be 'elpful. I'll keep me trap shut from now on, I ain't no ossifer!"

He ducked under the tree canopy, and was met by Maudie. She came bounding from the stern of the logboat, poleaxing the unsuspecting Noggo with a thundering right punch, followed by a swift left. There was no need for a third blow, the first two had done the job. Noggo was out for the rest of the day. As Maudie slid back into the boat, everything suddenly went wrong.

An otterbabe squealed out in pain, stung on her nosetip by one of the wasps which had been buzzing about. Before she could be silenced, the little one's piercing wails were echoing about widespread.

Barbowla appeared over the stern of the back logboat. "Ahoy, mates, git those paddles a-slappin', 'tis time we weren't in this place!"

The Guosim crews needed no urging, they shot their boats through the tree canopy and out onto the other side, paddles digging furiously. In the vessel to the rear, Maudie

168

and Osbil could see the first of the Brownrats, headed by Stringle, squelching their way along the muddy bank as they came hot in pursuit.

The sidestream was only wide enough to allow the Guosim craft to travel in single file. Prow bumped stern as they fled from Kurdly and his horde. Barbowla, and three of his sturdy sons, formed a rearguard behind the boats.

Maudie called to the otter, "Get up front, friends, I'll organise some sling throwers an' archers. They'll soon be close enough for us to get a shot at 'em, wot!"

Barbowla thrust his weight against the stern, shooting the craft forward. "No, miz, there's too many vermin, ye'd be overrun if'n ye tried to fight 'em. Speed, that's wot we need!"

Another shaded area of trees loomed up. Luglug could be heard calling from up in front. "We're runnin' into the forest, keep goin', mates, Redwall Abbey ain't far now, I recognise this area!"

Gruntan Kurdly was in the rear of the pursuit, bumping about as a score of Brownrats stumbled along bearing his litter. He was alternately urging his horde along, whilst cursing the litter carriers roundly.

"Avast up front, move yore sluggardly hides! I've seen snails wid shells on their backs that'd outrun youse lot. Argh! Go easy wid this stretcher, ye bumble-pawed nits, t'aint a bundle o' washin' yore totin'! Oof! Ye nearly spilt me into the water, watch where yore goin'. Where's the rest of 'em, they ain't all up front?"

Laggle, the old healer, who was trotting alongside the litter, gestured backward to the mainstream. "Heehee, half o' yore army are still on t'other side o' that mainstream. Prob'ly waitin' for a drought, so as it'll dry up an' they kin walk across."

Gruntan scowled sourly at the insolent Laggle, who was no respecter of rank or title. "Ho, are they? Well, go an' tell 'em if'n they ain't over 'ere in two shakes of a tail, there'll be a few attacks o' the Kurdlys runnin' through the ranks!"

He signalled to two vermin who were not engaged in carrying him. "Go an' see if'n we're gainin' on 'em, surely my rats kin run faster'n sh'ews kin paddle boats? Oh, an' when ye report back t'me, well, bring some vittles. I ain't gonna be bumped t'death an' starved inter the bargain. Yowch! Watch those tree branches over'ead, I near got me eye put out then. Can't ye carry an' crouch a bit, too?"

Maudie looked anxiously over the logboat's stern, not encouraged by what she saw. "I say, Osbil old lad, I don't wish to sound like a wet blanket, but those vermin types are gainin' on us, wot!"

The Guosim spotter nodded unhappily. "Aye, they're closin' the gap, miz, I can make out the paint on their mangy hides. We need more speed!"

Barbowla's wife, Kachooch, popped her head over the stern. "We're tryin', but ye can only go as fast as the boat in front when yore sailin' in single file."

"Ah, shure that's true, so 'tis. Ye talk good sense for a riverdog, so ye do!"

The logboat rocked as a creature dropped out of an overhanging beech into the vessel. He was a squirrel, small, but very wiry and agile. Four daggers were thrust into his broad waist sash, he wore a short, embroidered waistcoat, one hooped earring, and sported a woven, multicoloured headband, at a jaunty angle. He winked cheekily at Maudie, then bowed. "Rangval the Rogue at y'service, marm. Pray would ye impart t'me yore own dulcet title?"

Despite the peril of their position, the young haremaid took an immediate liking to Rangval, she curtsied formally. "Maudie (the Hon.) Mugsberry Thropple, pleased to make your acquaintance I'm sure."

Rangval the Rogue performed a somersault neatly. "Faith, an' that's a fine ould gobful of a name ye have there, marm. If'n I may, I'll just call ye Maudie, or prettyface, or beautybeast? Ah, but enough o' that ould flannel, I see ye've got problems. An' isn't it the bold Gruntan Kurdly an' his thickheaded horde!"

Maudie took another glance at the rats, who were getting closer by the moment. "It is indeed, I take it you know of him, wot?"

Rangval twitched his nose in the horde's direction. "Shure an' who doesn't know o' that 'un around here. I've been crossin' swords wid that boyo since he first showed his snotty nose in these parts. D'ye need my help now, Maudie, just say the word, me darlin', an' 'tis meself that'll put a spoke in his wheel!"

Osbil interrupted. "Wot could one squirrel do agin that lot?" Before he could speak further, the Guosim spotter was flat on his back with Rangval's dagger tickling his throat.

The roguish squirrel tweaked Osbil's snout. "When I want yore opinion, me ould son, I'll ask for it! Ah, shure but yore only a spiky rivermouse, what would ye know about anythin' or a hatful o' hazelnuts?" Rangval put up his blade and dismissed Osbil. "Now then, Maudie me darlin', tell yer friends to push on upstream an' don't hang about. When ye come to a tidy liddle cover with a sandstone overhang an' some pines nearby, wait for me there. Oh, an' when ye pass by Owch Mansions, hold y'breath an' keep yer head down, an' make no sudden movements."

Barbowla poked his head over the prow. "Owch Mansions, I've never heard o' that place."

Rangval grinned at the big otter. "Barbowla from the falls, isn't it? You don't know me, but I've watched you many a time, good, big family y'have. Shure, let's do the introductions later, I'd best be about me business now. I'll see ye later, so I will!" Rangval shot upward into the foliaged terraces and was gone.

Maudie turned to Barbowla. "I say we trust Rangval, he looks like a bit of a blinkin' laddo, but I'll bet he knows his bloomin' way round, wot!"

The otter slid back into the water. "Ain't much else we can do but trust him, miz. I'll pass the word along to Luglug, t'keep watch for the cove."

Smiling sheepishly, Osbil felt his neck, where Rangval's blade had been a moment ago. "I wonder wot Owch Mansions are, miz?"

Maudie shrugged as the logboat began making better way. "I expect we'll find out soon enough, old lad."

18

Abbot Daucus woke shortly after dawn. The skies were uniformly cloudy and dull, it was humid, and the dawn chorus of birdsong was absent. The good mouse wandered down to the kitchens, where Friar Chondrus was supervising breakfast preparations. Young ones on kitchen duty were scurrying around as the squirrel Friar issued orders.

"Don't put any hot bread or pastries to cool on the open windowsills, it's started drizzling. Folura, help me with this oatmeal, please."

Daucus took hold of the cauldron handle, his paw protected by a wrapping of sleeve folds. "Here, let me get that, friend, clear the table there!"

Chondrus made room for the cauldron as Daucus swung it quickly onto the tabletop. "Good morning, Father Abbot, have you been to the walltops yet, any news of the Sea Raider vermin?"

Daucus began adding ingredients to the oatmeal. "None yet, Friar. Skipper Rorc, Benjo Tipps, Foremole and Orkwil have been up there all night. I'll take them some breakfast and hear what they have to report. Then I'll have to organise a relief guard, they can't stay up there indefinitely. Have you heard from Sister Atrata, as to our badger, Gorath?"

Friar Chondrus bent to pull a tray of fruit rolls from the oven. "The sister will be here shortly, to collect breakfast for the sickbay. I'll let you know the moment she tells me about Gorath. Folura, Glingal, load up a trolley of vittles, and help Father Abbot up the ramparts with it, please."

Skipper's two fine daughters obliged cheerfully.

"Pore ole Daddy, he must be wet'n'starved."

"Never mind, we'll put a smile on his whiskers!"

Between them, the two ottermaids and the Abbot loaded up a trolley of hearty breakfast food, and headed off to the walltops. Benjo Tipps hurried down, to help them up the wallsteps with the trolley.

Orkwil rubbed a sleepy paw across his eyes, cheered up by the sight of breakfast. He was bone weary, but would not admit it. Abbot Daucus watched as the young hedgehog's snout drooped, almost dipping into his oatmeal bowl. Daucus tweaked Orkwil's ear gently.

"Wake up, mate, oatmeal's for eating, not sleeping in."

Orkwil protested. "I'm not a bit sleepy Father Abbot, honest I'm not!"

Skipper spoke through a mouthful of warm fruit roll. "Ho yes ye are, young Prink, but it ain't anythin' t'be ashamed of, ye did a good night's work on guard here!"

Abbot Daucus smiled at them through the thickening curtain of drizzle. "You all did a splendid night's work, and I thank you very much. But now you can go and have a good sleep, inside where it's dry and warm. Folura and Glingol will keep watch up here, whilst I go and organise some relief sentries. No arguments, off you go, please!"

Orkwil went straight up to the sickbay, where he was confronted by Sister Atrata. "And where pray do you think you are off to, sir?"

The young hedgehog tottered slightly and yawned. "Beg y'pardon, Sister, but I came to see how my pal Gorath is. I'd like to visit him if'n I may." Orkwil leaned up against the door, eyes drooping.

The good Sister shook her head pityingly. "My, my, just look at yourself, Master Prink, almost snoring on your paws. A sound sleep wouldn't harm you, I'm thinking. I had to put your friend in the little side room, since word got round the Abbey that we have a badger visiting us. I couldn't leave him lying on the floor of Great Hall in full view, because the whole population of Redwall wants to see Gorath. So I've hidden him in my private side room. There's an extra bed in there that you can use."

Orkwil was about to protest, but the Sister ushered him into the little room.

"There, that's better than sleeping in wine cellar barrels. Take these warm towels and dry the rain off. Hush now, your friend's still asleep, you can speak to him later, when you've had your rest."

Sister Atrata left quietly. Orkwil blinked in the dimly lit room. He opened one window shutter as he dried himself on the warm, soft towels he had been given. Gorath lay on the big bed, motionless, it was hard to tell whether he was sleeping or unconscious.

Orkwil snuggled beneath the counterpane on the small bed, staring across at his friend. The young badger seemed even more gigantic, stretched out there, though he looked haggard and ill from his shocking ordeal at the paws of Vizka Longtooth and his crew. His face was drawn, and hollow-cheeked, with the huge, red scar on his brow appearing like an angry, scarlet flame. On the bed beside him, still gripped in one paw, was Tung, his pitchfork. Even though he knew Gorath could not hear him, Orkwil murmured reassuringly to his sleeping friend.

"Rest easy, mate, yore safe inside Redwall Abbey now, an' I'm here to see you come to no harm. Guess what, they've made me an officer of the wall guard. I spent all night out on the battlements, watchin' for that fox and his scurvy crew. Hah, they didn't show a whisker. As soon as I've had a little rest I'll be back up on that wall with Skipper, Foremole and Mister Tipps. Father Abbot ordered us to take a break, y'see, there's a relief guard on at the moment. At least, I hope there is."

The young hedgehog turned away from Gorath, gazing out into the still drizzling morn. From the window he had a clear view of the northwest wall corner, it was well guarded by relief sentries. Beyond the ramparts, Orkwil could see some flatlands, the ditch running alongside the path and a portion of Mossflower woodland. He lay watching for any movement outside the Abbey, talking softly to himself.

"I know yore out there, fox, aye, an' you'd best stay out there if ye know what's good for you. Redwall isn't an easy nut to crack, it's made of stone, an' guarded by bravebeasts. . . ." The young hedgehog's voice trailed off, his eyelids dropped, sleep had overcome his weariness.

A piece of sailcloth had been erected to form a small shelter in the ditch. Vizka Longtooth and Magger sat beneath it, blinking in the smoke of a little fire, which had been lit to keep the numerous winged insects at bay. The rest of the *Bludgullet*'s crew either sought any cover they could find, or crouched there, suffering the persistent drizzle. Vizka stared bleakly at the closest group. "I don't s'pose youse thought ter bring any vikkles frum der ship wid ya?"

They avoided their captain's eyes and kept silent.

Vizka spat in the muddy ditchbed. "Oh no, I'm der one who has ta thinka dat!"

A voice from the huddled throng piped up swiftly. "But Cap'n, yew said dere was plenny o' vikkles in dat Abbey."

"Who said dat?" Vizka asked the question, knowing that nobeast was foolish enough to own up. The golden fox was no fool either, he knew the value of keeping a loyal crew about him. Thinking quickly, he explained their position, as if confiding in his followers.

"Right, I did say dere was plenny o' vikkles in de Abbey.

176

But we ain't gonna get 'em chargin' inter battle. Huh, wot sorta idjit does dat, eh?"

There was immediate agreement all round. Redwall looked too solid and forbidding to be attacked head-on.

Magger nodded eagerly. "So wot's der plan, Cap'n?"

Vizka's mind was racing as he spoke. "Er, this's wot ya do. First, we needs vikkles t'day. Magger, take der crew back up dis ditch, until yer outta sight. Den go inta der forest an' load up wid vikkles, must be plenty growin' in a forest, birds, eggs an' fishes, too. Stay in de forest an' make a big fire, cook everythin' up. Make skilly, an' soup, an roast stuff, to feed all me mates, all me good crew! Well, buckoes, 'ow'll dat do ya?"

There was a mass murmur of agreement. Magger started to move off, then turned to Vizka. "Wot'll yew be doin', Cap'n?"

The golden fox tapped his muzzle with a paw. "Plannin', Magger, figgerin' a way so's we kin get inta dat Redwall an' lay our claws on all dat loot, an' all der vikkles. Leave it ter me, nobeast can lay a plan like Vizka Longtooth, right?"

Magger saluted with his spear. "Right y'are, Cap'n!"

Vizka called after the departing vermin. "Don't let ole Magger scoff everythin', mates, save some fer yer old cap'n, I'll join youse later."

They went off in a lighter mood, bouyed by their captain's words.

When they had gone, Vizka sat alone under the canvas awning, pondering his dilemma. How to conquer an Abbey, which was not only well-defended, but contained a berserk badger who had sworn to kill him. It was not a prospect that he relished, but now that he had committed himself, he could not back down in front of his crew. He knew that if they lost confidence in him, he was little better than a deadbeast. There was always some creature wanting to be captain, he had already witnessed this with Grivel, Feerog and Durgy.

177

A noise from behind him on the path caused Vizka to creep out from his shelter and peer over the edge of the ditch. It was a party of moles who had ventured out to inspect the fallen watervole. He could not understand their speech.

"Burr, ee'm h'aloive, but that bee's ee gurt lumpen on ee'm 'ead, a roight mole'ill et bee's!"

"Burr aye, ole Benjo can surrpintly 'url a barrel stopper!"

There were six moles, they lifted the watervole between them and carried him inside the Abbey.

As the main gate of the outer wall slammed shut, Vizka mentally berated himself for a fool. He had missed a golden opportunity: the main gates had stood ajar for vital moments, and he had sent his entire crew off looking for food. They could have captured the moles, and rushed the gates! A huge sigh of regret and frustration came from the golden fox. He laid his forehead against the muddy ditchside, cursing fate for robbing him of a great chance.

Something tickled the tip of his nose, he drew back and inspected the object. It was a worm, boring its way out of the ditchside wall. Callously, Vizka nipped it in two halves between his pawnails. He watched the worm writhing, then stamped on it. His long fangs showed as a sudden smile came across his features. He had a plan, a superbly simple scheme. His crew would dig their way into Redwall from the side wall of the ditch. A bit lower down, close to the big gate. It would be a foolproof idea!

19

It was an unfortunate day for the Brownrats of Gruntan Kurdly. Hastened and bullied forward by their irate leader, they dashed along the squelching banks of the sidestream.

Rangval the Rogue, unseen to his enemies, skipped nimbly along in the middle terraces of the woodlands, chortling with delight as they blundered into his cunningly laid traps. He perched in a sycamore, watching the leading half dozen runners vanish amid screams of dismay. Down they went, straight into a deep, natural pit, which he had disguised with ferns and rotten branches. The hole was filled with water, overflowing from the stream.

The others veered sharply away from the bank, only to run into a grove of osier and purple willow, long, whippy branches and boughs. Rangval had tied back or intertwined a lot of the heavier limbs. He shook with laughter as the rats dashed into them.

Thwack! Splat! Whoosh! Thud! Their bungling passage released the lashing boughs. Jaws were shattered, teeth broken, paws damaged and stomachs had the wind driven from them as rats were felled, or cannoned into each other.

Rangval cast a backward glance at the chaos, wiping tears of mirth from his eyes. "Ah now, me bold buckoes, that's only a taste of wot ye've got to come. I'll teach ye to mend yore wicked ways. Hurry up, now, an' see the grand treat I've got in store for ye!" He halted long enough to hear Gruntan Kurdly roaring.

"Wot'n the name o' boiled eggs'n'bunions are ye doin' swimmin' round in that hole? Gerrout an' capture those boats! An' youse lot, who said ye could lay around in them bushes? Up on yore hunkers an' charge, afore I do a spot of ear slittin' an' tail choppin'!"

Rangval sped on his way, chuckling. "Shure that's the way, Kurdly me ould rat, keep 'em comin'. Boot a few bottoms, that'll move 'em!"

Rangval arrived ahead of the vermin, at his pride and joy, Owch Mansions. He had spent long seasons enticing wasps and hornets to the spot where two golden weeping willow trees formed a thick, low arch from bank to bank. He had specially placed lots of rotten fruit and dead vegetation, full of grubs and aphids, at the foot of each tree.

The wasps had built four nests there, large, globe-shaped structures, which perched between branches. For the hornets, he had a fallen tree, the long-dead and decaying trunk of a wych elm, that he had maneuvered to the waterside. There was a constant coming and going of wasps and hornets around the willow, and a steady, thin hum from the insects.

Rangval treated them with loving care, walking among them unafraid. He grasped the ends of two long, trailing ropes, which had been tied to the branches of both weeping willows. Rangval spoke soothingly as he paced carefully backward. "Ah, me little stripey darlin's, pay no attention t'me, 'tis only yore Uncle Rangval. But listen now, get those fierce ould stings of yores ready. There's a horde of fearful vermin comin' this way. I want ye to give 'em a good, hot, ould welcome, shure I know ye'll do me proud, bein' the fine, savage bunch y'are!"

180

Rangval retreated until the ropes were almost taut. Crouching in the undergrowth, the wily squirrel kept the wasp nests in view, listening for sounds of the Brownrats heading toward them.

Stringle's duty as an officer was to make the others carry out Gruntan Kurdly's wishes by hook or by crook. Having already blundered into a few of Rangval's minor traps, they were reluctant to pursue the logboats vigorously. Stringle knew that he would be the first to suffer, if the horde continued to advance in such a laggardly fashion. Gathering the two scouts, Noggo and Biklo, for support, he tried a strategy which he had seen Gruntan use successfully.

Pushing his way to the front, he halted the vanguard, waiting until the rest had caught up en masse. Gruntan was in his litter, somewhere near the middle of the mob. He listened to Stringle's speech, nodding approvingly, as his officer addressed everybeast jauntily.

"Scrag me tail an' plug me ears, wot's all this, mates? The terror o' Mossflower, the great Brownrat horde, an' ye can't catch a few wooden boats full o' scruffy liddle sh'ews! I'll wager they're laughin' at us right now. Them sh'ews is only just upstream, y'know, an' a stream can't go on forever. One good charge an' we'll lay 'em by the tails. All the boss wants is their boats. Once we've captured 'em the chase is over, we kin do wot we like. Go fishin', rob birds eggs or just lay round in the sun for a few days. So wot d'ye say, buckoes, shall we go an' get them logboats?"

Gruntan shouted from his litter. "Aye, go to it, mateys, I'll make a feast fer the first one who brings me back a sh'ews head!"

Stringle had to jump aside as the horde sped by him, roaring, bellowing and whirling their weapons.

Gruntan Kurdly was smiling, he winked at Stringle. "Haharr, well done, bucko, let's get after 'em!" He laid about at the litter bearers with a willow withe. "Cummon, yew bottle-nosed, slab-sided, doodly-tailed idlers, git those paws poundin' at the double!"

Rangval heard the horde long before he saw them. Standing out in full view, the roguish squirrel tugged gently on the ropes, which were tied to both willows at strategic limbs. "D'ye hear that, bhoyos, ye'll have company soon, shure an' I hope those stings are well sharpened!"

With Biklo and Noggo in the lead, the horde came thundering along both banks, splashing through the shallows and bulling through the reeds. Biklo was first to spot Rangval up ahead, he stabbed the air with his spear. "That looks like one o' the rascals, watch me take 'is 'ead!"

Rangval laughed. "Faith, an' aren't you the bold feller, take this, vermin, an' bad luck to ye!" He yanked hard on both ropes, then somersaulted up into the trees and vanished.

In a trice, the war cries and shouts of pursuit were transformed into piercing shrieks of agony, under the full onslaught of a wasp attack. The torture was heightened when several vermin tripped against the rotten wych elm trunk, releasing a veritable storm of maddened hornets. The air was filled with the zing and buzz of ill-tempered insects, as they stung and stung again at their helpless victims. Brownrats performed weird dances of pain upon the wrecked wasp nests and the pulpy wood of the hornet lair.

Gruntan leaned his weight sideways, upsetting the litter, as he launched himself into the streamwater. More than one rat died that day, overcome by hundreds of stings, each laden with wasp or hornet venom. Most of the horde fled into the woodlands, attempting to outrun their tormentors. Others, Gruntan among them, tried submerging themselves for long periods, and pressing on upstream.

Rangval the Rogue arrived at the cove as evening was on the wane. Maudie, the otters and the Guosim were standing ready for an attack, with weapons drawn. Rangval looked around, slightly disappointed. "Have ye not got an ould bite o' supper for a beast?"

Luglug sheathed his rapier. "We was expectin' Kurdly's crew, never cooked no vittles."

The squirrel chuckled drily. "I don't think they could make it, they was unavoidably detained by some little buzzin' friends o' mine."

Osbil shook a paw at Rangval. "The wasps an' hornets around those two willows, ye mean. Thanks for not tellin' us about 'em, mate!"

Rangval dismissed the indignant young shrew with a shrug. "Ah well, me ould tater, there wasn't much time for explanations, as I recall. I told ye t'watch out for Owch Mansions, tellin' meself ye weren't some thick'eaded horde rats, but intelligent shrews. I trust none of ye were stung by me liddle mates?"

Maudie wiggled her ears at Rangval. "Not to worry, old lad, our Guosim friends were jolly lucky to have one of the finest brains in the blinkin' land along with 'em, wot! 'Twas I who spotted Owch Mansions and brought us safely through to this fair haven!"

Barbowla murmured confidentially to the squirrel, "Miz Maudie's right, but it was she who wouldn't allow us t'cook, for fear we were attacked."

Rangval shook his head in mock sadness. "Ah, 'tis always the way with maids, beauty an' brains, but totally lackin' in the supper department. Right, if'n ye'd all like to get in yore boats, I'll take ye someplace where we'll get an ould bite o' grub!"

With Rangval in the lead vessel, they pressed on. It was fully dark, and drizzling, when the squirrel halted them. He pointed to a medium-sized hill, not far from the bank. "There's my lovely ould home. Rogue's Retreat, I call it."

It was a natural cave inside the hill, the entrance to which was a bushy screen. Portaging the logboats, they made their way inside. Setting steel to flint, Rangval soon had a torch lighted.

Maudie gazed around, it was a huge sandstone cavern. "I say, this is splendid, how'd you find it?"

Rangval touched light to several other torches. "Find it? D'ye mind, missy, I made it!"

Barbowla's wife, Kachooch, gave Rangval a playful shove, which almost sent him sprawling. "Ah, away with ye, great, treewallopin' fibber! I was brought up in a holt, just like this. It's a place where the river ran through, when the land was young."

Luglug agreed with her. "Aye, I've heard o' places like this, it was carved out by the water, over countless seasons. Then for some reason the river changed course, an' prob'ly dwindled to yon stream outside, leavin' this place."

Rangval did not seem at all put out by being caught lying, he grinned cheerfully at Maudie. "I'll allow ye the honour of cookin' supper for me, marm. On the way here these Guosim were after tellin' me wot a marvellous cook you are, so carry on, please!"

Maudie found herself smiling at the garrulous squirrel's impudence. "Right ho, you cheeky wretch, but only if you agree t'go a few rounds boxin' with me afterward. I'm the undefeated Champ of Salamandastron, y'know."

Rangval made a show of rolling up his nonexistent sleeves. "Shure, 'tis not often that I have to knock the block off'n a pretty maid to get supper, but I'll do it!"

Assisted by the Guosim helpers, Maudie put on a tidy spread, considering their limited resources. She made a pastry from cornmeal and chestnuts, filling it with preserved fruit and nuts, and working it into a long roll. To complement it, she made a thick, sweet, white arrowroot sauce. With some cheese and apples for starters, and coltsfoot dandelion cordial to drink, it proved a successful supper. They lolled about a fire as the Guosim servers apportioned it out.

184

One of the shrewbabes found, to her delight, that the cave had a pretty little echo. She began to sing a song which her mama had taught her.

"Don't run away from yore mamma's side,
'cos the woodland's big an' wide,
hold on tight to her apron string,
an' y'won't get hurted by anything.

"I'm a good likkle shrew so that's wot I do,
I'm not a naughty likkle shrew like you!

"When you go inna big logboat,
sit very still when it's afloat,
if you jump an' dance about,
my mamma says that you'll fall out.

"I'm a good likkle shrew so that's wot I do,
I'm not a naughty likkle shrew like you!

"Go near a fire an' you get burned,
this is a lesson I have learned,
one day I'll be big, you see,
an' I'll have a pretty likkle shrew like me.

"I'm a good likkle shrew so that's wot I do,
I'm not a naughty likkle shrew like you!"

Rangval lay back, both paws folded across his stomach. "Ah, charmin', well sung, liddle missy, that was grand, grand!"

Luglug drained his beaker, wiping a paw across his mouth. "Don't get too comfortable there, rogue, you've got to box a few rounds with Miz Maudie yet."

The roguish squirrel sighed. "Shure, I'm too stuffed t'move, an' I've never struck a pretty maid in all me life. Just suppose I slew her wid a single blow, which I'm quite capable of doin', havin' laid several o' me best friends low in that manner. Now I ask ye, who'd ever cook a fine ould meal like we've just had, widout the beautiful an' fascinatin' Maudie t'do the honours?"

Luglug lay back, closing his eyes. "I never thought of it that way, mate, yore excused boxin'."

Maudie added, "But only if you sing us a song."

Rangval leapt to his paws eagerly. "Faith, I thought ye'd never ask, I'll give ye a ballad that'd have a stone in tears. Silence now for the golden voice o' the woodlands." Placing a paw on his heart he began warbling dramatically.

"As I was lyin' in me bed the other night,
sewin' buttons on an' scoffin' skilly pudden,
when a thought flashed in me mind just like a light,
Shure bedad, said I, now isn't that a good 'un!

"So I hauled me pore ould body off the bed,
kicked the family frog an' put me greasy hat on,
an' roved forth to take a beneficial walk,
'cos lately I'd been pilin' too much fat on!

"Well, I'd not got very far along the way,
when I met a toad, all big'n'fat'n'warty,
Oh good evenin' to ye, sir, meself did say,
Shut yore gob, said he, which wasn't very sporty!

"So I gave him such a smack I laid him low,
I could see that his ould life was fast a-fadin',
He said, take me off this road, call me friends an' have
     me towed . . .
an' say you'll never strike a young haremaiden!"

Maudie kept a straight face, commenting, "Dreadfully sad tale, wot? So that's why you had to give up fightin'. Hmmmm. Er, I say, chaps, before we drop off to sleep, what's the jolly old plan for tomorrow? Always supposin' we have a plan, wot!"

Barbowla levered himself up on his rudder. "Well o'

course we have, beauty, the plan's to get to Redwall, safe'n'sound in one piece. Right, Lug?"

The Guosim Log a Log was already half-asleep, he muttered drowsily, "Sleep first, plan tommorer!"

Everybeast was in agreement, except Rangval the Rogue. He was up on his paws, pacing and gesticulating. "Shure, an' is it a plan yore after? Faith, me lucky bhoyos, look no further than meself, aren't I the grandest ould planner ye ever fell over on a day's march!"

Maudie stifled a yawn politely. "Carry on, old thing, the cave floor is yours, what super wheeze have you come up with, wot?"

Rangval gave up pacing, he sat down sulkily. "Ah, ye can go an' boil yore dozy tails for all I care. Saved ye from Kurdly an' his army, didn't I, brought yez all here unscathed. Hah, an' that's all the thanks I gets for me efforts. Here I am, tryin' to help ye, an' yore all yawnin', snorin' an' layin' round like a pile o' fractured frogs. Well, I'll keep meself to meself, thank ye kindly, an' you can all go an' pickle yore ears an' boil yore bums, so there. From now on me lips are sealed!"

Maudie was immediately sorry about their treatment of Rangval. Shaking Luglug and Barbowla into wakefulness, she tried to remedy the situation. "Good grief, sah, please accept our profuse apologies. Confound us for our atrocious bad manners, we never intended hurtin' your feelings. Moreover we are very grateful for what you've done so blinkin' far. In fact, we're all bloomin' ears, please carry on with your excellent scheme, ain't that right, chaps?"

Luglug and Barbowla agreed hastily.

"Right, matey, go on, I'm dyin' to 'ear yore plan!"

"Aye, it'll prob'ly be better'n anythin' we'd think up!"

The change in Rangval was like the sun coming from behind a cloud, he beamed cheerfully at them. "Haharr, wait'll ye hear this, me fine, furry friends. Now, wot ye don't know is that we're only a good day's march from the Abbey, by a secret path known only to meself. But first

we'll have t'get rid o' those ould boats, huh, can't be carryin' them along with us."

"Whaaaaat? Get rid of my logboats? Never!"

Rangval held up his paws, chuckling at Luglug's reaction. "Ah, shure I don't mean get rid of 'em altogether, ye'll
get 'em back easy enough when the time comes. But we've
got to travel light. By the mornin' Gruntan Kurdly'll have
scouts out all o'er the neighbourhood, searchin' for us an'
the boats. He'll be lookin' to the streams an' waterways,
but we'll be nowhere near 'em."

The shrew chieftain's face was the picture of misery. "But
where'll my six logboats be?"

Rangval patted the Guosim shrew's back. "Not t'worry,
me ould tater, they'll be no more'n a paddle's length from
where ye now stand. See this." The squirrel went to the
cave's north wall, suddenly shouting, "Now close yore
eyes tight, go on, close 'em!" They did as he ordered, there
was a minute scraping sound, then Rangval called out, "Ye
can open 'em now!"

Rangval was gone, vanished into thin air.

Maudie rubbed her eyes in disbelief. "Great seasons,
where's the blighter got to, wot?"

Rangval's echoing laugh boomed around the cavern.
"Ah shure, I'm right here, me darlin'!" He reappeared,
seeming to walk straight out of the wall. They hurried to
his side as he revealed all. "It's another small cave behind
this 'un, see this crack in the rock? Well, ye just pull on it,
like so." The whole rock seemed to move slightly, leaving
enough room for Rangval to use as a doorway. "An' that,
me ould Luglug, is where we'll hide yore boats. Aye, an' all
the other tackle, too, cookin' pots, an' the like. We need
t'cover a lot o' ground fast in the mornin', so we'll be travellin' light."

Maudie nodded. "I see, an' I take it you'll be comin' to
Redwall with us?"

The roguish squirrel raised his eyebrows. "I take it ye've

188

never tasted Redwall vittles, or you wouldn't be askin' such a foolish ould question. I'm with ye every step o' the way, me beauty, I wouldn't miss the chance of nourishin' me fine body with the good Redwall Abbey cookin'. Right, let's get everythin' stowed into the small cave, ready for an early start when day breaks."

20

Out in the woodlands, smoke billowed into the night, heavy smoke, thick and greasy. It came from wet, rotten vegetation, which had been piled onto a big fire. Hornets and wasps would not venture into the befugged area. Coughing, spitting, sneezing and constantly mopping at their eyes, Gruntan Kurdly and his Brownrats crouched around ten of these fires. None of them even resembled Brownrats. Everybeast who had lived through the stinging attack was heavily coated in greeny-black marsh mud.

Laggle, the old female healer, staggered about, dispensing advice. "Smear it on, thick as ye can, then leave it. No matter 'ow much it itches or stings, leave it. Tomorrer, when that scum an' ooze hardens up wid the sunlight, it'll peel off, an' bring all the stings out along with it."

Gruntan had missed most of the body stings by staying submerged in the stream, though his head was swollen and lumpy, where the wasps and hornets had attacked it. Stringle looked for all the world like a rat sculpture in mud, with holes for his eyes, nostrils and mouth.

Gruntan moved his head in Stringle's direction, slowly and painfully, he winced as he spoke. "Mim a thormem joo bikkupa pakth."

Stringle scraped some mud from his ears. "Wot was that, Boss?"

Gruntan huffed irately. "A thed, joo bikkup pakth mim a thormem, thoon adda blite!"

Not wanting to anger his boss further, Stringle whispered to old Laggle the healer, "Do ye think the wasps got down his ears an' stung 'im in the brains? 'E ain't makin' sense!"

Laggle waddled over to Gruntan, she tapped his chin. "Open yer mouth . . . wide."

Gruntan narrowed his already swollen eyes. "Moperamouff, fworra doodad form?"

The old healer was a no-nonsense type, she began prising his mouth open. "I said open yore mouth, Kurdly, yore talkin' rubbish, an' I want t'see why." Laggle took a swift peek inside his mouth, blanched at the odour of his breath, then gave her diagnosis. "Hah, no wonder ye can't talk proper, yore tongue's been stung, about nine or ten times I'd say, by the blisters on it!"

Gruntan touched a paw to his tongue, and winced again. "Me thongueth beed thtunged by d'wopth!"

Laggle shook her head resignedly. "That's wot I just said! Now, wot did ye want t'say to Stringle?"

Gruntan made an effort to speak clearly; it failed. "A thode hib doo bikkupa shooth pakth imma thormem!"

Fortunately, Laggle understood, she translated to Stringle. "He sez 'e told you to pick up the sh'ews tracks, in the mornin'."

The mud statue that was Stringle nodded forlornly. "Unnerstood, Boss!" He murmured miserably to Laggle, "Huh, that's if'n I'm still alive at dawn!"

Gruntan stirred the fire with a spear, causing fresh billows of stinking smoke to set everybeast hacking and coughing painfully. He crouched low, rubbing both eyes, and muttering darkly. "Wheb I gedd dode lobgoats I'll bake dode shooth thcreeb f'berthy, ho yeth, h'I bakem thnoddy!"

Noggo nudged his scout companion, Biklo. "Wot did the boss say just then?"

Biklo shrugged. "I dunno, but he'll bring bad luck on us all, usin' language like that, mate!"

Noggo licked mud from his muzzle tip, and spat distastefully. "Bring bad luck, does that mean we've been havin' good luck so far?"

The peace and comfort of the hill cavern was broken by Rangval the Rogue. Dawn had just broken when he marched in briskly. "Top o' the mornin' to ye all, the sun's puttin' on a grand show out there. 'Tis too fine a day t'be snorin' an snoozin', right, Maudie, me darlin'?"

Maudie, who had risen early with the squirrel, strode in, towelling her face dry of streamwater. "Right indeed, old lad! Come on, chaps, up on y'paws. Quick's the word an' sharp's the action, wot! Now, we've got some jolly hard paw-sloggin' today, everybeast will be followin' friend Rangval, who knows the secret route to Redwall. So, with the permission of our Log a Log, an' Barbowla, I'll organise the march, wot?"

Some of the Guosim looked as though they were about to dispute the haremaid's role (as was customary with shrews) when Luglug rebuked them sternly.

"The maid's got my say-so, anybeast wants to argue about the crackin' o' hazelnuts, can do so wid me afore we goes further!" The Guosim chieftain allowed one paw to slide down to his rapier hilt. It was sufficient, no shrew wanted to tangle with Luglug. He nodded. "Carry on with yore orders, miz."

There was no mistaking the haremaid's air of command, Major Mullein would have been proud of her. "Pay attention at the back there. We'll be travellin' light an' quiet, fast an' silent as the bloomin' breeze, wot! Files o' four'd be best, don't get strung out or trailed to one side, keep t'gether, that's the ticket. Rangval will take the lead, I'll bring up the rear, Luglug an' Barbowla to the midflanks, left'n'right. I want everybeast who's strong an' able enough to pack a babe on their backs. Sorry about brekkers, Osbil an' Belford will provide ye with vittles, to munch on the march. All clear, any questions?"

Kachooch held up her rudder. "Ain't we allowed to sing as we go? I likes marchin' songs, Miz Maudie."

The haremaid shook her head. "Apologies, marm, I like a jolly good marchin' song, too, afraid we'll have to do without 'em. Safety in silence y'know. No more questions? Lead off, Rangval!"

They left the cavern, emerging into the calm summer morn. Maudie listened to the distant trill of birds, the murmur of the nearby stream, and the swish of dew-laden grass underpaw. She kept her wits about her, and her eyes focused into the surrounding woodland. This was not at all an easy task, as she was trying to eat breakfast, a fine yellow pear, some shrewbread and a small amount of hard cheese.

Adding to her difficulties was the shrewbabe, a tiny pestilence named Yik. He had elected to ride on Maudie's shoulders, simply by climbing up there and refusing to come down. The haremaid could not really protest, as it was she who had initiated the idea, so she bore her burden stoically. For awhile, at least, until Yik started to make his presence felt. "Yowch, I say, old lad, don't pull my flippin' ears!"

"I norra hole'ad, jus' makin' ya go fasterer."

"Well, I don't wish to go fasterer, er, faster, so stop tuggin' on my ears, and don't keep kicking me with your confounded footpaws!"

"No kickin' ya, me paws gettin' itchy, I h'only scratchin' 'em on ya."

"Well, kindly chuck it, or go an' scratch y'paws someplace else. Whoops! What are you up to now, pestilential little bounder?"

"I savin' some breffkist for laterer!"

"Not down the back of my blinkin' tunic you're not. Eat

it up now, or I'll tell 'em not to jolly well serve you any lunch!"

Osbil dropped back to walk alongside Maudie. "Well, miss, are ye enjoyin' yoreself?"

Maudie treated the young shrew to an icy glance. "Are you blinkin' well jokin', enjoyin' myself, with this bloomin' miniature cad torturing me! Who does he belong to, where's his ma an' pa?"

Osbil took a closer glance at the shrewbabe. "That 'un's little Yik, he don't belong to anybeast in particular, miz, he just turned up one day, didn't ye, mate?"

Yik bounced up and down on Maudie's shoulders, gripping her ears for balance as he squeaked aloud. "Blinkin' flippin' jollywell bloomin'!"

Osbil tried to hide a smile. "That's very nice language to be teachin' a babe!"

This seemed to encourage Yik, who redoubled his efforts. "Blinkblink flipflip jolly jolly bloomers. Heeheehee!"

A low, cautionary whistle came from the flank Barbowla was patrolling. Everybeast halted, Maudie reached up and clamped a paw across Yik's mouth. The travellers stood stock-still, not daring to move. The big otter signalled twice with both paws, pointing off to the left. Barbowla balanced a short otter javelin, watching the four Brownrats, who were barely visible twixt the shafts of light and shade cast by the trees. The vermin moved slowly away, stooping with the mud and marsh ooze plastered thickly on their bodies.

Luglug came from the other side of the marchers. Both he and Barbowla, with weapons at the ready, stole noiselessly through the tree cover toward the Brownrats. They were gone a short time, whilst everybeast kept total silence, not moving a single muscle.

After awhile, the otter and the shrew chieftain returned. Luglug kept his voice low. "Relax, mates, they've gone, the opposite way to where we're goin', thank the seasons. Are you alright, Miz?"

As soon as Maudie had clamped her paw over Yik's mouth, the indignant babe had bitten into it. She could not shout out, or wriggle to free herself, but was forced to stand there, transfixed by the tiny, sharp teeth.

Luglug assessed the situation at a glance. "Pass the liddle scamp down 'ere t'me, Miz Maudie."

Still attached to the shrewbabe, the haremaid allowed Luglug to hold Yik. Pinching the babe's nostrils firmly, Luglug cut off his air supply, forcing him to open his mouth to breathe. Maudie withdrew her paw smartly.

Kachooch gathered a few dock leaves. "Put these on it, miz, 'twill stop the bleedin'. I'll fix ye up with a proper dressin' when we stops for a rest."

Barbowla interrupted, "I say we stops now, 'tis not far off'n noon. Once we're rested we'll carry straight on for the Abbey, widout any more halts."

They sat to rest in the covering shade of an ash grove. Kahooch put some salve on Maudie's paw, whilst Yik looked on with great interest. "I bited you 'cos you nearly chokered me, I cuddent breeve."

Luglug flicked the used dock leaves at him. "Be off, ye naughty liddle savage, shame on ye!"

The shrewbabe went off pouting. "I norra naughty samwich, h'I'm a Yik, h'an I not like youse anymore!"

Maudie could not help smiling at the aggrieved shrewbabe. "Ain't exactly the type to mince his words, wot!"

Rangval took stock of their surroundings. "By rights we should've pressed on further afore we stopped t'rest. Shure, we'll have t'step up the pace a bit, if'n we want to reach the Abbey tonight."

Luglug stood upright, signalling to the Guosim. "We're ready if'n everybeast else is, how's the paw now, Miz Maud?"

The haremaid went into a fighting stance, shooting off several jabs within a hairsbreadth of the shrew's chin. "Right as rain, old lad, shall we get goin', then? Form up again, chaps, an' let's see you march off smartly. Yik, c'mon, up on me shoulders an' see if you can jolly well behave y'self this time. Yik, where's that little terror got to?"

Osbil and Kahooch searched among the Guosim, the otters checked their own babes, to see if Yik was hiding among them. Luglug scratched his head. "That rascal's gone off somewheres, prob'ly found a spot to hide an' sulk, 'cos I spoke sharp to 'im. You lot best carry on t'Redwall, I'll catch up with ye after I've tracked Yik down."

Maudie nodded to Rangval and Barbowla. "You're in charge now, get goin'. I'll stop back an' help Luglug find the little rascal."

Rangval did not bother arguing. "Ah, yore right there, me darlin' commander, we can't hang about all day lookin' for the small villain. Just follow our trail once ye've caught Yik. Should ye get lost, then keep yore eyes peeled fer the two-topped oak, it was riven by lightnin', ye'll recognise it on sight. Right after the oak ye'll come out of the woodlands, Redwall's straight in front of ye then, across a patch of open land. Head for the liddle south wallgate, we'll be waitin' there for ye. Good luck now, an' give that fiend's tail a skelp for me when ye find him!" The main party moved swiftly off, leaving Maudie and Luglug to find the shrewbabe.

The haremaid's first move was to comb the area where they had rested. "He can't have got too far, a tiny babe like him will prob'ly be lurking under some shrubbery."

The Guosim chieftain was not of the same opinion. "Ye'd be surprised just how far some o' these little 'uns can go when they've a mind to, miss. Look 'ere." Away from the tracks where the main party had entered and departed the ash grove, Luglug pointed out some hard cheese crumbs. Maudie inspected them.

"That'll be Yik, he hadn't finished his mornin' meal. Aye, he's headed off this way, see the tiny pawprints." The babe's pawmarks stood out clear on a patch of damp soil. They came across yet more evidence, some blades of grass that Yik had knocked awry. Maudie surmised, "Prob'ly swipin' at things, with a twig he's found."

Luglug stepped up the pace. "'Tis a pretty straight path he's on, let's run 'im down!"

No sooner had they started to run than a bellow of pain rent the air, from somewhere up ahead. "Yaaargh! Gimme that stick, ye liddle murderer!"

Other voices chimed in.

"It's a sh'ew, grab 'im, mates!"

"Cummere, ye likkle maggot. . . . Yowch, me eye!"

Luglug and Maudie burst through the bushes onto a streambank, straight into trouble.

Yik had come across a half dozen of Gruntan Kurdly's Brownrats. They had been searching for shrews and log-boats along the bankside. Tiring of their task, the vermin lay down in the warm sun, letting it bake their thick mud poultices hard, and catching a much-needed nap. Yik had stumbled upon them, and decided to attack the foebeasts with his stick. The shrewbabe had struck several times, before the vermin were goaded into action. To the bold Yik it was all some kind of a game, he scuttled around the big Brownrats, jabbing and thrusting with his stick, as though it was a Guosim rapier. The rat who had been stuck in the eye by the stick kicked out at his tiny tormentor. He sent Yik headlong into the stream. One of his comrades waded in. Grabbing Yik, he shook him like a rag doll. "Shall we give 'im ter Kurdly, or eat 'im ourselves?" Then Maudie and Luglug arrived on the scene.

A look of surprise was stamped on the rat's features as the Guosim chieftain's blade pierced his throat. He staggered backward into the stream as Maudie skipped neatly forward, relieving him of the babe. Swinging Yik up onto her shoulders she spoke sharply to him. "Stay there an' hold on tight!" Whirling like lightning, Mad Maudie proved why she was the Salamandastron Regimental Boxing Champion.

197

Thudbangwallopsmack!

A Brownrat collapsed like a falling brick wall, under four thunderous punches from the haremaid. Luglug had crossed blades with another one, as Maudie spun around, kicking the spear from a vermin's grasp, catching it in mid-air, and breaking it over its owner's skull.

Little Yik was howling like a wolf, dancing on Maudie's shoulders and tugging at her ears. "Bangbang! Punch 'is nose! Jolly good, more, more!"

As Luglug ran his adversary through, Maudie, who could not duck and weave so well, with Yik dancing and yanking away on her, took a sharp blow to her ribs from a spearbutt. The shrew chieftain leapt in, fending off her attacker. He roared, "Let's git out o' here, miss, double quick!"

They turned and ran back from the streambank. One of the Brownrats took out a carved bone whistle, and began blowing the alarm. Two more vermin jumped from the bushes either side of the fugitives. Fortunately, they were as surprised to encounter the escapers as Maudie and Luglug were to see them pop out like that. Both the haremaid and the shrew kicked out fiercely, knocking their foes aside. They hurtled on their way, with shouts welling behind them from several directions.

"There they go, stop 'em!"

"Stringle, I sees 'em, they're up ahead!"

"Circle out an' cut 'em off, quick!"

Luglug judged by the hubbub building up either side of them, plus the shaking of shrubbery, that they would soon be surrounded. He cut off into the woodlands at a new angle, panting to Maudie, "If'n we don't shake 'em off, we're right in the soup, missy!"

Dodging round tree trunks, the haremaid followed him, with Yik clinging to her ears, thoroughly enjoying his wild ride, squeaking merrily. "Right inna soup, fasterer, mizzymiz, heeheehee!"

Now the pounding of vermin paws was all about them,

198

the area was teeming with mud-coated Brownrats. Then Gruntan Kurdly's shouts were heard. He had joined the hue and cry, and was running his litter bearers ragged, now that his voice was back to normal. "Move yore slop-coated carcasses! Noggo, can ye see 'em, where in the name o' hellgates are they?"

The scout bellowed back, "I can't see 'em, Boss, but they're somewhere round 'ere, I can 'ear a liddle 'un squeakin'!"

Maudie was reaching up to silence Yik again, when she stumbled and tripped. She had the presence of mind to grab the shrewbabe from his perch on her shoulders as she fell. Clutching Yik close to her, she landed faceup in an old, dried-out streambed. Luglug came leaping in after her. Fortunately the trench bottom was padded thickly, with seasons of moss and dead leaf loam. Maudie cast a swift glance up, at the inward-curving banks above them. A sudden ruse popped into her head, she whispered to Luglug, "Get under this ledge an' cover ourselves with loam, it's our only blinkin' chance, wot!"

They rolled under the curve of the overhead bank, and began building up the masses of crisp, brown leaves and damp moss around them. Yik wrinkled his little nose. "Us right inna soup, I not like it 'ere!"

Luglug muttered fiercely, "Give 'im t'me, miss!"

Maudie passed the babe over to the Guosim chieftain.

The intensity of Luglug's tone scared Yik into silence. "Now you lissen t'me, ye liddle pestilence. We're goin' to hide 'ere as best we can, an' just one word, one squeak, even one loud breath from ye, an' I'll paddle yore tail so 'ard that yore teeth'll hurt. Don't speak, just nod if'n ye unnerstand me!"

The chastened shrewbabe nodded vigorously.

The trio lay to one side of the ditch curve, under a blanket of dead vegetation. Two Brownrats came wandering up the middle of the streambed. Maudie tried to breathe quietly as they drew close to the hiding place. Both rats

199

carried spears, which they used to search the dead leaves with, jabbing the points wherever they fancied.

Sssshtukk!

An iron spearpoint almost grazed Maudie's ear as it buried itself in the loam. Gruntal Kurdly gestured irately to his litter bearers as they carried him close to the dry streambed.

"Down, put the thing down, block'eads, d'ye want to tip me inter that ditch, ain't I injured enuff?" The weary bearers placed the litter down gently. In the streambed, one of the Brownrats was raising his spear for a thrust, which if it had landed, would have pierced Luglug's stomach. Kurdly glared irately at the pair. "Wot d'yer think youse two are doin' down there?"

The vermin halted his spear in mid-thrust. "Er, lookin' fer the sh'ews an' that punchin' rabbit, Boss."

The Brownrat chieftain shook his head in disbelief. "An' pray tell me, d'yer see 'em anywhere?"

The rat let his spearpoint droop uselessly. "Er, no, Boss."

Dried mud cracked from their leader's blistered features as he bellowed at the hapless pair. "Then stop foolin' about an' git up 'ere! Go an' do somethin' useful, find me some eggs an' boil 'em up, afore I perish from 'unger, ye numb-brained nincompoops!" The two Brownrats scrambled to obey Gruntan.

Maudie breathed quietly to Luglug, "Good grief, mate, that was a lucky break!"

The Guosim chieftain snorted softly. "A lucky break, y'say? Lyin' no more'n a logboat's length from that evil monster, surrounded by a horde o' vermin. Y'don't mind me askin', miss, but do ye call that lucky?"

Aware of the importance of quietness, Yik whispered, "Wot's a punchin' rabbit, miz, the rat called you h'a punchin' rabbit?"

Maudie glared at Yik. "Don't annoy me, cheeky nose, or I may be jolly well tempted to show you!"

The shrewbabe wrinkled his nose insolently. "You punch me an' I bite ya again!"

Luglug placed a paw across the shrewbabe's mouth. He whispered urgently as he saw Maudie's paw clench, "Don't ye dare strike a babe, shame on ye. . . ."

Like lightning, the haremaid's paw shot between Luglug and Yik. She had heard the leaves rustle, and glimpsed the flat-scaled head rearing behind the shrews. In seasons to come, the Hon. Maude Mugsberry Thropple, known to her regimental comrades as Mad Maudie, would recall that she had gained the distinction of knocking a snake out cold, with one punch, that day.

And what a punch it was! A sharp, straight right, which hit the reptile's snout like a flying boulder. The snake's eyes immediately clouded over, the coils relaxed, and it lay amid the loam, like a wet piece of string. Luglug tightened his hold on Yik's mouth, he stared in awe at the snake.

"Seasons o' slaughter, where'd that thing come from?"

Maudie blew on her paw, watching the opposite bank-top with relief. The brief incident had gone unnoticed by Kurdly and his vermin, who were painfully occupied in cracking off the mud, which pulled the stings out as it was removed. The haremaid turned her attention back to the unconscious reptile.

"I say, quite a good-sized brute, doncha think?"

Luglug inched away from the snake, his eyes tightly shut. "Ugh, I wonder why I never smelled it, I kin always smell adders, long afore I sees 'em."

Maudie lifted the snake's head, inspected it and let it flop back down. "You couldn't smell it because it ain't an adder, old scout, it's a bally grass snake an' a bloomin' whopper of a beast if ever I saw one."

Luglug nodded agreement, adding, "It's big enough to swallow liddle Yik in one go!"

Reaching out carefully, Maudie broke off several strands

201

of hedge parsley, growing nearby. Plaiting them together, she fashioned a tough piece of halter. "Indeed, this brute most likely had friend Yik firmly on today's luncheon menu. Good job I got the old straight right in first, wot!" She began tying the snake's mouth tight with the tough parsley strands, knotting it securely.

Summoning up his courage, Yik struck the snake's snout with a small, chubby paw, scowling at it. "Yik hit ya, jus' like a punchin' rabbit!"

Maudie corrected him indignantly. "Now just a moment, young feller me shrew, there's no such thing as a punchin' rabbit. I am what is known as a boxin' hare, you little curmudgeon!"

The shrewbabe waved a clenched paw under Maudie's nose. "An' I norra likkle amudjin, I be a Yik!"

Luglug ducked his head into the loam. "An' yore both a pair o' noisy nuisances, 'cos I think the vermin's 'eard ye, an' they're comin' over 'ere to take a look!"

21

The moles carried the unconscious watervole into the gatehouse, laying him out upon the bed. Fenn Bluepaw sniffed in disgust.

"I take it you'll be removing that . . . thing from my bed as soon as it comes to. Hmph! Filthy paws and matted fur, I'll have to scrub the counterpane and drape it in the orchard, so a good, clean breeze can dry it!"

Abbot Daucus commented drily, "That's what I like about you, Miz Bluepaw, you're so kind and tenderhearted."

The squirrel Recorder bristled. "Well, it's not your bed that scruffy beast's laid out on!"

Daucus nodded. "Right, marm, but if you want him off your bed, you'd be better employed by fetching Sister Atrata, instead of being so harsh upon a senseless creature. Once the good Sister brings him around, then we can move him from your bed."

Benjo Tipps, accompanied by Orkwil Prink, wandered in to view the watervole. Redwall's stout Cellarhog looked slightly rueful. "Mayhap I shouldn't have chucked that bungstarter so hard at him. He might never waken proper."

Orkwil curled his lip when he looked closer at the patient. "It wouldn't be a great loss if'n he didn't, Mister

Tipps. I've had a few run-ins with this 'un, he's a mean-spirited an' bad-tempered ole watervole."

Sister Atrata entered the gatehouse with Fenn Bluepaw in attendance, still complaining bitterly. "The very idea of it, some raggedy-bottomed, barrel-bellied vole, cooling his paws on my nice, clean bed!"

The Sister silenced her with a single glare. "Yes, thank you, Miz Bluepaw, I've heard enough!" Leaning over the watervole, she opened one of his eyes, giving an instant diagnosis, as she unstuffed a pawful of feathers from the mattress. "Hmm, he's about ready to be wakened. Bring that lamp over here, Orkwil."

Igniting the feathers from the lamp flame, the Sister let them burn for a moment then extinguished them. Holding the smoldering material under the watervole's snout, Sister Atrata allowed him to inhale the acrid fumes. He shot bolt upright, gagging and gasping. The Sister smiled cheerily. "Up you come now, let's get a dressing on that head lump of yours, and a draught of my belladonna potion. You'll be right as rain before you know it!"

Skipper Rorc stepped in, taking charge of the vole. "Not so fast, matey, you've got some questions to answer. C'mon, let's take a stroll on the walltops, this place smells of smolderin' feathers, phew!"

The watervole hung back, he was in a surly mood. "Got to get me 'ead treated first, after wot that spikepig did t'me."

The burly otter squeezed his paw in a viselike grip. "If'n you call Mister Benjo Tipps a spikepig agin, I'll put another lump atop o' the one you've already got. Now watch yore mouth, vole, an' keep a civil tongue in yore 'ead when I talks to ye. Out ye go!"

Skipper pushed the vole in front of him. Together with Benjo and Orkwil, they mounted the steps to the walltop. Orkwil strode alongside Skipper, as he and Benjo walked toward the north parapet, keeping the watervole lodged firmly between them. As they drew close to the northwest

204

corner, the vole began dragging his paws, trying to hang back. Skipper shoved him onward, questioning. "Big, fat rascal like you ain't afraid, are ye?"

The vole ducked his head, so that he could not be seen. He crouched along in the cover of the battlements.

Benjo jabbed him in the ribs. "What are ye tryin' to hide down there for?"

Nodding toward the woodlands beyond the north wall, the vole whispered, "They're watchin' us, I'm sure of it!"

The stout Cellarhog hauled him up, above the walltop. "Who's watchin' ye, tell us?"

The watervole wriggled furiously as Benjo held him tight. "The golden fox an' his crew, there's a whole army of 'em!"

Benjo shook him. "Aye, an' yore one of 'em!"

The prisoner's nerve deserted him, he whined piteously. "No, I ain't, ask 'im, that young 'un!"

Orkwil had no sympathy for the vole. "He wasn't one of the fox's crew when I first met up with him, but that doesn't mean much. He's mean an' bad-tempered enough to have joined up with the vermin!"

Skipper stood on the north wall, peering down into the woodland, his keen gaze taking in the path and the ditch. "Well, they don't seem to be nowheres around now. Where d'ye think they've got to, young Prink?"

Orkwil shrugged. "I don't know, Skip, there was a lot o' crewbeasts aboard that ship. If they came chasin' me'n' Gorath, we'd have seen at least a few of 'em by now. Maybe they're hidin', waitin' for daylight."

Skipper hopped back down onto the walkway. "That don't sound like vermin t'me, mate, skulkin' round in the dark an' attackin' by night's more their style. You was with 'em, vole, didn't ye hear any plans?"

Still held in Benjo Tipps's grasp, the vole sneered. "Of course I didn't, they wouldn't tell me anythin'. But they never injured me like yore Mister Tipps did, nor stole my vittles like that young 'un."

205

Ignoring the vole's complaints, Orkwil ventured an idea. "Maybe they've moved position. Let's take a quiet patrol, right round the walls, we might spot the vermin."

Skipper nodded. "Good plan, young 'un, let's do it. Benjo, if'n the vole makes a sound, teach him t'be quiet, will ye?"

The Cellarhog drew a short stave hammer from his belt. "Why, thankee, Skip, 'twould be my pleasure. Move along now, my ole vole, an' don't even try to breathe aloud!"

Soft moonshadows dappled the walkway, as the four creatures padded softly toward the eastern walltop. From battlement to battlement they moved, with the three Redwallers keeping close watch on the trees and woodland floor outside the Abbey. It was a still and tranquil night. Orkwil was enjoying being back at Redwall, he felt very grown-up, and sensible to his new responsibilities. No more would he be the foolish young borrower of otherbeasts' property.

They covered the east parapet, without seeing any sign of life or activity outside, even the watervole was starting to walk more confidently.

Slightly ahead of his companions, Orkwil rounded the corner, onto the southern rampants. He was startled to hear a voice hailing them from below. "Ahoy the Abbey, matey!"

Immediately the vole panicked, breaking away from Benjo's grip, wailing fearfully, "It's them! I told you we was bein' watched, it's the fox an' his crew. . . . Yowhoooo!" In his excitement, the vole had stumbled and fallen down into the Abbey grounds. He made a distinct thud as he landed. This was followed by silence.

Skipper peered down at his slumped form, whispering to his friends, "Knocked senseless agin, an' just as well, too! That didn't sound like no vermin out there. Matter o' fact, I think I knows that voice. Leave this t'me." The otter chieftain shouted back in a gruff voice, "Who goes there, be ye friend or foebeast?"

206

An equally tough-sounding voice roared back at him. "If'n ye've got supper on the table an' a drop o' hotroot soup, then I'll be yore friend for life, cousin Rorc!"

A broad smile spread over Skipper's face, he murmured to Orkwil, "Nip down quietlike an' open the south wicker gate, they're friends down there sure enough!" Skipper leapt up on the battlements, grinning happily. "Well, sink me rudder if'n it ain't Barbowla Boulderdog! Ahoy, mate, who's all the gang ye've brought with ye?"

Barbowla chuckled. "Haharr, 'tis only me liddle family an' some shrewmates I brought along, now don't stand up there chewin' soup all night, Rorc, let us in, will ye?"

Skipper adopted a mock serious expression. "Let ye in? Huh, ye'd eat us out o' house'n'home an' the cook'd resign if I let you lot at our vittles!"

Barbowla's wife, Kachooch, steped forward, paws akimbo. "When yore finished playin' games, ye great pud-den, I suggest ye might think of openin' this liddle door down here. We've got a platoon of tired, hungry babes an' prob'ly a horde o' Brownrats on our tails!"

Skipper suddenly became serious. "Quick, Orkwil, open up an' let 'em in! Benjo, run an' fetch the Abbot, tell Marja Dubbidge to sound the alarm bells, we may need defenders on these walls if'n it's Brownrats!"

Orkwil was almost knocked flat as he unbolted the south wicker gate, a gang of shrew and otterbabes thundered by him, all agog to see what Redwall Abbey was like. These were followed by the Guosim, and Barbowla's clan. He enquired of the last one in, the squirrel Rangval, "Is that the lot, sir, any more to come?"

The roguish creature slammed the door, and locked it. "Ah shure, there'll mayhaps be another three shortly, sir, a haremaid an' two more shrews. But I think we'd best keep the ould door bolted until they're sighted, in case the rats make it here first, y'unnerstan'."

The Abbey's twin bells, Matthias and Methusaleh, rang

out the alarm, disturbing the peaceful night. Within an amazingly short time, the walls were being manned by Redwallers, armed with the first things that came to paw. Rakes, spades, hoes, ladles, window poles and a variety of odd implements.

Abbot Daucas accosted a passing shrew. "Where's your Log a Log, Guosim?"

The shrew tugged his snout respectfully. "Luglug stayed be'ind, Father sir, the haremaid, too, they went lookin' fer a liddle 'un who got lost."

Daucas signalled to Friar Chondrus. "Take these guests to Cavern Hole, please. See to it that they get a full supper."

The shrew, who was Osbil, saluted the Abbot with his rapier. "Beggin' yore pardon, Father, but all Guosim who are fightin' fit will be stayin' on yore walltops, in case o' trouble."

The Father Abbot shook his paw warmly. "The Guosim have always been our brave allies, thank you. Chondrus, just take the babes, old ones and mothers to supper. But have enough food prepared for everybeast defending the walls."

Abbot Daucas mounted the walltop, where he stood listening to the conversation between Skipper Rorc and his cousin Barbowla.

"I can't say for certain 'ow many Brownrats there are, Rorc, but there's a horde of the scum, an' Gruntan Kurdly's their leader."

"Kurdly eh, that 'un's been makin' a name for hisself round Mossflower fer a few seasons now. Well, let the rascals come, Redwall's ready for 'em, cousin."

Daucas interrupted. "I'm told there's still a haremaid, plus two more shrews to come yet, one of them is Log a Log Luglug. Keep an eye out for them, and be sure to get them safe inside quickly, if they're being pursued by Brownrats."

Skipper made way for a molecrew, who were trundling supplies of rocks, boulders and sling pebbles to the south-

208

ern walltop. The otter chieftain thwacked his rudder against the battlements, shaking his head at the Abbot. "Stripe me colours, Father, it ain't enough that we may have a crew o' seafarin' vermin on our paws, but now we got Gruntan Kurdly an' his gang callin' to visit!"

Abbot Daucus produced a sling from his voluminous sleeve, and began selecting stones. "Ah well, Skip, it never rains but it pours, or so they say. Let them all come, friends to receive a warm welcome, and foes to get a red-hot reception, eh!"

In the woodlands, a good hour's march north of the Abbey, Vizka Longtooth located his crew, having espied the light from their campfires. The weasel Magger, his second in command, made a place for him by the largest fire. "Yew was right, Cap'n, dere's plenny o' vittles fer everybeast round 'ere. Birds, fish, eggs an' fruit. Glurma! Fetch d'Cap'n summ supper, will ye."

The greasy old ratcook presented Vizka with two hazelwood skewers, laden with food, which she had been tending by her fire. "Been keepin' 'em special for ya, Cap'n, dat 'un's a woodpigeon, an' dis 'un's a bream!"

The golden fox tore into the roasted bird, spitting out fragments of feather as he gazed around. *Bludgullet's* crew seemed happy enough, those still not gorging themselves were dozing contentedly in the firelight. Vizka was pleasantly surprised, sea-raiding vermin were usually pretty hopeless at providing for themselves on land. He had expected them to be hungry, and sullen with unspoken complaints. He winked at Magger. "Pore ole Codj couldn't 'ave found vittles like dis, was it yore doin', mate?"

Magger showed his yellow, snaggled teeth in a modest grin. "Aye, Cap'n, me'n Glurma did it twixt us."

Glurma presented her captain with a beaker of liquid. "Drink up, 'tis only willowbark tea, but Magger sent Dogleg an' Patchy back to der *Bludgullet*, dey should be back by midday wid a keg o' grog for ya, Cap'n."

Vizka nodded his approval. "Hah, t'ings is lookin' up, mates, ya did good!"

As he ate and drank, Magger moved close to Vizka, speaking in a secretive murmur, "So, wot's da plan fer dat Abbey place, Cap'n?"

The golden fox threw a fishbone into the fire. "I been thinkin', would dis lot be any good at diggin'?"

Magger snorted contemptuously. "Sea Raiders diggin'? Ya mus' be jestin', Vizka, my crew's alright at shipboard tasks, or killin', but I don't see 'em as diggers. Why, are ya plannin' on diggin' inta dat Abbey place?"

Alarm bells began ringing in the golden fox's head. Suddenly he was looking at the weasel Magger in a new light, and he did not like what he had just heard. Magger was calling him Vizka now, not Captain. Also, he had referred to Vizka Longtooth's vermin as *his* crew. Now Magger was setting himself up as a favourite with Vizka's creatures, providing warm fires, and good vittles, even a keg of grog from the ship. Vizka continued eating in silence.

Though he did not know it, Magger had overplayed his cards. One thing a Sea Raider captain had to be constantly aware of was any threat to his authority. Vizka put aside his supper, lying back he half-closed his eyes, murmuring gently, "I'll let ya know me plans in der mornin'."

Magger nodded and turned away. He did not see Vizka smile, that long, toothy, dangerous smile, which always meant death for somebeast.

22

From their hiding place beneath the dead leaves in the curve of the dry ditchbed, Maudie saw four hulking Brownrats leaving the campfire. She covered little Yik's head, stopping him from bobbing up.

Alongside her, Luglug hissed urgently, "Y'see, I told ye the vermin heard us. Look, they're comin' over here, I'm sure we've been spotted, what are we goin' to do, mate?"

The haremaid instinctively knew their hideout would be discovered. Yik was wriggling to get out of her grasp, and the snake was moving, too. It had begun to come around, and was writhing feebly to rid itself of the halter, with which Maudie had bound its jaws shut. It was a time for rapid action. She swiftly imparted a scratch plan to the Guosim chieftain. "Got to get out of here jolly fast, old lad. Create some sort of diversion, then make a flippin' run for it, wot?"

The four Brownrats were already descending the far side of the ditch.

Luglug stared wide-eyed at Maudie. "Diversion, wot sort o' diversion?"

The haremaid hardly stopped to ponder the question. "We've got two things goin' for us, bucko, the advantage of surprise, an' this whoppin' great snake. Time for gossipin' is done, grab that confounded Yik an' follow me. . . ."

The Brownrats were completely taken by surprise. Whirling the maddened snake with both paws, and yelling like a banshee, Maudie rushed them. "Gangway, chaps! Eulaliiiaaaaaa!"

Two of the rats were knocked aside by the reptile's flailing coils, the other two stood rooted to the spot in dumb shock. With Luglug holding Yik tight to his body, running crouched behind her, Maudie breasted the ditchbank. The haremaid charged straight through the centre of the Brownrat camp, still flailing the big reptile. Gruntan Kurdly almost choked on the hard-boiled egg he had just popped whole into his mouth. Maudie looked like something out of nightmare as she bounded out of the night into the firelight. "Yahaaar! Blood'n'vinegar! Eulaliiiiaaaaa!"

More rats went down beneath the windmilling snake's body, then she flung it right at Kurdly. It was not a totally accurate throw, most of the reptile hit the Brownrat leader, but its tail landed in the fire. This move did not improve the snake's temper, it latched furiously onto the Brownrat's body, constricting as its tail shot out of the flames and beat a frenzied tattoo on Gruntan's head.

Spluttering hard-boiled egg widespread, he whooped aloud in terror, "Gerritoff! Waaaarrrgggh! Oo . . . oo! Gerritoffameeee!"

Clear of the Brownrat camp, Maudie slowed her pace for Luglug to catch up. From behind them she could hear angry shouts.

"Kill it! Slay the thing, ye mudpawed oafs!"

"Wot was it, 'ow many of 'em was there?"

"Round six if'n ye ask me, seven countin' the snake."

"It was the punchin' rabbit, I saw it with me own two eyes, came straight out the ditch it did!"

Gruntan Kurdly's voice rose to an enraged shriek. "I don't give a bee's be'ind who it was. Gerrem! Killem! Skin 'em alive an' bring their 'eads to me! Don't jus' stan' there, idjits, go. Go go go!"

Luglug gave a weary sigh as he heaved Yik up onto his shoulders. "We better git movin', fast."

Maudie held out her paws. "Give me the little chap, he'll hold you back."

For some reason best known to himself the Log a Log snapped back at her, "I said we'd better git movin', I can manage him!"

Yik tugged Luglug's ears. "I wanna go wiv 'er, she can run fasterer!"

The shrew chieftain growled at him. "Keep yore mouth shut an' stay up there, young 'un!"

Maudie shrugged. "As you wish, old chap, but let's be goin', wot. Don't want t'get collared by that scurvy lot!"

The haremaid took off at a brisk lope, but soon had to wait for Luglug to catch up again. They pounded on through the darkened woodland, with the noise of pursuit growing behind. Maudie adjusted her pace, running alongside Luglug. "Y'know I can run just as easy with Yik on my back, why don't you let me carry him, wot?"

Yik hauled on his bearer's ears, haranguing him. "Flippin' bloomin' wotwot, I wanna go wiv 'er!"

This made Luglug even more stubborn and irate. "You stop tuggin' my ears, an' watch yore language. I can carry ye as well as anybeast can."

An arrow zipped past Maudie, it quivered in a beech trunk. She glanced anxiously over her shoulder. "They must have a few fast front runners ahead of the rest. I wonder how far from Redwall we are?"

Luglug was beginning to pant, but he strove onward. "Keep to this trail an' we'll soon see the two-topped oak. After that we'll come out o' the woodlands an' cross some open fields t'the southside o' the Abbey. I remember this route now, came this way once afore when I was younger."

Maudie nodded. "Save your breath, old chap, those

blighters are closer than you think." An arrow buried its point in the ground, narrowly missing Maudie's footpaw, another flew close by Yik's ear.

The little shrew shouted, as if it were all some kind of game, "Yah, y'missed me! C'mon, we havta run fasterer!"

Luglug pointed ahead. "See, there's the two-topped oak, straight ahead, not too far now!"

Maudie spied the big, lightning-riven object. Even in the night it stood out above the other trees at the woodland edge. Wild cries of the Brownrats could still be heard behind them, but she knew the front runners would keep silent, hoping that they could outpace their quarry. On an impulse, she slowed, letting Luglug carry on ahead. Crouching down, Maudie scanned about for movement.

There they were! Two Brownrats, tall, slim vermin, running swiftly from tree to tree, pausing briefly to loose off arrows in the direction of the runaways. Now Luglug stopped, looking back at Maudie and calling, "What are ye doin', miz?"

Both the Brownrats were close enough to hear him. In a trice they had loosed off the shafts, which were lying ready on their bowstrings. Maudie ran without looking back, straight for the rats. The first one had another arrow almost ready to fire as the haremaid hit him like a thunderbolt. He collapsed to the ground immediately. Maudie grabbed his bow, whipped about to face the other, sighted and fired. The shaft struck true. With a strangled cry the other rat went down, grasping the shaft, which protruded from his neck.

Then the main body came running into view. Maudie dropped the bow and ran. Luglug was leaning against the riven oak, with Yik still on his shoulders. He was gasping heavily. Grunting with the effort, he lifted Yik free, holding him out to the haremaid. "You'd better carry . . ."

Maudie grabbed the Guosim infant, then saw the broken

arrow buried deep between the Guosim chieftain's shoulder blades, as he turned and slid slowly down the tree trunk. Half drawing his rapier, he gasped, "Take it to Osbil, save the little 'un. . . ." His head fell limply to one side as his eyes clouded over and he gave one last sigh.

There was no time to think. Maudie could make out the faces of the vermin as they came hurrying forward, shouting and yelling. Grabbing the rapier from Luglug's lifeless paw, she swung Yik up on her shoulders and ran. The sight of their victims-to-be spurred the Brownrats forward. However, they reckoned without the speed and determination of a Long Patrol hare. Mad Maudie Mugsberry Thropple ran as she had never run before. The shrewbabe on her shoulders hung on for dear life, with the night breeze blowing his fur back flat.

Out of the woodlands the haremaid rocketed, onto the flatland facing the Abbey's south wall. Her footpaws drummed the earth as she sped onward, with a screeching horde hard on her trail. "Eulaliiiaaaa Redwaaaaallll!" Maudie roared.

Skipper, Benjo, Barbowla and several stout young otters of the Boulderdog family came hurtling out through the south wallgate, running toward the haremaid who was speeding toward them. They shot right past her, halted, then flung a salvo of otter javelins. Unable to stop, the Brownrats stumbled over the bodies of the leading seven vermin who had fallen to the deadly, light throwing weapons.

It halted the horde only for an instant, but that was the short, vital time that saved Maudie and Yik. They were hauled through the gateway by willing paws, who slammed the little door shut as soon as the otters were safe inside. Now slingstones pelted like rain from the walltops, driving back those they did not slay or injure. A great cry rang from the ramparts. "Redwaaaaaaallll!"

A shrewmum took little Yik from Maudie's shoulders as the haremaid collapsed upon the ground. She was sucking in great gulps of air, her entire body quivering from the heroic efforts of her mighty run. Rangval and several of the Guosim defenders hastened from the walltop to congratulate Maudie.

The roguish squirrel pumped her paw and pounded her back heartily. "Ah shure, that was a grand ould run, with a horde o' rascals behind ye, an' carryin' a passenger, too. Not even their arrows could keep up with ye!"

Osbil was among the welcoming committee, Maudie passed Luglug's rapier to him. A silence fell over the shrews. Osbil stared at the blade for awhile, then his eyes met Maudie's gaze. Their exchange was subdued and brief. "Luglug?"

The haremaid nodded. "He was slain by an arrow. I had to leave him by the riven oak. They were almost upon us, I had to run with the little 'un."

Osbil ran his paw gently along the blade. "Did he die instantly?"

Breathing easier now, Maudie hauled herself upright. "He did indeed, or I wouldn't have left his side. We might've made it if he hadn't insisted on carryin' Yik. Right up to the moment he was hit, he refused to pass the little chap over to me. Why?"

Osbil was blinking back tears, but his voice was steady. "Because every Guosim is the responsibility of his chieftain. Luglug was duty-bound to carry Yik. Now I must go an' tell the rest of my tribe. Thank ye for bringin' me his blade, miz."

Maudie watched Osbil ascending the wallstairs. "Wonder why Luglug wanted me t'give him the sword?"

Teagle, one of the coracle paddlers, explained. "Luglug wanted Osbil t'be our new chieftain. That's Guosim law, the father passes his title on to the eldest offspring."

Maudie was surprised. "You mean Osbil is Luglug's son?"

Teagle wiped a paw across her eyes and sniffed. "Aye, an' a good son, too, miz, an' he'll make a fine Log a Log, just like his ole dad. Ye'll excuse me now, I've got to join my tribe for the Bladechant."

Piqued by curiosity, Maudie followed Teagle up to the south rampart, where she witnessed the strange Guosim ritual. Osbil was standing up between the battlements, in full view of the attacking Brownrats, singing a loud, dirge-like challenge, kissing the rapier blade, then pointing it toward the foe as he sang out threateningly. The Guosim warriors swayed slowly, chanting the chorus.

"I am Chieftain, son of Chieftains,
look upon my father's blade,
hark you vermin, spawn of darkness,
Guosim come now, be afraid!

"Hi hey oh Log a Log
Guosim hi hey ooooooooh!

"We will send your bones to Hellgates,
every single evil one,
bitter tears with blood must mingle,
ere your debt is paid and done!

"Hi hey oh Log a Log
Guosim hi hey ooooooooh!

"We are Guosim, born of Guosim,
all our words and steel are true,
none of ye will be left standin'
that's a warrior's vow to you!

"Hi hey oh Log a Log
Guosim hi hey ooooooooh!"

It was the most eerie thing Maudie had ever heard. Osbil was pointing at the Brownrats with his rapier, as the Guosim fighters either side of him swayed like a field of corn before the gale. So uncanny was the sight and sound that both the Redwallers on the rampart and the Brownrats below on the common land ceased fighting, they stood silently watching.

Then Osbil broke the spell. Leaping down from the battlements, he shook his blade on high, and roared in an ululating voice, which was taken up by all the shrew tribe, "Logalogalogalogalooooooog!"

Then the horrifying reality caught Skipper, he thundered down the wallstairs, shouting, "Bar the gate, they're goin' to charge out an' meet the vermin head-on!"

Rangval swiftly shot the bolts tight on the wallgate. Maudie, Skipper and Benjo ran ahead of the Guosim to render assistance. Barbowla and some of his family joined them, the big otter shook his head in disbelief. "Those shrews must be mad. They're outnumbered by vermin at least ten to one, an' they want to charge out an' do battle with 'em!"

Osbil came pounding down to the gate backed by his tribe, every one of them brandishing drawn blades. He bared his teeth at the guardians of the gate. "Stand clear, ye can't stop a Guosim once the Bladechant's been given. We'd be cowards if'n we didn't fight those stinkin' vermin after our Log a Log's been slain by 'em!"

Maudie stood forward until Osbil's blade was touching her. "Aye, and you'd be fat-headed dead fools if you did. Take it from me, old lad, you ain't goin' anywhere, an' I'm jolly well sayin' that for your own good, wot!"

It was a tense moment. The haremaid could feel the rapier point at her throat. Osbil meant business.

"Put that sword down at once. How dare you raise a weapon at a friend inside my Abbey? Put it down, I say!" Abbot Daucus pushed his way through the massed shrews, his face a mask of icy severity. Disregarding the rapier, he struck it to one side.

Osbil scowled darkly. "This is a Guosim thing, Father. It ain't yore quarrel!"

Daucus thrust his chin forward fearlessly. "Oh, isn't it?

Well, I'm making it my quarrel. As Father Abbot of Red-wall Abbey, I command that you cease this foolishness forthwith. Is that clear?"

Osbil began to wilt. He was still a young shrew, and in the face of the Abbot's superior authority, he became un-sure of himself. He replied with a touch of pleading in his tone. "But Father, we've sung the Bladechant, we lose face an' honour if'n we don't go now!"

Daucus began to feel pity for the young shrew, who had just been made Log a Log of his tribe. However, he was not about to back down to Osbil. "Hmm, loss of honour and face, I see. But are there no exceptional circumstances which might call the whole thing off, can you think of any-thing?"

On a flash of inspiration, Maudie interrupted. "Beg pardon, Father, I've just thought of a jolly wheeze, er, I mean, an answer to the problem." The haremaid edged a little closer to Osbil. "Er, suppose, just suppose I say, that you, bein' the bloomin' high old Logathing, were incapacitated?"

Not comprehending the word, Osbil repeated it. "Inca-pacitated?"

Maudie edged closer. "Indeed, incapacitated, you know, too hurt or injured to lead the charge. Could your chaps go out there to battle the vermin?"

Osbil shook his head. "Not unless they were led by their Log a Log, our law wouldn't allow that y'see . . ." Sud-denly he sagged, Maudie quickly supported him, but he was unconscious, out cold. The haremaid's face was the picture of innocence.

"Good grief, the poor chap's just swooned. Fainted away as sudden as y'like, wot?"

The Guosim began crowding round anxiously, but Rang-val took over officiously. "Shure, have ye got no sense, crowdin' round the pore beast like that, give him some air. Skipper, will ye take 'em up on the walltops agin, at least they can fight the durty ould vermin from up there wid slingstones. Go on now, buckoes, the Father Abbot'll do a grand job of lookin' after yore chief, hurry along now!"

The Guosim hesitated a moment, until Skipper mounted the wallsteps, goading them. "Don't waste yore breath, friend, there's plenty o' our Redwallers up there, if'n the shrews are afraid to go!"

In an instant he was thrust to one side, as the fiercely proud Guosim stampeded en masse up the steps. Aided by Foremole, the Abbot carried Osbil to the Abbey, for Sister Atrata's attention. Foremole Burff shook his dark velvety head. "Burr, oi do 'opes thurr bee's nuthin' badly amiss with ee pore beast, a-swoonin' away loike that."

Abbot Daucus was plainly perplexed by the incident. "Indeed, quite unusual for one so young and healthy. Still, it did solve a problem for us, didn't it?"

Back at the wallsteps, Rangval treated Maudie to a huge, sly wink, having seen the truth of it all. "Shure, I've seen lightnin' strikin' a lot slower than that, marm. Why, that was the swiftest an' neatest ould knockout punch I've ever had the pleasure of seein'. Faith, if'n I'd have winked I would've missed it!"

The haremaid threw a paw about the squirrel's shoulders, whispering as she drew him close, "Keep your blinkin' voice down, old scout, we don't want the whole bloomin' Abbey t'know. Actually, I was only carryin' out me duty, as t'were, doin' what had t'be done, eh wot!" She stifled a giggle.

"'Twas rather a scorcher of an uppercut, even though I say it m'self. Even better'n the one I gave big Blinky Swifleton when I first won the Inter Barracks Title. Nice chap, old Blinky, took an absolute age before he could see straight again, prob'ly how he got the name Blinky, wot!"

Rangval curled his tail in admiration of Maudie. "A real live boxin' hare, eh! Ah, 'tis a pleasure to see a perilous young darlin' like yoreself at work, marm!"

Maudie gave his shoulder a squeeze, imitating his brogue. "Get away, ye hard-faced rogue, yore no slouch yerself from wot I've seen of yore ould tricks! C'mon, shall we toddle up t'the walltop, just t'see how the battle's goin' on?"

The squirrel made a sweeping bow, indicating the steps. "After you, me long-eared, wallopin' beauty!"

23

The impetus of furious Guosim stone slingers added to the Redwall defenders had worked like a charm. Gruntan Kurdly had not yet arrived on the scene, and as a result of the ferocious retaliation from the south battlements, the few Brownrats with any authority were thoroughly cowed. Even with their superior numbers, they could make no impression on the high stone walls. So they did what was customary, retreated into the relative safety of the woodland trees, and sat waiting the arrival of their leader.

Skipper greeted Maudie and Rangval, pointing to the deserted field of conflict below. "I think they've had enough for now, mates. Though we'll stay alert up here an' see wot the dawn brings, eh?"

Friar Chondrus hailed them from the Abbey lawn. "Hello up there, are ye too busy fighting, or could you manage a bite o' supper?"

Rubbing his paws with anticipation, Barbowla shouted back as he ushered several of his family to the steps, "Ho, I think we could manage to nibble a few vittles, sir. I'm sendin' a few down t'lend a paw to ye!"

Much to the delight of the otters there was a big cauldron of their favourite soup, watershrimp'n'hotroot. The Guosim were very partial to a small cask of October Ale, plus a tray or two of shallot and mushroom pasties. There was white cheese with hazelnuts, apple and plum dumplings, a latticed pear tart with meadowcream, golden-crusted bread, hot from the ovens, and a choice of blackberry cordial or coltsfoot tea.

The cheese was almost melting as Skipper put it on his hot bread. He dipped the lot into his hotroot soup, exclaiming before he wolfed it down, "Eat hearty, mates, but tell me this. Wot beast in his right mind would allow a load o' scruffy vermin inside Redwall to steal this scoff from us, eh?"

Barbowla's sturdy wife, Kachooch, helped herself to a pastie. "I'd let 'em in, but not to eat the vittles. I'd use their heads'n'tails to scrub the pots out with!"

Roars of laughter rose to the summer night's sky. Maudie sat with Rangval and a young hedgehog, who introduced himself as Orkwil Prink. The haremaid sampled everything eagerly, commenting on each dish. "Absolutely topping, I must get the recipe for this pear'n'cream thing, and these pasties, top marks, I'd say! Steady the buffs! Now that's a real drop o' soup, watershrimp'n'hotroot, d'ye say? Hah, I wouldn't mind bein' a bloomin' otter if I could have this twice daily. Well, chaps, I only came here to find a blinkin' badger, but I'd have applied to be born at Redwall if the tucker's all as good as this!"

Skipper's two daughters, Folura and Glingol, were charming some of Barbowla's sons, they began tapping on two wooden bowls, singing a jolly song.

"I once knew an otter who liked apple pie,
why oh why, my oh my,
he could eat it both night and day,
if you asked him why he ate apple pie,
he'd laugh and he would say,
An apple's an apple, it ain't a pear,
some grows here an' some grows there,
bake 'em up in a pie an' serve it to me,

223

No strawberry y'see ever grew on a tree,
no sir no, dearie me,
strawberries don't grow in that way,
while carrots are found growing underground,
'cos that's a carrot's way,
some grow up and some grow down,
we gather them when the harvest comes round,
then the cook hangs 'em all in his old pan . . . tree
and we go to sleep in a dormi . . . tree!"

Using their rudders against the parapet stones, the sons of Barbowla applauded both ottermaids enthusiastically. Then, to display how tough and fearless they were, the young male otters began climbing on the battlements, and slinging stones at the woodland fringes. Naturally, they injured no Brownrats, who had retreated out of slinging range. Skipper's daughters looked suitably impressed, fluttering their eyelashes at every opportunity.

Maudie found herself sitting between Orkwil and Benjo Tipps. Being a hare, she was still doing full justice to the remains of supper, having exchanged introductions with the Redwallers whilst still expressing her appreciation of Abbey food. "By the left! I could get rather used to this scoff, is it always this good, Orkwil, old lad?"

The young hedgehog picked a crumb from his spikes. "Oh, this was just a quick meal the Friar and his helpers threw together. We weren't expectin' guests, y'see, or it would have been more carefully prepared. Er, by the way, Maudie, did I hear you say that you came here to find a badger?"

Maudie ran her paw around the rim of the empty soup cauldron, licking it longingly. "Oh, that? Well, yes, I have, actually. Secret mission from Salamandastron, all very hush hush, wot. Old Lord Asheye, he's my C.O. doncha know, sent me specially, prob'ly 'cos I'm jolly good at that sort o' thing. I don't suppose you've stumbled across this badger chap. Huge type, typical badger, wot. He's supposed not t'be a great lover of swords an' armour, simple salt o' the earth type, or so I'm led t'believe. Funny thing though, he's supposed to carry a flame an' walk with a thief. Sounds jolly silly, doesn't it, but who am I to argue? Badger Lord an' Major Mullein pleaded with me on bended paw. So I had to agree t'the task, I mean, what's a chappess t'do, wot!"

Maudie was totally unprepared for what Orkwil said next. "The badger's name is Gorath, he's up in Sister Atrata's sickbay, resting. It was me who brought him to Redwall."

Three things happened then. Maudie's ears stood up rigid, her eyes bulged wide and her mouth fell open. "You wha . . . Gorbadge in sick ratata bestray, an' you red him to broughtwall!"

Benjo Tipps chortled aloud at the sight and sound of the haremaid's confusion. "Better watch ye don't trip up over yore tongue an' fall down the steps, missy. Well, don't just sit there, young Prink, take the maid up to see yore badger friend. I'm sure she might start talkin' sense after a calmin' stroll o'er the lawn an' through our Abbey."

Skipper nodded after Maudie and Orkwil as they made their way across the lawn. "Where are those two goin', Benj?"

The Cellarhog sat down on the top step. "Orkwil's takin' Maudie to see the badger, she was sent from the Salamandastron mountain to find him."

Skipper watched the two entering the Abbey. "But Gorath didn't come from the badger mountain. I wonder how ole Lord Asheye guessed Gorath was here?"

Benjo took a sip from his tankard of October Ale. "Well ye may ask, Skip, Salamandastron's a mysterious place, plain, ord'nary beasts like us'll never fathom it."

As the pair made their way to the sickbay, Orkwil explained briefly how he was banished from the Abbey, and how he came to meet Gorath. After listening to his narra-

225

tion, the haremaid smiled ruefully. "Hmm, your tale isn't too far different from mine, old chap. We both came here pursued by foebeasts, eh!"

The young hedgehog winked at Maudie. "Aye, so we did, but what were you banished from Salamandastron for, were you a thief like me?"

Totally unprepared, Maudie blurted out, "Most certainly not! It was for fightin', actually, all I did was biff Corporal Thwurl an' a few other bods. But how did you jolly well know they were goin' to banish me, wot?"

Orkwil opened the infirmary door quietly. "Oh, it was just somethin' about you, a bit like me, I s'pose. Gorath's in the small back room."

Maudie gazed awestruck at the sleeping badger stretched out on the big bed. "Corks! He's bigger'n old Lord Asheye, though he looks a bit thin' an' wasted, is he ill?"

Orkwil touched Gorath's massive paw gently. "He's been through a lot. A lesser beast would've died from the treatment he received from those Sea Raiders."

Gorath's eyes came open, he struggled weakly to sit up. "Sea Raiders, where are they?"

Orkwil sat on the bed, pressing him back down. "Calm yoreself, mate, there hasn't been hide nor hair of those rascals seen anywhere around. At the moment we're more concerned about a horde of Brownrats outside the south wall. Listen now, there's someone I want ye to meet."

Maudie proffered her paw, introducing herself. "Maudie Mugsberry Thropple of Salamandastron, sah. I was sent to seek you out by Lord Asheye."

Gorath paused a moment. "Asheye, is that's his name? An old badger, completely gray all over, I've seen him in my dreams a few times. What does he want with me?"

The haremaid seated herself on the end of the bed. "Er, I'm not quite flippin' sure, sah. He said I was to observe you, probably has thoughts of me bringin' you back to Salamandastron."

Gorath interrupted her, the old fire seeming to smoulder in his eyes. "Not until Vizka Longtooth is dead by my paw! Orkwil, go and warn your Abbey friends, those vermin are somewhere near, waiting to attack Redwall. Bring me Tung, give me my weapon. . . ." Again he tried to rise, but Maudie and Orkwil held him down.

Sister Atrata appeared in the doorway. "What are you doing here, this creature is ill, he needs rest. You must leave immediately!" The Sister took a small bowl from the bedside table. Supporting Gorath's head, she raised it to his lips. "Drink some of this, friend, it will help you get well."

The badger took a long, thirsty draught and lay back. His eyelids fluttered, and he gave a deep sigh. Then he began murmuring as though thinking aloud. "Never saw them coming . . . no chance at all . . . have to bury the old ones . . . build a new dwelling . . . all gone now, home, kinbeasts . . . Getting cold now, so cold these Northern Isles . . . Ice, snow . . . Crops ruined again . . . Poorbeasts, poorbeasts . . . buried in Northern earth . . . So cold . . . So cold!"

Gorath began trembling and shuddering then. His great, wasted body arched against the bed, paws tightly clasped as his teeth rattled aloud. The pitchfork, Tung, which had been laid next to him, clattered to the floor.

Sister Atrata acted quickly, pouring more liquid from the bowl between her patient's clenched teeth as she snapped out orders at the two visitors. "You, miss, bring blankets from the big chest in the next room. Prink, get hold of Marja Dubbidge, tell her to get a fire lit up here. Look sharp now, both of you, your friend is in a fever!"

Orkwil scurried off to find Marja, the Bellringer. Maudie located the big chest, and pulled fleecy woven blankets from it as she murmured to herself, "Hope the Sis knows what she's doin'. Imagine me havin' t'go back emptypawed to His Lordship. What would one say? Sorry, sah, I found the badger who carries the flame, but I bloomin' well lost him. Huh, Major Mull'd have my hide!"

Stumbling over a heap of bedlinen and blankets, the haremaid tottered in to Sister Atrata. "Will that be enough, marm, d'you want me to fetch more, is he goin' to be alright, hadn't you better give him another dose of that jollop from the bowl, wot?"

The good Sister treated Maudie to a strict glare. "I'll do all in my power to help him, miz, but please don't start telling me how to do my job. Here, take a corner of this blanket, and help me to cover him."

The haremaid was tucking the blanket about Gorath's shoulders when she noticed the extent, the depth of the flame-shaped scar on his brow. "Great blinkin' seasons, what an awful wound, I saw it when I first got here, but I didn't realise just how jolly big it was, 'til I got up close!"

Sister Atrata nodded. "Yes, I'm just hoping it doesn't affect his recovery, but who knows?"

Maudie stared down at the awesome wound. "Hmm, there used to be an old hare in the veterans' barracks. Got a big rock broken over his head in the vermin wars. Funny old chap, used to sing songs in a language nobeast could understand. They reckon the bang he got from the rock sent him clear off his chump. Beg pardon, marm, made him act strangely."

The Sister lowered her eyes. "I understand, things like that have been known to happen. Though I don't think this badger will lose his mind, he's too fixed by one purpose, to avenge the death of his family."

Maudie gazed out of the window, watching the first pale streaks of dawn illuminating the night sky. "Sounds just like a badger to me, Sister."

24

Larks rose from the flatlands, twittering in the newborn summer morn at the misty blue sky, which promised a long, sunny day. It would have been an idyllic scene, except for two things, a horde of Brownrats in the southern woodland fringe, and a crew of vermin Sea Raiders to the north of the Abbey.

Vizka Longtooth had left the bulk of his creatures under cover, bringing twoscore along with him. They headed down the ditch to Redwall, ready to begin tunnelling operations. The crew he had chosen were not too happy with the scheme, but they kept silent, knowing the golden fox was only waiting on one protestor, to make an example of. Once the Abbey was in sight, they crouched low, approaching it with extreme caution. Vizka halted them when he was level with the main gates, and started issuing orders. "I t'ink we start tunnellin' right here, see." He scratched an X into the ditch wall. "Wot d'ya say, Undril, a gudd place, eh?"

Undril was a large, dull-witted weasel, whom Vizka had chosen to be in charge of the digging. He looked at the mark his captain had made, nodding. "If'n ya says so, Cap'n."

The golden fox gave his crew the benefit of a quick, dangerous smile. "Oh, I says so, ya can take me word on it. Now git diggin', all of ya!"

Without any proper tools they went to work, gouging at the soil with spear, sword and dagger points. Vizka toyed with his mace and chain, watching their clumsy attempts, whilst trying to keep his temper in check. He realised it was going to be a long, slow task, requiring a bit of patience, something Vizka was not used to. Already he was feeling irate.

"Dere's too many diggin' at once, yer gettin' nowheres. Undril, split 'em ina two groups. Firty, you'n Gerna go further down dis ditch, try der soil an' see if'n 'twould be easier ter dig a tunnel dere."

Firty and Gerna were both small and puny rats. Glad to be relieved of labouring, they scuttled off south, down the ditchbed. Vizka continued supervising the work. "Jungo, wot d'ya t'ink yore doin'?"

Jungo, the least intelligent of all the *Bludgullet*'s crew, pointed to the shallow depression they had made. "Huh huh, me spear keeps bouncin' back when I tries ter dig wid it, Cap'n."

Vizka explained, as though he were talking to a babe, "Dat's 'cos dere's a root in der way. Bilger, yew 'old der root, while Jungo cuts it wid 'is spearblade." The golden fox watched the proceedings, with a sense of hopelessness weighing upon him.

"Yowch! Der cap'n said cut der root, loaf'ead, not me paw. Ow! See, ya dun it again!"

"Huh huh, sorry, mate, yore paw's all full o' soil, I thought it wuz der root!"

Gruntan Kurdly had finally arrived at the south woodland fringe. His weary bearers set the stretcher down as he cast a scathing eye over his horde. He beckoned Biklo to his side. "Where's all the sh'ews got to?"

The scout, Biklo, nodded in the direction of the Abbey. "In there, Boss."

Assisted by two bearers, Gruntan wheezed his way to the edge of the trees. He had seen Redwall Abbey before, but not this close up; he tried not to look impressed. "Hmm, are the six liddle boats in there, too?"

Biklo shrugged. "Dunno."

For a rat of his size and bulk, Gruntan could move quite rapidly. He rushed Biklo, felling him with a kick. Standing over the fallen Brownrat, he made a pantomime of shrugging, and aping the scout's voice. "Dunno? Dunno?" Gruntan kicked him again, shouting, "Well, ye'd better get t'know, mudbrains!" He turned on Stringle, his leading officer. "Can't I leave ye alone fer a moment? Ye let the sh'ews git away, now they're in that place. Well, did ye try ter get 'em out, or did ye jus' sit on yore tails all night, waitin' fer me to do it for ye?"

Stringle nipped smartly out of kicking range. "We killed their chief, that Log a Lug sh'ew. They ran an' hid in Redwall. It wuz too hard t'get 'em out, we charged, but they beat us back. Not jus' sh'ews in there, Boss, they got streamdogs, 'edgepigs, treemouses, loads of 'em. Six of ours was slayed, an' more'n ten injured!"

Gruntan eyed the south ramparts sourly. "An' ye reckon they've got the place well guarded."

Stringle looked grim. "Nobeast could take Redwall!"

Gruntan's stomach wobbled as he gave a mirthless laugh. "Who told ye that? You lissen t'me, mate, there's more ways of killin' a mouse than tellin' it jokes until it dies laughin'."

Stringle scratched his tail. "Wot d'yer mean, Boss?"

Gruntan Kurdly was not prepared to give Stringle explanations, he waved a paw dismissively. "You go an' stay with the horde, tell the cooks to git my brekkist ready. Oh, an' ye'd best send out some scouts to take a look round that Abbey. May'aps one of 'em might 'ave the sense to find a way in." Gruntan continued to stare up at the Abbey walls, bright new prospects opening up before him. "Redwall, eh, now that's a place where I could be a real boss. Hah, wouldn't need no liddle boats then, I'd stop all me rovin' about. Oh aye, sittin' in a big, comfy chair, by a nice, warm fire on rainy days, Jus' givin' orders, an' eatin' vittles. Haharr, that'll be the life fer Gruntan Kurdly!"

Stringle dispatched eight scouts to sound out the perimeter of the Abbey. Two female Brownrats, Tantail and Dirril, were alloted to the west wall. Not wanting to walk along the path, which ran in front of the main gates, they chose to inspect the Abbey from the ditch. Ducking their heads, to avoid being seen from the walltops, the two Brownrats marched along the dry ditchbed, straight into Firty and Gerna. Unaware that they had company, both crewrats were digging into the ditchside, just as Vizka had ordered, trying to find a better tunnelling site. The Brownrats watched them in silence, until Firty stopped to mop a grimy paw across his brow. He turned and saw them, bringing his spearpoint to bear on the two big females, who stood head and shoulders over him and Gerna.

"Who are ya, an' worrya doin' 'ere?"

Dirril promptly kicked him in the stomach and wrenched the spear from his grasp. She pointed the weapon toward the Abbey. "Are you from in there?"

Gerna had been digging with his knife, and a sharpened stick. He looked up at the much larger Brownrats, gesturing uncertainly up the ditch with his blade. "Ya better not try anythin' wid us, we're wid Vizka Longtooth, an' he's cap'n of a big crew, see!"

Tantail advanced on him menacingly. "If'n ye don't come from inside o' that Abbey, we don't give a tailflick who y'are, 'cos we're part of Gruntan Kurdly's horde. Now give me dat blade!"

Gerna was scared, his voice trembled as he spoke. "No, I won't, dis is my knife."

With a swift move, Tantail knocked the knife from Gerna's paw. Grabbing the smaller rat by his ears, she

232

began pummelling him soundly. "Ye liddle snit, I'll teach ye to wave a knife at me!"

Firty protested as he tried to rise. "Yew leave 'im alone, wait'll Cap'n Vizka 'ears about dis. Git ya paws off 'im!"

All that this earned the unfortunate Firty was a severe beating from his own spearhaft. Both the Brownrats set about their victims, sniggering cruelly. "Cap'n Vizka, eh? Heehee, you've got us really frightened now, mate, he sounds a real terror, does Cap'n Vizka!"

Tantail had Gerna in a headlock, punctuating her remarks with stinging punches and slaps. "Never even heard of 'im. Lissen, snotnose, when ye get back to this Vizka idjit, tell 'im ye met up with two o' Gruntan Kurdly's Brownrats!"

Dirril had already broken the spearhaft over Firty's back, but she continued belabouring the helpless crewrat with the bottom half of it. "Take this message to yore cap'n. Tell 'im to run for 'is life, 'cos Kurdly's horde is here now!"

Back up at the start of the main excavation, Vizka Longtooth was in a calmer mood. The hole in the ditchside was actually beginning to take shape. It was almost the length of a stoat's body. He could tell this because there was a stoat digging in the hole, and just his tail was visible. He was working in there with a weasel, scrabbling out earth, which was being carried off and dumped by the rest of the team. The golden fox was sunning himself on the far ditchwall when Firty and Gerna staggered up. Nursing various injuries, the pair gasped out their report.

"Cap'n, we wuz attacked an' set on!"

"Dey jumped us an' battered us sumthin' fierce, Cap'n!"

Vizka held up a paw and they both fell silent. "Now, gimme straight answers! Who did this, Firty?"

The small crewrat was nursing a torn ear, he spat out a tooth before speaking. "Two big, brown ratwives I t'ink dey wuz, Cap'n!"

The workers had stopped to hear what was going on. When Firty said that he and Gerna had been beaten up by a pair of ratwives, they chuckled aloud. Vizka silenced them with a single glance. "Did ya tell 'em you wuz Vizka Longtooth's Sea Raiders?"

Clutching a broken tail, and squinting through a badly swollen eye, Gerna answered. "Aye, Cap'n we told 'em, but der one who was knockin' me round called me snotty nose, an' guess wot she said?"

Vizka shook his head. "I can't guess, so tell me."

Gerna told him, word for word. "She said, when ye gets back ter dis Vizka idjit, tell 'im ye met up wid two o' Gruntan Kurlie's Brownrats. Dat's wot she said!"

The golden fox picked up his mace and chain, addressing the twoscore vermin of the work detail. "Any of youse ever 'eard of a curly Brownrat?" There was a mass shaking of heads. Vizka began swinging his mace and chain, turning to Firty. "An' where'd ya run into dese two big, tough ratwives?"

Firty pointed. "Down der ditch a piece, jus' past der bend, Cap'n." As he spoke, the two Brownrats hove into view.

Whirling his weapon, Vizka broke into a run. "Let's gerrem! Chaaaarge!" Tantail and Dirril fled, with Vizka and twoscore of the *Bludgullet*'s crew hard on their tails.

Granspike Niblo was alone on the west wall, she hailed the defenders on the south walltop, shouting and waving her pinafore. "Skipper, hurry, there's something goin' on over here!"

Skipper came bounding across, with Barbowla and an assortment of otters, Guosim shrews and Redwallers following him. "We 'eard some shoutin' o'er there, marm, wot was it?"

Granspike's head only reached to just below the battlements. She stood on tip-paw, pointing. "Down there, in the

234

ditch I think. Somebeast shoutin' charge. I think it must've been vermin."

Barbowla looked down into the deserted ditch below. "Well, whoever it was has gone now, Skip. Brownrats, d'ye think?"

The otter chieftain leaned over the battlements. "Mayhaps 'twas, though it might've been them vermin who Orkwil said were chasin' him an' the badger. As y'say mate, they've gone now, so we might never know. Good riddance t'them, says I."

Some of the wallguards stayed to discuss the curious incident, but the majority began trooping over to the south walltop to patrol their former positions. Orkwil was still on the west wall, where he had been joined by Maudie.

The haremaid suddenly twitched her long, keen ears. "I say, what's that bloomin' rumblin' noise?"

The young hedgehog jiggled a paw in his ear. "What noise, I can't hear anyth . . ." His voice rose to an urgent bellow. "Here they come agin! Look!"

Everybeast hurried to the battlements, where they stood gaping in astonishment at the spectacle.

It was Vizka Longtooth and his twoscore vermin. This time they were the pursued, not the pursuers. Openmouthed, wide-eyed, they were running for their very lives, with most of Gruntan Kurdly's horde thundering along in their wake. A cloud of dust rose from the dried-up ditchbed, as the entire mad stampede rumbled by, heading north at top speed. The onlookers' heads swivelled from left to right, following the mad procession as it shot by, in a welter of noise, dust and churned-up weeds and vegetation. Then it was gone, north up the ditch and into the distance.

Orkwil was dancing up and down with excitement, shouting at everybeast. "That was Vizka Longtooth an' some of his crew!"

Barbowla chuckled as he blinked after the vanishing

dustcloud. "Aye, an' that was Kurdly's Brownrats after their blood. I wonder wot happened there?"

Foremole Burff was shaking with merriment. "Hurr-hurrhurr, who'd a-thought ee foebeasters wurrn't a-gettin' on together. Ho dearie oi!"

Abbot Daucus came skipping up the wallsteps, holding his robe like a mousewife with a trailing gown. "Will somebeast please let me in on the joke?" The Father Abbot's face lit up in a smile when he was told the news. Climbing onto a battlement, he peered northward, but both hunters and quarry were long gone. Daucus dusted off his paws. "Well well, what a lovely surprise, friends. I know this may not sound very charitable, but let me express the hope that the vermin wipe one another out, solving our problem once and for all."

Maudie helped the Abbot down from his perch. "Rather good, wot! I say, Father old thing, d'you think it'd be a jolly good idea to celebrate this cheerful moment, with something like a . . . er, er, what's the confounded word I'm lookin' for?"

The Abbot provided it. "A feast?"

Maudie shook his paw heartily. "What a wise mouse you are, t'be sure!"

Rangval seconded the haremaid slyly. "Ah sure, we'd all be delighted to attend yore feast, sir, 'tis a grand ould beast y'are for askin' us!"

Laughingly, the Abbot shook his head. "Well, I walked right into that one, didn't I? A feast, eh, well, why not? Orkwil, go and tell Friar Chondrus to get preparations under way. Skipper, where d'you suggest we hold this affair, Great Hall, or Cavern Hole maybe?"

The otter chieftain was ever practical. "I'd say somewhere outside, Father. We don't want t'be caught nappin' if'n there's vermin still abroad."

Maudie came up with a bright idea. "Why not have it up here on the walltop? Southwest corner, in fact. The scoff could be laid on the wallsteps, with us guard types up

236

here, an' other ranks, the oldsters an' young 'uns, down below on the lawn, by the jolly old pond, wot!"

"That's a great idea, then me'n you could have a little word t'gether, marm, about my sudden faintin' fit." The haremaid found herself staring into the angry eyes of the Guosim's new Log a Log, Osbil. Caught unawares, Maudie tried to woffle her way out of a quandary. "Wot, er, Osbil old lad, y'look remarkably chipper, wot! Well well, who'd have thought a stout chap like you would go into a faint, just like that, eh?"

Osbil's paw was on his rapier hilt as he replied. "Aye, just like that. Would ye like to try yore luck one more time, miz, then we'll see wot's faster, yore punch, or my blade-point?"

The smouldering resentment in Osbil's tone alerted Rangval, he stepped smartly between hare and shrew. "Ah now, don't be drawin' yore steel round here, bhoyo. Sure 'twas only to save ye bein' slaughtered by a rat horde that darlin' Maudie did wot she had to. Can ye not see that ye should be thankful to her?"

Now every eye was on Osbil and Maudie as they stood clear of the rogue squirrel. Keeping a watchful eye on the shrew's swordpaw, Maudie shrugged. "He's right, actually, I was only tryin' to save your life—"

Osbil interrupted her sharply. "Aye, an' shame me before all my Guosim, that's a great start for a new Log a Log. Tell me, would you be grateful to somebeast who knocked ye out with a trick punch, an' stopped ye avengin' the death of yore father by the vermin. Would ye?"

The full force of Osbil's predicament dawned upon Maudie; totally humbled, she bowed her head. "I did what I did with every good intention, but how can you forgive me? I wouldn't blame you for drawing your sword this instant, I acted like a thoughtless fool. If there is any way I can make up my stupid actions to you, just say the word, my friend."

Osbil, who had been expecting a challenge, was taken

237

aback by Maudie's sincere apology. He stood awkwardly, not knowing what to do. The situation was saved by Abbot Daucus, who joined the paws of them both.

"I think it was very big of Miz Maudie to apologize like that. If you could realise this, and forget your anger, maybe these Guosim may see that their Log a Log has the qualities of a good chieftain. Well, what do you say?"

Osbil gripped Maudie's paw. "Thanks for savin' my life, friend!"

The haremaid shook Osbil's paw in return. "Aye, an' thanks for sparin' my life, friend. We'll pay Kurdly's lot back tenfold before this business is done, believe me. Luglug wasn't only your dad, he was a fine leader, an' a good pal of mine. Remember, just say the jolly old word an' I'm with you 'til the end, sah!"

Rangval parted their paws, with an expression of comic concern on his face. "Ah sure, 'twas all well said an' grand, but can't we have a bit of an ould feast afore ye go chargin' off to pay back the Brownrats?"

25

Gruntan Kurdly was not built for speed. He stayed back in his position at the woodland fringe, facing the south Abbey wall. A dozen litter bearers, and the two scouts, Noggo and Biklo, were with him. The rest of the horde, led by Stringle, had gone off to chase the Sea Raiders. Gruntan lounged on the mossy sward, relishing a substantial clutch of partridge eggs, which the scouts had found in some long grass, not far from the ditchside. He swigged nettle beer from a small pail, wolfing down the hard-boiled eggs as fast as his lackeys could peel them. Wiping a grimy paw across his mouth, Gruntan belched happily. "By the 'ells teeth, I do like a good patteridge egg, more tasty than woodpigeons, eh, Laggle?"

The old female rat, who acted as his healer and physician, commented caustically, "I'll tell ye if'n I ever gits the chance to taste one. Sometimes I thinks yore goin' to grow feathers, ye eat so many eggs!"

Gruntan slung a pawful of crushed eggshells at Laggle. "Yew mind yore mouth, granny, go an' do summat useful, fetch me more beer. Noggo, cummere an' talk to me, tell me more about that raggedy bottomed bunch."

The scout had already told Gruntan all he knew, several

times, but he was obliged to recount it all again. "There wuz about twoscore of 'em, Boss. After our lot run 'em off, me'n Biklo took a look at wot they'd been up to. The main bunch had started diggin' an 'ole in the side o' the ditch, facin' Redwall."

Gruntan probed his snaggle teeth with a hooked claw, spitting out eggshell fragments. "Wot d'ye reckon they was up to?"

Noggo said what he had already surmised the first time. "Only one thing they coulda been doin', Boss, diggin' their way into the Abbey."

Again, Gruntan Kurdly became highly indignant. "But that's our Abbey, not theirs, we're the ones who's gonna take that place. Thud'n'blunder, the nerve o' those animals!" He took a deep swig from the beer pail, coughing and spluttering, as his resentment against Vizka Longtooth's crew heightened. "It ain't right, that's wot it ain't! By cracky, I 'opes Stringle collars a few o' those villains alive. I'll teach 'em to steal our Abbey, I'll skin 'em alive an' feed 'em their hides. Youse lot over there, can't ye even peel the shell off'n a patteridge's egg atween ye? I'm swallowin' more shell than egg. 'Ere, Laggle, lookit this 'un!" He tossed the boiled egg to the old healer, who immediately ate it whole. She shook her head.

"Nah, that wasn't fit for ye to eat, yore right. Git them eggs peeled proper, ye lazy lot!"

Gruntan moved back onto his litter, commenting sourly, "Ye can't git nuthin' done right these days. Noggo, wot's that noise, go an' find out. I dunno, can't even take a decent nap now, widout all kindsa funny noises."

Noggo saluted and crept off, following the direction of voices raised in song. It was coming from behind the southwest wall gable.

A small group of young moles were providing the bass line, swaying back and forth as they kept up a constant chant.

"Rubbledy dum be dum be dum,
rubbledy dum be dum be dum."

The main contingent, who were all young Redwallers,
marched in a circle, singing the verses aloud.

"I'll sit me down in my bestest gown,
an' joyfully I'll sing,
when a happy beast attends a feast,
he'll eat most anything!

"I think I'll start with a mushroom tart,
and some good Friar's cheese,
a pastie or two, or maybe a few,
and a salad if you please!

"O rumble tumble, fetch me a crumble,
that's what I'm yearnin' for,
if they're servin' second helpings,
I'll try to manage some more!

"Now bring me a pudd'n an' make it a good 'un
well-drenched with honey sauce,
an' a flagon o' rasp'berry cordial,
to swig whenever I pause!

"A trifle for me, a flan for you,
let's raise our tankards all,
what a happy day for a feast we say,
at the Abbey of Redwall!"

Before Noggo could return to make his report, Laggle
gazed wistfully in the direction of the Abbey. "Sounds like
they're 'avin' a feast in there, Boss."

Gruntan, who had been trying to ignore the song, found
his interest aroused at the mention of a feast. "Huh, I wonder wot they're 'avin' to eat. Did yew 'ear wot they wuz
sayin', Noggo?"

The scout, who was returning, began recounting various dishes. "Er, lessee, there wuz mushroom tart, cheese, pasties, salad, crumble, pudden with 'oney sauce . . . nyeeeerk!"

Gruntan had Noggo by the nose, twisting it viciously. "Yew rotten liddle fibber, nobeast has vittles as good as that!"

Laggle confirmed what Noggo had reported. "Noggo wasn't fibbin', I 'eard it meself, an' they was drinkin' raspberry cordial, an' scoffin' flans an' trifles. Me gob was waterin' jus' lissenin' to 'em!"

Gruntan released the scout's nose, turning on the old healer. "Then ye must be goin' soft in the 'ead, if'n yew believes all that. Huh, all sorts o' fancy rubbish like crumbles an' trifles. Did they say they was 'avin' 'ard-boiled eggs, betcha they never?"

Noggo kept out of Gruntan's reach. "No, Boss, they never said nothin' about 'ard-boiled eggs."

Gruntan Kurdly spat out an eggshell fragment contemptuously. "Hah, see, I told ye. A feast ain't no good widout 'ard-boiled eggs. Fetch me some nice, soft moss to plug me lugs with, I needs me nap!"

Vizka Longtooth's second in command, the weasel Magger, and the rest of *Bludgullet*'s crew were enjoying the good life in North Mossflower woodlands. They had brought grog from the ship, and gathered eggs, fish, birds, fruit and berries locally. Magger had become quite popular with the vermin crew, he was easygoing, and not given to making the others fear him, like Vizka did.

An air of enjoyment and relaxation pervaded the woodland camp. After grubbing about the cold seas for seasons, suffering hard chores and short rations, the warm climate and sheltered surroundings suited the vermin fine. Nobeast was overeager for the return of their captain, that would only mean more discipline, marching, orders and fighting, to fulfill the golden fox's ambitions. Accordingly they lay about, taking their ease, and enjoying the welcome respite whilst they were able.

Two shipmates, a stoat called Saltear and a ferret named Ragchin, were wandering along the ditchbed, picking blackberries. They had almost filled Ragchin's floppy old hat with the fruit, and were sitting on the side of the path, debating what use the berries might be put to.

Saltear sorted out a large juicy one, musing, "Wodja t'ink, Rag, we could make grog outta dese."

Ragchin shook his head. "Nah, takes too long, an' de uthers would only drink it on us. Worrabout cookin' 'em up in a skilly'n'duff?"

Saltear spat into the ditch, not relishing the idea. "Dat Magger'd soon yaffle it down, 'ave ya seen 'im eatin' skilly'n'duff, 'e's like a wildbeast!" He popped the berry he had been holding into his mouth, grinning. "Why don't we jus' eat 'em ourselves?"

Ragchin immediately grabbed a pawful, stuffing them into his mouth, and wolfing them down. "Yore right, Salt, it wuz us wot picked 'em, eh!"

Purple juice was running down both their chins as they devoured the blackberries. Saltear suddenly paused, a berry halfway to his lips, he held up a paw. "Ahoy, kin yew 'ear sumthin', thunder, I think?"

Ragchin stood up, gazing at the sky. "Thunder, on a day like dis, nah, give over, mate. . . ." Then he saw the dust-cloud rising in the south, it was coming from the ditchbed. He pointed. "Dat's wot's makin' der noise, lookit."

Saltear joined him, they stood watching the rising dust-cloud awhile, until a figure at the head of it came into view.

Ragchin could hardly believe his eyes, as more shapes became visible. Grabbing his shipmate's tattered jerkin, he fled, pulling him along. "It's der cap'n, bein' chased by an army o' durty, big Brownrats, mus' be a t'ousand of 'em. Come on!"

The two vermin came hurtling into camp. Magger and some other crew vermin had heard the rumbling, they were looking uneasy. Saltear and Ragchin shot past Magger, calling as they hurried to hide in the woodland depths, "Cap'n Vizka's bein' chased by t'ousands o' big rats, real big 'uns, dey're 'eaded dis way!"

Vizka Longtooth and the remains of his tunnelling party were running for their lives. Over a dozen of the *Bludgullet*'s crew were lying behind them, slain and trampled by Kurdly's horde. Though his breath was coming in ragged bursts, the golden fox drove himself on relentlessly, propelled by naked terror. The Brownrats pounded along in his wake, their weird, paint-striped bodies strung with necklets and bracelets made from the bones of past victims, waving clubs and spears.

Vizka plunged onward, out of the ditchbed, and into the woodlands. Magger and the rest of *Bludgullet*'s crew were to be his hope of salvation from the foebeasts. If he could make it to the camp, he would repel the Brownrat horde with the aid of his own considerable numbers. The Brownrats would be hit by a sudden retaliation from the vermin Sea Raiders. Behind him he heard one of his crew give an agonised screech as he fell victim to a stoneheaded axe. The golden fox leapt into the camp, his paws kicking up ashes from campfire embers as he shouted, "Magger, rally der crew! Magger . . . Magger?"

The realisation that he had arrived at an empty camp hit Vizka Longtooth like a thunderbolt. There was nothing for it but to keep running. Deserted by his own crew, traitors and cowards who had fled their captain! The golden fox sucked in air, running even faster, this time spurred on by rage. He was a fool to have left Magger in charge back at camp. Ducking and weaving around the trunks of mighty oaks, elms, conifers and other woodland giants, Vizka began outpacing his pursuers, their sounds grew faint in his wake.

He was in the heart of ancient Mossflower now. Sunlight rarely penetrated the overgrown tree canopy, it was a world of misty green gloom. The golden fox's eyes searched the area, he knew it was not possible to run ceaselessly. There had to be a refuge, someplace to hide. . . .

There it was! A massive, old beech tree, its huge, knotted trunk supporting widespread boughs, branches and foliage. Resting against it was a small spurge laurel, which had perished from lack of sunlight. Vizka Longtooth went up the laurel, into the lower forks of the beech, with all the agility of a cat. A lifetime spent on shipboard left him no stranger to scaling, after all the masts and rigging he had encountered.

Leaning down, he shoved at the slender, dead laurel, watching as it fell flat on the leafy, woodland floor. He went nimbly upward into the high reaches of the beech, choosing a wide, well-foliaged limb. Vizka settled himself there, knowing he was completely invisible from below. He lay there, tongue lolling, as he panted and gasped, relaxing his body, whilst his mind worked frantically, planning and scheming.

The golden fox was not a beast to be taken lightly. It would not be the first time he had snatched victory from the jaws of defeat.

It was night before the Brownrats ceased searching the woodlands for Vizka's crewbeasts. They retired to the camp, formerly set up by Magger, where they relit the fire and settled down to consume what food remained there. Stringle sat watching Tantail and Dirril, they were boiling a variety of eggs, which the *Bludgullet*'s crew had gathered. Stringle was quite pleased with himself.

"Haharr, lookit that now! Woodpigeon, coot, plover an' quail eggs. Ole Kurdly'd enjoy that lot, eh?" He watched Tantail and Dirril nodding their heads ruefully, then Stringle laughed aloud. "Hohoho, mates, well, Kurdly ain't gittin' none, 'cos we're gonna eat 'em ourselves!"

Giggling like three Dibbuns, the Brownrats began shelling and gobbling down the eggs. Tantail found the partially full keg of ship's grog, she sampled it, drawing in a deep breath. "Whfaw, this is the stuff t'put a curl in yore tail!"

Soon they were all enjoying the fiery liquor, laughing and gurgling uproariously at Dirril's imitation of Gruntan Kurdly, which was fairly accurate. She stuck out her stomach, belching cavernously. "Ahoy there, peel me more eggs, ye swabs, or ye'll find yoreselves sufferin' an attack o' the Kurdlys!"

Stringle swigged more grog, wiping tears of merriment from his eyes. "Heeheehee, the ole lardbucket, let 'im wait, we'll camp here an' go back tomorrer, mates. Make the best of it while ye can. Ahoy there, wot's this?"

A band of returning Brownrats swaggered in, dragging a prisoner. It was Magger, with his paws bound behind him and a rope halter about his neck. Their leader, Bladj, gave the weasel a kick, sending him sprawling close to the fire.

"We collared one of 'em, Cap'n, guess wot 'is name is, Maggot, ain't that a daft 'andle?"

Stringle placed his footpaw on Magger's cheek, forcing the terrified weasel's face into the dirt. "Maggot, eh, yore an ugly-lookin' cove. Wot'll we do with ye, Maggot, let y'live, or slay ye?"

Magger gazed fearfully up at the savage, painted face of the Brownrat captain, stammering, "Let me live, sir, I'm no 'arm ter anybeast!"

Tantail tickled his nose with a knifepoint, watching him flinch. "An 'armless maggot, eh, where's yore boss, Fizker summat, that's 'is name, ain't it?"

Magger pronounced his captain's name properly. "It's Vizka Longtooth, an' I don't know where 'e is."

Stringle took a burning stick from the fire. Magger yelped, arching his back, as the Brownrat ran the flaming timber down it, cautioning him, "Then ye'd better find out where this Vizka Longtooth is, if'n ye want to live. Is 'e alive or dead?"

Taking what he thought was the easy option, Magger whined, "Prob'ly dead by now, I t'ink."

Stringle took Tantail's knife, he held it against Magger's throat. "Prob'ly dead ye think, wot sort o' talk's that? I'll tell ye wot, shall I slit yore gizzard an' see if I think yore prob'ly dead, eh? Now, let me set ye straight about all this, Maggot. I can't go back to Gruntan Kurdly an' tell 'im 'is enemy's 'prob'ly' dead. My boss is a Brownrat warlord, wot 'e wants to 'ear is that ole Vizka Longtooth is stiffer'n a cold frog wot's been flattened by a fallin' tree in a snow-storm. There ain't no prob'lys with Kurdly. So I'm goin' to ask ye jus' once more. Is Vizka dead?"

Magger knew his life depended on the answer, he replied without hesitation. "He's dead!"

Stringle smiled and stroked his captive's head. "Well said, good ole Maggot! Now, tell me agin, but this time say it was me wot killed 'im."

Magger was past caring about the truth, he would have said anything Stringle wanted. "Aye, Vizka's dead, an yore der one wot slayed 'im!"

Stringle waggled the knifepoint close to Magger's eye-ball. "Very good! Now don't yew ferget it, keep sayin' it to yoreself, Maggot, ye'll live long'n' 'appy if ye do."

26

At about the same time the Brownrats had been pursuing Vizka up the ditch, Gorath opened his eyes. The young badger felt strangely calm. There was a little molemaid sitting by the bed, watching him. Raising his head slightly, he smiled at her. "Hello, what's your name, miss?"

She fell from the bedside stool, and shot up, throwing her small, flowered apron over her face as she fled. "Oi'm Dawbul, zurr, you'm ascuze oi, mus' be fetchen Sisarta, zurr!" Gorath could hear her cries as she tottered downstairs. "Eem gurt badgerer bee's wokened, Sisarta, 'urry!"

Gorath sat up. At first he felt dizzy, but the sensation died off as he breathed deeply. He had no idea where he was, except that it was someplace within Redwall Abbey. How long had he been here? Within moments he heard a rush of paws pounding the stairs. Next thing he knew, the little sickbay room was full of creatures. Sister Atrata hurried to his side, he sat quite still as she checked him out.

After awhile, the Sister announced to the visitors, "At least he's over the fever, thank goodness. How do you feel, Gorath?"

The young badger touched the deep, flame-shaped scar on his forehead, and spoke quietly. "I feel hungry, Sister."

Rangval muttered to Maudie in an audible whisper,

"Hungry, is he? Faith, an' 'tis goin' to keep the ould cook busy vittlin' that bhoyo up. Will ye look at the size o' the beast, shure I'd sooner be feedin' him for a day than for a season, that's for certain!" For some obscure reason, the roguish squirrel's remark amused Gorath, it made him chuckle.

Abbot Daucus observed the pleasure it gave all the Red-wallers, to see a happy smile on the face of their guest. The Abbot winked at Orkwil, indicating Gorath with a gesture. "Tell your friend why he's fortunate to wake up hungry at this time."

Orkwil grabbed Gorath's huge paw, and started tugging him out of bed. "'Cos we're havin' a feast out in the grounds, d'ye want to come, mate?"

Gorath allowed Maudie and several others to heave him upright, he shuffled once, then regained his balance. "It would be a pleasure to attend your feast, that's if it isn't too much trouble."

Skipper threw a paw around the big badger's shoulder. "Too much trouble, matey? Hahaarharharrrr!" Everybeast pointed their paws at Gorath, breaking out into an old Abbey feasting song.

"To the feast! To the feast!
Now don't be shy, goodbeast!

"Yore doubly warm an' welcome here,
don't stand on ceremony,
we've set a place so never fear,
just come along with me.

"To the feast! To the feast!
Now don't be shy, goodbeast!

"Ho move ye up an' make a space,
let our friend sit at table,
to drink the best our cellars brew,
an' eat all that he's able.

249

"To the feast! To the feast!
Now don't be shy, goodbeast!

"Come please us with yore company,
pray bring yore appetite,
sing loud if you've a mind to sing,
or dance throughout the night.

"To the feast! To the feast!
Now don't be shy, goodbeast!"

Surrounded by happy Redwallers, Gorath allowed
himself to be led downstairs, out of the Abbey building. It
was a perfect summer afternoon outdoors, with a gentle
breeze, and the sun beaming from a cloudless blue sky.
Maudie and Orkwil led him to the tables, which had been
placed on the lawn betwixt the Abbey pond and the
south wall.

Barbowla called down to them from the walltop, "Bring
the big feller up here, mates, those little 'uns will pester
the life out of him down there, that's if'n Gorath can manage the wallsteps."

Dibbuns, otterbabes and tiny Guosim infants were already clamouring around the big, young badger. Some had
perched upon his footpaws, and were beginning to climb
upward. Foremole Burff and Granspike Niblo disentangled
them from Gorath, reproaching the babes.

"Yurr, coom off'n ee pore beast, get ee daown, oi says!"

"You'm likkle villyuns, ee'm badgerer loike t'be toppled
o'er with you'm a clamberin' on 'im loike h'ants!"

Maudie took Gorath's paw. "I say, old lad, Barbowla's
right, are you able to manage the wallsteps, wot?"

The badger gave a rumbling chuckle. "I might just be
able to, if there's food up there."

There was indeed food to be had on the ramparts, the
best Gorath had ever tasted. Seating himself on the top
step, he allowed Benjo Tipps to press a tankard of finest

October Ale upon him. This was followed by Friar Chondrus, who placed a loaded tray close to Gorath's paw.

"This is one o' my mushroom an' leek pasties, I hope ye like it. There's some fresh made cheesebread, an' summer vegetable soup. Oh, an' a portion of tater, onion an' carrot bake to nibble afore dessert. Eat 'earty now, young sir!"

Gorath was joined by Orkwil and Maudie. As he ate with an astounding appetite, the young hedgehog and the haremaid related how Vizka Longtooth and some of his vermin had been chased off by the Brownrats.

Gorath expressed concern over the incident. "I hope Longtooth doesn't run off altogether, I've got a score to settle with that fox!"

Orkwil took a bite of pastie, fanning a paw across his mouth to cool it. "First you've got to get yoreself fit an' well, mate, then ye can think about slayin' yore enemies. I wouldn't worry too much over Longtooth, he'll come slinkin' back around Redwall sooner or later."

Rangval had been sitting close by, eavesdropping on the conversation. He called over to Maudie, "Why don't ye save a few of those good ould uppercut punches for the fox, if'n ye meet him, miss?"

Orkwil replied for the haremaid. "You don't trade punches with a vermin like Longtooth, have ye seen that wicked-lookin' mace an' chain he carries? One swipe o' that would be all it takes!"

Maudie was not impressed. "He could jolly well swipe with his mace all flippin' season, but he wouldn't touch a hair of me if I didn't want the rotter to."

Gorath looked at her curiously. "How so?"

Maudie took a kerchief from her sleeve. Spreading it on the walkway, she placed her footpaws on it, one slightly in front of the other. Then she gave forth a challenge. "Righty-o chaps, anybeast wants to try landin' a bloomin' punch on me, step up. I won't attempt to hit back, word of honour an' all that, wot!"

251

No sooner was the challenge out than Log a Log Osbil accepted it. He leapt up, paws clenched tight, milling about in small, businesslike circles. As he stood in front of Maudie, Osbil gave her a sly wink.

"My turn this time, marm, ye'll feel how hard I can punch. Are ye good an' ready?"

Maudie winked cheerily back at her adversary. "Ready as I'll ever be, bucko, you punch away whenever y'feel like. I won't move from this kerchief."

A crowd gathered along the walltop to watch. Some of Osbil's Guosim friends shouted out, "Go on, Chief, give 'er a good 'un!"

"Aye, an' belt 'er harder'n she hit you!"

Osbil never hesitated, he swung a big roundhouse right. Maudie seemed just to sway, ever so slightly. The punch spun Osbil around with its force, but it never touched the haremaid. The Guosim chieftain looked astonished. Maudie grinned at him. "Nice try, old chap!"

Osbil gritted his teeth and threw a huge uppercut. The haremaid bent gracefully backward, letting her opponent strike air. Osbil came back with a flurry of punches. Maudie evaded every one of them, swaying left, right, forward and back, with a lithe ease.

The Guosim were yelling encouragement to Osbil.

"Give 'er the ole one-two, Chief!"

"Try hookin' with yore left!"

"Go for the breadbasket, knock the wind out of 'er!"

Osbil tried them all, and a few more beside, but to no avail. Maudie could not be touched. He gave up and stood there, head bowed, panting heavily. Maudie folded up her kerchief, throwing a paw about Osbil's shoulders.

"Come on, friend, let's have a jolly old tankard of the good October together, what d'ye say?"

The shrew chieftain grinned ruefully. "How did ye learn to do that, mate?"

Rangval bounded between them, hopping about and

ducking. "Practice, me ould tater, that's how ye learn t'do anythin' well. Go on, go on, try to hit me, I dare ye!"

Osbil merely held out his clenched paw, and Rangval danced straight into it, knocking himself flat. Everybeast roared laughing, except Rangval, who sat up holding his chin. "I took lots o' bobbin' lessons, but none on the weavin'. So I bobbed when I should've weaved, an' that's how ye got me. Oh, an' then there's the duckin' an' divin' lessons, I'll have to start takin' those soon. Then I'll wipe the smiles off yore gobs. Maudie, me darlin', how's about givin' me a few tips?"

The haremaid issued a generous offer. "Why, certainly, old top, in fact I'll give anybeast a list of hints. Who wants to learn, any of you chaps?" Virtually everybeast on the ramparts, young and old, began clamouring for instructions. Maudie held up her paws for silence before giving them the benefit of her experience.

"Right, listen up now, chaps. My old pa was the finest boxin' hare ever to come out of Salamandastron. He could box the blinkin' whiskers off the best of 'em, an' that jolly well includes me. From the time I was only a totterin' leveret, he had me skippin' a rope an' singin' this song. I'll show you, who's got a piece of rope that I can borrow, wot?"

Abbot Daucus untied his white habit cord. "How would this do, miss?"

Maudie tried a few practice skips. "Nicely thank you, Father. Right, here we jolly well go!" She started with slow hops, twirling the rope easily as she broke into the song taught by her father in bygone seasons.

"Duck an' weave an' weave an' duck,
you'll learn the noble art,
don't lash out an' trust to luck,
use science, skill and heart.
Make your paws show him who's boss.

253

Hook jab! Punch jab! Feint jab cross!
Show commonsense, have confidence,
keep one eye on that blighter,
do what he least expects you to,
an' you'll become a fighter.

"Make your paws show him who's boss.
Hook jab! Punch jab! Feint jab cross!
Sway an' bob an' bob an' sway,
an' keep your guard up tight,
tuck in that chin, aye that's the style
the way you learn to fight.
Make your paws show him who's boss.
Hook jab! Punch jab! Feint jab cross!"

Maudie repeated the last two lines several times, skipping so fast that the rope became a blur. She finished to enthusiastic applause.

Abbot Daucus retrieved his habit cord, commenting wryly, "If they're all as good as you at Salamandastron, I wonder why they want a badger, you've got a real skill there, miss. Oh dearie me, it looks like you've started something, just look at that lot!"

Everybeast, including the Dibbuns and old ones, down on the lawn was using habit cords, belts, even pieces of trailing vine, as they leapt wildly about. Benjo Tipps, who was far too weighty for such exercise, donated his belt to a pair of shrewbabes. He chuckled as they skipped awkwardly off. "We'll soon be havin' an Abbeyful o' boxin' beasts. Lookit ole Foremole Burff there!" The mole chieftain had forgotten the words, but he bounced about solemnly, chanting. "Duck bobby duck bobby, 'ook duck bob!"

Maudie covered her eyes with a paw. "Good grief, if my old pa could see that, he'd have a flippin' purple fit, wot!"

The feast continued on into the warm summer evening, with other songs, dances and games taking the place of skipping. It was turning dusk as Maudie returned to the walltops, after helping to carry up more food from the kitchens. She plumped down beside Friar Chondrus, accepting a beaker of strawberry fizz from him. The haremaid cast a glance at Gorath's empty seat, calling to Orkwil, "I say, old lad, where's our big feller got to?"

The young hedgehog shrugged, but Skipper nodded toward the Abbey building. "Said he was goin' back to the sickbay to put his paws up."

Sister Atrata nodded sagely. "Probably the best thing for him, after recovering from the fever. Orkwil, why don't you and Miss Maudie go and check on your friend. Gorath might not know his way back to the infirmary."

Rangval joined them, rubbing his stomach ruefully. "Sure, a stretch o' the paws might do me a bit o' good, I think I overdid the ould feastin' a touch!"

Orkwil prodded the rogue squirrel's distended midriff. "Overdid the feastin' a touch, did you say? I think you must have a heavier touch than a regiment of starved squirrels, it's a wonder you haven't burst!"

Rangval wrinkled his nose at Maudie. "Faith, will ye lissen t'the creature, I suppose ye'll begrudge me second helpin's when we return t'the feast!"

As dusk darkened to night, lanterns were lit on the ramparts. Down on the lawn some of the elders lit a fire, to roast some of last autumn's chestnuts, which Marja Dubbidge had stored in the belltower. Skipper Rorc was helping Barbowla and Kachooch to carry sleeping Dibbuns up to the dormitory, when they met Maudie and her two friends hurrying down the stairs into Great Hall. The otter chieftain stood aside to let them pass. "Where are ye off to in such a rush, missie?"

The haremaid's jaw was set in a grim line as she explained. "We're looking for Gorath, he's not in his room."

Barbowla shrugged. "It's a warm night, Maudie, yore big badger might've chose to sleep out in the open. Maybe the orchard, or over by the pond."

Orkwil shook his head. "Then why would he want to take Tung, his big pitchfork, with him? It ain't in the room, an' Gorath's not in his bed. I'm worried!"

"Owow, git yer paws off me, I ain't done nothin'!"

Benjo Tipps pushed the surly watervole through the doorway. The burly Cellarhog had him tight by one ear.

Skipper Rorc eyed him with dislike. "Ahoy, Benjo, where'd ye come across this mis'rable sneak?"

The Cellarhog gestured with his free paw. "By the little north wallgate, Skip, he tried t'run off but I collared him smartish."

The vole, who had his head bandaged due to his fall from the walltop, squealed unmercifully. "Yeek, yowch! Lemme go, yore 'urtin' my wound!"

Benjo gave his ear an extra tweak, and spoke severely. "If'n ye don't tell us wot you were up to at the wallgate, yore in danger of losin' a lug. Now speak!"

The vole's explanation was a mixture of indignation and self-pity. "I went up t'the healers room, to see if'n that Atrata mouse'd change the dressin' on me injury, but she wasn't there. Suddenly I was grabbed, by that giant stripedog. He 'eld a big pitchfork to me stummick. I thought he was goin' to kill me!"

Orkwil had not liked the vole from their first encounter. He expressed this in no uncertain terms. "Listen, sourface, I'll kill ye meself if'n ye don't tell us where Gorath went. Get on with it!"

Hanging on to Benjo's paw, to ease the pressure on his ear, the vole explained rapidly. "The stripedog said he had business with the golden fox. He made me take 'im t'the north wallgate, said I wasn't to tell nobeast, an' told me to lock the gate after he'd left. So I did, an' that's when this fat spikepig laid paws on me. Yeeeek, yore draggin' me ear off, leggo leggo!"

Benjo squeezed the ear harder. "Tell me, slutchface, who was the fat hedgepig that laid paws on ye? I can't see no fat hedgepig round here, can you, Skip?"

256

The otter chieftain scratched his rudder thoughtfully. "We ain't never had a fat 'edgepig at Redwall, only a fine, big, 'andsome Cellarhog!"

The vole caught on fast. "Please sir, ye fine, big, handsome Cellarhog, release me, I beg ye!"

Benjo flung the vole from him contemptuously. "You've overstayed yore welcome at this Abbey, ye wretch. If'n I see ye around here come dawnlight, I'll throw ye from the walltops. Now get out o' my sight!"

As the vole slunk away, Skipper addressed Maudie. "Looks like yore badger friend's gone, miss, an' there's nought ye can do about it."

The haremaid looked at the otter. "Why so?"

Skipper gestured to the woodlands outside the walls. "Mossflower's teemin' with Kurdly's mob, an' a vermin shower o' Sea Raiders, far too dangerous for a young 'un like you t'be wanderin' about round the trees."

Maudie treated the otter to an icy stare. "I have only two words to say t'you, sah. Pish an' tush!"

Skipper looked nonplussed. "An' wot's that supposed t'mean?"

Rangval drew a dagger from his belt and twirled it skillfully. "Ah, shure, it means that darlin' Maudie has a mind of her own, bucko. She's goin' out there to find that great, ould lump of a badger. Oh, an' I'm the very beast who'll be goin' with her!"

Orkwil seconded the rogue squirrel promptly.

"Gorath's my friend, too, count me in, Miz Maudie!"

Skipper shrugged and heaved a gruff sigh. "I'll get some volunteers from the Guosim an' come along with ye. Barbowla, are you game for this?"

Maudie interrupted. "Not possible. I'm afraid, Skip, you'll need every beast available to defend these bloomin' walls if there's a vermin attack."

Abbot Daucus, who had wandered up, and eavesdropped on the conversation, stepped forward. "She's right, Skip, besides, I think a few might accomplish more than a whole band of Redwallers out in the woodlands. When do you three plan on leaving?"

Rangval sheathed his blade. "Soon as we can, Father. Now would be a good time, whilst the ould feast is rattlin' on atop o' the walls, an' the countryside's nice'n'quiet out there. Sure, nobeast'd notice us slippin' off quietlike."

The Abbot bowed slightly. "As you wish. Take some provisions from the kitchens, and whatever weapons you may come across. Though we're not greatly stocked with arms at Redwall. Go, and good luck to you. Maudie, should you find Gorath, would you be so kind as to bring him back to the Abbey, if only for a short visit and a brief farewell? Before you persuade him to be spirited off to Salamandastron?"

The haremaid curtsied elegantly. "It'd be my pleasure, Father Abbot. Right, stir your stumps, you chaps, quick's the word an' sharp's the action, wot!"

The Abbot accompanied them to the kitchen, where an obliging old molemum packed three small haversacks with foodstuffs enough to last several days. Maudie seldom carried a weapon, Rangval had all the arms he needed, and Orkwil still carried the knife and club he had taken from the vole. The trio had no need to go looking for more protection. As they were passing through Great Hall, Orkwil crossed to the alcove where the great tapestry hung. The Abbot commented to Rangval and Maudie, "He's probably taking his leave of our Abbey Champion."

The haremaid followed the young hedgehog. "A jolly good idea, from what I've heard of Martin the Warrior, think I'll pay my respects, too, wot!"

Before they reached the alcove, Orkwil's shout of alarm echoed around the vaulted hall. Rangval sprang forward, shouting, "Orkwil, what is it?"

The young hedgehog staggered toward them, dragging with him the limp form of Sister Atrata. Abbot Daucus intercepted him, gently he placed the Sister on the ancient floorstones, supporting her head as he made a rapid examination.

"She's taken a heavy blow to the back of her head, maybe she was pushed, and struck one of the columns."

Maudie knelt by the frail figure of Redwall's healer. "But why? She never hurt anybeast, the Sister was devoted to healing others. Who could have done this?"

Orkwil cried out, his voice rising to an angry shout. "Look, Martin's sword has been taken, an' I'll wager it was that vole who did it. The Sister must've tried to stop him!"

Maudie stared at the spot on the wall where the great sword had been mounted. "Good grief, you're right, old lad, it's not long since Benjo exiled him from the Abbey. He must have come straight here, committed the crimes and left pretty quick."

Rangval started toward the door. "Aye, well, the blaggard might've left Redwall, but he can't have gotten too far yet. Let's get after him!"

The rogue squirrel and Maudie sped off. Orkwil was last to leave Great Hall. He stood in front of the tapestry for a brief moment, gazing into the eyes of Martin's likeness, which was the centre of the wondrous fabric. The young hedgehog's voice was steely and resolute. "Martin, sir, I'll bring your sword back to Redwall, and I'll make that coward pay. I give you my promise I will." Orkwil Prink bowed swiftly and departed.

Abbot Daucus called for assistance to help with the unconscious Sister Atrata. "Our friend has been cruelly taken from us." He turned back to the picture of Martin the Warrior, his voice shaken by the violence in his beloved Abbey. "Rest assured, friend, Orkwil Prink will keep his promise."

27

A tranquil summer morn reigned over Mossflower. Dewdrops trembled, like tiny crystal pears, from bough and fern, birdsong echoed melodiously over the woodlands. Berries blushed from ruby to deeper purple as they matured, and flowers of the forest burgeoned into full blossom. However, all of this serenity was soon to be shattered. Gorath the Flame was on the vengeance trail.

The blood of berserk warriors coursed hotly through his veins, Gorath felt totally renewed as he stalked the woodland tracts. The sickness had left him, he was lean and gaunt, yes, but his dark eyes glittered with a frightening intensity. The big badger held his pitchfork, Tung, at the ready, as he passed, silent as a summer breeze, through the countryside.

Vizka Longtooth's deputy, the weasel Magger, had passed an unnerving night amid his captors. He was fearful of the Brownrats, they were big, painted savages decked out barbarously with bones, they treated their prisoners roughly. Their captain, Stringle, roped Magger's neck to a stake in the ground. He lay there helpless, dreading whatever fate lay in store.

The weasel Sea Raider had convinced himself that

the Brownrats were cannibals. Often in passing they would kick, slap or pinch him, sometimes terrifying him, with a hungry leer. However, for the moment they were satisfying their hunger by breakfasting on the remainder of the stores left behind by the vermin crew of the *Bludgullet*.

Stringle had commandeered the dregs of the grog barrel, he sat over Magger, gnawing at a roasted trout. As if suddenly noticing his captive, he winked at Magger. "Don't fret, matey, we'll soon be movin' out. Ye must be 'ungry, d'ye want some o' this?" He held the half-eaten fish in front of the weasel's nose.

Magger managed to mutter humbly, "Aye, sir."

Stringle dealt him a smack across the muzzle with the trout. He laughed, calling to a nearby Brownrat, "Ahoy, Bladj, this pore beast ain't 'ad no brekkist, wasn't you in charge o' dishin' out the vittles?"

Bladj was a wicked-looking piece of work, he seized Magger by the jaw, pulling him close and mocked the hapless prisoner. "I musta forgot that ye wanted brekkist, I 'opes you'll accept me apologies. I'll wager ye've not even 'ad a drink, 'ere, mate, try a liddle punch." He punched the weasel's snout so hard that it sent bells ringing in Magger's ears. Bladj patted his head. "Would ye like some more, or I can give ye lashins o' stick, a nice slap up soup an' a kick bottom pudden?"

Magger had the good sense to refuse. "No sir, der punch wuz enuff!"

Bladj communicated his reply to Stringle. "Sez he don't want no more brekkist, Cap'n."

Stringle smiled indulgently. "That's me trouble, I always spoils prisoners. Maggot, was that wot yore name is?"

Magger nodded dutifully, not wanting to disturb his captor's expansive mood.

Stringle untied the rope from the stake, passing it to Bladj. "Cummon, Maggot, we'll take ye to see yore Uncle Kurdly."

The Brownrat horde was moving out of the camp at a leisurely pace, when a horrible gurgling scream rent the morning air. Everybeast froze, Bladj cast an uncertain glance at the woodlands. "Wot'n the name o' 'ellgates was that?"

Stringle shrugged. "'Ow should I know, sounded like somebeast yowlin' t'me. It came from over yon, by that ole tree, go an' see wot it was."

Bladj did not sound too eager. "Wot, me?"

The captain turned his spearpoint threateningly toward Bladj. "Aye, you! Go an' see who's doin' the screamin' . . ." As Stringle spoke, another bloodcurdling scream rang out from the same direction as the first. This was followed by a great, roaring shout.

"Eulaliiiiaaaaa!"

Two slain Brownrat carcasses came hurtling out of the tree cover. As they flopped on the grass, another death screech cut the air, followed by a thunderous bellow. "Eulaliiiiaaaaa!"

En masse, the Brownrat horde turned and fled the scene. Stringle stood uncertainly for a moment, his voice hesitant. "But, but we don't know who . . ."

"Eulaliiiiaaaaa!"

The Brownrat captain fled after his command.

Completely forgotten in the panic, Magger fled straight up the nearest tree and clung motionless amid the foliage. He saw Gorath come striding out of woodlands onto the trail of the departing Brownrats, teeth bared, breathing like a bellows, eyes ablaze. Magger held his breath, not daring to move a muscle. The weasel had seen Gorath kill somebeast before, aboard the *Bludgullet*, he knew what he was seeing now, a badger in the throes of Bloodwrath. Magger stayed where he was, watching in horrified awe, until the huge, pitchfork-wielding beast was out of sight. Climbing swiftly down from his perch, Magger fled in the opposite direction.

Deeper into the woodland, another was also descending out of a tree. Vizka Longtooth had caught sight of several *Bludgullet* crew vermin, they were creeping cautiously about midst the tree trunks, trying to stay clear of Brownrats, whilst they foraged for food. Vizka concealed himself behind a fallen elm trunk, he watched, and listened, gleaning information from them.

Firty and Jungo were digging out some edible roots, debating as to whether they really were edible. "Dese looks alright, mate, wotjer t'ink?"

Jungo sniffed them, pulling a face. "Huh huh, dey smells a bit strong, but I s'pose dey'll do."

The ferret Ragchin upbraided Jungo. "Ahoy, don't yew be eatin' dem, 'tis share'n'share alike, chuck 'em wid der rest!"

Jungo looked highly indignant. "I wuzzent eatin' dem, I wuz only smellin' 'em. Any'ow, who made yew der cap'n, Raggy?"

Ragchin had made himself a spear, by tying a broken knifeblade onto a pole. He leaned on it nonchalantly. "Ain't no more cap'ns round 'ere now, but I'm in charge of youse lot, Glurma said so. Cummon, let's git dis lot back t'camp, so's Glurma kin cook dem up."

Gathering up their forage, the score of crewbeasts stole off through the trees, with Vizka quietly following them. The golden fox did not want to show himself, until he knew which way the land lay.

It was a day for wanderers and ramblers, in that region of Mossflower, one of whom was particularly pleased with himself. The watervole had come upon a magpie, it was fluttering feebly on the ground, dragging one wing, which was obviously injured. The vole finished the magpie's flutters, with a single thrust of Martin's sword. Gathering dry moss, he struck flint to the legendary steel, and soon had a small fire burning in the lee of a grassy knoll. Spitting the magpie carcass on a green twig, he set it over the flames, and settled down to admire the blade he had stolen.

The vole was ignorant of the sword's history, or value, to him it was merely something to replace the dagger which Orkwil had taken from him. Granted, it was a fine piece of work, razor-sharp, and perfectly balanced, but a sword was only a big, useful knife to the mean-spirited stream-dweller. He stirred the fire with it, not even bothering to clean off the flawless blade, which had once been part of a meteorite hurtling through space.

Magger had stopped running, he crouched amid some ferns, regaining his breath. Then he smelled the acrid odour of burning feathers. The weasel straightened up, judging the breeze direction until he knew the source of the pungent reek, a small, grassy knoll, only a short walk from where he stood.

The vole pulled the bird clear of the heat, raking away the black ash of burned feathers with the sword.

From directly overhead, a scornful voice caught his attention. "Hah, it's der 'airymouse!"

Bending backward, he looked up into the leering face of Magger. The weasel was standing atop the knoll, holding a boulder over his head. Before the startled vole could move, the big stone crashed down, slaying him outright.

Chuckling to himself, Magger kicked the deadbeast callously to one side. Sitting in his place, he continued roasting the magpie, commenting, "Shouldn't never waste good vikkles!" A moment later, the weasel was crunching into the carcass and spitting out feather stubs. He glanced at the dead vole, treating the body to another kick. "Ain't much of a cook, are ye, 'airymouse. Aye aye, wot's dis yer 'idin' from ole Magger?"

The vole's body had rolled over, to reveal the sword. Magger pulled it from the vole's deathgrip, appraising the wondrous weapon as he wiped it on his ragged jerkin. "By de 'ellfires, worra beauty!" Ignoring the roast birdmeat, he sprang up, waving the blade about, marvelling at its lightness and clean lines. "Hoho, blood'n'spit t'the bucko who tries ter stan' in my way, dis is a real cap'n's blade!"

Dashing headlong into the ferns, Magger swished about left and right, whooping with joy as the blade sent fronds willy-nilly, revelling in the feel of the thrumming weapon. He halted, to plant a smacking kiss on the red-stone-pommeled hilt. "Haha, king o' de forest, king o' de sea, king of everyt'ink, dat's me!" Surprised at his own rhyming eloquence, Magger sat down, gazing lovingly at his newfound acquisition. "Hah, I even feels cleverer now I gotten dis!"

Back at the deserted campsite, Rangval took food from his haversack, beckoning to his companions. "Take a rest now, mates, let's have a look at these tracks. Orkwil, try not to disturb anything."

Orkwil and Maudie made their way over to the rogue squirrel. Both opened their packs, they were hungry from hours of tracking.

Maudie cast a cynical eye about as she munched on a scone. "Hmph, it'll be jolly difficult tryin' to make one blinkin' track out from the other. It looks like there's a bloomin' stampede passed through here, wot!"

Taking a pull from a flask of damson cordial, Orkwil knelt. He outlined a broad footpad close by. "Well, here's where Gorath was, headin' that way toward the ditch. Lots of other prints, too."

Rangval gave them a cursory glance. "Brownrats, shure I'm no stranger to their trails. Nobeast passed over the big feller's marks, y'know wot that means?"

Maudie finished her scone. "Indeed, it means our badger was pursuin' the rascals. The way those rats kicked up dirt one could see Gorath was the last chap they wanted to face."

Rangval selected an apple. "Shure, an' I wonder why that was, Maudie darlin'?"

The haremaid replied nonchalantly, "Who knows, old scout? Gorath never looked to me like a chap who'd be fond of vermin. Perhaps he just got peeved with the blighters, wot!"

Orkwil snorted. "Peeved? Look at the way those Brown-rats churned up the grass to get away from him. Gorath's in the grip of Bloodwrath, that's why they were in such a rush to get away!"

Rangval took a bite of his apple. "Hmm, Bloodwrath, is it. I've heard o' that afore, ain't it supposed to drive badgers mad?"

Maudie nodded. "Somethin' like that. Oh well, chaps, up an' at 'em, wot! I suppose we'd best follow his trail. What d'ye say?"

Orkwil began packing his haversack. "You two go ahead, I won't be comin' with ye. I've got to bring Martin's sword back to the Abbey, so I'll have to cast about until I find that vole's tracks, he's the rascal who'll have the sword."

Maudie pointed to the main tracks. "But what about my blinkin' badger?"

Rangval found himself in the position of mediator. "Ah, c'mon now, Maudie me ould beauty. We know where the big feller's bound, he's chasin' the Brownrats. They'll run straight back to their boss, Kurdly, an' he's camped south o' the Abbey wall. Let's lend young Orkwil a paw to find his vole. We can always catch up with Gorath an' Kurdly's bunch later."

Maudie relented. "Oh well, righto, but remember, Ork-wil, if we find your sword then you owe me one."

The young hedgehog was frankly relieved. "Good, I'll be in yore debt, marm, let's go this way."

They marched off north, on Orkwil's supposition that the vole would be making for the River Moss. All three spread in a forage line, keeping their eyes out for tracks. Rangval was the first to break trail, he was slightly east of the other two.

266

"Ah shure, and ain't I the grand tracker! Look, here's the ould villain's pawmarks. I can tell 'tis him, 'cos there's the dragmarks he made by lettin' the sword point scrape the ground. See, an' here's a slash on this rowan trunk, where he's made a swipe at it, testin' out his fine, new blade I'll be bound, eh!"

Maudie cut across Rangval, getting ahead of him. "I say, chaps, blood'n'feathers on the ground here. The bounder's killed a bird. Hold on, can you smell scorchin' feathers? Quiet now, an' keep your eyes peeled!"

Rangval, who prided himself on his woodcraft, nodded toward the small hillock, which he glimpsed through the trees. "Smoke's still arisin' yonder, that's where yore vole will be, Orkwil."

Maudie took charge. "Rangval, you come over the rise from the back. Orkwil, skirt the hill from the left. I'll take it from the right. When you hear me shout a Eulalia, then charge the blighter. Spread out now."

Glurma, the old, female ratcook of the *Bludgullet*, looked up from her stockpot, as Ragchin and his group came wandering into the new camp, beneath some willows on a streambank. She challenged them in a harsh voice. "Tell me ye've caught fishes, or kilt birds, but don't say dem scabby ole roots is all yew got?"

There was a good number of the crew sitting about in groups. They watched in disgust as Ragchin's patrol threw their meagre offering on the wilted heap of vegetation, which was all that had been brought in.

Ragchin spat out moodily, "Dat wuz all we could find, ain't nuthin' much out dere."

Glurma flung a few pawfuls of their find into the pot. As steam rose from the boiling mixture, she wrinkled her snout distastefully. "Ugh, ramson bulbs, I could tell dat stink anyplace!"

Jungo's stomach rumbled aloud, he shrugged. "Smells awright ter me, I'd eat anyt'ink, I'm 'ungry!"

There was a whoosh of flying metal, the mace and chain missed Glurma by a hairsbreadth. The missile struck the cauldron, knocking it over. Sizzling steam and cascading hot water extinguished the fire noisily. Vizka Longtooth strode through the camp, and retrieved his weapon. He stood looking about in the hushed silence which followed his dramatic entrance. "Well, did ya t'ink I wuz dead?"

The haglike Glurma cackled aloud. "Heeheehee! I knowed ye'd come back, Cap'n, dat's why I kep' der crew t'gether fer ye!"

The crew did not know how to respond to their captain's appearance, everybeast kept dutifully silent.

The golden fox draped the chain of his mace round Ragchin's neck. He drew the petrified ferret close to him. "I left Magger in charge, where is he?"

Ragchin swallowed hard. "Gone, Cap'n, Magger's gone. We ain't seen 'im since dose big Brownrats attacked."

Vizka showed his long fangs in that familiarly dangerous smile, he spoke almost playfully. "Gone, eh, an' yew thought ye'd take 'is place as leader of der crew, is dat right, shipmate?"

Ragchin denied the accusation vehemently. "No, Cap'n, no, yore der leader, everybeast knows dat!"

Vizka was about to speak, when Maudie's distant cry rang out. "Eulaliiiaaaa!"

The golden fox released Ragchin immediately. "Dat ain't from too far off, foller me, buckoes, an' norra werd outta anybeast!"

Rangval sat by the embers of the fire, staring at the crumpled figure of the vole. "Orkwil, me ould mate, it looks like yore not the only one who wants t'get his paws on that sword."

Maudie placed her footpaw on the boulder that had slain the unfortunate creature. "Rather. Well, that poor fool didn't suffer much, wot. I wonder what scallywag did the deed?"

Rangval averted his face from the still-smoking remains

of the burnt magpie. "Phwaw! Can ye imagine anybeast wantin' to eat that?"

Orkwil had been casting about the scene, he wandered off toward some ferns, not too far off. "I think I've found tracks here, some kind of vermin. Aye, this'll be him, sure enough." He reached the fernbed, and went into it stooping. "Aye, this is the murderer, he's been slashin' round at these ferns, choppin' 'em all ways with the swo—"

Swooping out of the ferns behind him, the golden fox moved like lightning. Wrapping the mace chain around Orkwil's neck he crossed his paws and tugged hard, calling aloud, "One move an' I snaps 'is neck!"

Maudie and Rangval froze, the haremaid muttering, "You harm one spike of his head an' I'll kill you!"

Vizka tugged on the wooden mace haft. "Yer in no position ter give orders, rabbet. Ahoy, crew!"

There was a noise behind Rangval, he turned to see a whole crowd of vermin coming over the hill. "No good arguin', Maudie, the fox is holdin' all the acorns in this game. He's got us for certain!"

28

It was night. Gorath could look up and see the stars, countless numbers of them, some glittering, others still and unwinking. His grandfather had shown him stars when he was small, hanging in the skies above the Northern Coast, brilliant and cold as blue ice. Not like these stars, some almost gold, warm-looking, suspended in the soft, dark, Mossflower night.

A thought occurred to the young badger. What was he doing here, lying in a depression formed by three hilltops? He recalled a star, like some huge, flaming comet, exploding inside his skull. Then a black veil, enveloping his mind. Two creatures were talking nearby, their voices almost muted. One sounded young, feminine.

"But, Tabura, he looks far too big and powerful to have fainted away as you said."

The other voice was old, husky, with a rumble like far-off midsummer thunder.

"See the scar, he has been sorely wounded some time ago. A dangerous thing for a Warrior of the Bloodwrath. His rage overwhelmed him, he could not control the anger. It is well that we found him before his enemies did, Salixa. Try giving him a little water, he should be coming round. Not too much, just a sip or two."

Gorath was fully awake, but he held his silence, allowing the one called Salixa to raise his head. He drank sparingly from the scallop shell which was pressed to his lips. The water tasted cold and sweet. Sitting up slowly, Gorath could see he was west of the Abbey, on top of one of the few rises which dotted the flatlands.

Two badgers sat silently watching him. The old male gave a soft, homespun cloak to the younger one, a slender badgermaid. She draped it about Gorath's shoulders as the old one spoke.

"We did not make fire, for fear of being seen by foes."

Gorath felt the pitchfork, lying nearby. He picked it up. "This is called Tung. My name is Gorath, I fear nobeast!"

The old badger nodded. "I can see that you do not know fear, Gorath. This maid is my travelling companion, she is Salixa. I am called Tabura."

The young badger's eyes were wide with recognition. "Did you say 'Tabura'?" The name leapt unbidden to Gorath's tongue.

He detected a slight chuckle in the oldster's voice. "How does one so young know of the Tabura?"

"My grandmother used it often. If my grandfather and she were disputing anything, and he won the argument, she'd say, 'Huh, you're becoming a real Tabura.' Also, if I ever had a question that neither of them could answer, they'd tell me to wait until I met the Tabura, and ask him."

The maid, Salixa, refilled the scallop shell with water, passing it to her elder, who merely wet his lips with it before replying.

"We are different creatures, you and I, Gorath, each at opposite ends of the same scale. Once there were many badgers who were called Tabura, they devoted their lives to peace, and the search for knowledge. There were also the warriors, those who were born with Bloodwrath.

"As vermin conquerors arose throughout the lands, there was a need for more warriors, and fewer wisebeasts. I once had a brother, he was a Bloodwrath badger, just like

271

you, Gorath. It is seasons out of mind since I last saw him. Being the warrior he was, his bones have probably long whitened under some far sun. But enough of my meanderings, tell me, what roads in your short life have brought you here?"

Gorath felt he could immediately trust the Tabura, he related his whole life to him. However, as he spoke his gaze wandered constantly to Salixa. Even though she spoke not a word, and Gorath could not make out her features clearly in the darkness, he could feel understanding, and a silent compassion, flowing from the badgermaid. The Tabura sat with his eyes closed, never interrupting, or questioning. When Gorath had ended his narration, the old badger remained quiet for a long time before speaking.

"Tell me, would you wish me to help you? I can see you have much to learn. A Tabura can be of great assistance to one such as you. I do not require an answer right away, rest here with us tonight. We will speak again in the morning, Gorath."

Apart from his grandparents, Gorath had never known any other badgers. The kinship he felt with Tabura and Salixa was totally natural. He felt obliged to reply. "Tabura, thank you for your offer of help. I accept. Tell me what I need to do."

A rare, slow smile touched the old badger's face. "Salixa and I need to visit Redwall Abbey. It is a place I have heard much about. As you are already acquainted with its creatures, perhaps you'd like to introduce us?"

Gorath rose, pointing in the direction of the huge, dark shape to the east. "But of course, I'd be glad to. We'll go there now, it's no great journey, I'm sure they'll welcome us!"

The Tabura held out his paw. "Lend me your weapon, to use as a staff. Salixa, walk ahead with Gorath, I'll follow at my own pace."

They strolled over the flatlands at a leisurely pace.

Tabura kept a few steps behind, which Gorath suspected was the old one's way of allowing them to talk together. Salixa stayed quiet at first, letting Gorath take the initiative.

"Are you related to the Tabura, is he your grandfather?"

The badgermaid stooped to pick a small plant, she sniffed it briefly. "Scabious, it's said to be good for rashes, I like the flower, it's a pretty lilac colour. The Tabura is no relation to me, he is kind and wise, like a very old father. He's teaching me to be a healer, I know lots of plants and herbs, even tree barks and roots."

Gorath accepted the scabious flower from her. "How do you come to be with him?"

Salixa glanced back, satisfying herself that the old badger was not listening, before she replied. "I only know what he told me, I must have been too young to recall anything. I had no parents, or kin. The Tabura found me with a small vermin band. He took me from them, I did not even have a name, they called me stripedog and kept me on a rope halter. Tabura named me Salixa, an ancient name for willow trees, he said it was because I was so slender, like a willow sapling."

Gorath nodded. "Good for him, I know what it's like to be called names like stripedog, or stripehound. Were the vermin angry when he took you from them?"

Salixa replied in a matter-of-fact tone, "I recall asking him that same question. He told me never to mention those vermin, ever. Because he had sent them all to a place where they could never inflict their evil, anger or torment on any creature again."

Now it was Gorath's turn to glance back at the Tabura. He found it hard to believe that such a humble, mild-mannered creature could slay a vermin band. Then Gorath looked at Salixa, she was picking another small blossom. "Field gentian, see the little, star-shaped purple flower? The potion made from its roots is very good for wounds."

In that moment Gorath knew why the Tabura had done

273

what he did. He also knew that he would mete out the same fate to anybeast who harmed a single hair of the gentle badgermaid.

Osbil and some of his Guosim were on walltop patrol, he spied the three forms crossing the ditch below. "Show yoreselves an' be recognised, are ye friends or foebeasts?"

Gorath replied, "Log a Log Osbil, it's me, Gorath, and I have two friends with me."

Proud to be addressed by his recently inherited title, Log a Log Osbil detailed two of his shrews to admit the badgers. He called down in a loud whisper to Gorath, "Go round to the north wallgate, matey, we've got those Brownrats still camped south of us!"

Gorath and his friends were hurried inside by the Guosim. Abbot Daucus met them at the entrance to Great Hall.

"Gorath, they're out searching for you, come in and bring your friends. I'm afraid the news isn't good. Come into the kitchens, Friar Chondrus will fix you some supper. Then you can hear what's been going on."

The Friar served them a supper of vegetable soup and pasties, crisp from the oven. Gorath introduced his new friends as they enjoyed Redwall's delicious hospitality. When he heard the old badger's name, the Father Abbot was impressed.

"Welcome indeed, sir, most scholars know that the title Tabura is only bestowed on the wisest and most learned badgers. It is a great honour for us to have you as our guest, but what is the purpose of your visit to Redwall Abbey?"

The Tabura bowed courteously to the Abbot, his eyes twinkling. "Most scholars know very little about my title. It is a tribute to your knowledge of badger lore that you address me thus, Father Abbot. There are several reasons for my visit to your wonderful Abbey, not the least of them being a desire to sample your good Friar's outstanding cooking."

Chondrus acknowledged the compliment with a radiant smile.

The badger took the Abbot's paw firmly. "I could tell by your face, when we first met, that you are beset with urgent problems of your own, Father. In the light of this, let us put aside my minor requests, and concentrate on your troubles. Explain them, and I will see what help three badgers can offer."

As the Abbot spoke, Gorath found his attention distracted by Salixa, who was listening intently to Abbot Daucus. Gorath was plainly enchanted by the first badgermaid he had ever met. Calmness and serenity seemed to radiate from this slender, sable-furred creature. She possessed the most gentle and compassionate eyes. The young badger was studying her so intently that he had forgotten all about his food.

Everybeast thought that the Tabura had fallen asleep, by the time Daucus had finished relating the current situation, but they held a respectful silence until the wise badger's eyes opened, and he spoke.

"It is late, you all have things to do. Go about your business, or off to your rest. Leave me here, I need to think. See to your own needs, friends, please."

Skipper felt concern for the Tabura. "But wot about yore own rest, sir? You ain't young no more, ye must be tired!"

The old one shook his head. "I have learned discipline of body and mind long ago. The murder of one of your beloved creatures, the theft of your precious sword. One, possibly two bands of foebeasts threatening Redwall, and the three outside your walls, friends, who may be in mortal danger. What are the problems of one old badger, when you have troubles enough at your door? Leave me now."

Abbot Daucus showed the Tabura downstairs to Cavern Hole. "Sit in the big armchair by the hearth, I'll see that you aren't disturbed, friend. By the way, what problems, aside from ours, are on your mind?"

The Tabura patted the Abbot's paw, chuckling. "I care greatly for my ward, Salixa, as I am coming to do also for young Gorath. Did you not see them looking at each other? They are the sun and the moon, one is flame, the other is a calm lake. I know their fates are intertwined. I must see to it that no harm touches them, they are both very special creatures."

The Abbot recalled the looks that had passed between both young badgers. He smiled at the old one. "Surely you are the wisest creature that ever lived!"

The Tabura gave Daucus one of his rare smiles. "Or the most sentimental old fool. I bid you good night, Father. We will meet again as the sun rises."

29

Maudie, Rangval and Orkwil were strung up by their paws from the limb of a big sycamore, which grew at the edge of the camp. Their footpaws barely touched the ground. Four guards—two stoats, a weasel and a fat ferret—lounged against the sycamore trunk. Surprisingly, they had not been beaten or tormented by the *Bludgullet*'s crew. Vizka and his vermin were lounging on the other side of the camp clearing, virtually ignoring their three captives.

Orkwil muttered to his two friends, "It was my fault, gettin' caught like that, sorry, mates."

Rangval winked at him. "Ah, don't fret about it, bucko, shure, it could've happened to anybeast, ain't that right, Maudie darlin'?"

The haremaid looked up at her bound paws. "Right enough, old lad, I didn't spot that confounded fox 'til the last flippin' moment. Sneaky blighter!"

Orkwil could not keep the tremble out of his voice. "Huh, I 'spect they're busy thinkin' up 'orrible ways to slay us, what d'ye think?"

Rangval gritted his teeth angrily. "Shure, I'd give 'em a few ould things t'think about if'n I wasn't trussed up like washin' on a line."

Maudie agreed with him. "Indeed, the cowardly rascals.

277

If I was loose enough t'get a few punches at 'em, there'd be teeth fallin' like hailstones around this bloomin' camp!"

Rangval swung to face Maudie, grinning roguishly. "Tell ye wot, let's bait 'em up a bit, eh?"

Orkwil looked from one to the other, mystified. "Wot d'ye mean, 'bait 'em up a bit'?"

Rangval danced a little jig on his footpaws. "You just listen to us, me ould mucker, ye'll get the hang of it soon enough. Would ye like to start the ball, Maudie darlin'? Go on, give 'em plenty!"

Shouting so that she could be clearly heard, Maudie began insulting the golden fox and his crew. "I think they're goin' to leave us here to die of old age, 'cos they're too jolly scared to fight us!"

One of the guards ran in front of Maudie, waving a spear at her. "Sharrap, rabbet, or I'll gut ya!"

The haremaid swung forward, kicking him under the chin, and laying the guard out flat.

Rangval hooted. "Hahahaharrr! Did ye ever see anybeast so dim? Ahoy over there, any other idiot need a good kick? C'mon, line up over here an' we'll oblige ye!"

Vizka Longtooth saw several of his crew rising and pawing at their weapons. He snarled at them, "Stay where y'are, I'm tryin' ta t'ink!"

The small rat, Firty, piped up indignantly, "But dey're insultin' us, Cap'n, dey can't gerraway wid dat. Ain't ya gunna do not'ink?"

Leaning over, Vizka dealt him a fierce cuff on the ear. "I'll do sumt'ink ter you if'n ya don't shurrupp!"

The vermin crew were forced to sit glumly, enduring the prisoners' ribald comments.

Maudie sang out, "Oh, foxy, foxy, could you come over here please, whilst I kick your oversized choppers out?"

Emboldened by the vermins' lack of reprisals, Orkwil chimed in boldly. "Hah, I'm only little, but I can wallop weasels all day. Come an' try yore luck with 'orrible Orkwil!"

Rangval broke out into a raucous ditty.

"Oh the only good vermin is a dead 'un,
me dear ould mother used to say,
she was always puttin' paid to rats an' ferrets,
when they got in her way.
Ma was also very good at skinnin' weasels,
she made all the babies winter coats,
an' whenever we needed extra blankets,
why, she'd go an' collar two fat stoats!

"So the only good vermin is a dead 'un,
they're peaceful wid their paws turned up,
an' they're wonderful for fertilisin' roses,
but you mustn't dig 'em up.
We often had a ferret's nose to play wid,
a liddle game that we called hunt the snout,
and we had a sweepin' broom, made from a
fox's brush,
for dustin' the parlour out!"

Vizka began tying a knot into a rope's end. The slight
about the fox had got through to him. "I need dem alive,
but dat's all dey gotta be, alive. A taste of rope an' dey'll be
singin' a diff'rent song!"

One of the stoats on sentry duty at the camp fringes interrupted Vizka's intentions as he hurried in to report.
"Cap'n, dere's one o' der crew outside o' camp, 'e wants ter
speak wid ya."

The golden fox continued knotting the rope's end.
"Which one of der crew is it?"

The sentry, Dogleg, whispered confidentially, "Magger."

Vizka Longtooth's grip tightened about the rope he was
holding, his eyes glinting icily. Then he changed suddenly;
swinging the rope in a carefree manner, he called out
jovially, "My ole shipmate Magger, I t'ought he wuz
slayed. Bring 'im 'ere t'me if'n 'e's alive an' 'appy!"

Dogleg scurried off to get Magger, as Vizka sat smiling
from ear to ear.

The three prisoners were becoming weary of vermin bait-
ing, nobeast seemed to be taking much notice of them.
Rangval shouted out a final taunt. "Shure, the only difference ye can tell twixt a vermin's bottom an' his face is that
his nose ain't got a tail sticking out of it!" The roguish
squirrel gave up further efforts.

Maudie called out, almost halfheartedly, "Too right, old
sport, I always say that if looks could kill, then vermin
would never stare at each other!" The haremaid gave a
snort of disgust. "Oh, what's the bally use? A blinkin' plum
pudden's got more feelin's than that rotten lot, wot!"

But Orkwil was enjoying himself, he carried on with
his insults, undeterred. "Yah, go an' boil yore mouldy ole
bottoms, ye snipe-nosed, twiggly tailed bunch of frog
followers!"

Maudie sighed. "I say, old lad, d'you mind leavin' off,
wot, you're givin' me a flippin' earache!"

However, the young hedgehog was in full flow. "I could
lick ye all with a single quill! Ye droopy-bellied, snotty-
snouted, pongy-pawed, whiffle-eared scruffsacks! I'll bet
yore grannies were all snigglety wooflers!"

Bonk! One of the guards sprang forward, and dealt Orkwil a stunning blow with his spearhaft, muttering, "My
ole grannie wasn't no snigglety woofler, take dat!"

From where she was suspended, Maudie took a peep at
her senseless friend. "He's not hurt bad, but he'll have a
jolly red lump twixt his ears for a few days, wot. Anyhow,
at least we'll get a bit of peace for awhile, what d'you say?"

Rangval shook his head. "A snigglety woofler, wot'n the
name o' fur'n'feathers is that?"

The haremaid groaned as she tried to shrug. "Haven't a
bally clue, but I'll be sure to remember it whenever I'm
baitin' vermin. Hmm, snigglety woofler eh, I rather like
that! Good grief, eyes front, bucko, d'you see what I jolly
well see?"

Magger edged hesitantly into the camp. Every eye was

upon the fabulous sword he had thrust into his belt. The weasel nodded uncertainly at Vizka, acknowledging him. "Ahoy, Cap'n."

The golden fox left his mace and chain on the ground. Waving the knotted rope, he greeted his former second in command affably. "Ho ho, Magger, welcome, mate! Sit ya down an' get a bite to eat. It ain't much, but 'tis the best we kin do fer now."

The weasel glanced warily about, staying on his footpaws, and disregarding the offer of food. His paw never strayed far from the sword, as he enquired, "Ain't ya mad at me, Cap'n?"

Vizka's face was the picture of astonished amusement. "Mad at ya, wot would I be mad at ya for, matey?"

Magger replied, having first got his story prepared. "When dose Brownrats attacked I wuz out, lookin' fer vittles ter feed der crew. By der time I got back, yew was all gone an' der camp wuz empty, Cap'n." He avoided looking at Vizka, staring at the ground, and scuffing a footpaw to and fro.

Enjoying Magger's discomfort, Vizka pursued his interrogation, but in a lighthearted tone. "So, wot did ya do den, mate, an' where did ya get dat big, pretty knife, eh?"

One lie followed another as Magger embellished the tale. "I tuk it offen a big Brownrat, Cap'n."

The crew of the *Bludgullet* watched the exchange in silence, knowing the outcome as Vizka chuckled.

"Ye tuk it, jus' like dat?"

The weasel shook his head stoutly. "No, not jus' like dat, Cap'n, wot 'appened was dis. I surprised four of der rats, layin' round a campfire dey was. One of dem 'ad stuck der sword in d'ground. Dey was restin', so I sneaked in, grabbed der sword an' slayed 'em all. I been lukkin' fer yew ever since, Cap'n."

Vizka began advancing slowly on Magger, all the time keeping his eye on Martin's sword. The weasel sensed he was in trouble, he dropped his paw until he was grasping

281

the hilt of the weapon. Vizka stopped within a pace of him, shaking his head sadly.

"Don't do dat, Magger me ole mate. I left my mace on d'ground over dere. Wot could I do agin a blade like dat, I ain't armed, 'cept fer dis cob o' rope. Yew keep yore sword, messmate, ye deserve it after slayin' four Brownrats ta gerrit. Ain't dat right, mates?" The vermin crew nodded dutifully.

Magger looked around at them, relinquishing his hold on the sword. Stars went off inside his head as the knotted rope thudded into his eye. He fell backward with an agonised yelp as Vizka leapt on him, stepping on his sword paw and lashing mercilessly with the rope. Every stroke hit Magger's head, his eyes, jaw, snout, teeth, cheeks and chin. Vizka never let up the savage assault until he was certain Magger was finished.

The blade sliced through Magger's belt as Vizka pulled it free. Breathing heavily, he stood over his victim, bellowing with rage at the prone body. "Traitor! Turntail! Yew ran at the first whiff o' dose Brownrats! Ye deserted me'n'my crew, all yore mates! Now ya come runnin' back 'ere wid ya lies. Carryin' a fancy blade, an' thinkin' Vizka Longtooth is some kinda fool. Well, who's the fool now, scumbrain!"

The golden fox seized Magger by an ear. Raising the weasel's head he swung with the sword. The *Bludgullet*'s crew stared, horrified, as Vizka held up the severed head. His warning was not lost on them.

"Ya see, Magger ain't tellin' lies no more. I can't stand a runaway, or a traitor. Remember dat, all of ya!"

Rangval and Maudie had witnessed the whole shocking incident. Maudie whispered, "As soon as Orkwil wakens, we'd do well to tell him not to mention the sword. Right, bucko, mum's the word!"

The rogue squirrel agreed readily. "Oh, right y'are, marm, 'tis a good job the fox never had that grand ould blade afore we started baitin' him. He might've tried it out on us, just for practice."

The haremaid murmured urgently, "Don't talk too bloomin' soon, old chap, he's headed over here lookin' rather like he's become pretty fond of head-choppin', wot!"

Rangval swallowed hard as he watched Vizka approaching. "Shure, I hope he's not about to become a pain in the neck. I like bein' attached t'this ould head o' mine!"

Vizka held the sword forth, until it was at the captives' eye level. "Dis ain't no Brownrat weapon, 'tis a fine blade. Tell me, where've ya seen it afore?"

The keen blade came close to Maudie's throat as she answered. "Seen it before? No, 'fraid not, sah. But let me say, it suits you well. The sword was obviously made for you, it's yours by right of conquest I think."

Vizka stared up at the three friends, suspended from the branch by their paws. He drew back the sword and struck with a yell. "Yaaaaah!"

30

Soft clouds shrouded the dawn, lending the new day a pearllike sheen. The Tabura sat in the orchard, completely at one with his surroundings. Not a leaf or a blade of grass stirred, it was as if the earth lay still, enjoying the brief, peaceful moment, before the morning bustle of Abbey life.

A young robin landed in the folds of the badger's homespun garment. He sat motionless, watching the little bird. At the sound of approaching voices, the robin flew off into the trees. At his bidding, the badgermaid Salixa had brought Gorath, Abbot Daucus, Log a Log Osbil, Skipper Rorc, Barbowla, Foremole Burff and Benjo Tipps.

They seated themselves round and about the upturned barrow, which the old badger was using as a chair. Friar Chondrus and two helpers trundled up, pushing a trolley laden with breakfast food.

The Tabura declined a bowl of honeyed oatmeal, nodding at the trolley. "None for me just yet, thank you. I will eat after I have spoken. But please, do not let me stop you from breaking your fast, friends. Everything looks so delicious, I hope you will save me a little."

When everybeast was served, the Tabura gave voice to his thoughts. "Gorath, let us face your problem first. It is right and just that the murderer of your kinbeasts should

284

pay for his crimes. Therefore you must pursue this fox. I know by the vow you made to yourself that you will seek him, right to Hellgates if need be. But my young friend, it is not the fox that you must worry about, it is yourself that you must fear. Aye, fear I say, for your own Bloodwrath may be the death of you. Go now, but before you do, grant me just one wish."

The young badger took his pitchfork, the frown creasing his brow making the vivid, red scar look even more like a flickering flame. Gorath was frankly puzzled. "Tabura, I am bound in honour to obey one so wise. What is your wish?"

The old badger turned his gaze on the slender badger-maid. "That if Salixa so desires, you will allow her to go with you. To stay by your side and accompany you."

Gorath was lost for words, all he could say was, "But why?"

The Tabura was still staring at Salixa. "Would you go with Gorath if I asked you to do so?"

The badgermaid went to stand at Gorath's side, she replied without hesitation, calmly. "I will go with him because we both wish it."

The Tabura smiled at them both for a moment, then closed his eyes. "Go then, and may the fates be kind to you. With the Father Abbot's permission, I will be staying here, now that Redwall has lost its healer."

Abbot Daucus took the two young badgers' paws. "You must bow to your Tabura's wisdom. Friar Chondrus, will you see they are provided with supplies? Alas, your stay at our Abbey has been all too brief. We wish you well. Be kind to one another, remember, friendship is the greatest gift one creature can offer to another."

With the Friar following them, they departed without another word. The Tabura only opened his eyes after they had gone. There was a moment's silence, then Skipper shook his head in amazement.

"Gorath's a fine, young badger alright, but he's a Bloodwrath warrior, an' a dangerous beast to be around. I tell ye, I wouldn't allow any daughter o' mine to go off on the loose with one like him. Why did ye let yore daughter go, Tabura?"

The old badger stared at the spot where the pair had been standing a moment ago. "Salixa is no kin of mine, though I care for her as much as any father would for his daughter. You saw the two of them together, they need each other."

Benjo Tipps scratched his headspikes. "But suppose Gorath gets into one of his rages, what could a slip of a maid do then? She could be in peril."

Reaching into his belt pouch, the Tabura brought forth a small, round stone, which he passed to the Cellarhog. "Tell me, friend, what do you think that is?"

Foremole Burff took a swift glance, answering promptly. "Hurr, et bee's a pebble, zurr, make'd o' grannet, oi think?"

Everybeast present nodded in agreement. The old badger took the pebble back and held it up. "A simple pebble, which I took from a stream. One time, maybe before creatures ever walked the land, that was a chip of granite from some mountain. Somehow it fell into a stream, or a river. A small, sharp lump of stone, rough and misshapen. No tool, no chisel or hammer, turned it into a smooth pebble. Completely round, without any keen edges, a perfect little stone ball. It was water, streamwater, running softly through countless ages, which continually washed this stone, finally turning it into a pebble."

Skipper nodded. "You mean that the maid could smooth the rough edges off'n Gorath. But you said the water took countless ages t'do it, sir."

Abbot Daucus answered for the old badger. "Aye, but Gorath and Salixa aren't water and stone, they're living creatures who care for each other. It won't take ages, Skip, believe me!"

The oldster chuckled. "Well said, Father Abbot, maybe someday you might become a Tabura?"

Daucus smiled modestly. "I hardly think so."

The Tabura accepted a beaker of hot mint tea from Foremole. "We shall see. Now, let us face the problem of these Brownrats. What do you know of them, and their leader?"

The Abbot deferred to Barbowla's explanation. "Wot's to know, they're a vermin horde, an' Gruntan Kurdly's a big, fat, evil, greedy beast. First he wanted the Guosim's logboats, but then he set his twisted mind on Redwall. Now Kurdly wants this Abbey."

Abbot Daucus spoke out angrily. "But he won't get it, Redwall is too strong to fall into the paws of scum like that!"

Skipper slammed his rudder down hard. "That rat'll only get Redwall over our dead bodies, we'll fight him with everything we've got!"

The Tabura held up his paws until the indignant outcry halted. "Wait now, friends, what you're telling me is that Kurdly is a rat who takes what he wants by brute force and ignorance, because he has a horde behind him."

Osbil drew his rapier. "Aye, but if'n he wants war we'll give it to the villain, hot'n'heavy!"

Draining his beaker, the Tabura nodded to Friar Chondrus. "This is very fine mint tea, may I have more, please? Now, on the subject of your enemies, Father Abbot. I think you would agree that war is the last resort of intelligent creatures. It brings only death and destruction."

Abbot Daucus replied wistfully, "There's no doubt about that, friend, but what are we to do? Vermin aren't beasts you can reason with."

There was a twinkle in the old badger's eyes as he sipped his tea. "Indeed they aren't, that's what I'm relying on. They are not only our enemy, but they have no love for each other, these two vermin armies. My advice is, sit tight within your Abbey, defend it when you have to. Vermin are cruel, murderous, but most of all greedy. I think they'll cancel one another out. I have seen vermin conquerors and armies before, trust me."

287

At his camp, south of the Abbey wall, Gruntan Kurdly was reflecting also. He had become accustomed to the thunder of paws, either coming down or going up the ditch nearby. First it was Sea Raiders chasing Brownrats, then it was Brownrats chasing the Sea Raiders. Now it was his own horde again, madly stampeding from north to south. He watched with a jaundiced eye as they stumbled, slobbering and panting, into camp. As a change from boiled eggs, Gruntan was pigging down a mess of small, roasted trout. Hawking loudly he spat out in disgust, narrowly missing his old healer, Laggle. The Brownrat chieftain scowled sourly at her. "Wot did yer give me fishes for, ye ole frowsebag? Fishes ain't good vittles, they got bones in 'em, sharp ones, they got fish skin, too, an' . . . an' . . . bits, lots o' slimey bits!" Picking up another trout, he regarded it with disgust. "Yurgh! Fishes got eyes, too, an' they stares at ye when yore eatin' 'em!"

He grabbed the nearest Brownrat and slapped his face several times with the cooked trout. "I likes eggs, d'yer know why?"

The unfortunate Brownrat tried to duck another slap from the trout. "'Cos eggs tastes better, Boss?"

Tossing the fish at Laggle, Gruntan wiped his paws on the Brownrat's head before kicking him away. "No, stupid, it's 'cos eggs ain't got bones'n'skin, an' slimy bits, too. Leastways, not when they're boiled proper, an' peeled well."

He turned his attention on Stringle, and the rest, who were lolling about, still huffing and puffing. "So youse lot are back, eh? Hah, the way ye came bowlin' down that ditch, it sounded like you was bein' chased. So tell me, 'ow many was after ye, ten score, twenny score, or was it just a bad-tempered wasp? Stan' up, Stringle, an' let's 'ear the sorry tale!"

Stringle stood, well clear of Gruntan Kurdly, and did his best to put a brave face on things. "We chased those

288

seabeasts, Chief, jus' like ye told us to. When they saw us after 'em, they took off like scalded frogs, ain't that right, mates?"

There was a murmur of agreement, then Stringle carried on with his report. "Aye, they ran sure enough, but we charged after the gutless scum. Chased 'em right into their camp we did an' slayed 'em, left, right'n'centre!"

Gruntan raised his eyebrows. "All of 'em?"

Stringle tried hard to look injured and gallant at the same time. "Well, not exac'ly all of 'em, Chief, one or two of the cowards ran off, but we took care o' the main gang. Ye won't be bothered by that lot no more!"

Gruntan took a while to digest this information. "Hmm, an' wot 'appened to their chief, this fox, Fizzy Longteeth? Where'd he go?"

Stringle blurted out, "We catchered 'im!"

Gruntan picked a trout bone from his snaggled teeth. "Ye catchered 'im. Good! Well, where is he?"

Stringle hesitated, moving further away from Gruntan, or any missile he might choose to throw. "Well, that's wot I was goin' t'tell ye, Boss, it was like this, ye see. We 'ad 'im, all trussed up, comin' back 'ere along the ditch we was. When all of a sudden, there's this giant madbeast, wirra great big fork!"

Gruntan belched, then spat out another fishbone. "Wot sort o' giant madbeast?"

Stringle backed away even further. "One o' those stripe-'ounds, but big as a tree, wid red eyes. Stabbin' away at us with 'is big fork an' shoutin'!"

Gruntan halted his captain's flow again. "Wot was 'e shoutin'?"

Stringle replied promptly, "Yooleeyayleeyer!"

The Brownrat chieftain jiggled a grimy claw in one ear, staring hard at Stringle. "Yoolerwot? Say that agin."

Throwing back his head, and cupping both paws around his mouth for maximum effect, Stringle bellowed, "Yoooooleeeeyayleeeyaaaaaar!"

289

Gruntan winced at the volume of the piercing sound. "Wot's it supposed t'mean?"

One of Stringle's command ventured a reply. "Some kinda war cry, prob'ly."

Gruntan stared directly at the speaker. "War cry, eh, an' wot size d'ye say this stripe'ound was?"

The Brownrat soldier, who wished he had never spoken, echoed Stringle's original words. "'E was a giant, Boss, wirra great, big fork!"

Gruntan addressed his next remark to all the vermin. "Bigger'n me, was 'e?" It was common knowledge that the Brownrat leader could not stand the thought of anybeast being bigger than him. He was exceedingly vain about his size.

The horde hesitated, but Stringle shook his head. "Nah, nobeast's bigger'n the great Gruntan Kurdly!"

Swelling out his enormous stomach proudly, Gruntan pronounced, "Hah, then that must make me a giant. That don't make yore stripe'ound sound so big, do it?"

Stringle shook his head miserably, knowing he had fallen into the trap. "No, Boss, 'e ain't so big."

"Shame on youse all fer runnin' away from 'im then. Take 'em back out agin, Stringle, find the stripe'ound, bring me back 'is big fork, an' 'is skull, or 'is skin'n'bones, I don't care which, as long as ye slays the beast. Huh, Gruntan Kurdly ain't havin' giant stripe'ounds runnin' round 'is territory!"

Disobedience was out of the question. Stringle marched out at the head of his dispirited troop, back to the ditchbed.

Having dismissed them, Gruntan turned his attention to what he viewed as more important matters. "Now, about those eggs I mentioned, Laggle, where are they? Stir yore stumps, ye ole bat!"

The more Abbot Daucus saw of the Tabura, the more he was glad that the old badger had professed a wish to stay at Redwall as a healer and dispenser of wisdom. Even the

Abbey Dibbuns had fallen under the spell of the charismatic Tabura. At the moment, he was seated by the pond, surrounded by young ones, and quite a few elders. Daucus joined them, listening intently as the wise badger held forth on the merits of simplicity. He took a russet apple, snapping it into two halves with a twist of his powerful paws. The Tabura sniffed the peach-hued flesh of the russet and sighed. "Ah, the scent of quiet autumn afternoon!" Dibbuns crowded around to smell the apple, as the Tabura continued. "And the taste, my friends, it is different to all other apples, try it." He smiled as the Abbeybabes lined up to take a nibble, each one pronouncing an opinion.

"Umyum, tasters very nice an' sweet!"

"Bo urr, oi do loikes a gudd h'apple, zurr!"

The Tabura passed them the other half. "There are many ways that your Friar and his cooks can use a russet apple, in sauces, pies, crumbles, fruit salads, or baked in honey and spices. Each of these ways produces a delicious new taste for us. But, if you are really hungry, there's only one way to really enjoy a good russet apple."

Dawbil the molebabe wrinkled her little snout. "Ho aye, an' wot way bee's that, gurt zurr?"

The Tabura allowed Dawbil to scramble onto his lap as he explained. "Just pick the apple from the tree, take a crust of newbaked bread and a wedge of ripe cheese, then eat them all, a bite from each at a time. Apple, crusty bread and cheese."

Abbot Daucus nodded. "Right, Tabura, I've done it myself, many a time. There's no taste quite like it!"

The old badger looked around at his audience. "Father Abbot is right, life's greatest pleasures are the simple ones. A drink of cold, clear streamwater when you're hot and thirsty, or apple, cheese and bread when you feel the need of plain, homely food."

Granspike Niblo stood up, straightening her apron. "By golly, sir, you've made me feel quite 'ungry, a-talkin' like that. Those russets in the orchard ain't ready yet, but Friar

291

Chondrus has a big barrel of 'em, from last autumn, in his kitchen. I'm sure he could spare us some bread an' cheese. Would you little 'uns like t'come with me?"

There was an immediate clamour from the Dibbuns. As they set off in Granspike's wake for the kitchens, a Guosim sentry came running from the west wall. Osbil had been part of the Tabura's audience, the sentry hurried to his side, muttering urgently, "Come t'the walltop, Chief, we've just spotted vermin!"

Keeping low along with the other wallguards, the Guosim chieftain peered between the battlements following the sentry's directions.

"See there, just to the north, crossin' the path from the ditch, 'tis the Brownrats!"

Osbil watched. Stringle, Kurdly's second in command, was herding scores of Brownrats across the path and into the cover of Mossflower Woods.

The sentry shrew whispered, "Wot d'ye suppose those scum-faced murderers are up to?"

Osbil's teeth ground together audibly. "I don't care wot they're up to, we're goin' to be on them like wasps on honey, mate. Now's our chance. Rigril, Teagle, gather our Guosim. I want 'em armed t'the teeth and silent as pike in a midnight stream. Move lively now, we don't want to lose those villains!"

On hearing what had taken place, the Tabura, the Abbot and Skipper made their way to the north wallgate. The Guosim chieftain was marshalling the few late arrivals before setting forth.

Daucus, whilst not barring the shrew's way, tried reasoning with Osbil. "Think first, Log a Log Osbil, you haven't got the numbers to face the Brownrat horde."

Osbil smiled coldly. "We ain't goin' to face 'em, Father, this is goin t'be an ambush, hit and run, my Guosim'll defeat the vermin in any way we can."

Barbowla placed a paw on the Guosim chieftain's shoulder. "Me'n Kachooch started this journey with you and we

292

would be proud to come along. Skipper here will take charge of my otters, my band will stay as defenders at Redwall."

Osbil grasped Barbowla's paw. "Thank you, friend."

The Tabura stared levelly at Osbil. "Your friends are giving you good advice, young one. It is a dangerous course you are bound on."

Osbil had his paw on the wallgate latch. "But it is one that I must follow. This sword at my side, it was my father's blade. He was murdered by Brownrats. I am now Log a Log, as he was. It is Guosim law that he must be avenged, we have sung our Bladechant, yet his killers still live. Such a thing brings shame to me and my tribe. Can you understand, Tabura?"

The old badger clamped his paw over that of the shrew. He gave one swift tug, and the wallgate stood open wide. "I understand you completely, my young friend. Go now, exact the price of your father's blood from his killers! Banish shame and live on in honour. But remember this, do not let the enemy get behind you, sleep with one eye open and your blade drawn. May fortune go with you!"

Osbil saluted with his father's rapier. "And may wisdom attend your words always, Tabura, sir!"

A moment later the shrews and otters vanished into the fastnesses of the vast woodland.

BOOK THREE

The Battle of the Plateau

31

The great sword of Martin the Warrior sheared through the bonds which held Maudie, Rangval and Orkwil suspended from the tree. They were immediately surrounded by the *Blugullet*'s crew.

Vizka Longtooth snapped out orders. "Chop dat branch down an' yoke dem by dere necks to it!" The branch was promptly hacked down. Vizka spoke to his captives as they were roughly bound neck and paws to it. "T'ought ya was goin' ter die, didn't ya?"

Maudie could not resist a cool reply. "Actually, somethin' like that did speed through my agile, young brain, old thing. Rangval, d'you think our friend's savin' us for some fairly dreadful jape, wot?"

The rogue squirrel sighed. "Sure an' why wouldn't he, him bein' a double-dyed villain. I wouldn't put anythin' like that past him."

They were now standing shoulder to shoulder, with their paws and necks tied tightly to the branch.

The golden fox showed his long fangs in a sinister grin. "Ya won't be talkin' so fancy when I'm finished wid ya. We're takin' ya back to de Abbey, we'll see wot good friends ye've got dere. If'n dey don't open d'gates an' let us in fer a visit—"

Maudie interrupted. "Wait, don't tell me, you'll stamp your paws a lot, an' never speak to them again. Right?"

Vizka shook his head, still grinning. "Wrong, 'cos iffen dey don't open der gates, I'll roast an' skin ya. Right in front o' dem same gates." Brandishing his new sword in a flashing arc, Vizka signalled his crew. "Bring 'em along, we're bound for de Abbey. Steer clear o' dat ditch an' stay to der woodlands. March!"

Orkwil had to march almost tip-paw, even though both his friends crouched slightly to assist him. The young hedgehog had been warned not to mention the sword, but he could not take his eyes off Martin's blade. He strained his neck to one side, muttering to Maudie, "We've got to get the sword, an' make a break for it!"

Keeping her gaze straight ahead, the haremaid replied, "Certainly, old scout, but not right away. That foxy cad's a bit too taken with the sword, watch the way he swings it about. He'd probably chop us into fishbait if we tried anything too soon. Give it a little while yet, then we'll see what we can jolly well do, wot!"

A surly looking weasel slammed his spearbutt into Maudie's back. "Shut ya gabblin' an git marchin', rabbet!"

Despite the pain from the cruel blow, the haremaid managed to wink cheerily at him. "Right you are, sah, this rabbit's marchin', wot! But before our little jaunt's over, I'd like a word with you. Just the two of us, in private, eh."

Some distance to the south, the two badgers sat down near a sandstone outcrop. Salixa produced a flask of penny-cloud cordial, passing it to Gorath. "Would you like something to eat?" Her companion seemed somewhat preoccupied, he merely took a gulp from the flask, returning it with a nod of thanks. The young badgermaid tried not to stare at Gorath. He turned, facing the way they had come. His eyes roved restlessly as he touched the deep crimson scar on his brow. Salixa glanced anxiously at him. "Is your wound hurting you? It always looks so red and sore. If you like, I'll go and find some herbs to treat it."

Gorath gave her one of his quick rare smiles. "No thank you, the wound hardly ever hurts me now. Sometimes it will itch slightly, when I feel uneasy."

The slender badgermaid's voice sounded sad. "Is it me? I'm sorry if I make you feel uneasy. . . ."

Gorath's mighty paw covered hers, gently. "Oh no, you could never make me feel uneasy, in fact I've never felt so happy as when I'm with you. Salixa, look at me, I'm uneasy because we're being watched. No, don't look where I'm looking, just keep holding my paw and walk with me."

Salixa kept her gaze trustingly on Gorath. "Where are we going, are we still being watched?"

As they walked he nodded, answering her as if keeping up some trivial chat. "We're going to climb these sandstone ledges, all the way to the top. I've seen who is on our trail, it's those Brownrats. By the way the bushes are moving there's a lot of them, but I can defend our position from the top of those rocks."

As he helped her onto the ledges, Salixa replied, "Gorath, are you going to take the Bloodwrath?"

He swung her effortlessly up to the next level. "I can feel it beginning to press down on me, but it would be a mistake to give in to Bloodwrath. If anything happened to me, then what would become of you?"

The badgermaid clasped her big friend's paw tightly. "The Tabura has given you wise advice, Gorath."

Using his pitchfork, Tung, he vaulted onto a higher ledge. Salixa held onto the fork handle as he hauled her up. Gorath nodded. "Aye, the Tabura is wisdom itself, I wish I had met him long ago. Only a short way to climb now. We'd best hurry, I think they're coming."

Slingstones and a few arrows bounced off the ledges. Stringle stayed among the bushes, urging his Brownrats

299

forward, starting up a warchant as they charged the ledges. "Kurdly! Kurdly! Kill kill kill! Yeeeeaaaaahhh!"

Gorath pushed Salixa onto the plateau, leaping up beside her. "Keep your head down, they're shooting stones and shafts at us!"

Salixa immediately proved she was no helpless maid. Unwinding a slingshot from her slender waist, she gathered up a few of the hard streambed pebbles which had been thrown by the Brownrats and began retaliating vigorously. Gorath ranged the surface of the plateau, checking that there was no easy way up.

Stringle had not relished the idea of meeting up with the giant stripehound, more so when he saw there were now two of them. Admittedly, the female was much smaller and slimmer, but who could tell with stripehounds, maybe they were all berserk warriors. However, the moment he saw both beasts running off to safety, instead of turning to the attack, Stringle rapidly gained confidence. Still holding his position in the bushes, he worked himself into a fine old battle rage, just as he had seen Gruntan Kurdly do. "Yahaaarr! Gerrup them rocks an' toss 'em both down 'ere t'me. I'll git two spearpoints ready t'stick their 'eads on. Go on, buckoes, go on, up ye go!"

The rat who had led the charge, Bladj, came running back into the bushes, clutching his mouth.

Stringle prodded him with his dagger. "Wot are yew doin' back 'ere? I thought yew was leadin' the charge. Git back out there, ye worm!"

Bladj pulled back his lip angrily, exposing a bleeding gap. "See that? I jus' got two teeth belted out by a flamin' slingstone. Who are yew callin' a worm, why don't you lead a charge, instead of 'idin' back 'ere an' givin' yore orders!"

Stringle exerted his authority with high bad temper. Whacking the dagger handle hard against the uninjured side of Bladj's jaw, he covered the unfortunate in spittle as he roared into his face. "There, I 'ope ye've lost two teeth on the other side now. I'm in command 'ere, yew don't talk t'me like that! Lookit that 'ill, there's gangs of 'em tryin' t'get up t'the top, an' wot's stoppin' 'em, eh?" He struck Bladj on the nosetip with the dagger hilt. "One skinny stripedog wirra sling, chuckin' stones, that's wot! Now yew get back out dere, or it'll be yore 'ead I'll be takin' back to Kurdly on a spearpoint. Go on, show 'em yore not a worm, let's 'ear yew yellin' loud enough t'put the fear of 'ellgates inter those stripe'ounds. There's enough of us to eat 'em both!"

As the savage war cries rose in intensity, Gorath came hurrying back to Salixa's aid. He was holding a huge sandstone boulder above his head. Bladj had regained his position at the head of the charge, he was about two thirds up the slopes. Gorath roared out like thunder. "Eulaliiiiaaaaa!"

The boulder slew Bladj, plus the two Brownrats either side of him, who, following his example, had raced forward yelling lustily. Several more rodents were struck by the bodies, and the boulder, as they hurtled downward.

Salixa shot off another stone from her sling. She gazed keenly at her big friend, with his livid scar. "Gorath the Flame, how are you doing?"

He knelt on the edge of the plateau, watching the Brownrats retreat, fearing another boulder assault. "I'm coping, I think. I keep telling myself that I'm a Tabura, do I look wise to you, Salixa?"

She hid a smile, keeping her voice level. "You look so wise that for a moment I thought you were the Tabura himself. One thing your wisdom has accomplished, it's halted their charge, see?"

Gorath dusted off his paws. "Good!" He hurried off in search of another boulder.

Vizka Longtooth had heard the noise, but only faintly, as he stood waiting the arrival of his two forward scouts, the stoats, Dogleg and Patchy. They came stumbling along, pointing back over their shoulders.

301

Patchy called out excitedly, "A lorra shoutin' up for'ard, Cap'n!"

Vizka was trying to contain his impatience. "I know, we 'eard it. Did ye go an' see worrit was?"

Dogleg shook his head and scratched his stomach. "Er, no, Cap'n, sounded like sum sorta fightin' I t'ink."

Vizka stuck his wondrous swordpoint into the ground. He seized the two stoats, each by an ear. As he banged their heads together, he chided them like children. "You t'ink? Youse 'aven't got enuff brains between ya to t'ink. Scouts are supposed to scout, not t'ink!" He dropped both stoats and retrieved his sword. "Fall in wid der crew, we'll go an' see wot all der shoutin' an' yellin's about. Keep ya paws on dose blades, an' keep yer eyes skinned, all of ya!"

Rangval whispered to Maudie, "This could be a grand ould chance for us to part company with these rascals."

As if he had heard the remark, Vizka smirked at the captives. "Youse ain't goin' anywhere. Ruglat, Saltear, Undril, yew stay 'ere an' guard 'em. Lash dat branch off to a tree, an' see dey don't make no funny moves, an' don't take any lip off dem!" He signalled the *Bludgullet*'s crew with his sword.

When the main party had left, Maudie sized up their three guards. Ruglat was the surly weasel who had struck her with a spearbutt. Saltear was a fat, slovenly stoat, and Undril was a young weasel, fit and sly-faced.

Orkwil murmured to his two friends, "What d'ye think, could we handle 'em?"

Rangval winked at the young hedgehog. "Sure, I think we could cope with these three puddens, providin' we can deal with the ropes."

Saltear, who had commandeered Rangval's three daggers, drew one of them threateningly, glaring at the squirrel. "Ahoy, big gob, shut ya mouth, or I'll cut ya tongue off!"

Ruglat interrupted him. "Let's git dis branch tied off so

302

dey can't wander away." He pointed to a pair of small oaks growing close together. "Tie off de ends o' der branch atween dem trees."

Dragging the prisoners across to the oaks, they bound both ends of the branch to either trunk.

Maudie enquired politely, "Permission to speak, sah, if y'please."

Saltear scowled. "Wotja want, rabbet?"

Maudie smiled coyly. "I suppose a drink of water's out the question. . . ." She saw Saltear's scowl deepen, and continued. "I don't suppose you'd consider loosening off these confounded ropes, jolly uncomfortable on the old neck'n'paws, doncha know."

Ruglat thrust Saltear roughly aside. Springing forward, he punched Maudie on the cheek, hard. Ruglat bellowed, "Sharraaaaap! One more werd outta yew, rabbet, an' yer dead meat, do ya 'ear me?"

The haremaid's head was lolling loosely over the branch. Rangval answered for her. "Ah, faith, sir, ye've knocked her out cold, she won't be hearin' anybeast for awhile, I'm thinkin'."

Ruglat spat on his clenched paw, puffing out his chest. "Hah, dat should keep 'er quiet. Jus' one word out o' yew two an' I'll give ye der same, now sharrap!"

The three vermin retired a short distance away. They began building a fire, to roast some roots they had found along the way.

The branch bounced slightly, quivering under Orkwil's chin. He whispered urgently, "Maudie, are you alright?"

Contrary to the vermin's expectations, Maudie had not been knocked cold, she was wide awake. "I'm fine, thank you. Now then, you chaps, here's the flippin' plan, wot!"

Rangval chuckled quietly. "I knew 'twould take more'n some snotty-snouted ould vermin to knock ye out, Maudie me darlin'. We're all ears, wot's yore grand scheme, eh?"

Staying in her unconscious position, Maudie communi-

303

cated her ruse in hushed tones. "Actually, I've been testing this bally branch, an' I don't think it'll stand up to much. Now, here's what we do, chaps. Keep an eye on those clods while y'do this. Move together slowly, so as we're hunched together, like three peas in a bloomin' pod. Good, that's the ticket!"

Orkwil whispered eagerly, "What d'you plan on doin'?"

Rangval kicked the young hedgehog's paw lightly. "Give over now, an' lissen to the brainy beauty. Go on, marm, ye've got the floor, or should I say the branch."

The haremaid continued, "Righto, grip the branch tightly now, get your chins well settled on it. Good, when I count to three, give a great leap upward, an' lean down hard on the branch as you come down. I think this confounded branch will break under our combined weight."

With his chin anchored firmly on the branch, Rangval spoke through his clenched teeth. "Ye'll pardon me askin', marm, but wot happens if it don't?"

Orkwil growled. "Then we'll just bounce up'n'down 'til it does. Wot then, miss?"

"Then you two take the broken ends an' set about 'em. Rangval, you take the stoat, Orkwil, you tackle the smallest of the two weasels. Leave the one they call Ruglat to me, I owe him one or two good 'uns! Ready? Right chaps, here goes. One . . . two . . . three. Jump!"

The vermin heard the crack, and saw the three prisoners leap in the air again. Ruglat grabbed his spear, bounding upright. "Ahoy, wot's goin' on dere?" He and his fellow guards came running. There was another crack as Maudie shouted exultantly.

"One more'll do it, buckoes! One, two, three, jump!"

This time the branch snapped, right through the centre. The three friends sat down hard on the ground with the impact. Scrabbling furiously, they rid themselves of their bonds, leaping up to meet their foes.

Saltear had a dagger in either paw, he dashed toward

the trio, but was stopped in his tracks by Rangval. The rogue squirrel swung his half of the branch, catching the stoat a terrific blow to the side of his neck. Saltear died with an expression of shock on his face, with his neck tilted at an odd angle.

Undril dodged Orkwil's first attempt, he dragged a small cutlass out so forcefully that it severed his belt on leaving, which caused his pantaloons to fall down around his footpaws. He tripped and fell. That was all Orkwil needed, and he took full advantage.

Whack! Splat! Thud! Smack!

Orkwil battered away like a madbeast in a frenzy, screaming and yelling as he belaboured his fallen enemy.

Maudie dodged Ruglat's first three spear thrusts with contemptuous grace. On his fourth try at slaying her, she winded him, with a swift left to the gut. Knocking the spear from the big weasel's grasp, she challenged him. "C'mon, barrelbottom, let's see what you're made of, wot!"

Ruglat stayed down a moment, gaining his breath, then he jumped up, grinning viciously as he charged her with clenched paws and bared teeth. "Yew asked fer dis, rabbet!"

She merely swayed to one side, pummelling his head as he blundered by her. Maudie booted his rump, sending him sprawling. She stood over him, waiting. "Rabbit yourself, you overblown sloptub. C'mon, up you come, I'm not jolly well finished with you yet, laddie buck, you've got a lesson to learn, wot, wot!"

Ruglat threw himself at her, screeching with rage. Maudie feinted with a left, then delivered three rights, one to each eye, and a real stinger to the snout. Dropping into a crouch, she punished the weasel's stomach and ribs with a veritable tattoo.

Suddenly Ruglat could take no more, he lurched off to one side and grabbed his spear, snarling through battered lips, "Stay back, back! Foller me an' I'll gut ye!" He turned and ran, but Orkwil's outstretched footpaw stopped his headlong flight, quite by accident. The weasel tripped, and fell onto his own spearpoint.

Rangval threw a paw to his brow in amazement. "Ah, now haven't we got a grand ould warrior here? Shure he's polished off two vermin without even tryin'!"

Orkwil had sat down, dropping his piece of branch. Never having slain a living creature before, he was obviously in shock, hardly listening as Rangval carried on joking about the fight with the vermin.

"One vermin apiece, that was Miss Maudie's plan, but you had to have two. Haharr, you greedy liddle hog, where'd you learn to trip a vermin, at the same time ye were pulverisin' his pal, eh?"

Shaking her head, Maudie silenced the rogue squirrel with a severe glance. She had witnessed battle shock in several young Long Patrol hares, during their first encounter with the foebeast. It was not a thing to joke about. The sympathetic haremaid sat down beside her young hedgehog friend, giving him the benefit of her experience, he was younger than both she and Rangval. "Well, you're a warrior now, Orkwil, how does it feel, pretty awful I expect, havin' to kill or be killed, wot?"

Orkwil stared at her, a mixture of bewilderment and guilt in his eyes. "I feel terrible, did you feel like that when it first happened to you, marm?"

Maudie felt older, at being addressed as "marm," but she merely nodded, and patted his paw. "Blubbed my eyes out, actually, but old Sergeant Brassjaw soon straightened me out. Told me that if I were a mother with a few babes, or an old 'un, who was too weak to defend himself, I'd be thankin' the warriors. Aye, those who made the land safe for them to sleep in their beds, without fear of bein' left murdered in a blazin' homestead. You just think of what those vermin were plannin' for us, laddie buck!"

Orkwil stared at both dead Sea Raiders for a moment, then he spoke out indignantly. "Aye, they were goin' to roast an' skin us, right in front of the Abbey gates. Well, there's three vermin won't be doin' any more roastin' an' skinnin'!"

Retrieving his daggers, Rangval joined the pair. "Come on, mates, we don't want to be found hangin' about here if'n the ould fox comes back. Now, the second part of our plan has been thought up by meself. So, let's get ourselves rigged out in those vermins' rags."

Maudie and Orkwil spoke in unison. "What for?"

The rogue squirrel sheathed his daggers. "By me grannie's moustache, I can see you two wouldn't be much good as rogues. Suppose we runs into that vermin crew agin, eh, or the other mob, the Brownrats? Wouldn't it be far better if'n we looked as though we were villains like them? A spot o' disguise an' cammyflage never hurt anybeast, right?"

Maudie began divesting the carcass of Ruglat of its tatty finery, baggy blouse, ragged breeches, and a grubby turban. "Super wheeze, old lad. Come on, young Orkwil, get y'self geared up. We've got to go and see what all the hullabaloo over yonder's about, wot. Much better t'go in mufti. Well, how do I look, just call me maraudin' Maudie, chaps!"

Orkwil took a fit of giggling at the sight. Maudie had bound her long ears into the turban, and was rubbing mud over her face. She scowled at him.

"Haharr, one more titter out o' yew, landlubber, an' I'll gut yore mainstays an' keelwallop yore vitals, or whatever it is those seagoin' chaps say!"

Rangval had tied up his bushy tail into the back of Saltear's tawdry frock coat. He donned the stoat's floppy seaboots and slouch hat, then danced a comic jig. "Shiver me drawers an' drop me anchor, 'tis meself, ould Rangval the Rover. Hoho, an' who's this bully?"

Getting into the spirit of things, Orkwil had put on Undril's broad, brass-buckled belt, canvas kilt, striped waistcoat and fringed headband. He brandished the weasel's long knife, snarling. "Ahoy, I'm Orkwil the 'Orrible Outlaw! Rot me timbers, mateys, where are we bound? Haharr, hoho an' heehee!"

Rangval suddenly went serious. "Enough o' this foolin' about, now. We keep our heads down, an' keep ourselves to ourselves. Stick together an' look out for one another. Right, let's march!"

32

Evening shades were lengthening the shadows, the sun was washing the western horizon in scarlet as the three friends arrived at their destination. Sounds of warfare marred the closing of the summer day as Maudie surveyed the high sandstone plateau from the bushes some distance away.

Orkwil was behind the haremaid, jumping up and down. "I can't see properly from here, what's goin' on?"

Maudie stood on tip-paw, straining to find out. "I'm not sure, 'fraid I can't see all I'd like to. Mayhaps we'd do better if we got a bit closer, wot."

Rangval kicked off his floppy seaboots. "No sense in runnin' right into trouble. Stay here, mates, I'll climb that ould beech over yonder. From the top o' there I should get a fair view o' things." The rogue squirrel was an expert climber, he scaled up into the top heights of the beech. Perching among the swaying foliage, he called down to his friends, who were at the base of the wide trunk, "Maudie, it's yore badger, the bigbeast, Gorath, an' another badger I ain't seen afore, smaller, could be a maid, they're defendin' the top o' those rocks alone."

Maudie wished she could climb the tree to see properly

what was taking place. She called back to Rangval, "I can hear lots of noise, who is it they're fighting?"

Rangval climbed even higher before answering. "Shure, I can't see, but whoever it is, they're on the far side of those rocks. But I can hear a bit better up here, sounds like Kurdly's horde t'me. Oh no, they're really in trouble now, I can see the fox an' his crew, they're sneakin' up the back slopes o' the rocks. If'n they reaches the top they'll come up behind the badgers. Somebeast needs to warn 'em, quick!"

Maudie shot off toward the scene. Stopping short of the rocks, she looked up and saw Vizka and his vermin, almost halfway up. Throwing back her head, she sucked in a deep breath and gave out full blast with the Salamandastron war cry, several times. "Eulaliiiaaaa! Eulaliiiiaaaa! Eulaliiiiiaaaaa!"

From his vantage point, Rangval saw the big badger turn and run to the rear of the plateau. The warning had reached him in time. He began hurling rocks down at the *Bludgullet* crew. Vizka's vermin were spread out too wide for the missiles to wreak much damage, but they had the effect of stopping them in their upward climb.

Rangval came bounding down to earth, where Orkwil was awaiting him. Seizing the young hedgehog's paw, the squirrel raced off, panting as he explained. "Those badgers are bein' attacked from both sides, they ain't goin' to last long unless somebeast gets up to that flat hilltop an' helps 'em!"

As they neared the base of the rocks, Maudie signalled them from her cover in the bushes. "Over here, chaps!"

They joined her speedily, but there was no time for talking. Maudie held up her paw for silence. Rustling among the bushes and the sounds of vermin voices warned them that the area was being searched.

"Why ain't we serposed ta kill 'em?"

"'Cos der cap'n wants ta see who it was dat shouted der warnin' to dem stripe'ounds."

"Garr, we should be able ta jus' gut 'em!"

"Yew do dat, an der cap'n'll gut yew, now belt up an' git lookin'!"

The searchers were almost upon them, when Maudie had an idea. She whispered to her two companions, "I've just thought of a wheeze, chaps, follow me an' play along, we're sea vermin, remember." She began thrashing the bushes with her spear, giving a passable imitation as one of the *Bludgullet*'s crew. "Nah, I don't see nobeast round 'ere, 'ave yew spotted 'em yet, Grubsnout?"

Catching on quickly, Rangval snarled, "Dis is daft, bucko, dey wuddent 'ang around 'ere after shoutin out a warnin'. Woddya t'ink, Bloogle?"

Realising the remark was aimed at him, Orkwil acquitted himself well as he replied, "We ain't supposed ter t'ink, dat's Cap'n Vizka's job. Cap'n sez search, so we search. I says we try annuder place, mebbe up dere."

The stoat Bilger joined them. "Duh, I'll come wid ya, mates!"

Even though the night had fallen, Rangval caught Orkwil's look of alarm, as Bilger threw a paw about the young hedgehog's shoulders. He was about to act when Maudie stepped in. She tapped the stoat's back, warning him. "Watch out fer dat branch, bucko!"

The stoat turned, presenting the side of his jaw as a perfect target. "Duh, wot branch is dat?"

The haremaid's clenched right paw shot out. "Dat one! Huh, don't say I diddent warn ya!"

The weasel, Jungo, who was as dull-witted as Bilger, saw him fall. He hurried over to Bilger's side. "Bilge, are ya 'urted, mate?"

Emboldened by Maudie's swift solution, Orkwil scoffed at Jungo. "Walked inter a branch an' knocked hisself out cold. Huh, fancy sendin' dat t'ickhead out ta look fer somebeast, 'e cuddent find 'is tail iffen it wasn't anchored to 'is be'ind!"

Jungo found the remark quite hilarious. "Hahaw-hawhaw! Dat's a good 'un, tail anchored to 'is be'ind. Hawhawahaw! I must remember dat 'un!"

Trying not to draw further attention to themselves, the three friends ducked off, making their way uphill. Rangval went slightly ahead of the other two, being a swift and skilled climber, he soon made his way to the lip of the plateau. The rogue squirrel was halfway over the edge, when he saw Gorath striding toward him, brandishing his huge pitchfork, Tung.

Whipping off his floppy hat, Rangval hastily identified himself. "Go easy with that thing, sir, me'n me pals have come from Redwall Abbey to help ye. My name's Rang-val." He shook off the tawdry frock coat, displaying his bushy tail.

Reversing the fork, Gorath proffered the handle. Rang-val grasped it and was hauled up alongside the big, young badger.

Maudie's voice rang out from below. "I say, old sport, could you lend me a paw, too, wot?" In an instant she, too, was pulled up onto the plateau.

A moment of silence went by, then Rangval looked at her. "Where's Orkwil?"

The haremaid shrugged uneasily. "He's with you, isn't he?"

The rogue squirrel shook his head. "No, I thought he was with you?"

"Gorath! Heeeelp!" It was Salixa, the Brownrats had got past her, there were nearly a score of them on the plateau. The three defenders were forced to forget Orkwil for that moment. They charged headlong at the Brownrats, who were trying to hem Salixa in, and cut her off from Gorath.

Throughout his pursuit of Gorath, Stringle had been constantly sending runners back, these were to report the horde's progress, keeping Gruntan Kurdly up-to-date on the hunt. The Brownrat chief took these messages one of

312

two ways, either with bored disinterest or bad-tempered criticism. Gruntan was, as per usual, more concerned with his desire for food, specifically eggs. The hulking Brownrat leader considered himself to be a connoisseur, and an expert on the subject.

The latest messenger, a large, sleek-limbed female named Skruttle, was forced to stand and wait before submitting her report. Nobeast talked whilst Gruntan was speaking. At that moment he had an audience of young rats, and was holding forth to them on his favourite topic.

"Oh, aye, mates, I've et 'em all, every kind of egg knowed to bird or beast. From gooses to wrens, an' everyone atween. Seagulls, plovers, pigeons, thrush, starlin's, sparrers, rooks or cuckoos, you name 'em, I've boiled 'em!"

Gruntan could see Skruttle waiting, but he ignored her in favour of a young Brownrat, who piped up, "Do ye always boil yore eggs, Chief?"

Gruntan's formidable stomach wobbled as he chuckled. "Thud'n'blunder, wot other way is there, young 'un? Ye can take it from me, once an egg's boiled it's perfect. The only way it can be spoilt is by a lousy peeler, some dumble-pawed idjit who can't take the shell off'n an 'ard-boiled egg proper!" He scowled darkly at the older Brownrats, his servants. "Aye, an' there's enough of those round 'ere. . . ." He turned his attention to the runner. "Haharr, an' wot sorta bad news is Stringle sendin' me? Don't stan' there like a slug in a slopbasin, make yore report!"

Skruttle narrated the message. "Cap'n Stringle sez to tell you that he's got the giant stripe'ound surrounded, atop of a stone 'ill. But 'e sez there's two stripe'ounds now, the big 'un an' a smaller one, prob'ly a maid." She paused awkwardly, shuffling her paws. "So that's wot Cap'n Stringle told me to tell ye, Boss, we've got the stripe'ounds surrounded."

Gruntan cut in on the messenger. "Where's this stone 'ill where they're at?"

313

Skruttle gestured with her tail. "Up north in the wood-lands, 'bout a quarter day's march. Cap'n Stringle's waitin' on yore orders, Boss."

Gruntan heaved a snort of irritation. "Don't tell me, the great Cap'n Stringle's waitin' on me to come an' do the job for 'im. Well, ain't 'e?"

Skruttle nodded dumbly.

Gruntan climbed laboriously onto his litter seat, calling orders to his bearers. "Up off'n yore hunkers, ye layabouts! Break camp, we're movin' north. Stay outta that ditch, cut off around the Abbey an' go that way. Ahoy, you young 'uns, d'ye want a job?"

The young Brownrats stood to attention eagerly.

Gruntan called his old ratwife healer, Laggle. "Keep an eye on them, stay ahead o' me litter. See if'n ye can scout out any fresh eggs, there's none left in this neighbour'ood. Mind, I only wants good, big eggs, don't go bringin' me no wren or robin eggs. Go on, off with ye, I'll be followin', keep goin' north."

Back in the woodlands around the sandstone plateau, Stringle's fortunes had changed for the worse. Instead of being the hunter, he now found that his horde was being attacked by a tribe of vengeful Guosim. Log a Log Osbil's shrew warriors came hurtling out of the trees, yelling their battle cries as they hit the Brownrats' rear ranks. Stringle was forced to turn and fight, leaving those attacking the plateau to their own devices. The Guosim fought like mad-beasts, any Brownrat they seized was shown no quarter. Within a very short time they slew more than a score of the vermin. Guosim rapiers flashed in the dawnlight as Osbil and his tribe sent fear into the hearts of the foe while they started up a Bladechant.

"Hi hey Log a Log ho
Guosim lay the foebeast low,
Ho hey Log a Log hi

vermin 'tis the day ye die!
Logga Logga Logloglog!
Oh my blade is thirsting hard
not for ale or water
it will drink the vermin blood
brewed amid the slaughter!
Logga Logga Logloglog!
Ye who laid our chieftain low
Guosim wrath will feel,
take this payment of our debt
given with cold steel!
Logga Logga Logloglog!
Hi hey Log a Log ho
vengeance is a blood-red tide
Ho hey Log a Log hi
throw the Hellgates open wide!
Logga Logga Logloglog!"

On top of the plateau, Gorath and his three compatriots had repelled the Brownrats who had come over the edge. Working together, they beat the vermin back, though it was the young badger, armed with Tung, his weapon, who was carrying the fight. He was indeed an awesome sight, roaring forth his battlecry, swinging the pitchfork like a mighty flail.

Maudie was in top form. Avoiding spears and crude blades, she was lashing out with all paws, sending foe-beasts skittling over the rim, though several times the haremaid was almost struck by Gorath sweeping his weapon in wide arcs. Ducking Tung repeatedly, Maudie found herself appealing to Salixa, who was swinging a loaded sling further along. "Er, I hope you don't mind me sayin', old gel, but couldn't you have a blinkin' word with your chum? He'll sweep us all over the edge if he ain't careful. Oh, beg pardon a tick—" She broke off to deliver a walloping left to a Brownrat, sending him hurtling into space. Another came dashing up, wielding a spear. Before he could use it, the vermin was felled by one of Rangval's daggers. Maudie waggled her ears at the rogue squirrel. "Thanks terribly, I can't abide spear thrusters."

Rangval grinned as he bent to retrieve his blade. "Sure, think nothin' of it, miss—" As he stood upright the stock of Gorath's pitchfork swung too close, felling the squirrel.

Maudie wagged a paw at Salixa. "You see, I told you he was going to jolly well hurt one of us, swingin' that thing about!" Maudie helped Rangval up, rubbing the back of his head. "I say, old lad, are you alright? Still with us, wot?"

The rogue squirrel smiled crookedly. "Oh, I think I'll live, as long as the big feller doesn't give me another swipe!"

Salixa ducked and dodged until she was at Gorath's side. "You're not feeling an attack of Bloodwrath, are you?"

The young badger looked a bit pink about the eyes, but he stopped swinging briefly. "No, I've got it under control, Salixa, why, is anything wrong?"

She squeezed his paw reassuringly. "No, but watch out for your friends when you swing Tung around, you just hit poor Rangval."

Gorath was about to apologise to the squirrel, when a shout from the other side of the plateau alerted him. A gang of the *Bludgullet*'s crew came stampeding over the far rim, yelling madly.

Maudie picked up a fallen vermin spear and followed both badgers to repel the invaders. Rangval joined her, twirling a dagger in either paw. "Ah, miss, if only me dear ould mother could see me now, I know just what she'd say."

Maudie singled out a ferret, muttering as she went for him, "What would your dear old mater say?"

The rogue squirrel shrugged as he imitated his mother. "Here we go again, me son, what've I told ye about all this fightin', ye rascal!"

There were far too many Brownrats for Osbil and his

shrews to defeat, but they achieved a certain purpose with their fierce attack. One of the Guosim scouts, who had been ranging around the base of the plateau, reported back to his Log a Log. "Chief, there's a crew o' those seavermin attackin' the plateau from the rear!"

This was worrying information, requiring some quick thinking from the Guosim chieftain. Osbil cast a glance up at the rim, summing up his thoughts aloud. "Hmm, there's only the two badgers, Maudie an' Rangval defendin' up there, as far as I can see."

The scout interrupted. "There should be five, wot's happened to the young hog, Orkwil? There's no sign of him?"

Osbil shook his head. "Who knows, mate, he might be dead, or lyin' wounded somewhere. We can't stop everythin' t'go searchin' for him. One thing's certain, we can't leave goodbeasts up there to perish. Gather the tribe, we'll make a charge, stampede through the middle of Kurdly's rats an' carry on until we reach the plateau. That way we can join our friends an' make a proper stand!"

The Brownrats had now recovered from the initial Guosim assault. Under Stringle's command they were beginning to turn the tide against the smaller shrew force. However, they were not prepared for what came next. The Guosim warriors grouped into a mass behind Osbil and charged headlong at the Brownrats, roaring, "Logalogalogalooooog!"

They went like a gale through a wheatfield, whipping through the trees and shrubbery, with Brownrats being bulled and bowled in all directions. Straight through the centre, and onto the base sandstone ledges, Log a Log Osbil led his fighters, whooping and yelling like madbeasts.

Furious at being taken by surprise, Stringle, who had viewed the incident from safe cover, came dashing out to berate his Brownrats. "Why didn't ye stand firm, ye poltroons? We're bigger'n those liddle shrews, aye, an' we've got five times their number. Get after 'em, ye lily-livered layabouts. Form up an' charge, come on. Charge!"

"Why charge, my friend? Let dem carry on to der top, dey got noplace to go once dey're up dere, don't ya see!"

Stringle whirled around, coming face-to-face with Vizka Longtooth and half a score of the *Bludgullet*'s crew.

33

Gruntan Kurdly was in no hurry to join Stringle, the reason being that he was under the impression there was only one badger in the Mossflower region. Whilst passing around the back of Redwall Abbey on a northerly course, he sat back in his litter, gazing covetously at the east wall. The Brownrat warlord wondered if the time would ever arrive when he would be on the other side of that wall, master of all he surveyed. That was when he saw the badger.

The Tabura was being shown around Redwall, he strode the eastern rampart slowly, in company with Abbot Daucus and Foremole Burff, admiring the tranquil immensity of his surroundings. Stopping for a moment, the Tabura gazed out over the dense woodlands. He was about to turn away when a movement amid the trees caught his attention. The badger found himself looking straight into the eyes of a huge, overweight rat, being carried along, sprawled on a litter. Their eyes locked for a brief moment, then the rat was lost to view, being borne off midst the greenery.

Gruntan Kurdly furrowed his brutish brow, assessing the situation. Doubtless Stringle had been telling him a pack of lies. The minions of Kurdly often resorted to untruths, mostly to save themselves being exposed to his wrath, which often proved fatal. Every Brownrat knew what a dose of the Kurdlys meant. The Warlord dozed off, reflecting on how he would punish Stringle. The warm summer day, chirping insects, buzzing bees and silent butterflies winging their errant path amid the patches of shade and sunlight, lulled Kurdly into a comfortable doze for awhile.

He was rudely wakened by the cries of the young Brownrats, coming out of the woodlands. In a customary sour mood, which often followed his nap, Gruntan waved a grubby paw at the closest rat. "Gimme summat t'drink, me gob's like a sandpit!" He slopped grog down, casting a jaundiced eye over the young ones. "Wot d'yer mean, wakin' me with all yore shoutin', eh?"

A Brownrat maid came forward, holding out a nest for his inspection. "We found eggs for ye, Boss."

Poking about in the structure of woven vegetation, Gruntan pawed the two fawn-hued, brown-blotched eggs. "Moorhens, where'd ye get these?"

Laggle, the old healer, pointed off east. "They found a watermeadow over yonder."

Gruntan Kurdly immediately perked up, watermeadows were a prime source of eggs. He hid his pleasure, curling a lip at Laggle and the young rats. "Huh, an' that's all ye got, jus' two eggs atwixt the lot of ye? Aye, an' I'll wager these are addled an' rotten. Right, steer a course for these watermedders, we'll camp there, an' I'll take a look fer meself."

Noggo, who was one of the bearers, piped up. "But worrabout the giant stripe'ound, wot Stringle's got surrounded, Boss?"

Noggo was close enough, so Gruntan grabbed him, and broke both the eggs over his head. Gruntan gave a gaptoothed smile of vindication. "See, I told ye they was rotten. Never you mind about Stringle, I'll deal with that 'un. Durty great fibber, he ain't got no giant stripe'ound surrounded!"

Laggle made sure she was out of his reach. "An' how d'ye know that, eh?"

Gruntan smirked knowingly. "'Cos I just saw the stripe'ound on top o' Redwall, that's 'ow. I've seen the beast fer meself, so 'ow can Stringle've seen 'im, tell me that, clever whiskers!"

Laggle put forward her explanation. "Well, there might be three stripe'ounds, have ye thought of that?"

Gruntan shot her his meanest scowl. "Don't talk stupid, unless ye want to get a bad attack o' the Kurdlys. Now, where's that watermedder!"

It was a beautiful sight, a watermeadow in a woodland setting. Bulrushes and reeds flourished along the margins. Large dragonflies, mayflies and damselflies flittered and hovered amid widespread waterlilies, golden crowfoot, white flowering cottongrass and blue-starred brooklime.

All nature's splendour was lost on Gruntan Kurdly as his litter was carefully lowered onto the firm ground of the border. "Haharr, this is the place fer eggs, buckoes. Now if'n ye'd caught up with those sh'ews awhile back, I'd 'ave me a nice liddle logboat t'sail round 'ere in. Well, let's see if'n ye can make yoreselves useful now. Laggle, get some 'elp an' light a fire, git that water cauldron filled an' bubblin', ready for me eggs. Youse young 'uns, cast about an' see if'n ye can hunt up some decent nests, with lots of eggs in 'em. Go quiet an' easy now. If'n ye kills any birds, then ye can keep 'em to roast an' eat. But remember, the eggs are mine, off ye go now, an' don't dare come back empty-pawed, or I'll boil the lot of ye in this cauldron!"

The young Brownrats stole silently off to their duties. Gruntan amused himself awhile, swatting at any winged insect which came within range. Within a short time he was snoozing again.

Noontide shadows were lengthening over the tranquil watermeadows when Gruntan was gently shaken into

321

wakefulness by Laggle, who whispered in his ear, "Ye'd better wake up, Boss, they've found a swan's nest!"

Gruntan sat bolt upright, grubbing at his eyes. He breathed reverently, "A swan's nest!"

The one egg he had never tasted, a swan's egg. To the Brownrat chieftain the nest of a swan was his ultimate dream. The swan was the largest of all birds! Gruntan had never seen its egg, but he imagined it would be a thing of legendary proportions. He shuddered with unconcealed delight. All thoughts of Stringle, his lies and stripehounds were banished from his mind as he whispered orders to his Brownrats.

"Who was it wot found the swan's nest, which one of ye?"

A young male rat came hesitantly forward. "Me, Boss."

Gruntan gazed at him fondly. "Wot's yore name, mate?"

The young rat did not know whether to be proud or afraid. "Duggerlo, Boss, me name's Duggerlo." He blinked each time Gruntan patted his head.

"Duggerlo, eh, an 'andsome name for a clever young 'un. So yore the bright spark wot found the swan's nest, d'ye think ye could take me to it, Duggerlo?"

Feeling more confident, Duggerlo nodded vigorously. "Aye, Boss, 'tis over yon, where those willows are. There's a little stream runs through them into the meadows. The nest is right there, I saw it."

Gruntan turned to the other Brownrats. "Youse lot stay 'ere, keep the fire goin' an' the cauldron bubblin' 'til me'n Duggerlo returns."

At the far side of the watermeadow, Gruntan and Duggerlo stood waist-deep in the water, the willows were some distance away. It was not going to be as easy as the Brownrat chief first thought. He questioned the youngster. "Tell me, 'ow did ye make yore way across?"

"I waded most o' the way, an' swam a bit, Boss."

Gruntan scratched his stomach underwater. "Hmm, an' yore certain the nest is over there?"

Duggerlo pointed. "Ye can't miss it, Boss, right in the stream mouth, 'tween those far two willows."

After a few moments' thought, Gruntan reached a decision. "Right, young 'un, you stay 'ere, an' keep quiet, I'll go over there by meself. If'n I needs ye I'll shout."

Being much taller than Duggerlo, Gruntan figured he would not need to swim. Keeping his gaze fixed on the willows, he began wading. The going was slow, but steady; he squelched onward, feeling the ooze, old tree roots and vegetation beneath his footpaws. So obsessed was he with his quest for the fabled swan's egg, the Brownrat chieftain did not want any otherbeast sharing his discovery.

Wading closer, he could make out the nest now, a sprawling, unwieldy construction, probably based on some underwater willow roots. Gruntan could mentally picture the egg, lying there in solitary splendour, white as the driven snow, and big as a seaside boulder. His paws trembled with desire and anxiety as he pushed himself faster through the water, which was now lapping about his chin. He was spitting water by the time he reached the nest, but his footpaws found a hold on the underwater roots. Grabbing the outside of the huge nest, he hauled himself upward, gurgling with happiness.

Under the weight of the Brownrat's bulk, the entire nest came toppling sideways on him, in a hideous cacophony of sound. Two gangling cygnets and a fully grown female mute swan fell upon Gruntan. The young swans scrabbled back onto the half-capsized nest, trumpeting weakly, whilst their mother set about punishing the unwelcome trespasser.

Defending its nest and family, the mute swan was an awesome sight. It towered over the unfortunate Brownrat, hissing and snorting, thrashing him with both webbed limbs, beating him with wings like windmill sails. Then it pounded away at his head with its fearsome orange beak, which was backed by a hard, black protrusion at the base.

323

Once, twice, thrice the swan struck, each blow powered by its long, powerful neck. Gruntan Kurdly sank limply beneath the waters, with a fractured spine, and a cracked skull. Still hissing and snorting its wrath, the mute swan shepherded its two cygnets away to safety.

Duggerlo stood clinging to a clump of bulrushes, still waist-deep in the watermeadow. Shocked by what he had witnessed, his gaze was still rooted to the scene of the attack, watching the spot where Gruntan had sunk, expecting him to reappear, roaring orders to slay the swan. Duggerlo stayed quite awhile, until it finally dawned on him that only a fish could stay underwater so long.

The young Brownrat staggered into camp dripping wet. He had to impart the story three times, in full detail, before anybeast began believing him. Though there were a few cynics.

"Garn, Kurdly slayed, no bird could do that!"

"Hah, shows 'ow much you know, you've never seen a swan close up. One o' them things is even bigger'n a stripe'ound. It could finish off the boss, an' three like 'im. Swans is bigger'n giants!"

"Well, I don't believe the boss is dead, so there!"

Duggerlo lost his patience with the speaker. "Well, why don't ye go over there, an' swim under the water an' ask 'im?"

That ended the argument. They sat around the fire, boiling the few eggs that had been collected for the departed. Laggle, the old female Brownrat, made Duggerlo recite the tale once more, then she composed a dirge for the slain chieftain. Laggle considered herself an accomplished Dirger, a highly respected position in the Brownrat horde.

That night, by the light of the fire, she sang unaccompanied in a flat monotone the words she had put together for her former boss. The others wolfed hard-boiled eggs, some for the first time, as they listened to the dirge.

"O come listen, ye Brownrats, take heed o' my words,
all about Gruntan Kurdly our chief,
for he stood fat an' tall, well respected by all,
as a murderin', plunderin' thief!
Kurdly rose through the ranks, with his foul,
    wicked pranks,
but his stomach grew greater than he,
an' his awful downfall, I'll relate to youse all,
was he loved hard-boiled eggs for his tea!
He had every bird flappin' round, lookin' scared,
as he hunted for eggs without rest,
an' against every wish, he would never eat fish,
Gruntan Kurdly craved eggs from the nest!
'Til one fatal day, O it grieves me to say,
that his greed got the better of him,
he set his sights on the fine egg of a swan,
that he thought had gone out for a swim!
Thinkin' that he knew best, Kurdly swam to the nest,
where the bird sat with its family,
'There's a rat at the door, Ma,' the little 'uns cried,
'an' he's after some eggs for his tea!'
Mrs. Swan in a huff, lookin' rowdy an' tough,
honked, 'Come here now, ye fat, thievin' rat!'
An' with many a blow, she laid pore Kurdly low,
just by usin' her beak like a bat!
Now against Kurdly's wishes, he's feedin' the fishes,
they're nibblin' his ears, snout an' legs,
but his ghost's at Hellgates, where I'm tellin' ye, mates,
'tis a place where they don't serve boiled eggs!"

In the silence which followed the dirge, the Brownrats
sat gazing into the fire. Noggo, who was forced to sit apart
from the rest, owing to the stench of rotten eggs which
clung to his fur, sniffed brokenly. "We'll never get anudder
boss like ole Gruntan."

Laggle cackled. "Not if'n we're lucky we won't!"

325

Noggo's companion Biklo, the other scout, spread his paws in bewilderment. "But without the boss, wot are we goin' t'do about Stringle an' all the others?"

Laggle tossed more wood on the fire, she stared around at the company in disbelief. "Look at ye all, are ye dull, daft or just dozy? Who needs a boss anymore, or did ye enjoy carryin' Kurdly everywhere on yore backs! The great, bullyin' lard barrel, he's gone now, an' good riddance, sez I. Hah, as for Stringle an' the rest, let 'em get on with it. If'n they likes fightin' an' warrin', then I'll be the lastbeast to stop 'em, aye, or join 'em!"

The leaderless Brownrats sat openmouthed, taken aback by the old ratwife's attitude.

Noggo rose, pacing about in agitation. "But . . . but . . . wot are we goin' to do?"

Young Duggerlo suddenly blurted out, "Anythin' we wants to, that's wot!"

Laggle rocked back and forth, cackling wildly. "Heehee-heehee! There's a rat with more brains than the lot of ye. Lissen to 'im, ye thick'eaded clods! Ye don't 'ave t'do any-thin' fer Gruntan fattygut Kurdly no more, he's deader'n a fried frog. Ye can please yoreselves wot ye do, yore free!"

Biklo scratched his head hard. "An' wot are you goin' t'do, old 'un?"

Laggle snuggled down by the fire. "Me? I'm goin' to sleep late in the mornin'. An' I ain't movin' from 'ere. I likes these watermeadows, there's everythin' I needs right 'ere. Water, vittles, long, sunny days an' nobeast to give me orders!"

Duggerlo smiled. "I'm with ye, granny!"

The rest of the company were quick to agree.

"Aye, me, too, no giant stripe'ound's gonna slay me!"

"Right, mate, we can boil eggs for ourselves from now on!"

"Haharr, I'm goin' to break Kurdly's litter up, an' make a nice liddle shelter out of it!"

"You do that, mate, I'm sure ole Gruntan won't object."

"Aye, Kurdly's boss o' the fishes now, wonder wot they think of 'im?"

Laggle replied between cackles, "Heeheehee, they prob'ly think the boss tastes a bit eggy. Heeheeheehee!"

34

Stringle backed nervously away from the band of *Bludgullet* vermin, as their captain, Vizka, advanced, his long fangs showing in a broad smile.

"Don't be frightened, friend, I only wants ta talk."

Stringle blustered to hide his fear. "I ain't frightened of ye, fox, I'm cap'n of Gruntan Kurdly's Brownrats, we chased you up the ditch, remember?"

The golden fox continued smiling. "Aye, but it was us who chased yew down der ditch first." He shoved the magnificent sword he was carrying into his waist sash, and hung the mace and chain, which he was also armed with, across his shoulders. "Don't worry, I ain't here ta harm ye. We both wants ta put an end to dose creatures up dere on de rocks. So why don't me'n'yew join forces, we'd stan' a better chance together, don't ya t'ink?"

Stringle backed off farther, holding up a paw. "Wait." Grabbing a nearby Brownrat, he muttered furiously to him, "Get back to the boss, quick as ye can. Tell 'im I needs 'im 'ere, urgent!" Stringle turned back to the fox, who was lounging casually against a poplar. "Er, 'ow many warriors do ye have, we've got an 'orde."

Vizka chuckled, enjoying the Brownrat's discomfort. "A

horde, eh, dat could mean any number. I got enough to 'elp out 'ere. Wot d'ya say, Cap'n?"

Stringle hesitated. "Er, I dunno. . . . I mean, I'll 'ave to wait an' see wot Gruntan Kurdly sez."

Welcome paws reached out, helping the Guosim up onto the plateau. Osbil dispensed with greetings, joining Maudie and Rangval in a parrying movement against the *Bludgullet* vermin who were scaling the rim behind them.

"Drive those scum back, mates. Logalogalogaloooog!" Half the Guosim joined the charge, the remainder staying with the two badgers to defend the front edge of the plateau. The Sea Raiders were taken off guard by the wild sally, it was not long before the defenders had full control of the table-shaped sandstone top.

Introductions were made until Salixa was acquainted with everybeast. Gorath clasped Osbil's paw. "That was a brave charge you made, those Brownrats had you well out-numbered, you did well to break through."

The Guosim Log a Log sheathed his rapier. "What happened to young Orkwil?"

Maudie shrugged ruefully. "Can't say, old lad, one moment he was with me'n'Rangval, next thing he was gone. We're tryin' not to think the worst about him."

Rangval let his tail droop mournfully. "Ah, there's only one reason a pore creature goes missin' in the midst of a fight. Orkwil was a good little feller, I'll miss him, so I will!"

Maudie chaffed the rogue squirrel. "Come on, you old misery, tails up, wot! Look on the bright side, Orkwil might be fine an' well!"

Salixa turned in a slow arc, taking in the whole plateau. "Yes, let's hope he is. Meanwhile, we have other things to consider before this affair is over."

Osbil looked up from sharpening his rapier. "Wot sort o' things, miz?"

One of the Guosim, a gruff-mannered old shrew, snorted. "We ain't 'ere t'think, missy, us Guosim are 'ere to fight!"

Gorath silenced him with a severe glance. "Listen to what Salixa has to say, she has learned much from the Tabura, and does not talk just to hear the sound of her own voice."

Osbil tested the edge of his blade by licking it. "Aye, be quiet an' let's hear wot she has t'say."

The slender badgermaid did not have to raise her voice. There was a calmness about her as she spoke. "The one good thing to come out of this is that the Abbey need not fear attack. The enemies of Redwall are surrounding us at the moment, they cannot turn their backs on our force, small as it is. However, we are cut off up here, and out-numbered by Brownrats and the sea vermin. So, I think our main concern for the moment is, how do we defend our position?" By Salixa's tone, she was obviously looking for suggestions.

Rangval peered over the sandstone rim. "Sure, 'twas a charge that got these shrews up here, couldn't we make a grand ould stampede back down agin?"

There were murmurs of agreement from the Guosim, who were always headstrong, and ready for a fight.

Maudie shook her head. "Bad idea, old chap, not good form!"

The rogue squirrel deferred to the haremaid. "Well, it's the best I can do for ye, me darlin'. Though bein' a mem-ber o' that Long Patrol from Salamandastron, I suppose ye'll know a thing or two about warfare. So, Maudie me gel, wot's yore plan?"

Smiling ruefully, the haremaid scratched one ear. "Ac-tually, I haven't got a single bloomin' idea. But let's see if I can't think this thing out, the way Major Mullein would. Right, how are we in the jolly old weapons department? Osbil?"

The Guosim chieftain gave his estimate. "Slings'n'stones

aplenty, an' everybeast's carryin' a blade. There's a few spears we picked up from the vermin, an' few spare pikes an' axes. Oh, an' we've got almost a score o' bows, but not so many arrows. Apart from Gorath's great pitchfork, that's about it!"

Maudie began pacing slowly, back and forth. "More important right now, what's the position on food an' drink?"

Salixa interrupted. "Food and drink, why is that more important than weapons?"

Maudie was back into thinking like a Long Patrol hare now, she gave Salixa a quick salute. "Stan' corrected, miz, I should've said food'n'drink is as important as weapons, allow me to explain myself. Never underestimate the foebeast, y'see. Vermin are crafty blighters, wot! They're down below, where they can jolly well forage for vittles in the woodlands, and of course there's always water, streams an' such, down there. Meanwhile, here's poor old us, stuck on flippin' top of a stretch o' bare rock. Osbil, old scout, have ye sorted out how much fodder we've got, eh?"

Osbil beckoned to one of the Guosim cooks, who answered glumly. "Nothin' much, a few apples, two wheatloaves, a hunk o' hard cheese, an' three canteens, two of water, an' one o' shrewbeer. That's all. I didn't think we was goin' t'be away from the Abbey for too long."

Maudie carried on with her summary, to Salixa. "So there you have it, miz, virtually no rations at all. If those vermin cads down there happen t'make an educated guess, we're deadbeasts. They can lay siege to this plateau, which means do nothin' really, just lay about, eatin' an' drinkin'. They'll fire off the odd stone, or arrow, to keep our heads low. But in the end they'll starve us down. Either that, or wait'll we're too weak to fight back, then we'll be overrun an' slaughtered by the bounders. Pretty grim, wot?"

Rangval rubbed his stomach. "Grim, y'say, it sounds awful. Shure, I'm startin' t'feel hungry right now, an' I could do with an ould drop to wet me lips. 'Tis goin' t'get hot up here!"

331

Salixa tweaked the rogue squirrel's ear lightly. "Well, that sort of talk isn't doing anybeast a bit of good. The more we forget food, the less hungry we're likely to be!"

Rangval was forced to agree. "The very thought that just leapt into me own foolish ould mind, miz. But wot in the name o' seasons do we do, just sit up here an' wait t'get starved or slayed t'death? I'm not the one t'be doin' that in a hurry!"

Maudie knew she was clutching at straws, but a faint idea had formed in her mind. "I say, chaps, suppose we take the battle to the vermin from up here? What I mean is, we keep our heads well down, whilst keepin' a strong eye peeled on the villains, an' pick 'em off one by flippin' one, wot!"

Osbil unwound the sling from about his waist. "Let's do that, 'tis better'n sittin' up here twiddlin' our paws. Guosim, split up into four groups. Rigril, take yours to the rear. Teagle an' Frenna, you take your crews either side, t'the north an' south. I'll stay here at the front with my lot. How'll that do for ye, Maudie?"

Lying down flat, the haremaid peered over the rim to the woodlands below. "Aye, mate, let's see how much damage we can cause. Use slingstones an' bows, but go easy with the arrows, we're a bit short of shafts."

Lying alongside Maudie, Osbil shielded his eyes, peering intently at the scene below. "Wot's goin' on down there, between those two black poplars? Looks like some sort o' meetin', can't see 'em properly. You take a peek."

Maudie watched carefully, though her view, like Osbil's, was obscured by the dense poplar foliage. "Hmm, looks like Brownrats an' some o' the other vermin t'me. Let's wait an' see if they show their scruffy faces a bit clearer, wot!"

Vizka Longtooth was still silently enjoying Stringle's embarrassment, though he hid it well. Crouching down with his back to the poplar trunk, he feigned a yawn. "Where's dis boss o' yores gotten to, huh? I'm growin' old, hangin' round waitin' fer 'im."

Stringle paced back and forth, wracked by indecision. "Well, there ain't nothin' for it, Cap'n Longtooth, I've got me orders from Gruntan Kurdly 'isself, an' I've got t'wait on 'is word for any change in plans."

Vizka toyed with the pommel stone of his beautiful sword. "Well said, Cap'n Stringle, but I can't wait ferever. Wot were dese orders Kurdly gave ya?"

Stringle explained. "To slay those stripe'ounds, an' bring their 'eads back to the boss, on spearpoints."

The golden fox replied in a cheery tone, "Der very t'ing I wuz plannin' t'do! Lissen, mate, t'wouldn't do no harm fer us t'join forces an' get der job done. I'm sure ya boss'd be pleased, eh?"

However, Stringle continued hesitating, walking to and fro, trying to put Vizka off until the arrival of Kurdly.

On the rim of the plateau, Osbil peered down, his voice rising with excitement. "That's the Brownrat's officer, Stringle. Look, there he is now, wanderin' in an' out o' the poplars!"

Maudie could see the Brownrat down below, moving in and out of the covering foliage. "Indeed, that'll be the very blighter. But why's he so jolly important?"

Osbil gritted his teeth. " 'Cos he's the one who was leadin' the gang wot chased ye that night, you'n liddle Yik, an' our ole Log a Log. That scum must be the one who was responsible for my father's death. My Guosim told me Gruntan Kurdly didn't arrive at the south wall 'til long after you'n Yik made it inside the Abbey. Aye, he's the one who has to pay, gimme a bow, somebeast, an' a good, straight shaft!"

An older shrew passed Osbil his bow. "Try mine, Chief, 'tis the best bow in our tribe. Wait whilst I find ye a decent arrow." Sorting through his quiver, he selected one. Holding it to his eye, the older shrew sighted along the shaft, checking it. "Aye, this is a good 'un, straight'n'true. I made it meself out o' sessile oak, fletched it with a white gull feather, tipped it with best flint."

As Osbil set the shaft on the bowstring, Salixa joined him and Maudie, judging the target. "If you don't mind me saying, that will be a very hard shot to make. I know a little archery, would you like me to try?"

Osbil shook his head stubbornly. "No, miz, I won't be indebted to anybeast, 'tis my shot!"

Maudie whispered to Salixa, "Family honour an' all that, y'know, touchy types, these Guosim chaps, wot!"

They held their breath as Osbil hauled back on his bowstring. He sighted a moment, then dropped his paws with a snort of frustration. "Blood'n'fur, he's moved back into the trees. I'll have to wait for him to show himself agin!"

Salixa knelt by Osbil's side, advising him calmly, "Loosen up a little, you're too tense. That's better! Now, don't wait until the rat's right out in the open. Wait until you see him show, then fire your shaft slightly ahead of his position, aim at the spot where his next pace will place him. Now, pull back your bowstring in one movement, smoothly. That's right. . . . Fire!"

Vizka was beginning to lose patience with Stringle, who was still dithering over a decision, afraid to commit himself. "If'n 'twas up to me, I'd join ye right away, Cap'n Longtooth, but I've got to wait fer Grunt . . ." The Brownrat gave a strange gurgle and sat down. He swayed for a moment, then slumped forward, still in the sitting position.

Vizka had witnessed sudden death many times, he immediately dropped flat, calling to his crew, who were waiting nearby. "Git down, we're bein' fired on!"

Everybeast hugged the ground, waiting. After awhile it became apparent that no attack was being mounted. On his captain's command, the stoat, Patchy, crawled across to inspect Stringle.

"Deader'n a cold stone, Cap'n, de arrer went right atwixt 'is eyes. Dat's a fair birra shootin' from atop o' dose rocks!"

The golden fox spat at Stringle's carcass. "Saved me a job, I was gonna slay 'im meself. Dat fool was holdin' t'ings up. Right, Patchy, Dogleg, Ragchin an' Jungo! Git round to dose Brownrats, tell 'em Cap'n Stringle wants a werd wid dem."

Jungo looked at Stringle's slumped form. "But Cap'n, dat 'un can't say a werd to anybeast no more."

Vizka fixed the dull-witted weasel with a deadly smile. "Aye, an' yew won't either if'n ya don't do like I says!"

Rangval pounded Osbil's back. "I knew ye could do it, mate, shure it was a grand shot, so 'twas, clean as a whistle!"

Maudie shook her shrew friend by his paw. "Well done, sah! That's one rascal whose murderin' days are over, wot! So, how does it feel, bucko? You've done what you wished, put paid to your dear old dad's killer."

Osbil passed the bow back to its owner, commenting, "Too far off t'feel anything, miz. Wish I could've met the rat face-to-face, an' paw-to-paw, made him beg for mercy afore I slayed him!"

Surprised by his vehemence, Maudie shook her head. "Golly, you're a savage young feller, Osbil."

The Guosim Log a Log nodded. "I'm a Guosim an' I am wot I am. Tell me, miz, would you feel the same about some vermin who'd killed yore father?"

The haremaid was forced to concur with his logic. "You can bet your bally boots I would, bucko!" To change the subject, Maudie took stock of the scene, staring down at the woodlands. "Seems to have gone jolly quiet down there, wot? Nobeast chargin' or retaliatin', wonder what's goin' on?"

Gorath leaned on his pitchfork, watching the land below

335

the plateau. "Mayhaps they're getting ready for an all-out effort. What do you think, Salixa?"

The badgermaid summed up her outlook on the situation. "I don't think they'll be mounting any major attack, we're in too strong a position at the moment. If the fox is in command, he'll lay siege to us. Without supplies or reinforcements, time isn't on our side. The vermin still have us far outnumbered, I think they'll play the waiting game. It's the sensible thing to do, and it will save them losing more creatures on their side."

Rangval winked at Gorath, remarking quietly, "Ah now, there's a pretty maid who's as brainy as she's beautiful. Ye couldn't do much better'n to stick with her, if'n I say so meself!"

Gorath winked back at the rogue squirrel. "I intend to!"

The day rolled onward, with the sun mounting high on the shadeless sandstone plateau. Together with Salixa and Kachooch, Maudie helped to apportion and distribute their scant ration of food and drink. Like most hares, Maudie had always been blessed with a healthy appetite. She viewed her miserable ration gloomily, a slice of apple, a small piece of hard cheese, a tiny crust of bread and half a beaker of watered-down shrewbeer.

It was the same for everybeast. The normally cheerful Rangval scowled at his portion in disbelief. "In the name of pity, is this all we're gettin'? Shure, there's not enough nourishment here to keep fur'n'bone t'gether!"

Gorath caught the disapproving glance which Salixa shot at the rogue squirrel. Shielding Rangval from the Guosim with his huge bulk, Gorath lectured him tersely. "I know it's little enough, friend, but don't start complaining. You'll not only upset the Guosim, but should any of the vermin hear you, they'll know what a bad fix we're in, d'you understand?"

Rangval saluted smartly several times. "Ah, shure yore right, sir, aren't I the pudden-headed ould grouser. Now

336

don't you go frettin' yore grand self, leave it t'me, I'll soon put things right."

Gorath watched him as he sat on the rim of the plateau, dangling his footpaws. Salixa also watched Rangval.

"What's he up to now?"

Gorath shrugged his mighty shoulders. "I'm sure we'll soon find out, one way or another."

They did, as did everybeast on both sides, a moment later. The rogue squirrel began yelling at the top of his voice. His plan was to fool the vermin into thinking that there was no shortage of food or drink on top of the plateau.

"Ah, cook darlin', will ye take those mushroom an' gravy pasties out o' me sight. If'n I eats one more I'll burst. Just pass me a flagon of that grand ould October Ale ye've got coolin' in the shade, if y'please."

Rangval continued as though he were conversing with some imaginary cook. "What's that? No, no, I couldn't manage another crumb of that plum'n'apple pudden. No, I'm sorry, cooky, cheese'n'leek turnover, I've already had two. Are ye tryin' t'stuff me to death with yore fine vittles! Lissen, t'me, for pity's sake. I don't want any more to eat! No fresh-baked bread an' soft cheese, no summer veggible soup, meadowcream scones, strawberry preserve, fruit cake, elderberry jelly or cold mint tea. Just a drop of the October Ale, to settle me pore, groanin' ould stummick. Yowch!"

A well-aimed slingstone hit Rangval's bushy eartip. Wincing and rubbing his stinging ear, he grunted. "Ah, I'm gettin' through t'the scummy ould vermin at last!" He turned in time to see a Guosim shrew launch another pebble at him. Leaping to one side smartly, the rogue squirrel complained bitterly. "Cease fire, ye eejit, are ye tryin' to kill me?"

Osbil signalled the warrior to stay his paw. The shrew chieftain glared angrily at Rangval. "I'll do the job for him if'n ye don't shut up goin' on an' on about vittles!"

337

"Aye, matey, belay that talk!"

The squirrel countered indignantly, "Wasn't I only tauntin' the villains, to make 'em think we're not short o' a bite to eat up here?"

Both beasts were in a fine temper, threatening one another as they came nose to nose.

Maudie forced her way between the irate pair. "Steady on, chaps, there's no blinkin' need for all this shoutin' an' arguin', eh, wot!"

Osbil seethed, "Then tell that fool to shuttup about vittles!"

Rangval gritted his teeth aloud. "You tell that dimwit I was only doin' it to tease the enemy!"

Maudie felt herself drawn into the quarrel, she wagged a paw under Rangval's nose, raising her voice. "It's you who's the dimwit. Teasin' the enemy, if y'please, did it occur to you that it might jolly well be your own side who are bein' teased twice as bad, eh?"

It was Salixa's calm demeanour that halted the row. "What Maudie means is that we're the ones who have no food or water. Down there the foebeast can forage for their needs, and there's probably a stream close by. I'm sorry, Rangval, but yelling about delicious food is only upsetting your own comrades."

The sun beat down mercilessly on the bare rock plateau as the three creatures stopped their argument. There was an awkward silence, which was broken by Gorath as he peered down to the bushy shade, where Stringle's carcass still lay. "It's gone very quiet down there. I wonder what's going on?"

Rangval tried to get in the closing remark. "Maybe I made 'em hungry, an' they've toddled off to lunch somewhere, aye, that'll be it!"

Gorath's level stare silenced the rogue squirrel. Salixa patted the big badger's paw comfortingly. "Whatever's going on down there is nothing we can't take care of together."

Things were going better for Vizka Longtooth than he imagined they would. Suddenly the golden fox had more beasts under his command than ever before in his infamous career. He had two things to thank for this stroke of fortune, the death of Stringle and his own powers of eloquence. That, plus the fact that Brownrats were not the smartest of vermin. Without a leader, the Brownrat horde were fish out of water. Once the word got around that Stringle had been slain, the Brownrats did what they had always done, sat and waited for somebeast (usually Gruntan Kurdly) to galvanise them back into action. Stringle had been Kurdly's sole leading officer. Now that he was gone, the Brownrats were waiting for somebeast to tell them what to do.

Vizka was quick to realise this. He delegated each of his crew to act as group leaders. As tawdry as they were, the seafaring vermin looked superior to Brownrats, who were little better than primitive savages with their paint-daubed fur and stone-tipped clubs or spears. Vizka sent his crew among the horde, to order (not invite) all Brownrats to a meeting with him, in a clearing, west of the plateau.

Wielding the sword of Martin in one paw, and carrying his mace and chain in the other, he watched them file silently into the woodland clearing, they outnumbered his crew by at least six to one. The Brownrats seated themselves on the sward, whilst the *Bludgullet*'s crew stood around behind them on the fringe of the gathering. The golden fox took the floor, smiling as he made his address, his quick eyes watching everybeast closely.

"I'm Vizka Longtooth, cap'n o' der Sea Raiders. I just seen yore cap'n, Stringle, killed by dat lot up dere. Bunch o' cowards, wouldn't come down an' fight proper, slayed pore Stringle wid an arrer from far off. Jus' when we'd reached an agreement!"

Vizka paced up and down, eyeing the silent rats, waiting for a reaction. They stared dumbly back at him. He put a paw to the side of his mouth, as if imparting a secret. "Aye, an agreement, an' ya know worrit was?" There was still no reaction, so he continued dramatically. "Dat we all join t'gedder in one big 'orde to defeat dat lot up dere. Me'n Stringle woulda commanded t'gether, but now dat yore cap'n's been merdered, youse'll have ta take orders from me. Unless ye've got anudder cap'n?" Sticking the sword point down into the soil, Vizka draped the mace and chain around his neck, allowing his gaze to range over the assembly.

A voice spoke out. "Worrabout Gruntan Kurdly, 'e's our chief, Stringle always waited fer him afore doin' anythin'." The speaker was a big, lean, tough-looking rat.

Vizka began moving through the seated throng toward him. "Wot's yore name, mate?"

The Brownrat met the fox's stare. "Gurba, me name's Gurba."

Vizka stopped in front of him. "Well, let me tell ya sumthin', Gurba. Yore Cap'n Stringle was waitin' on der big chief. Aye, waitin', while youse Brownrats was gettin' slayed by dose stripe'ounds an' shrews atop o' dat rock. But Stringle couldn't stand ter lose no more mates, 'e got tired o' waitin' fer Kurdly. Dat's why me'n 'im made de agreement, see!"

Something about the twist of the Brownrat's lip warned Vizka. He took a pace back as Gurba stood, holding his big, flint-tipped spear loosely, but ready for action. There was open defiance in his tone as he told Vizka, "I ain't agreed to nothin', neither 'ave the rest o' my mates. We'll wait for Gruntan Kurdly, an' see wot 'e sez!"

Vizka seemed to wilt in front of the bold, lean rat. He turned away shrugging his shoulders. "Fair enuff, if'n dat's 'ow ya feel. . . ." He spun around without warning, Gurba was taken by surprise. A clank of chain and the whirr of the steel-spiked ball was the last thing the Brownrat heard. There was a sickening crack of metal on bone, and Gurba lay dead on the ground with a smashed skull.

The golden fox stood smiling, his overlong fangs exposed as he toyed with the mace, flicking it with one paw, and catching the ball in the other. His tone was almost playful as he addressed his dumbfounded audience.

"We'll leave Gurba 'ere, to wait fer Kurdly. Jus' put ya paw up if'n ya wants ter join 'im . . . anybeast?" Not a single paw moved, the Brownrat horde sat in shocked silence, staring in awe at their new leader.

Vizka nodded, then got down to serious business. Retrieving his sword, he pointed to the plateau. "Wot's up dere, a coupla score o' liddle shrews, one rabbet, a squirrel an' two stripe'ounds. Dat's all wot stands atween us an' vict'ry. An' look at us, mates. A fine crew o' Sea Raiders, an' a full 'orde 'o fightin' Brownrat warriors. One good charge'd wipe all our foes out, a force our size couldn't lose. Nobeast but a few ole cooks an' a pack o' toddlin' babes would be left in dat Abbey. Jus' picture it, you'n'me an' Gruntan Kurdly, marchin' through der gates o' Redwall t'gether, wotja say, eh?"

The *Bludgullet*'s crew knew what to do, they took up the cry. "Aye, Cap'n, we're wid ya! Yaaaahaaarrr!"

Caught in the wild moment, Brownrats leapt upright, waving spears, clubs and slings as they roared. "Kurdly, Kurdly! Kill kill kill!"

Vizka let them carry on awhile, even encouraging them by waving both sword and mace. He allowed them to carry on until they began to sound hoarse, then he stood on a boulder, calling for silence. "Enough, all of ye, I knows yer all good beasts an' true!" He glanced toward the westering sun. "We'll camp 'ere for der night. Glurma, get some 'elp an' feed dis lot, git some cookin' fires lit. Rest now, me buckoes, look to ya weppins, eat'n'sleep, 'cos at dawnlight tamorra we got some slayin' ta do!"

Vizka wandered about, quietly contacting several from his crew vermin. "Ragchin, Dogleg, Patchy, Bilger, Firty. Set up a fire, away from dose Brownrats, I wants werds wid ya!"

35

It was the end of a hot, dry, dusty day on the high plateau. Osbil and Barbowla walked around the rim checking on the sentries. They paused at the western edge to see the scarlet orb of the sun descending amid strata of purple and gray clouds, some with gold-tipped underbellies.

Barbowla sighed, "A pretty picture, Log a Log, but I'd much sooner be seein' it from the doorstep of my holt up-river."

"Aye, me, too, mate, but we're up 'ere 'til the party ends for better or worse."

Barbowla pointed to a glow some distance off. "That clearin' in the trees yonder, I think the vermin are campin' there, that light looks like their fires."

Osbil studied the glow. "About six, maybe seven fires by the look of it."

"Ah well, we might get a bit of peace seein' as the foe's camped down for the night. I'll warn the sentries to keep their eyes peeled in case any vermin tries an ambush in the dark."

Osbil and Barbowla reported back to Gorath, who was sitting with Salixa, Maudie and Rangval around a small, boulder-ringed fire.

The big badger yawned. "I think you're right, those not on guard can rest tonight. Vizka will probably be having his supper and planning his next move."

A moan came from Rangval. Barbowla turned to him. "What's the matter with your face, rogue?"

Rangval stirred the flames with his dagger tip. "Ah, 'twas just the mention of supper . . ."

Maudie prodded him. "Don't even think about it, sah, we don't want you goin' off into vittles raptures again, wot."

The rogue squirrel looked injured by her attitude. "Ye've a harsh tongue, me beauty, but 'twas Gorath who mentioned vittles, not meself. Ah well, seein' as me freedom of speech is forbidden, I'll just have to give ye a bit of an ould song, eh?"

Maudie smiled. "You warble away to your heart's content, old lad, a jolly good ditty might cheer us up, wot!"

Rangval sat up straight, making ready to launch into song. "Thank ye kindly, miz. I'd like to start with a little thing entitled, 'Please pass the plate of peach'n'pear pudden.' "

Osbil waved a clenched paw. "Oh, no you won't!"

Rangval swiftly changed his selection. "Oh, right y'are, sir. Well, how about, 'Don't chomp cheese while yore mother's chewin' chestnuts'?" Rangval saw several Guosim shrews glaring at him and toying with their rapiers. He took the hint. "Er, as me third choice I'll give ye a rendition of me ould auntie's favourite. It's called 'The battle of the boiled beetroot an' how d'ye slice strawberry soup.' "

Maudie dived at the rogue and got him in a headlock. "Righto, you bushtailed bounder, now you've got two blinkin' options. You'll either hear me sing one called 'How to strangle a senseless squirrel,' with actions to suit the words, of course. Or you can simply belt up an' go t'sleep. Take your pick, sah!"

Rangval wailed as the haremaid's hold tightened.

343

"Mercy, marm, if'n ye throttle me ye'll never forgive yore-self. Desist from squeezin' me ould windpipe, an' I'll take me rest with sealed lips, so I will!"

After that, silence fell over the plateau for awhile as some slept, and others lay there, thinking of what the dawn would bring. Gorath sat alongside Salixa, letting the little fire burn low. They both lay back, gazing up at the star-spangled wilderness of dark night skies.

Salixa chaffed her big friend quietly. "I thought you were going to sing for a moment back there."

Gorath gave a deep chuckle at the thought. "Who, me, sing? No thank you, I only ever sang to myself as I worked on the land in the Northern Isles. Sometimes it was just to break the silence and loneliness. I think I've got a pretty awful singing voice, I'd never break into song whilst oth-erbeasts are listening."

The slender, young badgermaid turned toward him, she saw the starlight reflected in his huge, dark eyes. "It must have been very hard for you. Did you ever get angry about your lot, stranded there with your aged grandparents? Tell me, were you aware of the Bloodwrath?"

Gorath passed a paw over the scarlet wound on his brow. "Not really, but looking back on things, I know that my grandfather could see the Bloodwrath in me. He never spoke of it, but he knew, I realise that now."

Salixa frowned thoughtfully. "How so?"

Gorath explained, "When Grandfather was still able to work, we toiled side by side, getting the earth ready to plant crops. Often we would come across a big boulder, or an old tree, barring our progress. We'd try together to move the boulder, or uproot the tree. When we failed, Grandfather would stop work and sit down, then he'd say, 'It's too much for a young one and an oldster, but your fa-ther could have done it alone. Aye, he'd get into a temper with that boulder, or that tree, he'd shout Eulalia at it, and kick the thing with his paws. Go on, young one, give it a try.' So I did."

The badgermaid continued questioning. "What happened?"

The big, young badger flexed his mighty paws as he recalled the incident. "The first time it was a rock, a huge granite boulder, half-buried in the frozen earth. I shouted Eulalia at it until I was roaring, I struck the bare rock with my clenched paws. I didn't feel any pain, just a mighty surge of power building within me. My chest was heaving as I sucked in huge gasps of air. Suddenly I was yelling, panting and seeing the boulder through a red mist. I flung myself upon it, thrusting both paws deep into the soil either side of the stone. Grandfather told me later that I plucked that rock from the earth, as easy as if I were lifting a babe from its cradle. I lifted it and flung it from me. Either I passed out after that, or fell asleep, but I couldn't remember anything, except what Grandfather told me. I uprooted trees in the same way. I became bigger and stronger, my muscles grew hard."

Salixa picked up one of his hefty paws, she studied the tracery of old scars crisscrossing the pad. "So your grandfather goaded you into Bloodwrath to get the heavy work done. That was so unfair."

Gorath smiled. "That's what Grandma used to say to him, she said he was making me into a Berserker, who would die just as my father had. But it never bothered me then, I did the work of three badgers. Often I enjoyed the feeling, the rage and power, the knowledge that nothing could withstand my wild strength."

Gorath could see Salixa beginning to wince, he had unconsciously tightened his grip on her paw. Embarrassed, he quickly released her, changing the subject. "Enough about me. What about you? I'll wager you can sing."

She nodded. "I like to sing, but quietly, to myself. Sometimes I have sung for the Tabura, he enjoys my voice. Would you like me to sing for you?"

Gorath closed his eyes, afraid to look her way. "I could think of nothing I'd like better."

345

Everybeast heard the plaintive sweet voice, which, though gentle, seemed to radiate around the plateau.

"Let me wander here forever, through the glades
where once I played,
Long ago in carefree seasons, mid the noontide
sun and shade.
I will see again before me, all those smiling
friends I knew,
gone alas to memory's keeping, faithful comrades
good and true.
Oh, those days of youth and splendour, when we
dreamed of glorious war,
vows were made to keep forever, and return back
here once more.
Then the clouds began to gather, winter came,
we marched away,
singing songs of love and valour, off we went
into the fray.
Comes a warrior returning, to old autumn's gold-
clad trees,
where the leaves do fall like teardrops, on the
gently sighing breeze.
Casting sword and shield aside now, I stand
weary and forlorn,
in the silence of the woodlands, I will rest
until the dawn.
Let me sleep and dream forever, of the golden
days of yore,
and those friends who marched off with me,
who'll return alas no more."

Gorath opened his eyes. Gazing into the embers of the fire, he murmured, "I've never heard a song so sad and beautiful, where did you learn it?"
Drawing her cloak closer, Salixa lay down to rest. "The

Tabura taught it to me, he said it was something he had written a long time ago."

Gorath closed his eyes again. "Your Tabura is a wise and wonderful creature. I would like to spend some time with him—say, a few seasons. I'm sure he would have much to teach me."

The badgermaid paused before speaking again. "He was only my Tabura for a certain time. Now I will never see him again, and nor will you, friend."

Gorath was mystified. "How do you know this?"

Salixa replied, "Because he told me that the parting of our ways would come when we reached Redwall Abbey. I was sad at first, but the Tabura explained. He said that he had taught me many things, now it was my turn to go out into the world, to teach and help others. He also knew you and I would meet on the western plain, not far from Redwall, because we were destined to travel together, while he lived out his days at the Abbey. Now I know what he meant, I am sad no longer. I have you to look after. Sleep now, Gorath the Flame."

Gorath obeyed her. He did not know what to think, he was happy, quite puzzled, but certain he would never leave Salixa's side. They both slept then, the badgermaid to her own dreams and Gorath to his. Visions of heroic and wise warriors visited them both as they dwelt in the Halls of Slumber. Martin the Redwall Abbey Warrior, the Tabura, Lord Asheye and one whom Gorath recognised as his long-dead father. Each had their own special message to impart to the young badgers, each had a different instruction for Salixa and Gorath.

Maudie found she could not sleep, the feeling of impending battle on the morrow hung over her. Also, sleep was out of the question with Rangval close by, snoring like two wild hogs guzzling soup. She went and relieved a couple of Guosim sentries at the plateau rim, where she was joined by Barbowla's sturdy wife, Kachooch. The otterwife winked at her knowingly.

"For somebeasts like us, sleep's hard t'come by on a night like this, Miz Maudie."

The haremaid nodded. "Indeed it is, marm, an' twice as hard with a rogue squirrel snorin' nearby."

Kachooch chuckled quietly. "Aye, an' maybe thrice as hard bein' surrounded by shrews with growly stummicks. I thought the battle had already started with all the noise that gang was makin'. Have ye been in many battles afore, Maudie?"

Keeping her gaze on the glow from the distant campfires, Maudie answered, "Oh, one or two y'know, pretty difficult to avoid skirmishin' bein' a fightin' hare o' the Long Patrol. Tell me, marm, d'you think those vermin fires are beginnin' to die down, or are they still as bright?"

The otterwife peered hard at the distant glow. "I'd say they've died down a mite, why d'ye ask?"

Maudie explained, "If the fires are allowed t'burn low, that usually means the vermin are sleepin'. But if they burn fresh'n'bright, that means they're jolly well up to some mischief."

Kachooch scratched her rudder. "What sort o' mischief?"

It was the haremaid's turn to wink at the otterwife. "It's an old trick, marm, pretty stupid one if you ask me. If the rascals want to sneak up an' ambush us in the dark, they always leave a couple of vermin behind, to keep the fires burnin' bright. Just so we'll think they're still in camp."

The otterwife was puzzled. "Doesn't sound too stupid t'me."

Maudie tapped the side of her head. "Think. Who'd stay awake on a summer night, to pile wood on fires? Wouldn't it be more sensible to sleep before the battle, like our chaps are doin' right now?"

Kachooch grinned. "Yore right, of course, but if'n 'tis more sensible t'sleep, why are we sittin' here wide awake?"

Maudie shrugged. "I suppose because the most highly sensible of us has to stay alert, to watch the foe."

Kachooch shook with silent mirth as she cast an eye over the snoring plateau defenders. "Don't say much for that lot, do it?"

Maudie smiled. "Indeed it doesn't. Let's hope the blinkin' vermin types are snorin' their thick heads off twice as flippin' hard, wot!"

At the vermin camp, the Brownrats were complying with Maudie's wish. However, Vizka and his cohorts were wide awake, the golden fox was explaining his plans for the battle. "Lissen, mateys, we've got der Brownrats on our side now. If'n we kin get dem up on dat rock tommorer dey'll slaughter dem Abbeybeasts, der Brownrats'll 'ave 'em far outnumbered."

Ragchin ventured an opinion. "I was t'inkin', Cap'n, wot if'n dis Gruntin' Kurly shows up before de attack, wot then?"

"Gudd question, bucko, 'ere's wot ya do. Yew keep Kurly talkin' 'til I gets be'ind 'im . . ." Vizka brandished his mace and Martin's sword under Ragchin's scruffy beard. "Den jus' leave 'im t'me!"

The small crewrat Firty wanted to know more about his role in the coming fray. "Wot ja want us t'do, Cap'n, lead der charge?"

Vizka beckoned them closer, dropping his voice. "No, Firty, mate, I wants youse, dat's yerself, Dogleg, Ragchin, Patchy an' Bilger, ta stick close t'me. I've told de other crewbeasts ta go up the rock wid der Brownrats, dey should be able ta do der job." He looked from one to the other of the chosen five. "But jus' in case dey don't, or if'n everythin' goes wrong, youse are de ones I trusts, ter get me away safe, see!"

Bilger, who was the slowest witted, enquired, "Er, getcha away, Cap'n, where to?"

Vizka looked as if he were going to strike Bilger for his

stupidity, but he smiled, patting the stoat's cheek good-naturedly. "Off through dese trees, to dat path we came down. Back up it dis time, to the *Bludgullet*!"

Bilger chuckled. "Oh, d'ship, I'd fergot about dat!"

Patchy nudged him roughly. "But der cap'n 'ad'nt."

Vizka winked at Patchy. "Right, mate. A good cap'n always takes care of 'is trusty crew, yore d'ones I chose ta go wid me. Now lissen, youse all keep t'der rear wid me, we'll take care of any backsliders wot doesn't join in der charge. Like I said, we should win 'cos we've got der numbers on our side. But, if'n somethin' does go wrong, ye'll 'ear me shout dis. 'Fight on, me brave buckoes!' Dat's der signal, we leaves 'em to it an' makes for der ship. Hah, dere's plenty of other ways to de easy life, we'll sail off to der far south t'see wot der pickin's are like, eh, mates?"

The five vermin agreed readily, happy they would not have to fight, and maybe die, with the rest.

Ragchin spoke for them all. "We're wid ya, Cap'n!"

Vizka nodded. "Right, we'll set off for der rock just afore dawn. One good charge'll catch 'em still nappin'. Firty, tell Glurma to keep two Brownrats back. Dey can keep der fires goin' so 'twill look like we're layin' about eatin' brekkist."

Firty went off to find old Glurma, shaking his head in admiration at Vizka. The golden fox had thought of everything, he was a smartbeast sure enough.

36

Dawn broke in a gray haze, without a single ray of sunlight, or wisp of breeze. It was like an autumn day instead of late summer. Swathes of fine drizzle dampened the woodlands, causing heavy mist to rise amid the trees. Maudie stood at the edge of the plateau with Rangval and Osbil, surveying the scene below, the rogue squirrel spoke in hushed tones.

"Shure, will ye look at it? I'll wager ye couldn't see yore paw behind ye in all that fog!"

Maudie reprimanded him smartly. "Yes sah, but we're not lookin' for that. If we're not jolly well wide awake an' alert, 'tis quite likely we'll find ourselves ambushed an' overrun by the bally enemy, wot. So keep those eyes peeled!"

Kachooch came hurrying over, from where she had been standing with the haremaid during the night. "Miz Maud, I can see the campfires glowin' bright, even through this mist!"

Osbil scowled sourly as his stomach rumbled. "Aye, that's 'cos that scum down there ain't short o' vittles, they're prob'ly cookin' brekkist."

Maudie licked at the drizzling rain which clung to her lips. "No such thing, bucko, this is it, stand fast the buffs, 'tis death before dinner. Right, now, you chaps have a word with our badger chums, then put the word about quietly. Muster to the edges in full fightin' order. Let's see if we can't turn the ambush on the confounded vermin, wot!"

Vizka Longtooth drew his cloak close, against the prevailing drizzle. He sheltered in the bushes, surrounded by his chosen aides. Raindrops glistened on his fangs. "Dis is perfect for der surprise attack, no wind, rain, fog. Dey won't know wot hit 'em. Dogleg, Patchy, go an' tell 'em t'start the first wave climbin'. Once dey're outta sight, send der second lot up. Don't fergit, tell 'em ta keep silent. Now go!"

With ten of the *Bludgullet*'s crew to lead them, and another ten at the rear to urge them on, half of the Brownrat horde began scrambling up toward the plateau. They were a barbaric sight, daubed with plant dyes, armed with primitive spears and clubs, escorted by the vermin Sea Raiders. Once they were about a third of the way up, the second wave came in their wake, with the remainder of Vizka's crew shepherding them.

The going was not easy, with rocks made slippery by the drizzle, and any patches of earth rendered slick and muddy. The Sea Raiders, fearing their captain's wrath, urged the Brownrats on. Trying not to betray their position by shouting, they swiped out with the flats of their blades, muttering, "Git movin', ya big, dumb savages, c'mon, shift yer paws!" and "Ahoy there, bucko, no backslidin', up y'go!"

Gorath patrolled the defenders on the plateau rim, checking that their weapons were at the ready. He was accompanied by Salixa and Maudie, both of whom had armed themselves with slings. The haremaid could see that the Guosim were eager for action, so she constantly cautioned them.

"Don't go hurlin' stones, spears or arrows until you can

actually see the blighters. All this fog an' mist can create false impressions, y'know."

A young shrew twirled his sling restlessly. "I know, marm, I keep thinkin' I kin see their ugly mugs comin' at me through the mist, but it ain't nothin'. Plays tricks wid the eyes, all this fog."

Maudie patted the young warrior's shoulder. "You'll be alright, just trust your own best judgement. Don't worry, we're all a bit edgy, wot!"

Rangval loomed up chuckling. "Ah well, 'tis no surprise we're edgy. Sure, aren't we standin' on the edge here?"

The haremaid half-grinned. "Oh, very droll indeed, sah . . ." At the sight of a painted Brownrat face materialising out of the fog behind Rangval, she whirled her sling.

However, Gorath the Flame was even quicker. Leaping forward he thrust his pitchfork, catching the Brownrat in the throat. The vermin vanished with a horrible gurgle.

Like lightning, the war cries of the defenders rang out. "Eulaliiiiaaaaa! Logalogalogalooooooog!"

They were echoed by the advancing horde. "Kurdly Kurdly kill kill kill! Blood'n'bones! Hahaaaarr!"

The battle was on.

Maudie was everywhere at once, swinging a loaded sling at vermin heads, stamping and kicking at paws that came over the top, yelling like a wildbeast. "Yaaarrr! Blood'n'vinegar, chaps!"

Rangval, with a dagger in either paw, scuttled, crouching crablike as he circled the rim, stabbing out left and right. "Arrah, step up, ye villains, an' meet the rogue!"

Osbil saw a shrew take a spear through his heart, the Guosim chieftain ran to fill the gap as his comrade fell. His rapier weaved a flashing pattern in the ceaseless drizzle as he carved and thrust, howling aloud. "S'death to ye, vermin, an' I'm the beast to bring it! Logalogalooooog!"

Salixa tried to keep at Gorath's side, fearing that he might take the Bloodwrath and fling himself over at the enemy. The huge, young badger was a fearsome sight, often he would cast Tung, his pitchfork, to one side, and grab a vermin from the edge. Lifting the foebeast high above his head, he would hurl him, screaming, into the mist-filled void. Salixa felt the rain driving on one side of her face, she called out in her excitement, "A wind is springing up!"

Maudie whooped. "Eulaliiiaaaa! That'll shift this bloomin' mist, wot! Come on, you vermin, let's see your foul faces. Come and face us!"

Like a magical spell, the driving wind cleared the air. Rangval groaned. "I wish ye hadn't said that, me darlin', just look at this mob comin' up at us!"

Brownrats and crew vermin could be clearly seen now, swarming up the cliffsides in their masses. There was enough of the enemy to swamp the plateau twice over. Maudie was beyond reason in her mad fury. She battered away with a captured Brownrat spear, roaring, "Yaaahaaar, let's see how many of 'em we can take with us, make 'em pay a dear price for this rock!"

Vizka Longtooth stepped out from the brush cover, his teeth bared in a triumphal grin as he turned to look at the plateau, where vermin were starting to clamber up onto the flat summit. "Guts'n' 'ellsteeth, dey've made it!"

Almost half of the first wave were on top, the second wave were only a short distance from joining them. Ragchin performed a little dance of delight. "Ya did it, Cap'n, we're winnin'. Yeeehoooo!"

A crew member, who was leaping up onto the plateau, heard Ragchin's shout. He turned, waving his blade, roaring back down to his shipmate, "Yeeeeh—"

Vizka saw him topple forward, with an arrow through him. The golden fox stared at Ragchin. "Wot's goin' on up dere?"

From behind him a bloodcurdling war cry rang out. "Redwaaaaaaaaalllllll!"

It was Orkwil Prink and Abbot Daucus, heading the

largest, most motley crowd of creatures ever assembled outside of Redwall Abbey. Scores of squirrel archers were sending flights of arrows zipping into the climbing vermin. These squirrels stayed in the upper treetops, moving neither backward or forward. In serried ranks upon the boughs they kept a constant shower of shafts, winging like angry wasps, dealing death widespread into the enemy. Moles, hedgehogs, mice, otters and more shrews, wielding a staggering array of makeshift weapons, came bulling through bush and shrub, howling fiercely. "Redwaaaaaaalllllll! Redwaaaaaaaalllllll!"

Some crewbeasts and Brownrats came hurrying back to where Vizka was standing with his aides. The weasel named Jungo was clearly perplexed. He stared dully at the golden fox.

"We was up dere, Cap'n, I t'ink we was winnin', den arrows started bringin' our beasts down. Who is it, Cap'n, wot's all der shoutin' about?"

Vizka laughed, he shook Jungo by the paw, and moved among the others patting backs and nodding. "It ain't nothin', friends, I'll take care of it!" He gave a significant wink to Ragchin and the others. Gesturing Jungo to go back to attacking the plateau, Vizka called aloud, "Fight on! Fight on, me brave buckoes!" As Jungo and the Brownrats charged off to do his bidding, Vizka whispered to his five crewbeasts, "Time ta get outta dis place, take me ta the *Bludgullet*!"

The tide had turned on top of the plateau, now there were not so many vermin about. Maudie glanced down at those who were about halfway up. They had retreated from being a hairsbreadth from their goal, they seemed bewildered. Vizka Longtooth's shouts urged them to go forward, he was waving sword and mace as he called for them to fight on. However, the victory cries of vengeful Guosim shrews, and the carcasses of vermin hurtling down on them, swiftly decided their course of action. They turned and fled in retreat, attempting to avoid their new assailants. The shouts of the Redwall supporters were everywhere. It was retribution time for Sea Raiders and the once-feared Brownrats of Gruntan Kurdly.

The fire of battle was in the blood of Mad Maudie (the Hon.) Mugsberry Thropple. She feinted with a right uppercut, and dealt a double flying footpaw kick to a large, fat Brownrat, who shot off into empty space with a despairing wail.

Rangval shook her paw cheerily. "We're saved, me darlin', look at 'em, the grand ould gang, an' wid our Orkwil leadin' the charge like the hero he is!"

The pair were almost knocked flat by a rush of Guosim, headed by Osbil, waving two rapiers like windmill sails. "We'll be singin' a Bladechant tonight, mates, c'mon, let's get 'em. Logalogalogaloooooooog!"

Caught up in the moment, Maudie and Rangval scrambled over the rim, and went sliding downhill in the mire, chasing the remnants of their enemies. Gorath and Salixa stood watching the pursuit for a moment, then the big badger went and retrieved his pitchfork from where it lay nearby. He turned to Salixa. "I must go now, swiftly, I had a dream. . . ."

The badgermaid silenced him with a upraised paw. "Go then, I will follow you as my dream told me to."

Without another word, he touched Tung to his flamelike scar, in salute to her, and vanished down the opposite side of the rim. A moment later the plateau was deserted, apart from the bodies of the slain. Salixa had followed the trail of Maudie and the rest. She, too, had a dream to fulfill.

37

By midmorning the rain had ceased and the wind became a mere whisper of breeze. Mossflower came back under the spell of halcyon summer. Watching the back trail, to see they were not being followed, Vizka and his five cohorts emerged from the woodlands. Dripping with dew and drizzle from the foliage, they halted on the path, panting as they got their bearings. Redwall Abbey's bell tower was visible to the south, the golden fox turned to face north. "Dat way to der ford an' d'ship."

Firty cocked an ear at a sound from the woodlands. "Somebeast comin', Cap'n, we been follered."

Vizka ran across the path. "In der ditch, quick!"

They leapt into the ditch, which separated the path from the flatlands. It was full of mud and nettles, and was a sticky and uncomfortable landing, but nobeast made a sound. Crouched on the ditchbed, the crew vermin held their breath as Vizka risked a speedy glance over the bank. He uttered a sigh of relief as a familiar cackle sounded from the underbrush.

It was Glurma, the fat, old cook of the *Bludgullet*. She waddled across and peered into the ditch, treating her shipmates to a snaggletoothed grin. "Heehee, ya wuddent t'ink o' sneakin' off widout ole Glurma, now, would ye?"

Vizka scowled. "Anyone else follerin' us?"

Glurma sat down on the path. "Only me, Cap'n, jus' ole Glurma. Der rest of ya fine crew's prob'ly waitin' at 'ell-gates right now, pore fools."

The golden fox glared at her. "Alright, ya better git down 'ere wid de others."

Glurma twitched her snout at the rank odour of mud and wet loam. She shook her head. "Nah, I'm too long in me seasons t'be wadin' round in dat lot. I'll jus' walk on der path alongside ya."

Vizka beckoned, as though he had something secret to impart. The fat cook bent, so he could whisper in her ear. She did not even see the spiked metal mace, which snuffed out her life in the wink of an eye. Vizka stepped back disdainfully. "Stupid ole fool, she'd give us away walkin' along in clear view. Stow 'er down 'ere, Glurma ain't goin' nowheres!"

Shocked into silence by the swift and callous murder, the crewbeasts obeyed their captain's order. Vizka thrust the sword of Martin through his waist sash, he shouldered the mace without a backward glance at his victim. "Git goin', 'tis safer down 'ere where we can't be seen!"

Back amid the woodlands near the plateau, Orkwil was being reunited with his friends. Rangval ruffled the young hedgehog's headspikes fondly.

"We thought ye were a goner when ye went astray. Where did ye go, mate?"

Orkwil related his story. "I was climbin' up to the top o' that rock, with you an' Maudie, in the dark. Then I tripped an' fell, right down the hill. Must've banged my head agin a rock, 'cos I blacked out for awhile. Then I came around a bit, an' went wanderin' off. I was still only half-conscious, an' there was vermin all over the place, Brownrats an' Sea Raiders, far too many of 'em, I thought. So I made me way back to Redwall, an' reported everythin' to the Abbot an' that good ole badger, Tabura I think ye call him."

358

Abbot Daucus took up the tale. "We knew you had to be rescued, so the Tabura and I took a chance. I marched from the Abbey, taking every able-bodied beast with me. The Tabura, with only the Dibbuns and old ones, stayed back to guard Redwall. He sounded out an alarm on both our Abbey bells. Such a din! I wonder you didn't hear it back here. The Tabura made those bells ring! They never have been so powerfully tolled.

"As our friends arrived to answer the call, from all over Mossflower, they were sent to join with us. We arrived in sight of the plateau, surrounded by a veritable army. Kinbeasts, tribal relatives, some we had helped or befriended in bygone seasons, even a bunch of Riverdogs and some roving Guosim. It made my heart soar to see so many who love Redwall!"

Maudie came running to congratulate Orkwil. "By the left, right, front'n'centre, you've done us proud, young Orkers. What a show, hoorah to you, sah!" She threw a paw around Rangval's shoulders. "Well, well, what d'ye think, Rangee, isn't our little pal the absolute bloomin' bees' knees, wot?"

The rogue squirrel agreed heartily. "Ah, t'be shure he is, miz, but yore only lookin' at half the crowd him an' the good Father Abbot fetched with 'em. Hah! The other half of yore warriors are chasin' the tails off Brownrats an' vermin all over the woodlands, aye, an' I'll stake me tail they won't be takin' many o' the bad ould scum prisoners. I think by nightfall that Mossflower won't be bothered by invaders an' plunderers no more!"

Maudie chuckled. "Especially if friend Gorath is huntin' 'em, wot wot! By the bye, has anybeast seen him of late? He's partially my responsibility y'know."

Osbil pointed with his rapier. "Here comes Salixa, she'll know if anybeast does!"

Abbot Daucus took the badgermaid's paw. "That was a brave show you put on up there at the plateau, miz, and your friend Gorath. Where is he?"

359

Salixa explained in a word. "Gone!"

Maudie's ears stood up like pikestaffs. "Gone? Where's he flippin' well gone to, who's gone with him, is he on his own, why didn't you stop him? Gone, is that all you've got to bloomin' say, marm, gone?"

The Abbot stared Maudie into silence before turning to Salixa. "I can tell by your eyes that you know where Gorath has gone. Pray, would you enlighten us?"

The badgermaid explained, as briefly as she could. "Gorath has gone to fulfill a dream he had last night. I, too, had a dream, I must follow him. Orkwil, if you wish to regain Martin's sword you'll come with me. Maudie, you must come, too, if Gorath is to realise his destiny. Now we must go quickly."

Benjo Tipps enquired, "Who sent your dream, miss?"

Salixa replied tersely, "My Tabura and your Martin."

The Abbot settled any further comment. "Then you must go right now. Good fortune attend you!"

Rangval grasped his dagger hilts. "I'm with ye, missy, if'n ye'll have me along?"

Skipper Rorc nodded to his cousin Barbowla. "I've been out the action too long, I'm comin', too, are ye with me, Barb?"

As Barbowla picked up his javelin, Osbil spoke out. "Looks like ye be needin' a few Guosim to round the feast off, we're with ye!"

The slender badgermaid bowed gracefully. "My thanks, friends. Follow me!"

Gorath the Flame was following his fate. The big badger's footpaws pounded the earth like triphammers as voices echoed through his head, directing him. North through the vast tract of Mossflower he raced, with a speed which was surprising for one of his size. Pictures raced through his mind, the flicker of firelight and shadow, a smiling fox swinging a spiked metal ball at his head. Once! Twice! As he lay helpless on the floor of a little farmhouse.

Gorath the Flame was following his fate. Like a runaway juggernaut, smashing through bushes which barred his path, plunging through streams in a welter of icy spray. The coarse laughter of Sea Raiders rang in his ears; branch, twig, plant and thorn were crushed in his headlong flight through the silent woodlands. Mingled with the laughter, he could hear the anguished screams of two ancient badgers, his blood kin, struggling feebly in the locked and burning building.

Gorath the Flame was following his fate, still directed by unseen forces. Nausea, an iron chain, a padlocked waist manacle. The ship plunging wildly over the cold Nothern Seas. Starvation, a flailing rope's end, the pain lancing through his head. More laughter, the glitter of a golden fox's long fangs, the taunts and insults he was forced to bear in silence.

Weaving around the moss-clad trunks of mighty forest trees. Breath rising like a bellows in his cavernous chest. His paw grasping the pitchfork like a vise. Sunlight and shadow racing by, fernbeds that his footpaws bulled a swathe through. Startled birds flapping skywards, to avoid this giant, heading onward to the river, like a coming storm. Aye, Gorath the Flame was following his fate!

38

When he was confident that they were not being pursued, Vizka Longtooth slowed his pace. The fact that his ambitions of conquering Redwall, plus the cowardly, cut-and-run retreat he had been forced to make, rankled him deeply. Now he had to reestablish his authority over what was left of his once-numerous crew. The stretch of ditchbed they were travelling now was nettle-free, and drying out nicely in the late summer sunlight. The golden fox seated himself on a stone, allowing the crewbeasts to continue onward before he called to them.

"Where are ya runnin' to, dere ain't no 'urry. Sit ya down an' rest awhile, mates."

Sheepishly the five vermin came back to sit with him.

He stared pityingly at them, there was contempt in his tone. "Hah, wot are ya all dashin' off like frightened liddle insects for, eh?"

Jungo, who was not the brightest of weasels, said by way of explanation, "Yew said ya wanted t'get away quick, Cap'n. Prob'ly 'cos ya was scared o' dat big stripe'ound follerin' ya."

There was a sickening thud as the mace smote Jungo. He crumpled, lifeless, to the drying mud. The golden fox did not even rise, he grinned as he turned Jungo facedown, with a shove of his footpaw.

"Wot's dat ya said, scared? Me, Vizka Longtooth, de greatest o' Sea Raider cap'ns, scared! Ahoy, speak up now, anymore o' yew mis'rable scum wants ta call me scared?"

Knowing there would be no response, Vizka put aside his mace and drew Martin's wondrous sword. He waved it, making the blade flash in the sunlight, then thrust it, point first, into the ditchbed. Watching the weapon quiver, he ignored the four remaining crew, speaking to Jungo, whose lifeless eyes stared up at the sun. "Dis is der greatest sword I ever seen, but I ain't slayed anybeast wid it yet. Haha, mebbe I shoulda tried it out on yew, eh? Nah, a pretty blade like dis is too good fer a fool weasel. But der next one who strokes me d'wrong way, dat'll be der beast who'll taste der sword, right, shipmates?"

There was, however, no reply. Whilst Vizka had been admiring the sword, and addressing the dead Jungo, the four vermin had crept away and climbed out of the ditch.

The golden fox stood on the stone, which had served him as a seat, and peered over the ditchtop. They were not on the path, or in the woodland fringe. Turning, he saw them, running off over the flatlands to the west. The golden fox would have traded either of his weapons for a longbow and quiver of arrows at that moment. Instead he was reduced to shouting after them.

"Git back 'ere, ya cowards, I'm yer cap'n, an' dat's an' order. Git back 'ere right now!"

But they had a head start and they kept going. All but one, the small rat, Firty. He halted and yelled aloud, "We ain't comin' back, Longtooth, let's see 'ow far ye'll get widout a crew, go an' sail yer own ship!"

Vizka waved the sword and mace aloft. "Git back 'ere, ya gutless worms, or I'll slay youse all!"

Firty scoffed. "Hah, ya don't stan' a chance o' catchin' us! C'mon, try it, stupid!"

Firty took off after his shipmates. Enraged by the impertinent little rat, Vizka scrambled out onto the plain and gave chase.

It was pointless. Fear lent speed to the crewbeasts' paws, beside which they began to split up, fanning out as they went. With the handicap of sword and mace weighing on him, Vizka soon gave up. He stood panting, tongue lolloping out over his two long fangs.

Firty halted, too, nimbly he skipped back a few paces, mocking his former captain. "Yore on yer own now, ya dirty murderer!"

For the first time, there was a whine of self-pity in Vizka's reply. "Firty, mate, wot did I ever do to harm ya?"

The little rat picked up a stone and slung it. He stood gritting his teeth as it fell far short of the target. Firty gave vent to all his stifled feelings as he replied to the golden fox. "Ya never did nothin' to 'arm me, apart from the kicks an' insults I put up wid from ya. But worrabout the ones ya killed . . . ole Glurma, an' pore Jungo who never 'armed anybeast. Yer no good, Longtooth! Wot sorta cap'n sneaks off an' leaves all but five of 'is crew t'be slain by de enemy? An' yore a coward, too, ya ran 'cos yer frightened o' d'big stripe'ound. Well, yer on yer own now, ya murderer. An' I 'opes I never sees yer ugly mug agin!" Firty turned and bounded off without a backward glance, leaving Vizka completely deserted.

Vizka reviewed his position aloud. "Let der maggots run, dey was never any use t'me, ungrateful blaggards, leavin' dere cap'n widout a crew to sail 'is ship, how'm I supposed t'do dat?" Venting his rage on the earth, he stabbed at the ditchbed with Martin's sword, thinking back upon the *Bludgullet*'s ill-starred voyage, and his subsequent failure to possess Redwall Abbey.

At the thought of his ship, it suddenly occurred to Vizka that he had left two of the crew to guard it. He could not recall their names, but that did not bother him unduly. Fortune had taken yet another turn for the golden fox. With himself and a pair of able-bodied vermin, he would manage to sail the *Bludgullet*.

Considerably cheered, Vizka briskly continued his journey, with a jumble of future plans revolving in his fertile imagination. Crewbeasts would not be difficult to recruit as his ship skirted the coastlands on its southern voyage. Vizka had two ways of bringing stray vermin into his service, the first of which was eminently simple: join my crew or die! The second method was for those he judged to be valuable as Sea Raiders. These he could flatter, offering them plunder, the good life and promotion aboard ship.

Vizka Longtooth could not resist laughing aloud, where were they now, his former crew, either dead alongside a horde of Brownrats, or deserters, running for their lives. He marvelled aloud at his own cunning and resilience. "I gotta fine ship, a good mace an' chain, aye, an' a sword like no other beast alive owns. Hah, a new crew? I kin pick dem up anyplace, me, Vizka Longtooth, der boldest sea raidin' cap'n dat ever strode a deck!"

Maudie trotted up front with Orkwil, Salixa, Osbil and Skipper Rorc. They had skirted the base of the plateau, and were now following Gorath's well-defined trail, northward through the woodlands. The haremaid observed wryly, "There's one jolly good thing, chaps, we don't need any blinkin' expert tracker, t'sniff the breeze an' look for bent blades of grass. Friend Gorath left a trail like a bloomin' pack o' stampedin' wolves, wot!"

Salixa nodded as she viewed the trampled and broken vegetation ahead of them. "I think he's back to his former strength. How far is it to the ford, Osbil?"

The young shrew was not sure. "Couldn't say for sure, bein' in the woodlands an' not on the path, miss. Wot d'you reckon, Skip?"

Skipper Rorc glanced up at the position of the sun. "Oh,

if'n we keep goin' at this rate, we should see the ford come early evenin'. But why d'ye think the big feller's makin' for River Moss?"

Orkwil leapt over a half-flattened bush. " 'Cos if'n Gorath's after the fox an' his crew, they're bound to get to their ship. Once they can make it t'the sea there'll be no catchin' the villains, right, miss?"

The badgermaid kept her eyes on the trail. "I only know what my dream told me, my fate is intertwined with that of Gorath, it's my duty to follow him."

Maudie merely shrugged. "As for me, I'm only doin' my duty under orders from a Badger Lord an' my commandin' officer. If I return to Salamandastron minus a blinkin' badger, good golly, one shudders t'think of it, wot, I'd be on a fizzer for the rest o' my bloomin' life!"

Rangval winked at her. "Don't you go frettin', me bold beauty, shure we'll find Gorath for ye."

Maudie sniffed indignantly. "Huh, these confounded heroic types, you'd think instead o' rushin' off to face their fate, they'd jolly well sit still an' let the Fate come to them, wot!"

Salixa smiled grimly. "A pleasant thought, but let's save our breath and step up the pace. There's no telling what we may find, if and when we catch up with Gorath."

39

Just short of the actual ford, the *Bludgullet* lay at anchor in the tranquil waters of the River Moss. The two ferrets who had been left to guard the ship, Baul and Widge, had become accustomed to their life of happy idleness. Both beasts lay on the stern deck, sharing a flagon of ship's grog. Attached to their footpaws were fishing lines, Widge watched his float moodily, urging it to move.

"Bob up'n'down why don't ye, we ain't 'ad a bite all day."

His companion had fashioned himself a sun hat, from a large dock leaf. He pulled it down, shading his eyes. "I t'ink dose fish are like us, mate, too lazy t'move."

Widge yawned. "Go'n git another flagon o' grog, mate, dis one's empty, lookit." Sticking out his tongue, he upended the flagon, a single drop trickled out, landing on his nose. He tossed the empty flagon into the river.

His companion, Baul, closed both eyes, mimicking a snore. "Can't 'ear ya, mate, I'm asleep, git it yerself."

Widge halfheartedly threw the flagon cork at him and missed. " 'Tis yore turn t'go, I went last time."

Baul sniggered. "Aye, so ya did, but I can't go 'cos I'm der laziest beast aboard dis ship."

Widge decided to play the game, he shut his eyes. "No

367

ya ain't, I am. If'n dis ship started t'sink right now, I wouldn't move. Dat's wot ya call real lazy."

Baul thought for a moment before replying. "Ya call dat lazy? Lissen, mate, I wouldn't even budge if'n dis ole ship went afire!"

A cavernous rumble sounded out, almost above their heads. Before they could stir, both vermin were pinned to the deck by the stout wooden handle of a pitchfork, which pressed down on their chests. Gorath the Flame leaned on the shaft, his deep, growling voice turning the blood in their veins to ice water.

"My kinbeasts weren't lazy, they were old and weak, so they couldn't better their way out of a burning dwelling, after sea-raiding vermin locked them in!"

Baul and Widge found themselves staring up into a pair of burning, bloodshot eyes, surmounted by a flamelike crimson scar. Panicked words tumbled from the ferrets' mouths.

"It wasn't us, lord, on me oath it wasn't!"

"We knew nothin' about it, sir, honest!"

"Aye, we're allus left be'ind ter guard der ship!"

"Cap'n Vizka ain't let us ashore fer seasons, ya gotta believe us, sir, please!"

The huge, young badger pushed down harder upon the pitchfork shaft. "Has Longtooth returned here yet?"

Grunting and wheezing as the breath was crushed from them, the crewbeasts gasped painfully.

"No, lord . . . 'e ain't returned . . . yet."

"We d-don't know when ta expect 'im . . . uuuunnhh!"

Gorath released the pressure from their bodies. "Get up, quickly!"

They staggered upright, tenderly holding cracked ribs. As the pitchfork, Tung, was levelled at them, both vermin wept brokenly. "Aw, sir, ya ain't gonna slay us are ye, 'ave mercy!"

"We ain't nothin' but pore shipwatchers, 'tis Cap'n Vizka ya wants, but watch yoreself, 'e's an evil fox."

368

With a massive effort, Gorath fought to shake off the Bloodwrath, which threatened to engulf him. *Whump!* He slammed the tines of Tung deep into the deck timbers. Grabbing the two ferrets by the scruffs of their necks, he lifted them up bodily. They screeched in terror as he shook them like rag dolls.

"Yeeeeeek! Oh mercy, sir, mercy!"

The young badger's chest expanded as he sucked in a huge gulp of air. He threw them from him, clear over the stern rail into the River Moss. Leaning over the rail, he bared his teeth at Widge and Baul. "Go! That way, north. Go now before I change my mind and kill you both. Go while you still have your lives!" Gorath turned his back on them, knowing that when he looked again, all he would see was the muddied water they had churned up in their mad flight.

Retrieving his weapon, Gorath stood there shaking, forcing himself to calm down. Making his way to the galley, he went in and sat down. Overcome by thirst, he drank a full pitcher of water. Then he sat still, awaiting the arrival of the fox.

Shimmering calm had settled over the ford as noontide softened to early evening. Blue damselflies hovered over the River Moss, tiny, winged insects flitted about in myriad patterns, whilst a trout made a halfhearted jump at a mayfly, which skimmed gracefully out of harm's way. A meadowbrown butterfly stretched its dun-hued wings, settling close to the golden fox's footpaw.

Vizka was oblivious to the tranquil charms of the summer's day. Shielded by clumps of knotweed and hemlock, he lay watching the *Bludgullet* from a short distance. There was no sign of movement from on board the vessel. Had he brought crewbeasts with him, he would have sent them to investigate his apparently deserted ship. Several times since his arrival, he had flicked pebbles at the side of the craft, with no result. He rose slowly. There was

369

nothing for it, he would have to board her and see for himself.

Placing one paw cautiously in front of the other, he approached. Still no sound from the ship. Gripping one of the midship mooring lines, he pulled gently on it. The *Bludgullet* drifted smoothly to the bank until it scraped bottom. Martin's swordblade clattered against the rail as he boarded. Vizka held his breath a moment, waiting for any reaction to the sound. There was none. Drawing the blade, he unhitched the mace and chain from about his shoulders, calling in a voice barely above a whisper, "Ahoy dere, guards, show yerselves!"

Silently cursing himself that he could not recall the names of the two vermin he had left to watch his ship, he called out again, this time in a normal tone. "Ya slab-sided idlers, where are ya?"

A startled wren darted off from the bowrope. Vizka whirled to face forward. He thought he saw a shadow flitting somewhere near the galley. The old smile, which had given him his name, Longtooth, appeared on his face. It was the usual tale with crew vermin, leave them alone for awhile, and all they were interested in was sleeping, and feeding their faces with grog and vittles. He tip-pawed toward the galley. The two guards, whatever their names were, would have to learn a harsh lesson, for disobeying Captain's orders.

He was about to place his paw on the door latch, when some inner instinct made him stop. If the ship's guards were in there, why had they not responded when he called? Perhaps they were asleep, but then why were there no sounds of snoring or ragged breathing from within? There was a tiny crack in the door planking, the golden fox squinted his eye against it, peering in.

Gorath had heard Vizka come aboard. The young badger stood facing the galley door, his pitchfork aiming squarely at it. He thought he heard his enemy's footpads approaching, and readied himself. Then there was complete silence from outside, nothing but a thin sliver of sunlight from a crack in the door, playing on the floor in front of Gorath. Then it vanished.

Alarm bells began ringing in the badger's head, he knew the fox was watching him through the crack. Without giving a second thought to the consequences, Gorath put all his muscle behind Tung, giving the pitchfork a ramming thrust as he roared, "Eulaliiiiiaaaaa!"

Vizka leapt to one side, he saw the twin metal prongs of the weapon come thundering through the shuddering timbers, almost to their full length. The golden fox was an expert fighter, the most feared among the sea raiding brethren, he saw the immediate chance and took it. Avoiding the prongs, he threw himself hard against the galley door, slamming it wide open. Gorath was thrown against the bulkhead, still gripping the pitchfork haft tight as it snapped, leaving him holding only the end piece.

Vizka bounded in, flailing his mace, and brandishing the sword. The advantage was all his in this battle to the death, he grinned wolfishly. "I'll finish ya dis time, stripe'ound! Haharr!" He held Gorath against the bulkhead, swinging the mace and hacking away with the sword in a frenzied attack.

With his back to the wall, armed with just a broken piece of wood, Gorath could only try to weather the vicious onslaught. Splinters flew as the spiked ball struck the bulkhead timbers, he ducked and swayed, trying to avoid the whirring mace and flashing blade.

Vizka found himself imbued with a new confidence, this was no seasoned warrior he was facing, merely a big, young beast, armed with only a bit of stick. Moreover, the stripehound's eyes were not blood red, as he had seen them before. Had he lost the power to go into one of his berserk rages?

The golden fox slowed his assault, laughing as his victim tried to wriggle out of harm's way. Vizka performed a clever maneuvre with the mace, grazing the side of

Gorath's head. "Ya want me ta give ya another fancy mark on yer skull? Mebbe I'll knock one of ya eyes out dis time!"

Now that he had the upper paw, the old Vizka returned, swaggering as he taunted the young badger cruelly. What he did not realise was that as he mocked and toyed away, Gorath had been gradually edging round the galley until he was close to the door, still trying to parry his foe's random sallies with the battered little section of wood. Almost chopping Gorath's paw, Vizka hacked a chunk from the broken haft, he waved the sword of Martin proudly in Gorath's face, as the badger tried to parry it away. Vizka was really enjoying himself now.

"D'ya like me new blade, ain't it a beauty? I tell ya, I could take yer 'ead off wid one swipe. Dat'd be nice'n'quick, wouldn't it? Stan' still, stripe'ound, an' I'll show ya. . . ." He swung the sword back as far as he could.

That was when Gorath made his move. Throwing himself out of the open doorway in a sidelong roll, he grabbed at his pitchfork, which had pierced the door through, to the length of its prongs. The handle snapped, right at the socket where it joined the metal fork.

It was at that point the tracking party arrived alongside the *Bludgullet.* Rangval seized a pair of his daggers, but was halted from boarding by Salixa.

"Leave Gorath, this is his fight, he wouldn't thank you for helping him!"

Maudie was aghast. "I say, that's a bit thick, ain't it? The other rascal's armed to the bloomin' teeth!"

The badgermaid warned the others, holding her paws wide, "My friend is facing his fate, we cannot alter what's about to take place. Have faith in him. Watch!"

The combatants faced each other on the deck. Vizka did not seem unduly put out by his quarry's escape. "Ya had yer chance t'die quick, stripe'ound, now I'm goin' to carve ya up nice'n'slow!"

Gorath swung the long part of the haft like lightning. *Crack!*

372

It struck his adversary's paw as he slashed out with the sword. Vizka screeched with pain and shock, his paw totally numbed, and broken, by the blow. The sword of Martin arced through the air, ending up point down in the shallows. Gorath's eyes were calm, he stood waiting until his opponent came at him again. This time it was with a long, flailing swing of the mace. The young badger switched his hold; seizing the wooden haft in both paws, he held it forth horizontally. The iron chain of the mace wrapped thrice around it, the spiked metal ball dangling useless in the tangle. One wrench from Gorath tugged the weapon's handle out of the fox's grasp. Vizka watched, horrified, as Gorath tossed the shaft and the mace into the river.

A cheer went up from those on the bank. Gorath the Flame hardly noticed it as he wrapped a mighty paw about Vizka. His other paw clamped around the fox's muzzle. Lifting Vizka until their eyes met, Gorath growled, "I was never your slave, and I am no longer the slave of Bloodwrath, that is my fate, fox. Now here is yours!"

Maudie winced, as did everybeast. The sound of Vizka Longtooth's spine snapping sounded like a dry twig. There was a splash as Gorath tossed his enemy's limp carcass into the River Moss.

Salixa allowed her friend to assist her aboard the ship, she clasped his paw tightly. "You defeated him without resorting to Bloodwrath. Though I had my doubts when I heard you calling the war cry."

Gorath smiled. "Oh, I only shouted that cry because I like the sound of it. Also because I knew that I was in full control of myself."

On the bank, Orkwil Prink was waving a hefty staff of yew wood, which he had garnered with the sword of Martin the Warrior. "I found ye a new fork handle. Permission t'come aboard, Cap'n Gorath!"

The young badger shook his head. "You'd best ask my first mate."

Salixa laughed. "Permission granted, but only if you can shout out the password. Maudie, coming from Salamandastron, you should know it well."

Mad Maudie (the Hon.) Mugsberry Thropple threw back her head, bellowing the time-honoured cry in a most unmaidenly manner. "Eulaliiiiiaaaaaa!" She bounded aboard, followed by the rest of the company.

Orkwil was beside himself with happiness, he waved the sword of Martin in the air, yelling. "Friends, I've just thought of a new name for this ship, guess what it is?"

The answer came in a deafening roar from everybeast. "Eulaliiiiiaaaaaa!"

The young hedgehog looked slightly crestfallen, but a moment later he was joining in the general laughter and backslapping.

40

As evening shadows gathered, a meeting was held on the deck. By unanimous decision they voted to sail the newly named vessel on a voyage that would fulfill Maudie's mission. Both Gorath and Salixa were enthralled at the thought of seeing Salamandastron, that fortress of legendary Badger Lords. There was no lack of volunteers for the trip, everybeast wanted to go.

The next three days were spent profitably. Foraging parties scoured the woodlands for food supplies, whilst Guosim shrews and otters cleaned the ship from stem to stern, eradicating all trace of vermin habitation, and making *Eulalia* shipshape for the coming adventure. Rangval proved to be quite artistic, obliterating the name *Bludgullet*, and installing the new title skillfully.

Many suggestions were put forward, as to who should captain the *Eulalia*. Skipper Rorc, Barbowla and Log a Log Osbil were all well-favoured, capable beasts. However, it was Salixa who settled the matter, both she and Gorath nominated Orkwil Prink. This was enthusiastically seconded by Maudie and Rangval.

On the evening before they sailed, Rangval whispered to Maudie, as he watched Orkwil swaggering around the deck, "Shure, an' will ye look at the bold, liddle hog there. Faith, ye'd think he was a cap'n born t'the command. I wonder where he found those floppy, ould seaboots an' big, feathery hat?"

Maudie stifled a giggle, saluting the young hedgehog as he strode by. "Good evenin', Cap'n Orkwil, lookin' forward t'the jolly old morrow, wot wot?"

Orkwil waved a paw nonchalantly. "Oh, one voyage is much like another y'know. . . ." The floppy hat fell over his eyes, and he tripped as the sword came loose, dangling between his outrageous boots. He stumbled, fell and bounced back upright, all in the one movement. Orkwil glared at both of his friends, as if daring them to laugh. "Ahem, river's a bit choppy tonight, watch how ye go!"

Rangval stared over the side at the River Moss, which was as still as a millpond. He nodded. "Yore right, Cap'n. I'll take first watch in case those waves come a-washin' o'er the sides an' sink us!"

The young hedgehog nodded officiously. "Right, Mister Rangval, I'll be in me cabin if'n ye need me. Good night to ye both!" Trying to control the sword, boots and hat, he staggered off to the stern.

Salixa and Gorath joined Maudie and Rangval, watching their new captain's progress. Gorath smiled fondly.

"I owe my freedom to that one, he's learned a lot since we first met."

The gentle badgermaid clasped her big companion's paw. "I think we've all learned a lot, don't you?"

Maudie interrupted. "Aye, friend, we have, an' we're all young enough to learn more, wot!"

Afternoon sunlight flooded the forge room at Salamandastron, softening the rough, rock walls. Old Lord Asheye sat on the broad stone windowledge, enjoying the late summer warmth. Blindness did not stop the ancient badger from appreciating the day, he could even judge the time by the position of the sun upon his face. The outgoing or incoming tides, he knew by the sounds of the sea, the cries of seabirds and, often, the feel of wind or breeze. The familiar sound of Major Mullein's swagger stick beat its brief tattoo on the chamber door. Lord Asheye's response was correspondingly brief. "Come!"

The Major entered, shepherding Furps and Tringle. Both young hares were in charge of the afternoon tea trolley. Mullein cautioned the pair as they negotiated the rock floor. "Steady as y'go now. Furps, slow down, laddie buck, you ain't in a race. Now, what dainties have we here, wot?"

Tringle fluttered her long eyelashes. "Hot mint or chamomile tea, sah, a selection of sandwiches, some of Cook's dark fruit cake, an' the usual scones an' whatnot, sah. With the jolly old trimmin's of course."

Lord Asheye nodded approvingly. "Very nice. I hear you passed your Running Scouts test yesterday. Congratulations t'you both!"

Furps and his sister saluted smartly. "Thank ye, sah, it was jolly hard, but we passed with flyin' colours, didn't we, Tring!"

"Oh rather, we're both wearin' green pawbands at the moment, new uniforms ain't ready yet, m'Lord!"

Asheye reached out and ruffled their ears. "I'm sure you'll both be a credit to the Long Patrol. But remember the old saying, It ain't the uniform that counts, 'tis the warrior who wears it, eh!"

Major Mullein took charge of the trolley. "C'mon now, chaps, back down to the Mess Hall, you'll only tire Lord Asheye out with all this chatter."

Furps and Tringle saluted, but before they dashed off, the Badger Lord spoke out.

"Leave them, Major, I enjoy their company. Sit down here and take afternoon tea with me, young 'uns. Mull, you can be mother, pour for us, please."

Honoured and delighted to be invited thusly by their Badger Lord, Furps and Tringle smiled cheekily at the Major. "Two spoons of honey in my tea, Mother!"

377

"Me, too, an' could you pass the cucumber sand-wiches, mum?"

Mullein fixed them with a comical glare. "I'll mother you two when I get you out on the parade ground, it'll be tails for tea an' drill for dinner!"

Asheye chuckled. "Young ripscallions, here, come and be my eyes for awhile. How d'you see the sea today?"

"Blue as usual I suppose, sah."

"No, it's a sort of greeny blue."

"Don't y'mean bluey green?"

"Well, alright, it's a kind of light bluey pale green, with tiny white flecks here an' there."

Asheye spread a huge old paw to indicate the expanse. "Oh come on, you can do better than that. Are there no patterns of breeze ripples on the surface? How big are the waves as they break on the shore? Any gulls or cormorants diving out there? Use your eyes, describe!"

Furps took a try. "Lots o' jolly big waves comin' ashore, sah, makin' that swishy noise they always make. Some of that seaweed gettin' washed up also, long, dark, green stuff. Er, some seabirds, too, gulls I think—"

Mullein interrupted him. "You think, laddie buck? Are they guillemots, geese or gulls, have ye been taught nothin' at nature study, wot?"

Tringle cut in, attempting to help her brother. "Actually there's some puffins an' guillemots, ordinary gulls, an' a few kittiwakes, sah. Oh, there's also that small thing, right out there, could that be a ship?"

Lord Asheye stood bolt upright, his head turning this way and that. "A ship . . . Where?"

Leaving the tea trolley, Mullein hurried to the broad win-dow space. He peered hard, following the direction of Tringle's paw as she explained.

"Over there, sah, away to the far west, comin' from the north. I think it is a ship, eh, Furps?"

Her brother, who had the keenest sight of those in the forge room, climbed up onto the sill, taking hold of Major

378

Mullein's paw as he leaned out. Shading his brow with his free paw, Furps stared intently at the object. His shout echoed around the forge chamber. "It is! It's a bally ship alright, sah, an' it's headin' this bloomin' way, straight t'the blinkin' mountain, if'n y'flippin' ask me!"

Major Mullein lifted him from the sill, with a stern note in his voice. "Less of the barrack room lingo young 'un, Badger Lord present, y'know!"

Furps held a paw to his mouth. "Oops, my 'pologies, sah!"

The ancient Badger Lord seized his walking staff, issuing orders urgently. "Major, gather all officers immediately, tell them to turn out the Long Patrol, full complement, well armed!"

Mullein saluted with his swagger stick. "Right y'are, Lord. I'll have 'em linin' the west shore in full fig, armed t'the eartips. Will ye be attendin'?"

Asheye nodded vigorously. "Send old Ecrea up, tell him to attend the lord's wardrobe, I want to be dressed in full regalia. Oh, I'll need to be bearing some kind of arms, a sword do you think?"

Tringle spoke out boldly, before the Major could answer. "Beg pardon, Lord, but a battleaxe might be better. It looks fearsome, but you can use it to feel your way, just like the staff you have to help you along."

The haremaid winced as Asheye's big paw descended thankfully on her shoulder. "Good idea, young 'un! You and your brother stay here. When I'm ready you can both walk me down to the shore."

Major Mullein did an about turn in the doorway. He beckoned Tringle and Furps to him, whispering to them. "This is your first assignment as Scout Runners. Lord Asheye is under your protection. Guard him with your lives, your very lives, d'ye hear?"

Mullein turned and marched off, leaving behind him two young hares almost bursting with pride.

Drums thundered and bugles blared as Salamandastron roused itself to meet the newcomers.

379

The *Eulalia* dipped its prow to the heaving sea, bucking playfully as it rose, dropping to meet the next wave. Every scrap of sail canvas was taut as the breeze whistled through the rigging. Gorath the Flame stood in the bows with Salixa, watching the majestic mountain growing larger with every moment. Gorath wiped a big paw across his eyes. "Salamandastron, it's like a dream. If only my old grandparents could have lived to see it."

The slender badgermaid patted his shoulder. "They did their best for you, and you lived to see it for them. That would have made them happy."

Orkwil trundled by holding the sword of Martin over his shoulder so that he would not trip. The young hedgehog swept off his floppy hat in an elaborate bow. "Good day, friends. The weather's holdin' fair I trust!"

Salixa smiled at him. "It is indeed, Captain, and how are you today pray tell?"

Reveling in his role as Shipsmaster, Orkwil replied. "Well, marm, exceedin' well, as is all me gallant crew, 'ceptin' ole Rangval, who swears he ain't long for this world. Still y'know wot us saltwater beasts say,

He's far better on land,
be it soil, rock or sand,
an' quite good up a tree,
but he don't like the sea!"

Rangval the Rogue was the only beast aboard to be seasick. The wretched squirrel lay on the afterdeck swathed in a mass of blankets.

Maudie brought him a beaker of fresh water. "Golly, you look like bloomin' death, mate. Try a sip o' this, 'tis only water, but it might help, wot!"

He pushed the beaker away with a plaintive groan. "Water, d'ye say, get it outta me sight, darlin'. Sure an' wasn't it water that's got me this way? Water, goin' up

380

an' down, back an' for'ard, side t'side, rollin' an' sloppin', an' never stoppin'. Me ould body'll be dead by the time we make land. No need t'dig me a grave, no, just toss me ould remains anywhere, up in a tree, or down on the grass. Sure, there's not a beast that'll notice me. Bein' so green I'll blend right in!"

Osbil was passing by, he shook his head sorrowfully. "It's been a pleasure knowin' ye, Rangval, me ole mate. Would ye like to do me a partin' favour, seein' as yore dyin'?"

The rogue squirrel managed a weak smile.

"Anythin' fer you, me ould Guosim messmate, name it."

Osbil replied promptly. "Those good daggers ye always carry, could ye let me have them now, just to save us all arguin' over 'em when yore gone."

Salixa arrived in the nick of time, she helped Maudie to restrain Rangval as he tried to hurl the blades at Osbil, ranting furiously.

"Arr, let me at the villain, I'll give him me knives sure enough. One through his black heart, one through his fatpot belly an' one more through his thievin' paws!" He appealed piteously to the young badgermaid. "It ain't bad enough, havin' to die of the seasickness, miss, but that blaggard wants to rob me lovely daggers!"

Salixa took a small flask from her beltpurse. "Die of seasickness? Nonsense, a good swig of my medicine should put paid to that. Open your mouth!"

Rangval had a horror of medicines. Shaking his head vigorously, he clamped his mouth tight. Salixa passed the flask to Maudie. "Give our friend a good dose when he opens his mouth." She pinched the squirrel's nose, cutting off his air. He struggled wildly to resist, but in the end he had to open his mouth to breathe. Maudie acted swiftly, pouring almost half the flask into Rangval.

The rogue squirrel's tail stood up like a flagpole. "Yooooaaaaarrrrgh! Ye murderers, ye've killed me!"

Amid the laughter he sprinted up the mast, where he sat quivering with rage as he glared down at them.

Gorath called from his place in the bows as they drew closer to shore. "Look, there's almost tenscore hares in uniform waiting on the tideline for us. I take it they're the famous Long Patrol, Miz Maudie?"

The haremaid began brushing her tunic down and generally trying to look presentable as she answered. "By Jove, there's a sight t'do your jolly old heart good. They've turned the full complement out t'greet us. Stap me scut, there's Major Mull, Corporal Thwurl, Biffy Bigelow, Lanky Lockben, Stinky Scarbuttle an' Big Beau Sullagan. Colour Sarn't O'Flugg an' Colonel Cragglow. Oh look, there's young thingummy an' his sister wotsername, see who they're escortin', it's Lord Asheye himself, wot! Halloooo, milord, ahoy!"

The ancient badger raised his battleaxe to the incoming vessel. Wild cheering broke out on the shoreline. Not to be outdone, the crew of *Eulalia* added to the din with their joyous shouts. As soon as it was possible, mooring lines were hurled to the vessel from the shore. Scores of willing paws hauled the ship to land. Osbil and his Guosim furled sail, slacking off all rigging. The prow nosed up through the shallows until the entire craft lay heeled onshore.

Maudie leapt down onto the beach, closely followed by Gorath and Salixa. The ranks of warrior hares parted as Lord Asheye and Major Mullein walked to meet them. The haremaid threw a smart salute.

"Hon. Maudie Mugsberry Thropple reportin' back as ordered, sah! Mission accomplished, found Gorath the Flame, er, an' one other, Salixa, very pretty maid. Hopin' you approve. Sah!"

Major Mullein returned the salute. "Well done, Miss Thropple, you're to be commended on an exemplary completion of a difficult assignment."

The ancient Badger Lord confronted the two young badgers. Reaching out, he found the badgermaid's face, smiling as he ran his paw gently across her features. "Salixa, the slender willow tree. At times like this I would wish to have my sight for a moment. Truly I can tell you are as beautiful as your name implies. Salamandastron bids you welcome, young one, it is your home for as long as you wish it to be."

Salixa placed her brow against the lord's paw. "Thank you, sire, I will never leave this place as long as I can stand at Gorath's side."

Both the Badger Lord's paws now found Gorath's face. He stood silent as the blind one inspected his features thoroughly. Asheye nodded as if in confirmation. "So, you are Gorath the Flame, I have seen you in my dreams many times. Though now you stand before me I feel you are bigger than in the visions, taller. Truly you are marked deep by the flame, the forge of life branded you thus. Let me touch the weapon you call Tung."

Gorath placed Asheye's paw on the pitchfork, he familiarised himself with it from butt to tines. "A stout and honest implement, Gorath, it can be used either in combat, or to tend growing crops. Which do you prefer?"

The young badger thought for a moment. "I would sooner grow food from the land than dig graves for our enemies. But I can do both if need be, sire."

Asheye gave him back the pitchfork. "Welcome to your mountain, Lord Gorath!"

The crimson westering sun cast long shadows on the three badgers. Gorath and Salixa took Asheye's paws, allowing him to lead them into the mountain fortress of Salamandastron. Maudie borrowed Martin's sword from Orkwil, it flashed scarlet in the last rays as the shores resounded to the mass roar of a single word . . .

"Eulaliaaaaaaaaaaaa!"

Epilogue

"Extract from the writings of a badgermaid."

Fourteen seasons is no great length of time to most elders, but to me it is the sum of my entire life so far. A few days ago I finished reading the Family Chronicle, which was written by my mother, Lady Salixa of Salamandastron. Maybe I have not lived through the adventures of my parents and their friends, but I have a lifetime ahead. So this morning I started to write my own Chronicle. Who knows, mayhaps I have inherited some writing skill from my mother.

However, with all the goings on around here, it is hard to concentrate. Did I tell you, tonight is the Great Midsummer Eve Feast. The shore in front of our mountain will be decked with lanterns, and garlanded with blossoms. It's going to be a time for wonderful food, happy music and great entertainment. Then guess what? Tomorrow afternoon I will be boarding the good ship *Eulalia,* bound on a voyage to Redwall Abbey. Such excitement!

But let me tell you how all this came to be, back to my Chronicle. You must remember that being young, I rely on family and friends for certain information about events that occurred when I was a mere babe, or even farther back, before I was born. I have a few to thank for their time and patience in assisting me. My mother, Salixa, and my father, Gorath, Lord of Salamandastron. My Grand Uncle, General Mull; Aunt Maudie, the regimental Colonel Cook and Caterer; and rascally old Uncle Rangval, unofficial Scout in Charge to the Long Patrol. Also the various Guosim shrews, otters and Redwallers I have encountered when the *Eulalia* makes her annual voyage from the River Moss, which they tell me is not far from the Abbey.

Well, it seems that when *Eulalia* first came to our mountain, in the final days of that long-gone summer, there was widespread rejoicing. A feast, which lasted four days, took place. It was during the final evening of the celebrations, everybeast was seated around a fire on the shore, singing, feasting and enjoying those last warm days of the season. A young hedgehog, Orkwil Prink, made the remark that soon the falling leaves of autumn would be sticking to his headspikes. This seemed to affect Old Lord Asheye greatly, his jovial mood deserted him, and he sat there in a state of deep depression. Everybeast present thought the ancient badger had merely fallen asleep, because he was very old, and it was getting quite late. Not wishing to waken Lord Asheye, the Long Patrol hares stopped roaring out rowdy barrack room ditties. My father turned to my mother, who had not sung thus far. Knowing she possessed a sweet, gentle voice, he persuaded her to give a rendition of the little ballad she had performed for him that night beneath the stars on the plateau. Obligingly, she began singing.

"Let me wander here forever, through the glades
where once I played.
Long ago in carefree seasons, mid the noontide
sun and shade.
I will see again before me, all those smiling
friends I knew.
Gone alas to memory's keeping, faithful comrades
good and true—"

386

She was interrupted by Lord Asheye, who rose up calling, "I know that song, Melutar composed it! How do you know it, lady, tell me, please?"

My mother was startled, but she answered readily. "Lord, I learned it from a good and wise old badger, but his name was not Melutar, they call him the Tabura."

Asheye clutched my mother's paws and wept. "Did you know this Tabura, does he still live?"

Gorath my father answered for her. "Aye, Lord, like you he is heavy with seasons, but he is alive and well at Redwall Abbey. Why do you ask?"

A hush fell over the assembly as Asheye began speaking. "Long ago in another life, there were two brothers, Melutar and Ferlon. They were like the sun and moon. Ferlon, the eldest, was big and strong, silver-coated, hot-tempered and wild. Melutar, the younger, was of medium size, dark-coated and placid. He was a dreamer, a seeker of knowledge, a writer of poems and songs. They were destined to walk different paths. Melutar stayed home, caring for their aged parents, and growing in wisdom. Ferlon followed the drums of war, his road took him to Salamandastron, and his savage reputation grew by the seasons. Vermin foebeast feared Ferlon, wherever he cast his wild gray eyes, death and destruction came like a roaring fire, leaving only ashes. That badger was me, I became known as Lord Asheye, the beast cursed by Bloodwrath. Melutar was my younger brother, I thought he had long gone to the land beyond the seasons. Something told me that soon I would be joining him."

Asheye turned his face toward the recently promoted General Mullein, his constant companion. "Remember I told you of the voices that haunted my dreams? They said that never again would I be seen at Salamandastron, once the autumn leaves fall. Well, old friend, it looks like the shadow of fate has finally fallen upon me."

Mullein nodded sadly. "Aye, sah, who can escape it?"

That was when my father said his piece. "When I was taken captive I thought many times that I would die never having seen Redwall, or Salamandastron. But I was mistaken, as I believe you are, Lord. There is a ship lying in the bay, it will take you to be united with your long-lost brother, whom you thought dead. When autumn leaves fall, you will be far from this mountain, bound for the Abbey of Redwall. I think that is what your voices were trying to tell you, sir. The fates are being kind to you!"

Mullein helped the ancient badger to stand upright. "Well, stap me, sah, I believe Lord Gorath's right. I'll jolly well wager your brother, the Tabowot'sisname, will be over the blinkin' moon t'see ye, wot!"

Lord Asheye clasped his friend's paw. "It would be a pleasure if you were to accompany me, Mull."

The General saluted gallantly with his free paw. "Hah, t'would be an honour to travel at y'side, sah!"

I have heard that story many times from my father, he calls it the happy fate of Lord Asheye. My mother also related how Asheye, and Mullein, sailed away on the *Eulalia*, bound on a rosy dawn tide for Redwall, to meet again his brother, the Tabura.

I think this is a fitting start to my Chronicle. Redwall Abbey is a place of my dreams, many times I have pleaded to visit there. However, my father always said I was too young, until this season, my fourteenth. With the aid of Aunt Maudie, Rangval and my mother, he was finally persuaded. I am to spend four seasons at the Abbey. Can you imagine it, four whole seasons! Mother has given me to understand that I will spend time being educated by my two adopted grandfathers, Asheye and the Tabura. Father says that education is the key to both happiness and wisdom, I am sure this is true.

But Auntie Maudie and Uncle Rangval told me there is lots of fun to be found at Redwall, and lots of new friends to be made. There'll be feasting, singing, sporting, log-boating with Guosim, ranging the streams with Barbowla and his otters. . . . And I'm actually sailing tomorrow at noon, I'll be lucky if I sleep a wink tonight!

I know I'm repeating myself, but Redwall really is the place of my dreams. They say that there is always a welcome there for those who are good of heart, and true to their friends. Who knows, perhaps we'll meet there one sunny day?

Rowanbloom, daughter of Lady Salixa and Lord Gorath of Salamandastron